RAZORHURST

JUSTINE LARBALESTIER

SOHO
TEEN

Published in the United States by Soho Teen
an imprint of
Soho Press, Inc.
853 Broadway
New York, NY 10003

Library of Congress Cataloging-in-Publication Data

Larbalestier, Justine.
Razorhurst / Justine Larbalestier.

1. Criminals—Fiction. 2. Organized crime—Fiction. 3.
Ghosts—Fiction. 4. Sydney (N.S.W.)—History—20th century—Fiction.
5. Australia—History—20th century—Fiction. I. Title.
PZ7.L32073Mah 2007
[Fic]—dc23 2014030128

HC ISBN 978-1-61695-544-1
PB ISBN 978-1-61695-625-7
eISBN 978-1-61695-545-8

Map by Hannah Janzen

Interior design by Janine Agro, Soho Press, Inc.

Printed in the United States of America

10 9 8 7 6 5 4 3 2 1

For Ruth Park and Kylie Tennant,
who lived in and loved and wrote about Surry Hills
decades before me,
without whom this book would not exist.

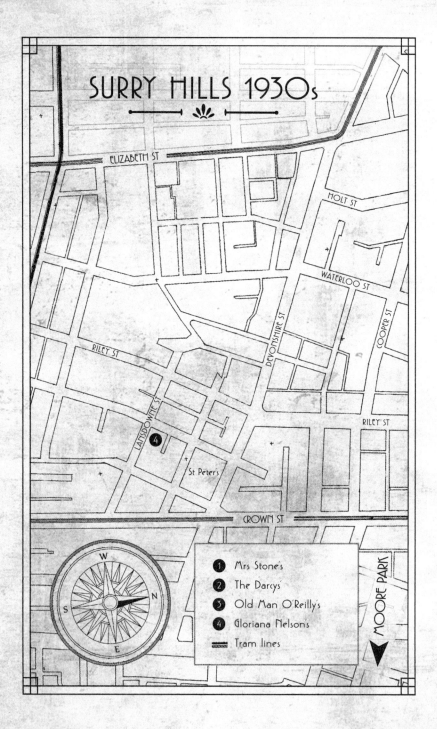

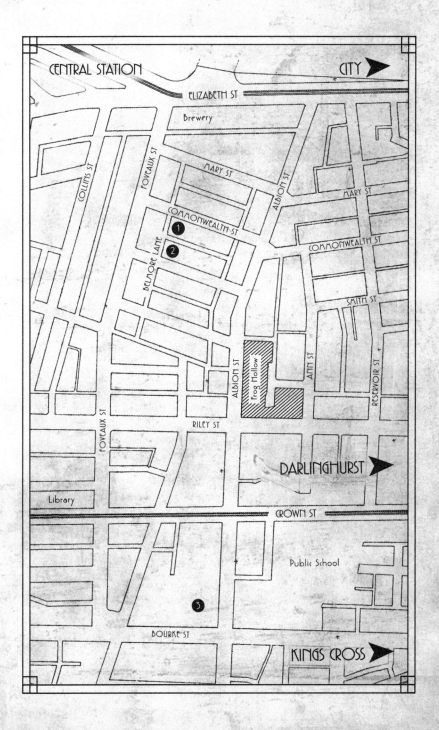

✂ KELPIE ✂

Tommy was a talker and didn't much like the other ghosts, so he was forever talking to Kelpie. That's how she divided them up: talkers and silent ones. Most ghosts were silent. Most ignored the living. Kelpie thought that was just as well.

She wished Tommy was a silent one. She wished she hadn't listened.

Most ghosts haunted a person or a place. Pimply Tommy had Belmore Lane. He didn't like the word *haunt* because it implied he had a choice, but no matter how many times he tried, he could not leave. Tommy had been born in that lane, he had been killed in that lane, and that kept him there for eternity, looking at the backyards of houses and the rear entrances of warehouses and factories, unable to set foot in either.

It made him cantankerous and tricksy.

"Barefoot again, eh?" Tommy said, his voice cracking on the word *barefoot*. "And this the coldest winter in forever."

Tommy's world was so constrained he noticed all the changes. Because he was a ghost, he could see in the dark, and though he could not leave that all-too-small lane, he could hear and smell farther than a human. All ghosts could. Tommy knew everyone's business.

"Where your shoes?"

Kelpie'd taken them off once she was sure Miss Lee had faded. Miss Lee was a ghost too.

Had been a ghost. She'd looked after Kelpie, which was why Kelpie'd worn shoes—to please her. They pinched Kelpie's toes, and besides, the soles of her feet were tough as any shoe. Cold didn't bother her as much as shoes did.

"Here to see your boyfriend?" Tommy asked. "You do know every girl in the Hills is after that ugly mick, don't you?"

Neal Darcy was not ugly, and he was not her boyfriend. Though she was there to see him. She hadn't once since Miss Lee had gone, and he'd promised he was going to show her how to use his typewriter. Her stomach growled.

"Hungry, eh? Darcys' ain't got no food. Piles of apples in there, though." Tommy pointed at Mrs. Stone's boarding house.

Mrs. Stone's was not what Miss Lee would have called respectable. It was what Kelpie's other living friend, Snowy, called dangerous. Hardly a one of the men who lived there didn't have an L- or an X-shaped razor-etched scar on one side of his face. Hard men, Snowy called them. He'd know. You'd have to be mad to venture in uninvited.

Or invited, for that matter.

"I never seen such shiny apples. Reckon they're for that Gloriana Nelson's party. Lot of her boys live at Mrs. Stone's."

Kelpie wished her stomach were quiet. She would not listen to Tommy. Miss Lee never had. *No one has ever lied as much as that young man*, she'd told Kelpie. *Just because sometimes he leads you to a meat pie. Well, a stopped clock is right twice a day.*

Kelpie wished Tommy told the truth that often.

"All you gotta do is climb in the back window. The one off that side."

Kelpie couldn't help looking past Mrs. Stone's fence, which sagged in the middle like an old horse. The window was open. A tattered curtain fluttering over the sill looked silver in the moonlight.

"Back door's always locked. Kitchen's second door down past the room you'll climb into. And there's your apples. Dead shiny, they are."

Kelpie knew better than to go in. Apples or no apples.

She wasn't even sure she remembered their taste. A bit sharp, a lot sweet. Or was that plums? Hadn't had one of them since Old Ma was alive. They were softer, juicier. Apples were the hard ones. Like cricket balls. She felt the water enter her mouth.

"Never seen so many apples," Tommy said.

"Why do you want me to eat?" Kelpie asked instead of walking on like she would have if Miss Lee hadn't faded. "They poison?"

Tommy grinned.

If Miss Lee was still here, Kelpie wouldn't be talking to him. She wouldn't be hungry either. Miss Lee found food for her and safe places to sleep.

"She's gone now, ain't she? You talking to me again and no shoes. No one's looking out for you." He paused and then said, "'S not right." Almost as if he cared.

That should've been Kelpie's warning. Tommy didn't care about anything. If he wanted her to go into Mrs. Stone's, it weren't for any good reason.

Ghosts couldn't hurt you directly. They couldn't push you off a cliff, but they could lead you off one, if you were stupid enough to follow.

But Kelpie was hungry. Hard to think when you're hungry. She had to scrounge food where she could, because Miss Lee was gone, because Snowy was still in gaol and no one else living looked out for her, because she had no money to pay for food, and because she couldn't beg. Kids who begged got swept up by Welfare.

Tommy nodded at Mrs. Stone's. "Ain't none of them home. Too early for that lot. And you know Mrs. Stone's deaf as a post."

The sun wasn't up. For the razor men, the standover men—all of that mob—their working day ended at noon. Didn't start till after the sun went down.

"I used to love me some apples."

Tommy kept showing teeth. *Happy as a pig in shit*, Old Ma would have said, with no approval at all.

"Go on then." Tommy pointed at the gap in the collapsing grey fence, edged with splinters longer than Kelpie's thigh. "You'll fit through easy." He leaned back, arms folded, all nonchalant like he owned the lane.

Kelpie was hungry.

She slipped through the gap, crept past the pile of bricks that was the dunny leaning against the fence. Smelled like the night-soil men had missed this one. She threaded her way past a broken curved-backed chair and a rusting bicycle without seat or handle-bars or wheels. Weeds growing high between paving stones brushed the backs of her calves.

Kelpie tried the back door, not putting it past Tommy to make her enter through a window when she didn't have to.

Locked.

She stood on her toes to look through the window. The dirty curtain brushed across her nose. An empty bedroom. Narrow unmade bed in the corner. A pile of clothes on top of suitcases and a side table covered with old newspapers, an overfull ashtray, and empty bottles. One was filled with desiccated brown flowers. Kelpie wondered at a razor man having flowers, even dead ones, and then hauled herself over the sill.

Outside she could hear the *clip clop* of horse and cart, the clatter of a truck down Foveaux Street, further away raised voices. The house creaked, settling in the wind. The place smelled damp and dank and dusty. She heard no movement inside the house.

Kelpie peered out the open door. The carpet along the corridor was so worn the floorboards peeked through. Near the front door empty hooks protruded from the wall. On an afternoon, they'd hold hats and coats. Behind her the back door's bolt was thick and heavy.

As Kelpie crept along, a board groaned. She stilled. Listened hard. Nothing.

Her skin tightened, as if her body heard something her ears didn't. Kelpie could slip out the way she came. Go to Paddy's Markets. There was sometimes fallen fruit and vegetables, provided she wasn't run off before she could lay hands on any of it.

These apples were closer.

Kelpie went up on her toes, making herself lighter. She'd spent so long among ghosts she'd become almost as quiet.

Something smelled worse than damp. The closer she moved to the kitchen, the worse the smell grew.

The first door on her left was closed, but the second was open.

It wasn't a kitchen. Tommy'd lied.

It was another bedroom.

A lady in a fancy blue suit with matching hat was leaning over a dead man on the bed. Her hands were shaking. She held a card. She handed it to Kelpie.

"Mr. Davidson did it," she said. "See?"

Razorhurst

Nineteen twenty-eight had been a banner year for blood. Throughout the east of the city—Surry Hills, Darlinghurst, Woolloomooloo, Kings Cross, Paddington—blood flowed. Razors cut up faces, sliced off ears, opened up chests and bowels; went in through the eye, the ribs, the throat. They maimed, crippled, and killed.

Why razors?

Because they banned handguns at the beginning of the twenties, didn't they? To keep them out of the hands of the Commies. To stop the much-promised revolution. The one that never came.

Not that banning guns made them go away, but it did mean if you was caught with one, they could arrest you without you even pulling the trigger. Catch you with a razor, and all you had to do was point to your none-too-smooth cheeks: *Was gunna give meself a shave first thing, wasn't I, constable? A very close shave. That's why it's so sharp, see?*

The razor men became artists of the blade. Where was the artistry in squeezing a trigger? In the rough outlines of a bullet wound? Nowhere. Not like the *L* you could carve on a man's face.

You didn't have to kill your enemies. Just let them know you'd been there and weren't never going away. That scar lived on a mug's face for the rest of his life. He would always be marked, broken, less than.

Or not.

The hardest razor men had the biggest scars.

Get cut up like that? And live? Now *there* was a man.

Angry Carbone, Snowy Fullerton, Razor Tom, Jimmy Palmer, Bluey Denham. Real men with real scars and real razors.

Proud inhabitants of Greater Razorhurst. Dubbed so by *Truth*, a newspaper that never lied, in the bloody year of 1928—when Frog Hollow had only just been torn down, Old Ma was barely dead, and Kelpie was being raised by ghosts. Dymphna Campbell was beginning her first year in her chosen profession, and those gang bosses, Gloriana Nelson and Mr. Davidson, were crawling to the top of the bloody remains of Razorhurst and brokering the peace that still held.

And could well hold for a while longer on this cold winter morning in 1932.

Or not . . .

✂ KELPIE ✂

Kelpie didn't look at the card between her fingers. She could feel it there, but she was staring at the red splashes on the walls, on the mirror of the wardrobe, across the two paintings. At the blood sliding down in thin rivulets. Her nostrils flared at the smell from the dead man, and she wished she could close them.

She did not see or smell apples.

She had to run. This was trouble. This would bring police, Welfare. Her feet would not move.

"That's Mr. Davidson's handwriting," the woman said, as if handwriting mattered while a man lay dead. Newly dead.

Kelpie knew who Mr. Davidson was: the boss of all the crime in the Hills and beyond, him and Gloriana Nelson. She ruled where he didn't and vice versa. They did not like each other.

The man's face was all cut up, his throat slashed open. Kelpie saw something white in the midst of all the red. The bones of his neck?

Kelpie couldn't help touching her own throat.

Blood had soaked into the top of his trousers, his jacket, his shirt, the pillows under his head, the sheets. There was blood across the ashtray and magazines and books and empty glass on the bedside table. On the coats hanging from the hooks on the wall. Blood dripped from the dead man's shoes hanging over the edge of the not-big-enough bed.

Kelpie wondered how his blood had hit the wall behind him. She tried not to imagine his body spinning.

She'd seen dead bodies before. But not like this. She needed to get away. Fast.

Why wasn't she moving?

"Davidson did this," the woman said. Her voice caught on his name. "Do you understand? Look at the card."

His eyes were as open as his throat, staring up at the ceiling as if that's where his killer was. Kelpie looked up.

The ceiling sagged, the plaster rose in the centre mostly gone, damp brown stains spreading out from where the rose had been, but no killer. No blood either. The splashes didn't reach that high.

One of his hands lay palm up on the bed, scored with deep cuts. The other hung over the edge.

"Can't you read?" the woman asked. Her voice was as posh as her clothes.

Kelpie blushed and looked at the card. There was blood on it, and neat handwriting:

For you, Dymph

That was when Kelpie knew who the woman was: Dymphna Campbell. She was famous in the Hills. Most beautiful woman any of them had ever seen.

Kelpie had never seen her this close. She was prettier, shinier, cleaner than Kelpie had imagined. The cold didn't seem to affect her: Dymphna's eyes weren't red or running. Her blue suit was matched by her hat, by the small bag jutting out of her pocket, by the shoes on her feet. The silver watch on her wrist sparkled in the moonlight spilling through the window. Her hair was almost the same colour.

Kelpie half disbelieved Dymphna Campbell was real.

She didn't have a drop of blood on her.

There was blood everywhere.

"The card was on top of Jimmy. A warning for me."

Kelpie could hear Dymphna breathing. Dymphna worked for Glory Nelson. But the card was from Mr. Davidson. This was worse than trouble.

"I thought he'd last longer," Dymphna said, her voice shaky, looking down at the body, one hand covering her nose. "Now what? Shit." She glanced at the card in Kelpie's hand, breathed in, and straightened, stepping away from the bed. "Kelpie, isn't it?" Dymphna asked, as if they'd been introduced on the street, as if there wasn't a dead man in the room.

Kelpie nodded without meeting her eyes, surprised Dymphna knew her name. She lowered her head, saw drops of blood by her feet. Everyone in the Hills called Dymphna Campbell the Angel of Death. All her boyfriends died. Not one had been with her longer than a few months.

"Snowy told me," Dymphna said. "I saw him give you peanuts."

"My Snowy?" Kelpie asked. Why wasn't she running?

"Snowy Fullerton."

Snowy was one of Mr. Davidson's men. Why would he be talking to Dymphna, Glory's best girl? Their people were not friendly with one another.

A jarring thud made them both look away from the dead man.

"*Shit,*" Dymphna said, grabbing Kelpie's hand and pulling her from the room. Kelpie's feet finally cooperated.

The thumping came from the front door.

Dymphna dragged her along the corridor, dropping Kelpie's hand to pull at the bolt on the back door. It didn't budge. She pulled harder, her knuckles going white.

The banging grew louder.

"In here," Kelpie whispered. She shut the bedroom door behind them as wood splintered at the front of the house. The room looked different from this angle. The dead flowers cast a shadow the shape of a twisted hand.

The house shook.

"Christ," Dymphna breathed. "Sounds like they've ripped the door off. Not the cops. It can't be the cops."

Kelpie swallowed. Cops. Cops meant Welfare. She pulled Dymphna towards the window, scrambling onto the sill and over, silent as she could.

Behind her Dymphna hitched her skirt up and slung a leg over, ducking her head.

A ghost appeared beside her. A big bloke with a scar on his cheek. Kelpie didn't startle. She'd expected there to be ghosts. Most houses had at least one.

"There's worse things than cops, Dymphna love," the ghost said. He tried to pat her shoulder. His hand went straight through. He stared at it. "Why does my skin look wrong?"

As if she'd heard, Dymphna whispered, "Though Davidson's men are as bad as coppers."

Kelpie didn't think so. Mostly the hard men left her alone. Coppers though . . .

Dymphna dropped to the backyard, breaking a flowerpot.

They both froze, crouched low beneath the sill. Kelpie crept to the gap in the fence, hoping Dymphna realised the noise from inside drowned out their pot shattering.

"Dymphna," the ghost began.

Kelpie slid through the gap into Belmore Lane.

Dymphna turned sideways, fit one leg through, sucked her belly in, and pushed with both hands. She didn't shift. But the wood groaned.

The ghost tried to pull one of the boards from the fence. When his hands went straight through, he bellowed.

"Here," Dymphna said. "Take my hat."

Kelpie took the small, blue-veiled thing that wouldn't keep rain or sun out of your eyes. It looked like something you could eat.

"Her arse is too big," Tommy said. "She's gunna break the fence."

He was leaning against the warehouse opposite, not grinning now, laughing. "Good apples, eh?" He slapped his thigh. "*That* was a corker. Don't think I've ever done better. Heard the coppers coming, didn't I? I seen her watching you, see? Plenty of times. Reckoned it might be fun to see what'd happen."

Kelpie ignored his stupid blather. If he weren't already dead, she'd do for him herself. Not another word to the rat-featured little bastard, she vowed.

Tommy grinned widely. "Looker, ain't she? I never seen a chromo look as good as her. Most of them hard-faced sluts'd make a rat look good. She almost glows."

The other ghost shot Tommy a poisonous look and tried to help Dymphna. Kelpie was sure now that he was the dead man—what had Dymphna called him? He didn't know he was dead yet.

"Hard to imagine her killing anyone," Tommy said, though he was doing just that. "She's too pretty."

Kelpie wasn't going to correct him. Whoever killed that bloke would be covered in blood. Not shiny clean like Dymphna Campbell. Kelpie put the hat down, grabbed Dymphna's hands, and pulled, both feet braced against the kerb. Fabric tore.

"Harder," Dymphna said. "Don't worry about the skirt."

"Don't hurt her!" the ghost cried.

"Leave the fat cow!" Tommy yelled. "Save yourself!" He laughed harder. "Pity you ain't invisible, like us. Stupid breathers."

Kelpie heard metal on metal. Louder even than Tommy's maniac laugh. The bolt on the back door. She strained so hard tendons stood out along her arms, so hard it felt like her eyes would pop.

Dymphna ripped through the fence, knocking Kelpie over. Kelpie scrambled out from under her and onto her feet. Dymphna grabbed Kelpie's arm and used it to stand up. The back of her skirt was torn. She bent to pick up her squashed hat.

"You have to stick with me," she whispered harshly in Kelpie's ear, gripping harder as Kelpie tried to shake free.

Why did she have to stick with Dymphna? That dead man had nothing to do with her.

Dymphna staggered a few more steps away from Mrs. Stone's. It was obvious she had no idea where to go.

Behind them Kelpie could hear shouting. They must've got the back door open.

"They'll kill us both," Dymphna said. "We're both in this."

No, they weren't. It wasn't Kelpie's name on that card what'd been on a dead man's chest.

Tommy snorted. "Jeez, sounds like there's an army after you! Don't fancy your chances, Kelpie. Wonder where you'll haunt. Right here on the lane with me? Won't that be cosy?"

"This way," Kelpie said, Tommy's comments deciding her. She pointed at the Darcy place. No one would be awake but Neal Darcy, and he'd be too focused on his writing. "Let's go."

Dymphna complied but kept a grip on Kelpie's arm. Kelpie dragged them three doors up past leaning fences covered in choko vines that were still months away from fruiting.

Kelpie pushed the loose board aside and scrambled into the Darcys' backyard on hands and knees, landing next to the dunny. Dymphna scraped through behind her. Kelpie turned to stop the board from swinging. They were both breathing too hard.

The ghost of Dymphna's dead boyfriend appeared next to her. Cripes but he was a huge bugger.

"It's me, Dymph," he said. "I know it's all gone bung, but we can fix it."

His hands pawed uselessly at Dymphna's side. Kelpie shuddered. She hated when ghosts touched her.

"Why won't you answer me, Dymphna?"

Kelpie could hear men on the lane stomping and yelling.

"I'm sure it's the cops," Dymphna breathed. Her gloved hands shook. They weren't shiny clean anymore.

Someone cleared his throat.

Kelpie turned to see Darcy sitting on the back steps, cigarette in hand, staring at Dymphna.

"And who the fuck are you?"

Miss Lee

Miss Lee had been dead wrong about Kelpie's age when they first met. Not that she ever knew that.

Miss Lee had a heart as soft as bitumen on a stinking hot day and thought it a disgrace that Kelpie had been abandoned on the streets to fend for herself. What was the world coming to? The little girl was skeletal, dressed in rags, and all alone. When Miss Lee had discovered Kelpie could see ghosts, the little girl wasn't even wearing shoes! Miss Lee had determined at once that she would find the poor child food, clothes, and shelter; she would protect her.

Miss Lee would have been even more shocked had she known that Kelpie was not a child. When they had met, Kelpie had been about to turn fifteen. Malnourishment had stunted her growth and prolonged her childhood. If you could call it a childhood, out on the streets, ignored by all but ghosts and that hardened standover, Snowy Fullerton.

But Miss Lee did not know how old Kelpie truly was. How could she when Kelpie herself had little idea? If she had, Miss Lee would have seen it as her duty to prepare Kelpie for womanhood. How would the child know what to do when her monthlies began? Kelpie knew nothing of what her body had in store for her. Miss Lee would have taught her.

Miss Lee liked to teach. It had been both her profession and her vocation.

Kelpie was grateful to have found Miss Lee, for the prim ghost had the run of the Hills. Miss Lee was one of the few talkers who could move around. She spent her time going from house to house looking for open books or, best of all, someone reading.

"Could be looking at anything," Tommy grumbled. "*Anything*. A picture show. Could go to one of Glory Nelson's houses. Watch them girls. I'd like to see *that*."

Miss Lee ignored Tommy, something Kelpie all too often failed to do.

"Can't turn the pages," Miss Lee explained. "Have to peer over their shoulders and hope they don't put the book down right when it gets exciting."

It was spring when they met. The first hot day. Miss Lee had been so thrilled to find someone alive who could see her that she'd urged Kelpie all the way to the public library. Kelpie had let herself be bullied because she liked Miss Lee. She was enthusiastic. All most talkers did was complain or be mean.

Not Miss Lee.

Besides, a ghost who could travel without haunting someone was a novelty.

Kelpie had had to sneak past the woman at the front desk. Kids weren't allowed, and even if they had been, it was school time—still a few more weeks before they were released for the summer. The librarians would have handed her to Welfare if they'd caught her.

She'd never been inside a library before. It was dark, full of dust, and echoingly quiet, but it wasn't damp, and nothing was rotting.

"Over here," Miss Lee yelled. "Get down *Great Expectations*." She clapped her hands. "*Finally.* Died less than halfway through, didn't I?"

Kelpie reached for where Miss Lee was pointing. She wasn't quite tall enough. She pulled out a big volume from the bottom shelf and stood on it.

"Oh no, not on a book!"

"Won't hurt it," Kelpie said, quiet as she could. "It's thick as a brick. Which one d'you want? This one?"

"*Great Expectations.*"

Kelpie slid a red volume from the shelf.

"No, no. Didn't you hear me? *Great Expectations.* The one next to it. Oh," Miss Lee said. "You can't read, can you?"

Kelpie's face got hot. Miss Lee thought she was stupid. She wasn't. She wasn't!

Kelpie ran.

Bolted out of the aisle of books, past the librarian with her mouth wide open, and onto the footpath, almost knocking over a pedlar's wheelbarrow full of several-days-old fruit and veg most likely scrounged from the ground at the markets. She ran hard and fast until she pulled up in Moore Park, scrambling up the nearest fig tree.

Miss Lee appeared beside her, and Kelpie was less charmed by her ability to go wherever she wanted. She screamed at her to "Bloody bugger off!"

Miss Lee disappeared. That sudden vanish all ghosts could do that never stopped making Kelpie's skin crawl.

Though worse was the slow fade. Because then they never came back.

Next morning Kelpie woke to Miss Lee whispering in her ear. Kelpie had kipped down in what had been Frog Hollow, inside a broken packing crate on a pile of discarded fabric, wishing Old Ma was back.

Miss Lee whispered a story about a selfish giant. Kelpie pretended to be asleep until she was finished. When she opened her eyes, Miss Lee was smiling.

"I'll teach you to read," she said. "It's easy."

⟩━ DYMPHNA ━⟨

Dymphna Campbell smiled at the handsome young man smoking on the back steps. She held a finger to her lips, curving them as charmingly as she could, meeting his eyes, willing him not to betray them, trying to slow her breath, the beating of her heart, all while the ghost of Jimmy Palmer begged her to stop ignoring him.

"Please," she whispered to the young man, who almost smiled back at her.

Jimmy Palmer dead. Jimmy Palmer a ghost.

Dymphna did not glance his way. She kept her eyes on the young man. Watching him watching her.

She had plenty of practice not looking at ghosts. Most of her life she'd concealed her ability to see and hear them. Unlike Kelpie she knew ghosts could drive you mad.

She could even ignore a ghost like Jimmy—a man she'd known, a man she'd tried to love—while he loomed over her, taller than a house, stronger than an ox; big, Jesus, he was big. Take two of that young man to approach the size of Jimmy Palmer. Though the boy was much prettier.

Jimmy waved his hand back and forth in front of her face. Dymphna didn't blink.

He tried to put his arms around her. They slid through as if he were separating Dymphna's body from her soul. She didn't shudder, though it made her guts quail. She was already quailing—huge Jimmy Palmer, robbed of heft, light and airy as any ghost half his size.

Much harder than not looking at him was not asking him what had happened. How did Mr. Davidson know they were going to kill him and take over Razorhurst? Who else knew?

How did he get to Jimmy first? Was Mr. Davidson going to kill her too? Did Gloriana know? If Glory knew that Dymphna and Jimmy had been planning to take over from her, then Dymphna was twice dead and would end her days haunting the bottom of the harbour.

Between Mr. Davidson, Glory, and the coppers, Dymphna couldn't see a way out.

But at least her blood was still inside her, not like Jimmy Palmer. Walking in on him like that . . . she wasn't going to forget it any time soon. So much blood. Almost as much as . . .

Dymphna gulped.

If she'd arrived a little earlier, would she be dead too? Had she missed death a second time?

How had Mr. Davidson found out about their plans? There was no one to tell him. Jimmy and Dymphna had kept it all to themselves. But he would not have had Jimmy killed without knowing for sure. For more than three years now, Gloriana and Mr. Davidson had respected the truce. Each sticking to their own slice of Razorhurst. None of their men going after each other except when it was personal. It would take something big for Mr. Davidson to break the truce. Something as big as a plot to kill him.

But then why had Mr. Davidson left that card? Identical to the cards on all those flowers he'd sent her?

For you, Dymph

Dymphna had almost dropped her bundle reading those words. But perhaps she was reading it wrong. Perhaps it was exactly like the other cards he'd sent her with their messages of *Be mine* and *You are in my thoughts* and *I want you*. Yet another attempt to woo her. Only this time with blood.

Perhaps it was Mr. Davidson announcing he was getting rid of his competition; clearing the path so she'd be his.

Like hell that was going to happen.

Perhaps the card meant Davidson *didn't* know about her and Jimmy's scheming.

If Davidson didn't know, perhaps Glory didn't know either.

Perhaps . . .

The young man took another drag on his cigarette, still staring at her. She hadn't lost him. She had to make sure, too, she did not lose herself.

The yelling in the lane was louder. She thought she recognised Boomer's voice. He was almost as big as Jimmy and one of the few coppers not in Davidson's or Glory's pockets.

Dymphna did not want to go back to gaol.

"Coppers," the young man said, quietly. "What'd you do?"

Dymphna shook her head. "Nothing," she whispered.

He took another drag, let the smoke curl slowly out of his mouth. "Sounds like something."

"It was what we saw."

He nodded. But she couldn't tell if it was in agreement or if he was merely acknowledging that she'd answered his question.

All he had to do was call out.

Dymphna was no longer sure he was looking at her with admiration. It was more like he was considering. She would not let herself panic.

If the coppers did grab her, well, gaol was better than being dead.

Not that coppers meant gaol for sure. Plenty of those cops were Davidson's or Glory's. They owned a few judges too.

Jimmy Palmer was dead.

She hadn't been with Jimmy because of his looks or his personality. He was tall and strong, and almost everyone in Razorhurst was afraid of him. He was smart too, and ambitious, and knew everyone who mattered in their world. That's how he'd become Glory's right-hand man.

Dymphna had been sure he would keep her safe. Thought him not being an underling meant he'd last longer. She'd been right. He had lasted longer than her other men. By a matter of weeks.

Now Jimmy's blood was everywhere and her own soon to follow.

Beside her Kelpie shifted against the fence, causing a faint creak in the timber. Dymphna told herself no one would have heard it over the hullabaloo behind them.

"Kelpie?" the boy said softly, as if he had only just noticed she was there. He raised an eyebrow. Kelpie shrugged, smart enough to be quiet.

Dymphna had to focus on getting out of this mess, getting *them* out of this mess.

She almost laughed that now, in the midst of this disaster, she had finally spoken to Kelpie, the girl who saw ghosts same as her, the girl she'd planned to rescue someday—and had found by accident over Jimmy's dead body.

Jesus wept.

She still had hold of the girl, but her grip had slipped to the girl's hand, as if Kelpie were a littlie and Dymphna her mum. She would be happy to mother her. Kelpie needed it.

But Jimmy Palmer was dead. Which meant Dymphna had no protection until she lined up her next man, who would not be Mr. Davidson. There would be no next man if Glory knew what she and Jimmy had been planning. If Dymphna was merely waiting to be a twice-murdered chromo.

Dymphna wanted to hold her head in her hands and weep. To ask Jimmy what he knew. Even though once you let a ghost know you could see it, it started to eat away at you. Even though it would give her away to Kelpie too soon. Even though that young man might hear her, the coppers too.

Instead she watched the young man smoke his cigarette. The smoke curled up in wisps past his curly dark hair, clear as day in the full moon's light. She smiled a little wider. He could *not* give them away.

Kelpie shook off Dymphna's hand and stood with her back pressed to the fence. Dymphna breathed in sharply. But it was all right. Unlike Dymphna the girl was shorter than the fence. Dymphna took hold of the girl's ankle. Gently. She didn't want to hurt her.

"They're coming for you," the ghost on the lane screamed. "You're doomed, Kelpie, doomed!"

Bloody ghosts. Dymphna was going to have to teach Kelpie to be a lot less friendly. Mind you, the girl had wandered into Mrs. Stone's as if it were a gingerbread house and not full of standovers and gangsters and dead men. She didn't seem to know how dangerous *anything* was.

The young man ran the glowing tip of his cigarette gently against the step's edge, and the ash floated gently onto the garden.

"Please," Kelpie whispered. "Please don't give us away."

Dymphna doubted he'd heard. Kelpie repeated her plea.

Dymphna smiled again. Surely he wouldn't call out? But what if the coppers started searching each yard? They were done if . . .

She could not let herself think through all the dead ends.

A brown and yellow bundle of fur jumped over the fence, streaking across the yard and over the next fence. Dymphna choked back a scream as the cat flashed past. Chickens squawked loudly in the next yard. Almost as loud as the cops.

Dymphna's heart beat too fast. She had to calm herself. Focus. Smile, she told herself. Win him over.

"Please," Dymphna whispered, trusting to the strength of her charm.

Old Ma had the misfortune of owning a building in Frog Hollow. Built when the frogs that gave the Hollow its name were still there. When the water that ran through it was clean.

Back then there wasn't more than a few homes in the Hollow, and none of them built to last. You don't build on swampy, sandy land hoping for permanency. But the people were mostly decent, even if they was poor. Didn't last long: the Hollow turned bad before the Great War. Before the men came slinking home missing legs and arms, eyes, their minds.

Old Ma had taken some of them in. At least they was honest. Mostly. Times were always bad down there, even before all them banks closed and the jobs dried up so's the only blokes working were the ones with the quickest hands and the sharpest razors and the meanest faces, and the women could only earn their keep turning chromo, flat on their backs.

But no regular jobs. Not in Frog Hollow.

If you weren't sick before you lived there, you were soon after you moved in. Everyone turned pale and concave chested. Everyone's coughs rattled through their bodies, looking for escape.

You didn't go there unless you were wicked or there was nowhere else.

Nothing reached down into Frog Hollow, not even sunshine. Bordered on two sides by sheer cliffs not even the wiliest monkey could climb, and the poorer it got, the more houses they built, one on top of the other.

No running water and no night-soil men to come and take the shit away.

Kelpie had known Old Ma before she became a colourless ghost, when her cheeks were mottled red, her legs a ropey mess of blue and red veins, and Kelpie could feel her warmth and smell milk and flour and tobacco when Old Ma drew her into her arms.

Old Ma wasn't Kelpie's real ma, but she told Kelpie stories about her parents. About how she'd been there when Kelpie's real ma died bringing her into the world. How her pa died a few scant hours later.

Other times she said that Kelpie's ma had died alone. Or that it was her pa who brought the wee babe to Old Ma and was still watching over her when he could. One time she said she'd found Kelpie in a bucket on her doorstep.

Kelpie hated variations in the tale, insisting that Old Ma stick to one, correcting her when she changed any details. The story they stuck to went like this:

Grief was what killed your pa, Old Ma would say, *though they was sickly getting off the boat, leaning in on each other, unsteady-like, coughing all the time. As if they was still on the water. Skin too yellow, too dry.*

But they were always looking at each other, smiling. Must've seen something good there. He never raised his hand to her. Nor her to him. No yelling neither. They were decent people. Even though they never paid for more than that first week. And them staying on another two.

Or was it three?

No, Old Ma, Kelpie would say. *It was two!*

Old Ma didn't like to rent her rooms for free. But times being as tough as they were and no jobs that weren't dodgy, she'd had to get used to it. She didn't like to throw people out on the street. There were enough evictions without her adding to their number. She'd only toss you if you stole from her or got mean when you was drunk. Kelpie's parents didn't do neither.

That was all the staying they did. Three weeks in Old Ma's falling-down, broken home in Frog Hollow, and then dead and gone.

Or—

No or, Kelpie said. *Tell it the proper way.*

If her parents were ghosts, it wasn't in Frog Hollow. Kelpie wondered if they'd flown back over the seas to haunt the island they came from. But Old Ma was from the old country, and when she died, she had haunted right there in the Hollow.

Old Ma said Kelpie's parents died before they named her. Old Ma had called her Petal. But everyone in the Hollow called her Kelpie, which you'd think was after the water spirit because her parents were Irish, but no, it was after the dog. They said she was a wild pup.

KELPIE

Neal Darcy opened the back door. Kelpie kept low, skirting the dried-up veggie garden, the water pump, the tub, the line hung only with old pegs, and up the wooden steps. Dymphna slipped past her and inside first. Darcy shut the door behind them.

"Don't say nothing," Darcy said from outside. The door bowed inward under his weight. "Walls are thin."

Kelpie leaned against their side of the door breathing through her nose. Quieter that way. Outside she heard men's boots thudding on the lane, whistles and sirens, and so many raised voices they overlapped. Inside she heard Dymphna's breaths, her heart pounding too. Though that could have been her own noisy beater ringing in her ears.

The curtains at the window were white and transparent. If they moved beyond the safety of the door, they'd be seen. She hoped Dymphna knew to stay still.

The big, tall ghost planted himself on Dymphna's other side and yelled at her to stop ignoring him. Yelled at the world to tell him what was happening. Why was his skin wrong? Why did he feel wrong? Kelpie wished she could yell at him to shut his big, fat gob.

Dymphna gripped Kelpie's hand again. Kelpie'd never felt such a soft hand. No calluses. No scars.

Outside: more yelling.

Kelpie would have to escape soon. She didn't want to make trouble for Mrs. Darcy. Wouldn't be long now before she would be up making breakfast.

She'd never been inside the Darcys' home. She'd stood on the other side of the window watching Darcy bashing out his stories while Miss Lee leaned over his shoulder and read out the words. There'd been two faded ghosts in the kitchen when Miss Lee first led her to Neal Darcy. Now there was only one, so insubstantial Kelpie could see through it as it wafted from the front of the house to the kitchen door. She could barely feel the ghost as it drifted through her.

After Darcy'd caught her peering through the window, he'd invited her in. But Kelpie said no. It didn't seem right. She'd said no again even after Mrs. Darcy had given her a piece of bread and asked her in for a cuppa. Kelpie didn't belong with a family.

She liked being able to see the kitchen. It reminded her of Old Ma's. A kitchen table took up most of the room. Stools and crates were shoved underneath. A stove, a gas meter, an icebox, and two rickety cupboards whose doors did not quite shut leaned against the wall. On the wall, hanging from hooks, were ladles and spoons and pots and sieves and graters and things Kelpie couldn't identify because Old Ma hadn't owned anything like them.

Through the mottled glass of the front door, Kelpie saw dark shapes moving out on the street. Lights shone through. Coppers searching, most like.

Kelpie's stomach growled. It was the half-full glass of milk on the table that did it. She wished she could take a sip. But there was no way to get her hands on it without being seen.

Next to the milk, Darcy's typewriter rested on a pile of newspapers. Beside it was an uneven stack of pages half covered by a towel. She wished she could touch those keys, that one day she could make the typewriter clatter and ding the way Darcy did. He'd promised to teach her.

Outside Darcy coughed, loud and sudden, and Dymphna flinched beside her.

"That you, Darcy?" someone called. Kelpie couldn't be sure if it was from the lane or next door.

"What's the barney, constable?" Darcy replied. The door shifted as he must have leaned forward.

Dymphna stilled. Kelpie breathed even quieter.

The gate creaked, so loud Kelpie wondered that the whole Darcy household didn't wake.

"Bit of bother at Mrs. Stone's. You seen anyone about who shouldn't be, Darce?"

Kelpie thought of that poor bloke on the bed, who was now a ghost trying to make Dymphna see him. Bit more than a bother, wasn't it? *That smell.* She'd heard some people wet themselves when they died. He'd done worse than that.

"Almost everyone at Mrs. Stone's shouldn't be about," Darcy said. Kelpie heard him take a drag on his cigarette. The copper snorted.

"Seen any young women? Well dressed?"

"Well dressed? Around here?"

The copper laughed again. "This one's known for hanging out with a rough crowd."

Darcy didn't say anything.

Kelpie wondered how they knew to look for Dymphna Campbell. Kelpie was going to get shot of her as soon as she could. Dymphna squeezed her hand, and Kelpie's face felt hot. Dymphna was right-o. But Kelpie couldn't afford to keep company with anyone the coppers was after.

"Let us know if you hear anything."

"Will do, Boomer. Only you blokes so far," Darcy said. "And those chooks and some screaming and breaking glass from the Kellers."

"All as it should be then?"

Darcy gave a short laugh. The gate creaked again. "See ya later."

The copper shouted something back that Kelpie didn't hear.

"Too right!" Darcy called after him. "You owe me a drink, Boomer."

The door bowed in again. "Imagine they'll keep searching," Darcy said quietly in between drags. "Best you two stay put a while longer. Don't move. I'll be in when I finish this."

Dymphna made a little noise. "Does he want us to stop breathing?"

"That'd help," Darcy said.

Kelpie tried not to worry about Darcy's ma and his brothers and sisters and their lodger. The house was quiet, but with all that racket from the cops, they'd be up soon. Then what?

"Don't think you should stay here, Dymph," the scarred-cheeked ghost said. "It's not safe."

"You all right?" Dymphna whispered.

Kelpie nodded.

Darcy hissed at them to *shh*.

Kelpie pulled her hand from Dymphna's and slid to the floor, letting her muscles relax. Like Old Ma had taught her: sleep when you can, never be tense unless you have to be. Only led to grief and headaches.

The kitchen ceiling was stained and bowed in as if a little more weight from above, and it'd come crashing down. It wouldn't be the first. Before they'd torn down Frog Hollow, some of the houses had collapsed on their own. *All it took was breathing a little too heavy*, Old Ma had said.

Kelpie kept her breath quiet and slow, watched it make condensation in the air as if she were smoking like Darcy.

"Jimmy Palmer was a good bloke," Dymphna said softly. "Kind. Probably why he didn't last."

Kelpie had heard that name before. One of Glory's standovers. Did Dymphna mean the ghost? He didn't look kind. He looked big and ropeable.

"Shh," Darcy whispered. "Killing my cigarette now."

"I'm *still* a good bloke," the ghost said. He waved his hand in front of Dymphna's eyes. She didn't even blink. "I'll always be a good bloke."

But Kelpie could tell from the way he said it that Jimmy Palmer knew he was dead.

The door shifted, and the back step creaked as Darcy stood. "There's a fair few eyeballs out on the lane. Duck down, then move below the windows."

Kelpie slid right, Dymphna left.

"Opening the door now. Slowly."

"Hey, young Neal," Mrs. Keller shouted from next door. "What's the barney? My chooks are going mental."

Darcy stepped back out and shut the door. Kelpie flattened herself against the wall, pulling her knees to her chest and squeezing her eyes tight. She was even closer to the milk now.

"Morning, Mrs. Keller," Darcy said. "There's trouble at Mrs. Stone's."

"Oh, aye," said Mrs. Keller with a loud exhale. She didn't talk so much as boom. Tommy called her Old Bellow Lungs, but her husband was louder. "Well, there would be, wouldn't there? Up at all hours. Doing God knows what. All of them scarred like, like, I don't know what. It ain't right."

"No, it's not, Mrs. Keller."

"I don't suppose them coppers are doing anything about it for all their running about and shouting," she continued without pause. "It's a wonder anyone's still asleep. It's not like that lot at Mrs. Stone's didn't already keep us up all night with their goings-on. Women laughing too loud! Bottles smashing! Automobiles driving up at all hours! Louder than a herd of elephants! Here it is almost five and soon time to be awake and off to the factories. It ain't right at all."

"Why don't you bloody shut it then?" yelled a voice so loud and penetrating it could only be Mr. Keller. "Not like *you* work in a factory!"

"Don't talk to me like that!"

"I need all my sleep, you stupid cow! Glory's party's tonight, or had you forgotten? Free beer and sausages! I'm not gunna miss it 'cause I can't keep me bloody eyes open!"

"Free beer! Free entry to corruption and dissolution and the end of your natural days, more like!"

"Oh, shut your flapping mouth! You know what her party's for, don't you, you silly sow? She's shafted her own husband. I'da thought you'd be the first one to celebrate a woman doing wrong by her husband. Divorce! And her a Catholic. Well—"

"Divorce is the only thing that—"

"They're off," Darcy whispered. The door opened, and he slipped inside—straight through Jimmy Palmer, who snarled and tried to punch him. Kelpie slid in front of the door and stood up. Dymphna did the same. They were so close Kelpie could see the yellow stains on Darcy's fingers.

"Thank you," Dymphna said quietly.

Kelpie muttered the same. She doubted Darcy heard. He was staring at Dymphna, she was staring at him.

"I'm Dymphna."

"Neal."

They didn't shake hands. They didn't stop staring either.

Kelpie wondered why Darcy was pretending he didn't know who Dymphna was. He'd written a story about her. He'd changed her name to Kitty Macintosh, and her eyes were green, not blue, but her hair was blonde like Dymphna's—though in the story he called it "silvery." Kitty ran with the same bruising men—that's what Darcy called them in the story—as Dymphna. In the end, the man Kitty loved killed her.

"Do you think it'll be safe if we slip out the front?" Dymphna asked.

Darcy shook his head. "Cops everywhere."

"I'm supposed to be helping set up for Glory's party," Dymphna murmured.

Kelpie heard footsteps upstairs. A door slammed. Someone called out, "Ma!"

A woman replied softly. Kelpie couldn't make out the words.

Dymphna and Darcy stared at each other.

The Kellers were still shouting. Kelpie heard the words *mongrel*, *proddie*, and *shiv*. Other voices screamed at them to bloody shut it. And that shouting from the lane—was that the police? Maybe the coppers were gone. Further away a whistle blasted from a freight train.

The stairs groaned loudly, one for each step, and then Mrs. Darcy stood at the bottom, her arms crossed tight. "Who are youse? What are you doing in my kitchen?"

"Friends, Ma," Darcy said softly, turning to her, leaning over the kitchen table and kissing her cheek. "You remember Kelpie."

Mrs. Darcy didn't say anything, but she smiled when she saw

Kelpie, patting her head while Kelpie resisted squirming. She did not like being touched as if she was a littlie. She might be small, but she wasn't a child.

Mrs. Darcy's gaze hardened when she turned to Dymphna. Kelpie could tell she knew who she was and how she made her money. Kelpie could almost see the word *chromo* balanced on her lips.

"They're in a spot of bother, Ma. We can give them breakfast, can't we?"

"Kelpie's welcome," Mrs. Darcy began, "but—"

"There's not enough time," Dymphna said. "We have to be going."

Jimmy Palmer looked agitated.

Outside the siren from a police motor-car sounded. Neal Darcy looked at Dymphna. "You won't get far."

More footsteps on the stairs.

"Who's that then?" one of Darcy's brothers asked. A little one. Snot dribbled from his left nostril to his mouth.

"Our guests," Mrs. Darcy said, shooting her eldest son a dark look.

Darcy carefully wrapped the typewriter in towels and put it under one of the crates they used as chairs. All six Darcy kids and the lodger, a tall thin woman wearing a worn suit and a hat, crammed around the kitchen table. Mrs. Darcy moved to the stove to warm the porridge.

The ghost belligerently pushed his way through them, and not a one noticed. Palmer looked like he was ready to explode.

"We should leave," Dymphna said, sounding even posher than Miss Lee.

The youngest Darcy girl was staring at her and making faces. Kelpie averted her eyes.

Someone banged so loud on the front door it rattled.

Kelpie and Dymphna looked at each other. Kelpie began to ease the back door open, readying herself to slide through and away.

"Cops, Ma," Darcy said as the pounding on the door continued.

"Upstairs, you two," Mrs. Darcy said. "Not a sound."

Kelpie's Theories of Ghosts

The dead weren't forthcoming about their lives as ghosts. No more than the living were about their strange rituals and customs. When drinking with your mates, you clink glasses. When you meet a man, you shake his hand. Very few could say how those customs began or what they mean. Or explain why they close their eyes when they sneeze. Or why so many living presume they are the centre of the universe.

Kelpie had no idea why only some dead stayed with the living. She had no idea where the rest of the dead went. Was it the same place ghosts went when they disappeared quick as a pickpocket, only to pop back just as sudden? Was it the same place they went when they faded away forever?

She had asked Miss Lee where she went.

"Not here."

"Not here as in somewhere else in the Hills or . . . ?"

"Not here. I can't explain more than that."

Kelpie asked other ghosts. Most didn't answer. She asked the cauliflower-eared boxer, Stuart O'Sullivan, where he went, and Stuart said, "Why don't you go tell off some hard man? You'll be killed dead, and *then* you'll know where we go."

She didn't ask Stuart anything like that again. Only questions about boxing and how to defend herself against the likes of Bluey Denham.

His main answer was, *Run.* But he also gave her useful tips on how to roll and duck, and tricksy ways to move from one spot to another slick fast, and which parts were most vulnerable: knees, between the legs, throat, eyes. *Not that you'll be able to reach the last two. Not unless he's already down. Hit 'em hard in one of them, then RUN!*

She didn't know why ghosts were grey. Though grey wasn't exactly right because they weren't like the colour grey of the living. It was more that all their colour was gone. Maybe it was life that gave the living colour, and when a person died, their colour died too.

She didn't know why some ghosts haunted people and others haunted places, or why Miss Lee could go wherever she wanted.

Tommy had been in Belmore Lane always. She'd never seen him anywhere else because he couldn't go anywhere else. Tommy was always complaining he was gunna be stuck on the lane until the end of time.

She didn't know why Miss Lee was free to roam. Miss Lee didn't either. *Do you know why the living have to breathe?* Miss Lee had asked.

Kelpie didn't know why only some ghosts could talk. She didn't know why most of them didn't talk to each other. Or maybe they did, but not when she was around.

Maybe they could all talk if they wanted. Maybe some of them had nothing to say. Or nothing to say to her. Most ghosts avoided the living.

She didn't know why so few of the living could sense ghosts. She'd see some people shiver and shift out of the way. But as far as she knew, Kelpie was the only one who could see them.

Why couldn't some living see her if she was near a ghost? Could they really not see her, or was it because she was little and inconspicuous? Nothing to do with ghosts at all?

Why could the dead see and smell and hear farther than the living? Why couldn't they touch or be touched?

What was the point of ghosts? Might as well ask what was the point of the living.

Kelpie knew almost nothing.

But she still knew more about the dead than the living.

Though as Miss Lee told her, there was an ocean more to know about the living than about the dead.

⊁ KELPIE ⊁

Kelpie scrambled up the stairs fast as she could, Dymphna behind her.

"Faster," Dymphna breathed, putting her hands to Kelpie's shoulders, pushing her. Each step creaked so loud Kelpie was sure they'd be caught. At the top of the stairs, Dymphna pushed her hard, and Kelpie stumbled into what had to be Mrs. Darcy's room.

It was dominated by a large, sagging bed with a chest at its foot. On the walls, clothes hung from hooks and wires running from corner to corner. Faded curtains covered the windows. Beside the bed was a small table with a sewing machine and a pile of cloth on top. Judging by the shoes along the wall, the three littlest must sleep with their ma.

"Under the bed," Dymphna said as Kelpie dived beneath. It wasn't as if there was anywhere else.

Dymphna did not close the door behind her. Afraid to make more noise, Kelpie reckoned.

Kelpie pulled herself up to the head, curling into a tight ball so she couldn't be seen. The chest blocked them from view, but it didn't hurt to make herself as small as she could. Dymphna crawled up next to her, hand over her mouth to keep from coughing. Dust didn't bother Kelpie. She was used to it.

She could hear raised voices below, but she couldn't pick apart the sounds to find the words.

Dymphna was still, her breathing quiet and even. Kelpie wondered if she'd fallen asleep.

"You're so beautiful, Dymphna," Palmer said. He was so close to Dymphna that his nose was pushing inside her cheek. His legs angled out through Dymphna's and past the end of the bed. Kelpie shuddered. Dymphna was lucky she couldn't feel ghosts. "I was looking forward to dancing with you at Glory's party. Didn't know I could dance, did you? My ma taught me. I can even waltz."

He had been by Dymphna's side since they left Mrs. Stone's. Kelpie was certain he was haunting her. Lucky for Dymphna, she couldn't see or hear him.

Kelpie hoped no ghost ever haunted her. Then wondered if that's what Old Ma had done. The thought had never occurred to her before, but Old Ma had been with Kelpie wherever she went. Kelpie had always assumed Old Ma haunted Frog Hollow, not her. After all, she'd faded after Frog Hollow had gone.

Kelpie felt a tightness in her chest. If Old Ma had been haunting her, why had she stopped? Why had she abandoned her?

"I never told you, Dymph, but I love you. Or should I say I *loved* you. I'm dead now, so I guess it's all past tense, even though I still love you. We were going to rule the world, you and me. Then Snowy killed me."

"Snowy Fullerton?" The name exploded out of Kelpie. No! He couldn't have. Not with all that blood. Snowy didn't kill people unless he had to, and he didn't make a big show of it when he did. Blood everywhere? The body lying about for anyone to find? With a card on it? That wasn't Snowy.

Palmer turned to stare at her.

"What about Snowy?" Dymphna whispered.

"Nothing," Kelpie said just as quietly. "I was wondering when he'd be out of gaol. I was, um, hoping to see him. He gives me chocolate. I miss him."

Dymphna put her fingers over her lips and closed her eyes.

"You can hear me," Palmer said. "How can you hear me?"

Kelpie closed her eyes too. She didn't owe this ghost anything. Snowy couldn't have killed him because Snowy was still in gaol. Besides, if Snowy had killed Palmer, his body would be in the harbour or buried somewhere. Snowy wasn't a butcher. Not like that Bluey Denham. Maybe Bluey had done it? Everyone knew Bluey would kill you as soon as look at you. Even if you had the same boss as him.

Jimmy Palmer reached through Dymphna, trying to touch Kelpie. Kelpie felt her insides crawl. She concentrated on the voices downstairs. But everyone was yelling. It was one thing she preferred about ghosts: mostly, they were much quieter.

The first of the factory whistles blew. A lorry rattled along Albion Street. The Hills were waking up.

"Tell Dymphna that Davidson made him do it. So she shouldn't be angry with Snowy. But she needs to get away. Pretty sure Davidson knows. It ain't safe. I know you can hear me. Go on, tell her."

Kelpie opened her eyes. He was leaning through Dymphna, less than an inch from her face. That close, his scar looked even worse.

She shook her head. She didn't tell the living about ghosts. Old Ma had taught her that.

"Tell her."

Dymphna might think Palmer was a good man, but the way he said those words made Kelpie want to run far away—despite knowing he couldn't hurt her.

"I saw the way that Neal Darcy was looking at her. You can tell him to stop and all. He'd be useless. You can tell he's never killed anyone. How would he keep any of those bastards at bay?"

Kelpie could tell he meant not like himself, Jimmy Palmer. Must be a lot easier to be hard when you were that big.

"Though maybe what she needs is someone who's not dangerous. Maybe he'd tell her to go back to her folks. She's from the North Shore, you know. From respectable people. She could be a doctor's wife if she wanted."

Downstairs a door slammed. Footsteps. Voices raised.

"She's bloody calm, don't you think? Like she doesn't realise how bad this is. I mean, look at her!"

Kelpie didn't.

"She's asleep. How could she fall asleep?"

Kelpie didn't think she was asleep. She'd just closed her eyes.

"Snowy sliced my neck open!"

"Shut up," Kelpie whispered. "He didn't."

"Was I snoring?" Dymphna asked quietly against Kelpie's ear. "Because I don't remember falling asleep."

"No," Kelpie whispered.

The stairs creaked.

"Just me," Darcy said. "Cops are gone."

Kelpie skidded out from under the bed as fast as she could, not caring about going through Palmer, though the sensation of moving through his not-there-ness made her stomach heave.

Dymphna followed more elegantly than should have been possible. Her white gloves were smudged and torn. She ran them along her skirt, pushing some dust to the floor.

Darcy followed every gesture.

"I'm not quite as presentable as I was."

Kelpie could tell that Darcy thought she looked fine.

"They were looking for a big man," he said. "Or men. Standovers and a well-dressed, blonde woman."

"That's what they said? They didn't ask for me by name?"

Darcy shook his head.

They stared at each other. Darcy's lips were slightly parted, as if he was hungry.

Kelpie couldn't see how that was going to help. They could stare at each other all day long, and the coppers would still be looking for Dymphna Campbell. How many other well-dressed, blonde women were there in the Hills?

"Tell him to stop looking at her like that," Palmer said. He tried to push Darcy out of the way. Kelpie bit back a smile as he pushed right through Darcy, who didn't even shiver. That would teach him to tell lies about Snowy.

Jimmy Palmer roared.

Kelpie put her hands over her ears and glared at him. *They can't hear you*, she wanted to tell him. *Only I can and I don't want to.*

"I fucking hate this!" Palmer shouted. "Why can't she fucking hear me?" His face had gone darker. It would have been red if he was still alive. He disappeared.

"Are you all right?" Dymphna asked Kelpie.

Palmer reappeared beside her. "Bloody hell," he said. "Where'd I go?"

Kelpie shrugged, answering both Dymphna and Palmer with the same gesture.

"Neal! You going to eat your breakfast?"

"Hungry?" he asked Dymphna.

Kelpie was starving. She nodded even though Darcy wasn't looking at her.

"We have to go. I have to get back to my place." Dymphna brushed dirt from her skirt again. She'd taken off her jacket to tie around her waist and hide the tear in the back of her skirt.

"Still plenty of cops out there. How far you reckon you'd get?"

"Tell me where I went, kid," Palmer said, walking through Darcy to loom over Kelpie. "Why can't she see me? Why can you? If I'm dead, why the fuck am I still here?"

Kelpie had no idea. No ghost had ever told her where they went. Palmer's face went dark again, and then he was gone.

"All right," Dymphna said. "But after that we have to leave."

Kelpie wondered who she meant by *we*. She sure as buggery wasn't going anywhere with no Dymphna Campbell, who was wanted by the coppers. How daft did she think Kelpie was?

Neal Darcy

Neal Darcy was a published writer. He was not the Hills' only author. In the streets surrounding the Darcys' home, there were novelists, playwrights, poets, and reporters, not to mention scribes of polemics, catalogues, advertising, and greeting cards. Writers being not well paid and Surry Hills being cheap, it was only natural the Hills had more than its fair share of scriveners.

Kelpie treasured the day Miss Lee led her to Neal Darcy. She'd known who he was. She knew about everyone on Belmore Lane because of Tommy. But she hadn't known about his writing.

He is the most wonderful discovery of my life, Miss Lee told Kelpie. Kelpie didn't point out that Darcy was the most wonderful discovery of her *death*.

Neal Darcy was the oldest of the Darcy brood. The big gap to the next child was because Darcy's father had been off shearing for a decade. Then the old man came back, and there were five in a row while he worked odd jobs, drank the proceeds, and didn't gamble on the horses because that was how *his* old man had ruined the family. Each generation of Darcy men had to find a different way to blight their families. The youngest of the Darcy brood was barely four years old. Before she was born, the old man went bush again.

Miss Lee did not hold a high opinion of Darcy's old man. Neither did Neal Darcy.

"G'day, little doggie," Tommy'd said.

Kelpie'd smiled. He'd led her to a fresh-baked pound cake the day before. Kelpie had never tasted anything like it.

Miss Lee had ignored him as she walked through the Darcys' fence. "Come on, Kelpie."

"She's not got you mooning over him too? Why watch 'im when you could listen to me? I'm a proper bloke! Don't see me arseing around with some maggoty, girlish—"

Miss Lee was already in the Darcys' kitchen. Kelpie snuck in through the loose board in the fence and peeked over the sill. Darcy was draped in a towel bashing away at something on a pile of newspaper, which was half covered with another towel.

He shook both towels off and yanked a piece of paper out of his

odd machine. The machine looked like a colony of metal spiders.
The paper tore. "Lucy, you bitch!" Darcy yelled.

Kelpie wondered who Lucy was.

"Cork it!" someone screamed, setting off a round of yelling from
the rest of the household.

Darcy swore again. Quieter this time. Then he straightened the
piece of paper, turned it over, and put it back into the machine, then
draped it and himself with the towels again.

"He's a writer," Miss Lee said, as proudly as if she had invented
writing. "Writers express themselves colourfully, so don't be
alarmed."

Kelpie grinned. Far as she could tell, everyone swore—other than
Miss Lee. Besides, she liked the sound of Darcy's voice, even when
he was going off about his *bloody, fucking, bastard, no-good, bung-
headed, sodded-up, so-called typewriter.*

Miss Lee leaned over to read from the page at the top of the stack.

Kelpie liked what Miss Lee read. It was the kind of story you'd
hear from the old fellas in front of Castle's, but funnier, less ram-
bling. His story was about people like him, living in the Hills or out
bush.

"So authentic!" Miss Lee breathed. "Oh, excellent word choice!
Aromatic." She continued to read aloud. "Oh, no," she said a little
later. "I hope he's going to change that. *Strewth?* I know he's writing
about the Hills, but he doesn't have to use such common vocabulary."

Kelpie liked the word *strewth* and vowed to use it more. When
Miss Lee wasn't around.

"Oh no! *That* word's even worse." Miss Lee's lips pressed together.

Kelpie wanted to ask what word, but she could tell Miss Lee
would never say. Besides, Neal Darcy was barely two feet from
where Kelpie was crouching. She peeked over the edge of the sill.

There was a patch of sweat in the middle of Darcy's back. She
found it strange that banging away at those metal spiders made
him sweat. Like he was chopping wood, or shifting furniture, not
making up stories in his head and writing them down.

The harder he pounded at the typewriter, the more he sweated
and the more the towel on his head started to slide, until it fell to the
ground and his hair fell forward into his eyes, so he had to push it
back, sending droplets of sweat flying.

"Such passion!" Miss Lee said. "Once his face went purple, he was so infuriated that the writing was not proceeding as he wished. He almost hurled his typewriter at the wall! He had it poised above his head. I would have held my breath if I had any to hold. But then he put it down, said, 'Sorry, Lucy,' and punched the wall. His knuckles bled, Kelpie. Can you imagine? I was most concerned."

The stairs creaked and Kelpie ducked.

Miss Lee sighed. "The rest of the household is stirring. Mr. Darcy's packing up. He must go to work in that dreadful brewery. Such a shame."

Kelpie scrambled into the lane before any of the Darcys came out to use the dunny. Miss Lee appeared beside her.

Tommy was where he'd been. "Don't know why you'd waste your time watching that ugly mick."

Kelpie didn't think Neal Darcy was ugly.

"Wish I could smoke," Tommy said, watching old man Miller passing by, sucking on the last dregs of a cigarette. Miller's cough was wet and echoed in his chest. "Only thing I really miss. Well, that and fucking."

Kelpie pulled a face.

"Ignore him," Miss Lee said. "Nothing he tells you is true. But it is *all* unpleasant. Let's find you some food. Are you ready for your first reading lesson?"

Kelpie nodded.

Those precious minutes watching Darcy write, listening to his words, had made Kelpie want to know everything about letters and words and sentences. She wanted more of Darcy's stories, more of any stories.

⤝ DYMPHNA ⤞

Dymphna felt her left leg trembling. Soon her right leg would shake too. Usually she could conceal it. Especially if she was sitting down.

She was in the Darcys' kitchen, wedged against the back door. Kelpie by her side. Jimmy on the other. Her leg's tremor causing the door, already loose on its hinges, to vibrate. Kelpie must know she was shaking. But surely Mrs. Darcy's brood were gobbling their porridge too loudly to notice? Even though they were seated mere inches away. Even though the ones without their backs to her were staring at Dymphna, barely blinking.

She had to steady herself. If she wasn't calm, she couldn't plan her way out of this imbroglio.

"Why are you so pretty?" one of the little Darcys asked.

Dymphna smiled. "Thank you."

The littlie goggled at her.

"'Cause she's got money, silly," an older one replied.

"Money don't make you pretty," the younger one protested. "You is or you ain't."

"It helps," Dymphna could not resist replying. Money kept you clean and housed and eating well and wearing beautiful clothes and having your hair styled and your nails done by other people. She was quite sure she spent more on a jar of face cream than the Darcys spent on food in a month.

"How much did your hat cost?" another of the little Darcys asked.

Dymphna laughed, though her leg did not stop shaking.

"Mary!" Mrs. Darcy glared at the girl. "Ain't polite to ask about money. Finish your breakfast, the lot of youse. Now."

The police hadn't asked after Dymphna by name. She could take comfort in that, couldn't she? But their description fitted her. Well-dressed, blonde. Surely she wasn't the only one in Surry Hills. There was that girl who worked at the florist's on Taylor Square. Very pretty she was, blonde like Dymphna, and always smartly dressed.

What did the police know? She was sure she and Kelpie hadn't been seen. If they had, surely they would already have been dragged from the Darcys' yard and thrown in the lock-up. Or Dymphna would be. They would hand Kelpie over to Child Welfare. Dymphna didn't know which was worse.

Even if they knew nothing about what had happened last night, everyone knew Jimmy was her man. They would be coming by to question her. They always did.

Snowy Fullerton had killed Jimmy.

What if she'd arrived when Snowy was still there? Would he have killed her too? She didn't think so. Snowy and she, they were friends. She could make a sly comment and he'd understand. Make a similar observation of his own. She liked Snowy.

Snowy did not pick fights, and he didn't kill unless his boss told him to. Had his boss told him to kill Dymphna too? Was he looking for her now? If Snowy had to kill her, he would be sorry about it. She wasn't sure what difference that made. She didn't doubt he'd been sorry to kill Jimmy. That didn't make Jimmy any less dead.

Or any less of a ghost railing at being dead.

His face was getting darker because Kelpie wasn't answering any of his questions. When he was alive, his face would turn bright red when he was angry, when he laughed too hard, when they had sex.

Dymphna had thought Jimmy was smart enough to realise why Kelpie was ignoring him in a room full of the living. His adjustment to being dead was going to be slow. From what she'd seen, it was slow for most people. No one believed they were going to die, and once dead it was hard to let go of that disbelief.

At least Jimmy wasn't trying to touch her or talk at her now.

He was focused on Kelpie. Poor Kelpie.

If Dymphna's leg hadn't been shaking, if her man weren't dead, if she weren't afraid that Mr. Davidson or Glory would find and kill her, she would have laughed. She was in a none-too-clean room full of Irish tykes, their overworked mother, handsome eldest brother, Kelpie, and the ghost of her dead man.

Kelpie and Jimmy Palmer in the same room.

Chance had thrown Dymphna and Kelpie together. Left to herself, she would have gone on waiting for the perfect moment to introduce herself to the girl. She was too nervous about frightening her off. Dymphna's desire to win Kelpie over was too intense.

But here Kelpie was, and for the first time in Dymphna's life, she was with someone who could hear every word the dead said.

It made Jimmy harder to ignore because she couldn't help but watch Kelpie interact with him, which led her gaze back to Jimmy, whom she could not look at without giving herself away.

Jimmy had been alive yesterday; Jimmy had been alive mere hours ago. Her leg shook harder.

Focus. Where had the lodger gone? To the police? The shakes were in her hands now. She put them behind her back.

"We should go," Dymphna said. "Your lodger . . ."

"Miss Pattinson won't say nothing to no one. She's here to escape her husband. Ain't even her real name. She won't do nothing that'll help him find her."

"Her old man tried to dead her," one of the smaller Darcys announced.

"With an axe," another added breathlessly.

Dymphna breathed in sharply. Did it have to be an axe?

Kelpie turned to look at her and then away.

Dymphna shivered. She had to calm herself.

Sheep's brains.

Dymphna's mother used to make brains for her and her twin sisters when they were wee. Strained so that they became a delicate, tiny-bubbled sauce. They called it fluffy. It was the one savoury dish Mama always prepared, though Isla, their cook, made most of their food.

Mama had made it for them whenever they were upset. When the littlies, faces streaked with tears, begged, "Fluffy, please, Mama." Or when Dymphna's leg started shaking. She'd had these tell-tale tremors all her life. Set off by anxiety, by fear, by death.

Mrs. Darcy handed a half-full bowl of pale, grey mess to Dymphna. The uneven, muddy porridge was not fluffy. "You'll have to share."

Dymphna gave the sludge to Kelpie, who ate until she was scraping the spoon at nothing. Dymphna didn't wonder at it. There was almost no meat on the girl's bones.

Mrs. Darcy and Neal Darcy stared at Kelpie. The girl kept her eyes low.

"When's the last time you ate, girl?" Mrs. Darcy asked. "It wasn't when I gave you that scrap of bread, was it?"

"Her bones are sticking out," one of the little Darcys said.

"Most everyone's bones stick out round here," an older Darcy said.

"Not like hers. She's like old Mr. Farrow's horse that fell down dead in the middle of Crown Street. Nothing but bones with a bit of skin tying them together."

Dymphna saw the suppressed smile in Neal's eyes and smiled too. She liked a fella who could laugh. Jimmy was not much for laughing.

"Shush, Eoin," Mrs. Darcy snapped. "Don't repeat what you don't understand."

"I understand bein' hungry!"

Dymphna could see that all the Darcy children understood that.

"Shush, Eoin."

Mrs. Darcy opened the cupboard behind her and unwrapped a half loaf of grey bread. Dymphna doubted much wheat had gone into the making of it. Mrs. Darcy cut off a bit, leaning heavily on the knife, and handed it to Kelpie.

The girl took the bread and ate it as though she worried that Mrs. Darcy might change her mind and snatch it back. Mrs. Darcy handed her another piece. The girl gobbled that down too.

Mrs. Darcy shook her head.

"You'll be all right, Kelpie," Neal said. "I promise."

Kelpie edged closer to the back door, scrupulously avoiding Jimmy. Dymphna could see she didn't like going through ghosts. Jimmy moved closer to Kelpie. The girl twitched.

"You can stay with us, love," Mrs. Darcy said. Neal smiled.

"There's no room—" one of the younger Darcys began.

"I'm looking after her," Dymphna said.

A factory whistle sounded. Then another and another.

"Time to finish up," Mrs. Darcy announced. "Got to get youse all to school. Mary, you with the dishes. Seamus, take the little ones out to wash."

"*Ma*," Seamus whined.

"Now."

Seamus led the three youngest through Jimmy, not a shiver among them, out back to the rusted tub, but not before shooting a look at Mary. The back door crashed shut behind them.

"Upstairs," Mrs. Darcy said, pushing Dymphna towards the stairs. In any other situation, Dymphna would have let the woman know how much she presumed. "You too, Kelpie."

The Angel of Death

They called Miss Dymphna Campbell the Angel of Death because every man she was with for more than a couple of days wound up dead.

It started as a joke.

But some believed that she really was.

Dymphna believed that she really was. Dymphna *knew* that she really was.

Dymphna Campbell should have been dead. She should have died with her mother and her sisters. But she escaped death, only to live the rest of her life tainted by Death.

Dymphna Campbell saw ghosts. Had done so since before her name was Dymphna Campbell; from the moment she came into this world. Her mother's parents died the day she was born. The very hour she was born. In the same house. Spanish flu took them both.

Death swarmed around that house. Took the three siblings that followed her.

Spared the twins: Vera and Una.

Until the night her father did for them and did for her mother too.

He used an axe.

He tried to do for Dymphna-who-was-not-yet-Dymphna too.

She did for him.

With a knife from the kitchen. She didn't know what she was doing.

It was the middle of the night. Still, balmy. She hadn't been able to sleep. Tiptoed down to the kitchen, holding her breath as she passed her parents' room, poured herself some milk. She heard one choked-off scream. She dropped the glass. It must have shattered.

Heard footsteps, a slammed door.

There was a carving knife in her hand. Sharp, it was. Isla kept all the knives sharp. *Fewer accidents that way*, she said.

Her father was there, in the kitchen, axe held high, blood all over him, dripping from his chin, from his hands.

She remembered wondering where the axe had come from. They had no fireplace. No wood to chop.

The carving knife was in her hand, and then in him.

She didn't remember how she did it. How she knew to push up under his ribs. But she did. Again and again. She could not say how many times.

Her father dropped the axe. Tried to bring his hands to her throat. Fell.

There was blood everywhere.

The kitchen was bathed in it. She stepped over her father, knife in hand, followed the blood along the hall, up the stairs, into her parents' bedroom where her mother lay in blood-soaked pieces, her eyes still open.

She tried not to wonder how that was possible. She closed them, kissed her mother good-bye, followed her father's bloody footsteps to the twins' room.

Vera and Una looked like tiny, red, broken dolls in the middle of their bed. Four years old. She could not bring herself to touch them. She blew kisses at them and turned away.

She left home to escape the place where they died, where she almost died. She left because it could never be home again.

She left because, as she walked down those stairs, her father rushed at her, arms aloft as if he still held an axe, as if he still had the power to kill her. Even though he was dead and would always be dead.

He ran straight through her.

Then the ghost of her father screamed that she was a no-good slut. Screamed at her dead, unmoving mother that she was a foul temptress. *Like mother, like daughter,* he roared, face turned dark. Then he screamed the same at tiny Vera and Una.

As he had when he was alive.

She ignored him as she had tried so hard to do when he was alive. She would close her eyes and pretend he wasn't there. It was much easier now that he was dead. He couldn't lay a finger on her any-more. She could ignore him with her eyes open.

Dymphna put the knife down while the ghost of her father screamed that she was trash. She went to the bathroom and washed and washed and washed. She had to fill the tub three times before it drained away with no trace of blood. Her father stood over her calling her a dirty whore, pointing to the parts of her body that offended him most.

She went to her bedroom, careful not to step in any of her father's bloody footprints.

The door had come off one hinge. Bloody handprints were streaked around the knob. She dressed and packed one small suitcase. Swung her warmest coat over her shoulders, though it was summer. It wouldn't always be summer.

She pulled all the money from her father's wallet, from her mother's purse, from the jam-jar hidden behind the breadbox, while her father called her a thief and a liar.

Almost fifty pounds in all. It seemed like a fortune.

Her mother and the twins did not become ghosts. For which she was grateful. She could not have faced them enduring her father a second longer. Or the ache of seeing Vera and Una unable to hug or kiss, unable to pick flowers from their mother's beautiful garden. Her mother's arms going through her . . . It would have been too much.

She could not have pretended not to see them; she could not have borne leaving them.

She left home before dawn not knowing where to go.

Her father followed her down the hall to the front door, across the porch, where she bent to put her keys under the empty flowerpot.

Down the path to the front gate, past her mother's peonies, irises, roses, lilies, delphiniums, sweet peas, pansies, sunflowers, larkspurs, Queen Anne's lace. Dull in the darkness, but come dawn the garden would sparkle with whites and yellows and oranges and pinks and blues and purples. People stopped from miles around to admire her mother's garden.

Her old man walked with her every step of the way, even as she paused at each new cluster of flowers to bend and inhale. She loved the sweet peas best. They smelled exactly as fresh and sweet as her mother.

She was sure she would never smell their like again.

Those bloody flowers, her father snarled in her ear.

She shivered with fear that he would haunt her forever. But she opened the gate and stepped out of her mother's garden alone.

She took a few more steps along the footpath beside her mother's white picket fence. Her father walked through the flowers on the other side, his face contorted.

At the edge of the property, she turned, looked past him, at her mother's beautiful cottage, surrounded by flowers, knowing she would never see it again.

That's when she would have cried if she had not long since learned that it did no good.

She turned away, walking towards the water. She would walk the whole way. Not wait until the buses started running at five.

Her father screamed one last thing: *But I loved you*, he bellowed, calling her by her long-forgotten name. *I loved you all*.

She told no one. She renamed herself before she boarded the first ferry of the morning. *Dymphna* for the saint whose life was all too like her own. *Campbell* because it was the name of the athletics coach at school who had encouraged her to run, far and fast.

Dymphna Campbell sat on the ferry bound for the city, watching tiny waves break against the hull, seagulls diving down across the water searching for fish, and wondered where to go, what to do. Her left leg began to shake.

Dymphna's father was the first one to touch her. He was the first one to die. He was the only one she didn't want to touch her, the only one she killed herself. She did not know if her father's death had made her the Angel of Death or if she was born marked. Perhaps it didn't matter.

All Dymphna knew was that Death had been with her from the beginning. She saw Death everywhere, and no one else could. But she hoped there was someone else.

Then she saw the crazy old man living on the streets in the Rocks. He talked to ghosts. They taunted him. Here was proof of what she had always thought: acknowledge the ghosts and they drove you mad and out onto the streets. Might as well be a ghost yourself.

Better to keep them at arm's length. Avert your eyes.

Then Dymphna saw wee Kelpie, who might have been a darker Una or Vera if they had escaped their father, if they'd had more years of life, if they had not died.

So many ifs.

Dymphna saw Kelpie talking to ghosts and knew she had to save her.

✂ DYMPHNA ✂

They sat on the bed with Mrs. Darcy in between, her bulk causing them both to slide towards her. Dymphna held on to the head-board to keep herself upright and pressed her leg firmly against the bed in an attempt to stop the shaking. Neal leaned against the closed door.

Dymphna wondered what he'd be like to kiss. His lips were. . .

She looked away. She should not be looking at his lips. What would it be like to live in a world where she could kiss a good man instead of worrying if she was going to survive until nightfall?

"We'll make sure you're okay, Kelpie," Mrs. Darcy said, putting her arm around the girl. Gravity meant Kelpie couldn't extricate herself. Not that she was trying. She looked content. Dymphna knew that she should leave Kelpie with the Darcys. But she couldn't stand the idea of losing her. She'd only just found her.

Jimmy paced the room, glowering. Dymphna wished she could make him stop. But she had no more power over him than she had over her leg. She stared at the floor and then at Neal. His eyes were green flecked with brown—hazel, she supposed. Jimmy paced faster.

"You're really the only one who can see me?" he asked Kelpie.

"It'll be all right, love," Mrs. Darcy said.

Kelpie nodded. But Dymphna couldn't tell if her assent was for Mrs. Darcy, for Jimmy, or for the both of them.

"Why can't they see me?" Jimmy demanded.

Because you're a bloody ghost, you arse-brained moron, Dymphna wished she could say. She had thought he was cleverer than this.

"What's happening, love?" Mrs. Darcy asked Kelpie. "Why are the coppers after youse?"

Kelpie shrugged. Again the answer served for the dead and the living. *Nicely done*, thought Dymphna.

"You don't know?" Jimmy asked.

Kelpie looked down, shaking her head slightly. She straightened as much as she could given the bed's sag and then gave up, sinking back against Mrs. Darcy.

"She saw something she shouldn't have," Dymphna said, which was true, but no one knew that except Dymphna. "There are bad men who want to kill her. I'm protecting her. I have to get the both of us somewhere safe."

The coppers had only mentioned a well-dressed blonde woman, not a young girl. Dymphna didn't care that she'd given Mrs. Darcy the impression Kelpie was in trouble. She wanted Mrs. Darcy to think Dymphna knew more than the police, which she did. Though she had no idea how the police knew she had been at Mrs. Stone's.

"*You're* protecting her?" Mrs. Darcy said to Dymphna. "How do you expect to do that?"

"It's dangerous," Dymphna said, which had the virtue of being true and revealing nothing.

Mrs. Darcy's lips whitened. She patted Kelpie's knee.

"We'll go soon. I promise," Dymphna said. Though she had no idea where. Or if she could convince Kelpie to leave with her. Had the cops been tipped off?

Then she remembered the card. The one from Mr. Davidson. The one with her name on it. Where was it? She'd given it to Kelpie. Had Kelpie dropped it at Mrs. Stone's? Her leg's tremolo movement increased. She willed it to stop; it didn't even slow.

"You're cold," Neal Darcy said.

"Is she?" his mother said. "We're *all* cold. Only heat's in the kitchen."

Neal Darcy looked away. Dymphna wondered what he was thinking. She should not be wondering what he was thinking.

"Dymphna's the one who needs protecting," Jimmy Palmer told Kelpie. "She needs to get away from here, and she needs to hide."

Kelpie said nothing.

"We really do have to go," Dymphna said firmly. "It's not safe here."

"Won't be safe anywhere," Jimmy said, which might well be true, but Dymphna could do without him saying it. Now both Dymphna's legs were shaking.

"No one's keeping you here," Mrs. Darcy said. "We can look after Kelpie. She's welcome. She'd be welcome at St. Peter's. About time she went to school. How old are you now, girl? Ten? Eleven?"

Dymphna was not going to let that happen; Kelpie stayed with her.

"They're *both* in trouble, Ma," Neal said. "We need to help them. How many times have we been helped? When Da shot through—"

Mrs. Darcy's glare was enough to freeze flames. "You don't need to tell me what's right, young man."

Neal grinned. Dymphna felt her face mirroring his.

Jimmy threw a punch at Neal which went straight through him. Dymphna bit her lip to keep from laughing. Her right leg stilled and the left slowed.

Mrs. Darcy stared at her eldest son, who was looking at Dymphna. For a moment, Dymphna thought she was going to be thrown out. Her right leg began to shake again.

"I wasn't going to make her leave right off," Mrs. Darcy continued. "How far do you think you'll get, young lady, with your skirt torn like that and your gloves ruined? And look at the state of wee Kelpie! People will wonder how a lady like you wound up with a street urchin. Better she stay with us."

Dymphna looked down at her gloves and then at Kelpie. Kelpie looked like she'd never washed in her life. "You're right. Thank you. We'll clean up as best we can. Then we'll be out of your way. I will take good care of her."

Everyone looked at Kelpie, who squirmed from their gaze.

"You don't have to go with her, Kelpie," Mrs. Darcy said. She turned to Dymphna. "You're too young to be looking after a child."

"She's older than you were," Neal said, "when you were first married and had me."

Dymphna did not like to think about how old she was, how old her dead sisters weren't.

"She's *much* older than I was," Mrs. Darcy said, flicking her eyes from her son to Dymphna so that she needn't say *and much older than you* out loud. Dymphna almost laughed. "But she doesn't know the first thing about young 'uns."

"She's a woman," Jimmy said. "Women're all tougher than they look." A minute earlier he'd been proclaiming that she needed to be protected.

"I have friends," Dymphna managed to say. "Powerful friends. No one touches me."

"What, like that Gloriana Nelson? Or that Mr. Davidson?"

"He's not my friend!"

"They're not the sorts of friends I'd like. They might not touch *you*"—Mrs. Darcy sounded sceptical—"but they touch them that's around you. We've all heard what they call you. Angel of—"

"Don't call her that, Ma," Neal said. His hand twitched to his chest and then back to his side. As if he wanted to cross himself.

"I can protect her," Dymphna said. "You can't."

She knew it probably wasn't true. She knew she should leave Kelpie with the Darcys, but she *couldn't*. Dymphna had to save her, make her life less of a hell than her own had been.

If Dymphna lived through the day; if she didn't get Kelpie killed.

"You're barely old enough to protect yourself," Mrs. Darcy said.

"I've lots of money," Dymphna said, aware of how crass that sounded.

Mrs. Darcy snorted.

"Money that can buy a lot of protection." Her money would be worth nothing if Mr. Davidson or Glory wanted her dead.

"They could *both* stay here," Neal said.

Dymphna almost laughed. Where exactly? With the lodger?

"Everyone knows who Miss Campbell is," Mrs. Darcy said with a little too much emphasis on the *Miss*. "How long could we keep her hidden?"

"There's no need. We'll be gone from the city before the day's out," Dymphna said confidently. She'd go back to her flat, grab the coat she'd lined with money, her passports, then they'd get passage out: overseas, safety.

"You can't do that," Mrs. Darcy said. "You're not blood relations. I've a good mind to tell the authorities."

On the other side of Mrs. Darcy, Kelpie flinched.

"You wouldn't," Dymphna said, cursing herself for saying it out loud.

"Sister Josephine or Father O'Brian would have something to say about your plan."

Kelpie jumped up. "I'll go with her," she said, putting her hand awkwardly in Dymphna's.

Scared of the nuns, thought Dymphna, squeezing Kelpie's hand.

"You're sure, lass?" Mrs. Darcy said. The expression on her face made Dymphna brace for Mrs. Darcy's arguments against anyone going anywhere with the notorious Dymphna Campbell. But Mrs. Darcy said nothing, waiting for Kelpie to reply.

"I'm sure," Kelpie muttered.

Mrs. Darcy did not look pleased.

"Good," Jimmy said. "You can tell Dymphna everything that happened when youse get away from this mob. You can tell me what's happening and all. I going to stay like this forever? This what being dead is?"

Dymphna wondered how on earth Jimmy expected a kid like Kelpie to know all about death. "Would it be all right if we cleaned up now?" she asked.

Mrs. Darcy stood up. "I'll mend your skirt." She grabbed a small basket from underneath her sewing table. "You can sponge your jacket in the kitchen. Neal, you should be off to work already. We can't have you speared."

Neal nodded, not taking his eyes from Dymphna's.

None of Dymphna's hard men had eyes as pretty as his.

Old Ma

Old Ma fed Kelpie and clothed her. Though shoes were a problem. Old Ma wasn't made of money, and Kelpie kept growing. So they didn't bother. Before long her feet grew tough as the streets she walked on. Besides, Old Ma said, it wasn't like it was as bitter cold here as it was back in the old country.

Kelpie had never been anywhere but the Hills. Before Old Ma died, she'd never been outside Frog Hollow. She thought it was plenty cold. Especially at night in winter when the damp set in and you were so far down in the Hollow you'd forgotten what the sun looked like.

Her first memory was of Old Ma washing Kelpie's face. Ma wasn't gentle, but Kelpie could tell it was done with love. She remembered the smell of soap, the feel of the cold water hitting her skin, and Old Ma smelling like freshly baked bread, though most often the only bread she made was damper because that was cheaper. Old Ma made Kelpie drink the milk she couldn't always afford. *You're still growing*, Ma said, *up and up. I'm growing out and out.*

Old Ma died in the winter. Went to sleep and didn't wake up.

But Old Ma stayed. She kept looking after Kelpie. Led her to places to sleep. Led her away from the bad men who took over Old Ma's house. Led her to rooms where there really were apples.

But she wasn't a talker like Tommy. When she was alive, Old Ma hardly ever shut up. Jabbering all the time with stories and opinions and telling Kelpie what to do.

Surry Hills, she'd say. *Sorrow Hills, more like.* Then she'd tell the tale of someone who had died before they should have, which they all did in the Hills.

Mostly though, when she was alive, Old Ma had warned Kelpie to stay away from *them. They're no better than they should be.* Old Ma's *them* was wide and varied. The rich, the poor, the coppers, the crims. The only person Old Ma had a good word for was Snowy Fullerton. *Good man, Snowy. Always mind what he says to you, Petal. He'll look out for you. Leastways he will when he's not in the lock-up.*

Old Ma had little time for the living or the dead. Not that Old Ma had been able to see ghosts, but she knew they were there, knew they were up to no good. Besides, Kelpie talked to ghosts often enough. Old Ma's grandma had been the same way. Look at what happened to her! *Down the well*, Old Ma had said darkly. Kelpie tried not to giggle.

Old Ma couldn't see ghosts after she died neither. Or if she could, she ignored them.

The damp and the dark that killed Old Ma was why they tore Frog Hollow down. Men in suits following up their evictions with wrecking crews and demolitions. Said the Hollow wasn't clean what with the mould creeping up the listing walls.

It wasn't too long after they'd torn down every last bit of rusted corrugated iron and rotten wood that Old Ma started to fade.

As if she had been clinging to those sodden timbers.

Kelpie was on her own.

Kelpie did not like being on her own.

She ventured all over the Hills. Even further than Moore Park— all the way to Centennial Park. There were ghosts everywhere she went. Most of them ignored her. But not all. A few of them helped her the way Old Ma had. Steering her towards food and away from bad men.

A few of them did the opposite.

Even so, ghosts were what kept Kelpie alive.

✂ KELPIE ✂

Kelpie said yes to Dymphna Campbell because she didn't want to go to school, because Mrs. Darcy had said she'd tell the authorities, which meant Welfare, and because she'd mentioned Sister Josephine and Father O'Brian, who were almost as bad as Welfare.

She wanted to stay.

She wanted to learn how to use Darcy's typewriter and read more of his stories. She especially liked the ones set out bush, with strange things like wallabies and shearers and rouseabouts. Maybe he would let her write a story of her own. Kelpie had too many questions she wanted to ask: Were his stories all about real people, like, how Kitty Macintosh was really Dymphna Campbell? Or did he make some of them up? Was he going to write a novel some day? Or was that Miss Lee dreaming?

But it wouldn't be like that. Darcy was down the brewery every day but Sunday. Besides, the Darcys couldn't afford another mouth to feed.

Mrs. Darcy would hand her over to Sister Josephine or Father O'Brian, who would hand her over to Welfare, who would give her to some do-gooder family, who wouldn't know nothing about ghosts or the Hills or anything important, who'd make her wear clothes that itched, and make her wash once a week, and beat her when she said the wrong thing, which she would, because Miss Lee said she only knew wrong things, from growing up on the streets and not knowing any better, and they'd make her go to school where there would be itchy clothing and pinching shoes and cracks across the knuckles with rulers.

No, thank you.

She liked the Darcys. Darcy and his ma had been kind to her. Mrs. Darcy hardly ever smacked her kids. They laughed and sang together, which was not what she'd seen through most family windows. Miss Lee had said they were decent people. Old Ma would have agreed.

She would leave with Dymphna Campbell, who most definitely wasn't a do-gooder or decent people and was as scared of the coppers as Kelpie was. Dymphna wouldn't hand her over to anybody. Besides, getting away from Dymphna would be a darn sight easier than getting away from Mrs. Darcy. Darcy's ma was used to keeping littlies in line, to giving orders and having them obeyed. Dymphna had soft hands and a soft face and didn't know anything about bossing people around. Mrs. Darcy scared Kelpie a lot more than Dymphna did.

Kelpie would walk out the door with Dymphna Campbell and then scarper before the coppers caught Dymphna. Easy.

Kelpie doubted Dymphna would get far. Not in the daylight.

The kitchen was bright with sunshine now. Mrs. Darcy's clean plates were drying on a cloth. They gleamed despite the crazing across their surface.

Kelpie sat on a crate with her legs tucked up under her and the back door behind her and hoped for more food. She eyed the icebox. Mrs. Darcy was bent over Dymphna's skirt, stitching up the tear, while Dymphna sponged off her face and hands over a bowl of water.

Palmer was pacing and asking her more questions about being a ghost. None of which she could answer with two of the living sitting right there. Was he daft? Kelpie was pretty sure he was. He'd said Snowy did for him, and Snowy would never.

He couldn't have. He was in gaol. If he was out, he'd come looking for her. He always did.

Besides, Palmer's throat had been cut open. Take someone tall and strong to do that. Snowy was tall, sure, but he wasn't as big as Palmer. Palmer's arms were thicker than her waist, and his legs might as well be trees.

Stuart O'Sullivan, the boxer ghost, always said if you needed to take down a bigger opponent—outside the ring—your best bet was to surprise 'em. From behind was always the ticket. Even then you'd best be quick about it. Bringing down a big fella was always harder than you'd think, he'd say. Half the time you'd bottle 'em and they'd barely blink! They'd keep coming at you, like nothing had happened. Might as well walk up to 'em and say, *Give me a hiding, please.*

It would've taken at least two big men to surprise Palmer. Snowy worked alone. Everyone knew that.

Palmer asked why he couldn't touch anything. Kelpie didn't say, *Because you're dead, you arse-brained bugger.*

He was so stupid he could have mistaken Snowy for someone else. Kelpie didn't doubt that one of Mr. Davidson's men had killed

Palmer. Why wouldn't Davidson's men be killing Glory's men? Or Glory's killing Davidson's? That's what hard men did: killed each other.

"Is that thing like me?" Palmer pointed to where the faded ghost wafted past him. "Is that where I'm heading? Turning into a wispy cloud trapped in someone's kitchen?"

Mrs. Darcy handed Dymphna a cloth, and she used it to dry herself.

"How do I look?"

Like an angel, Kelpie thought. Dymphna had no scars or pimples or cysts or moles or warts or freckles. Her skin looked like it had never been touched by anything, not even the sun.

"Too beautiful for this place," Palmer said, scowling.

"You'll do," Mrs. Darcy said, laying down the skirt. "I'll get more water."

When she was gone, Dymphna said, "I'll take good care of you. Unless you really want to stay here."

"Tell her about Snowy and Davidson," Palmer said. "Before the old lady comes back."

Kelpie shook her head slightly, answering them both.

"You'll leave with me?"

Kelpie nodded. Leaving with her didn't mean *staying* with her.

Outside was awake now. All the factory whistles had blown. The morning was filled with the splutter and roar and clip clop and buzz of automobiles and trucks and carts and horses and a thousand different conversations up and down the length of Foveaux and Albion, and Elizabeth Street too, with the hammering and shuddering and staccato whirr of sewing machines, giant fabric cutters, the thunderous clap of barrels at the brewery slammed together. Tommy might still be yelling at Kelpie from Belmore Lane, but she could no more hear it than she could hear a butterfly in the backyard.

Dymphna stood and removed her torn stockings.

"Look at those legs," Palmer said. Kelpie did not look at them.

"Those are done for," Mrs. Darcy said, closing the door behind her and putting a fresh bowl of water in front of Dymphna. "Silk, eh?" She touched them reverently.

Dymphna nodded. "Toss them. Plenty more where those came from."

Mrs. Darcy slipped them into her apron pocket. Kelpie was pretty sure she'd be keeping them.

She handed Kelpie a cloth, a sliver of soap, and a bowl of water.

Kelpie hated soap. It got into her scabs and cuts and made her eyes
sting.

She ignored the sliver, wetting the cloth with the icy water and
rubbing at her face while watching Dymphna pick up her hat, brush
the dust off, and carefully push the tiny thing back into shape. She
borrowed Mrs. Darcy's shears to trim the veil, then turned the hat
around several times, adjusting it, dabbing at it with a cloth. When
she put it down, the hat looked like nothing had happened to it.

"She's an artist," Palmer said. "I bet she could make her own hats
if she wanted to. Probably made that one."

Kelpie didn't think so. It had a little label stitched inside. She'd
seen them sewing labels into clothes in the factories on Foveaux. If
you made something yourself, why would you put a label in it? She
rubbed her hands together in the now-grey water.

"There's no fixing those," Mrs. Darcy said, pointing at Dymphna's gloves lying on the kitchen table. Two of the fingers were torn,
and they were filthy. White gloves were stupid.

"I won't be a minute." Mrs. Darcy went upstairs.

"I will keep you safe," Dymphna said.

Kelpie said nothing, wishing there was more food.

"She'll do her best," Palmer said. "But if you'd tell her about me
and Snowy and Davidson, she'd be in a much better position to take
care of both of youse."

Kelpie shook her head.

"I will, Kelpie," Dymphna said. "I promise."

"God damn it!" Palmer roared, then disappeared. Kelpie hoped
he'd stay gone this time. He talked almost as much as Miss Lee, but
none of it was useful. She was not going to tell Dymphna lies about
Snowy Fullerton.

Mrs. Darcy returned carrying tissue paper. She placed the crin-
kled sheets in front of Dymphna. "Go on then. Unwrap them."

Dymphna carefully peeled back the paper. Nestled inside were a
pair of cream-coloured gloves. Dymphna stared at them.

"My wedding gloves, ain't they?" Mrs. Darcy looked almost teary.
"Made 'em myself. Lost count of how many I've made since then.
But these are still the finest I ever made."

"I can't."

"You have to. Wouldn't look right you in that suit and no gloves.
Might as well wear no shoes. You'll get them back to me."

"I will."

Dymphna opened her purse and fished out a red note and handed it to Mrs. Darcy who gasped, staring at it.

"A brick! Ten pounds! I never seen one of these before. That's more than Neal makes in weeks!"

Kelpie didn't reckon anyone round here had ever seen that much money. Not unless they were Old Man O'Reilly, or some other nob, or worked for Glory or Mr. Davidson, and even then. She'd never seen Snowy with a note that big. Ten shillings, maybe.

"I gave her that," Palmer said. "Remind her."

"Don't say no," Dymphna said. "You've run a risk hiding us. You've fed us, let us wash, loaned me your gloves. You have to let me repay you."

Mrs. Darcy looked as if she was going to say no, but then she tucked the note into her apron next to the torn silk stockings. "I won't forget this."

"Nor I."

"Now, what are we going to do about her hair?"

"It's a disgrace," Palmer said. "Look at Dymphna and then look at you. Hard to tell you're a girl."

Kelpie itched to point out that his hair hadn't looked especially wonderful after he was killed, sticking up in all directions, stuck together with blood.

Mrs. Darcy tried to pull her fingers through Kelpie's hair, but the snarls were too tightly stuck together. It hurt, but Kelpie didn't flinch.

At one time, her hair had been plaited and tied with string. Kelpie had done it herself, copying how Mrs. Darcy did her girls' hair with Miss Lee giving her instructions and encouragement. But that was likely months ago now. The string had become part of Kelpie's hair.

"It's more like carpet than hair. Dirty old carpet." Mrs. Darcy lifted up a clump and let it drop. Her nose wrinkled.

"It will be prettier short," Dymphna said, as if Kelpie cared about pretty.

Mrs. Darcy began to saw at it with a kitchen knife. "It'll grow back soon, love."

Kelpie knew that. It was the main problem with hair. Always growing. Mrs. Darcy threw the hair into the fire. It smelt awful.

Then she attacked Kelpie's head. Pouring water over it so that her coat got wet and rubbing at her scalp so hard Kelpie wanted to scream.

"You call that washed, lass?" Mrs. Darcy's voice was stern again. "You've just spread the dirt around your face. Let me."

Mrs. Darcy pushed the sleeves of Kelpie's coat up past her elbows and put her hands in new cold water, then scrubbed at them with a stiff brush and soap like she was washing clothes. Kelpie's eyes watered, but she refused to cry. Even when her fingers started bleeding around the nails and the soap got in.

Mrs. Darcy began scrubbing at Kelpie's face only marginally more gently than she had scrubbed at her hands. "And behind your ears. Don't think you've ever washed here, have you?" Mrs. Darcy shuddered. "Water's all dirt already. You're filthy, you are. And your neck." She pulled the collar of Kelpie's coat down, and it came away in her hand.

"Don't break it!"

"I'm not, love. Your coat's old. That bit of water washed away whatever it was that was holding it together."

Kelpie wasn't convinced. That coat had to last her through the winter.

Mrs. Darcy wiped her hands on her apron then started rubbing Kelpie dry with a towel. It hurt.

"So many scabs. So many scars. You're brown as an acorn. How long you been living wild, lass?"

Kelpie didn't say because she didn't know. Most of her life. However long that had been. When Old Ma had been alive, Kelpie had known how old she was. Old Ma always lit a candle on her birthday. But then she died and only Snowy knew. He'd given her a woollen hat for her tenth birthday, but that had been . . . two winters ago? Or was it three? Kelpie didn't think she could be thirteen yet.

"How long since you had a proper wash?"

Kelpie didn't know that either. She'd dunked herself in the pond at Centennial Park many times last summer. But Miss Lee said that didn't count 'cause there was no soap. She hadn't had a wash with soap since Old Ma died.

"We're going to have to do something about her clothes," Dymphna said, putting her finger through one of the holes in Kelpie's coat. "Holes in all the pockets too. Where d'you keep your things?"

Kelpie had hiding places. She wasn't about to tell Dymphna about them.

"All your clothes are falling apart. I can see your knees."

Kelpie looked at where they stuck through her trousers.

Mrs. Darcy reached to undo the buttons. Kelpie stepped away. She wasn't taking her clothes off.

"She's about the same height as my Seamus. I'll get some of his clothes for her."

Kelpie scowled and hugged herself tighter.

"You're skinnier than he is, lass. His clothes can go over the top of yours. All right? You won't have to take them off. You'll be warmer that way too."

Mrs. Darcy returned with trousers, shirt, shoes and socks, and a coat that was bigger and warmer than hers.

Kelpie started unbuttoning her own. The first button broke apart in her hand. She hadn't touched those buttons in weeks. The second fell off. The third would have stayed, but the fabric around it disintegrated. Miss Lee had found this coat for her. It had been almost new. For a moment, Kelpie thought she might cry.

Dymphna squeezed Kelpie's hand as if she was her mum. Kelpie didn't know what to make of it. She wanted to shake Dymphna off. She wasn't a littlie who need comforting. But it felt nice too. Old Ma had held her hand.

"I'll wear his coat."

"How charitable," Mrs. Darcy said, but she was smiling.

Snowy Fullerton once punched a man twice his weight so hard that the man fell to the ground and didn't get up again for hours. Snowy was strong, six foot four inches tall, and in a line of business that meant he was challenged all too often by hard men desperate to prove they were made of that fancy new metal, tungsten carbide.

Always turned out they were more tin than steel.

Snowy did not start fights. Nor did he hit anyone without provocation. If he believed it was an option, he'd've never hit anyone, let alone killed them. But working for Mr. Davidson was all he had ever known. Snowy had a long scar on his left cheek. Six inches long and half an inch thick. It stood up from his face almost a quarter inch. Claimed he cut himself shaving, but everyone knew different. Knew, too, that whoever did it was most likely six feet under. That or fish food.

People called him Snowy because he bleached his tightly curled hair platinum blond. Because he was that tall his head was like a mountain top. Because you were more likely to get an answer from actual snow if you asked it a question than you were from Snowy. Because they thought it was funny. "Doesn't make sense," Tommy complained. "Snow's white; Snowy ain't."

No one laughed to Snowy's face.

Snowy always had food for Kelpie. Though she liked him best when it was peanuts or chocolate or a small bag of lollies. Snowy said if she ever needed anything, she should tell him. If she was ever in trouble, she should come get him and he'd fix it.

But the few times she did, he was away in gaol.

Snowy always answered her questions. Kelpie didn't ask many. She had never looked him in the eyes and not just because he was so tall. Sometimes he would sit beside her, smoke a cigarette while she ate, and occasionally he would tell her a little about his childhood. He grew up in Frog Hollow, like her. He was raised by Old Ma, like her. Old Ma had told Kelpie she could trust Snowy. So she did.

The only time they didn't see eye to eye was not long after Old Ma died and Snowy said maybe he should take Kelpie to the orphanage and have the nuns look after her. That it would be better than her living on the streets. Kelpie ran away and wouldn't talk to him until Old Ma's ghost persuaded her by leading her to Snowy day after day.

He asked his landlady if Kelpie could stay with him. She wouldn't have a bar of it. No women, no kids was her rule. Single men only.

He hinted at finding Kelpie somewhere to live off the streets a few times more: asked if she was doing okay, if maybe she'd like somewhere clean to stay for a while. Every time Snowy asked, Kelpie ran. So he stopped asking.

Snowy was as good a man as you could be living in the Hills, working for a man like Mr. Davidson, being in and out of gaol, and wearing that mark of trouble across his face.

✕ DYMPHNA ✕

It was almost nine when they finally slipped out the Darcy's back gate onto Belmore Lane. Much later than Dymphna had wanted. The brewery was in full motion, the smell of hops and yeast so strong she had a sudden craving for her mother's bread spread thick with butter.

There were no coppers around. Just a couple of old blokes hurrying down the lane towards the brewery—late for their shift, probably—and that awful pimply ghost with the Adam's apple dancing up and down his throat shouting at Kelpie that she was done for and would be joining him soon. Dymphna was glad the boy appeared to be haunting the lane and not Kelpie.

She held Kelpie's small hand firmly in hers while the girl squirmed. Dymphna did not walk quickly, though she was longing to. Rushing would attract attention.

Besides, Dymphna hadn't decided what to do, where to go.

Chances were good the police would be at her flat. Chances were good that Glory would be looking for her. Whether Glory knew that Dymphna had plotted against her or not, she'd know by now that Jimmy was dead. One of Glory's boys. She'd want to know what Dymphna knew.

If Glory didn't know, then Dymphna needed to stay in good with her, tell her what had happened, head to Lansdowne Street—much as she hated it there—to help get ready for the party.

If Glory *did* know, she needed to run.

Then there was Mr. Davidson.

Shit.

Her flat was where her money was, some of it hidden in the lining of her warmest coat. Her passports were there too. One under the name of Dymphna Campbell. One not. That was Jimmy's idea. *Just in case*, he'd said. Neither one dreaming that they really would have to run away. They'd laughed about it. They were sure they'd thought of everything.

Home or Glory. Glory or home.

Which was safer?

She wished she could ask Jimmy without risking him haunting her for the rest of her life. But she wasn't sure if Jimmy knew. She doubted

Snowy would have said *why* he was killing Jimmy. Snowy probably didn't know. He was doing what his boss told him to do. Mr. Davidson was not the kind to share his plans.

Neither was Glory, for that matter.

"Stop pulling, Kelpie. I'm stronger than you. I'm not going to let go of your hand."

Kelpie stopped pulling, but Dymphna knew she was waiting for a chance to run. She didn't blame her. Dymphna would have run away from herself right then if it was possible.

"No matter what happens, you can't tell anyone what you saw," Dymphna said, though she was pretty sure Kelpie would keep her mouth shut. But perhaps it would get Jimmy talking. He hadn't gone into much detail about what happened to him.

Kelpie nodded without looking up. The girl avoided eye contact. Wise.

"I'll do for you if you don't," Jimmy said, leaning into Kelpie's face.

He still hadn't realised there was little he could do to the living. Except drive them insane, and that took time.

"You've got to tell her about Snowy killing me."

"You promise?" Dymphna asked Kelpie, as if she didn't hear Jimmy.

"I promise."

"That card I gave you, the one from Mr. Davidson—" Dymphna began.

"Hoo roo," Snowy Fullerton called from the top of the lane. Kelpie twisted around to see him.

Dymphna turned and smiled, ignoring her impulse to run. The two of them had always been friendly—despite him being Mr. Davidson's, despite his having killed Jimmy. He probably wasn't the first man of hers that Snowy'd killed. She was almost certain Snowy wouldn't hurt her, and if he meant to take her to Mr. Davidson, there was not much she could do to stop him. She would not let herself be scared.

Jimmy ran his finger across his throat. "He did this."

Kelpie looked away.

Snowy lifted his hat briefly. The scar on his right cheek stood out pale against his dark skin. Even so, he was handsome. One of the few hard men never to make a play for Dymphna. She'd heard rumours as to why. She didn't know enough to credit them.

His left eye was mottled red and purple. Did Jimmy give him that?

"Morning, Kelp. Been looking for you," Snowy said, reaching down to ruffle the girl's hair. "You look different. Someone attack you with shears and a bucket of water?"

Kelpie ducked her head, but Dymphna could see she was pleased. She shifted towards him. Dymphna held her hand a little tighter.

"Dymphna," Snowy said.

"Snowy."

Snowy's knuckles were red. They'd probably be blue with bruises later. Did he bruise them on Jimmy or someone else? Dymphna tried to find it in herself to be angry. She wasn't. It wasn't Snowy's doing; it was Mr. Davidson's.

"Bound to happen one day, Kelp. Clean's not so terrible, is it?"

Kelpie's head was still down, but Dymphna thought she saw the hint of a smile.

"Didn't realise you were out already," she said.

"Yesterday morning. Good behaviour," Snowy said, his eyes on Kelpie. "Been a while, hasn't it, Kelp?"

Kelpie nodded a little.

They'd missed each other, Dymphna could see. Kelpie had called him *my Snowy*, hadn't she?

He handed the girl a Cherry Ripe and a bulging brown paper bag. Dymphna could smell the salted peanuts inside. Kelpie went straight for the chocolate, taking longer to get it out of the wrapper than to eat it.

"Didn't know you two were acquainted," Snowy said to Dymphna, as he watched Kelpie dig into the bag of peanuts.

Dymphna smiled but said nothing.

"Where you both headed?"

"Don't tell him!" Jimmy shouted at Kelpie.

"Around," Dymphna said. "It's a perfect winter day for a stroll."

Snowy looked up as if he hadn't noticed that the sun was out and the sky cloudless.

"Might get us something to eat. Kelpie reminds me of my niece," Dymphna said. "I don't like to see her hungry."

"None of us do," Snowy said. "Thought I might take you for a meal myself, Kelpie. Whatcha reckon?"

Kelpie took another step towards him.

"Don't go with him, kid," Jimmy yelled. "Tell her, Kelpie. You want to stay with Dymph, don't you?"

Dymphna wished he would shut up. Getting away from Jimmy was an excellent reason for Kelpie to go with Snowy.

"Flanagan's missus is doing a big spread," Snowy continued. "She'll be serving it midday. Paid for the beef myself. When's the last time you ate meat, Kelpie?"

Kelpie didn't say anything, but she edged even closer to Snowy.

"Sheila Flanagan?" Dymphna asked, wondering why Snowy was lying.

Snowy nodded. His eyes were on Dymphna's now. She would not be afraid of him.

"Sheila's gone back to Dural," she said. "Her mum died."

Sheila's oldest, Lettie, worked for Glory too. She'd been distraught about her grandma passing. Lettie was as close as Dymphna got to having a friend. She'd eaten at the Flanagans' more times than she could count. Snowy should have known better.

He bent to Kelpie's level and leaned in to whisper in her ear. Dymphna couldn't hear the words. She didn't need to. Snowy wanted Kelpie to go with him. Kelpie's head dropped lower; she shook it. His hand went to her shoulders, making Kelpie seem even tinier than she was. Kelpie wiggled away, shaking her head, and ducking behind Dymphna.

Snowy stood and addressed Dymphna softly. "She's not safe with you. I heard about Palmer."

"*Heard* about what happened to me? That's a fucking laugh!" Jimmy said without laughter.

"I can look after myself," Dymphna told Snowy.

"Maybe," he said, but he didn't sound like he believed it. "Can you look after Kelpie?"

"I can try."

Snowy did not look impressed. "You should consider getting away. Far away."

Snowy might as well have told her Mr. Davidson was after her.

"You're a good man, Snowy. Have you . . ." She trailed off, then took courage. Snowy was warning her, wasn't he? "Have you heard anything specific?"

"The boss wants you. You know that. Everyone knows that. This time though he wants us to bring you to him."

Dymphna swallowed. "Alive?" she whispered.

"Unharmed. He was very definite about that. No one's to harm you," Snowy said.

"Are you going to take me to him?"

"Going to *try* not to," Snowy said. "The boss is, well, he's not himself. He's not thinking straight. You need to scarper. Let me take Kelpie. She's safer with me."

"Do you want to go with him?" Dymphna asked Kelpie, hoping the girl was still shaken by whatever Snowy had whispered to her.

Kelpie pressed closer to Dymphna. "Not going to the orphanage."

"I'm not taking you there, Kelp. I promised you I wouldn't. How long have I been looking out for you?"

Kelpie nodded, then shook her head. "You lied about Mrs. Flanagan."

"Because I didn't know if I could trust Dymphna here." He ruffled Kelpie's hair. "We're mates, you and me. What would Old Ma think of you going off with a stranger like this?"

Dymphna could feel Kelpie wavering. "How's a single man like him going to look after you, Kelpie? He'd have to give you to someone. Or Welfare would take you away."

Snowy could pick Kelpie up in one hand and walk away with her. But Dymphna could see he wouldn't do it if she was unwilling.

"We have to go, Kelpie," Dymphna said, pressing her advantage.

He shook his head but said, "Go." Then he walked down the lane at a fast clip, looking back only once.

Dymphna followed, dragging Kelpie with her. But where to go?

"Shouldn't let an abo touch you," the ghost in the lane told Kelpie. He hadn't said a word while Snowy was there, even though Snowy wouldn't have heard him.

"That's ignorant," Jimmy said. "Snowy Fullerton's father was as white as you and me. His mother was from the Caribbean."

"How would you know?" The ghost stuck out his lower lip.

Dymphna wished they'd shut up. Mr. Davidson wanted her unharmed. Surely that meant he didn't know that she and Jimmy had meant to kill him, had meant to take over Razorhurst. So perhaps Glory didn't know either. Which meant she'd be safest going straight to Glory, who could protect her. Jimmy Palmer was dead not because of their scheming but for being her man.

"I know a lot of things," Jimmy said. "Snowy is a good man. Even though he did kill me. You can't hold a grudge against a man doing his job."

Kelpie looked sick. Dymphna was going to have to explain to the girl that you could be a killer and a good person at the same time. You could kill no one at all and be worse than Satan. She'd heard Mr. Davidson never lifted a hand to anyone. He didn't ask any of his men to kill for him either. Instead he gently requested that they *see to someone* or *sort out the problem with so-and-so*. So much worse than Snowy could ever be.

Glory was much more honest. Besides, Glory had killed with

her own hands more than once; she knew what she was asking. Mr. Davidson kept his hands clean, but his soul was putrid.

"I'll admit I done plenty I shouldn't have," Jimmy said.

"What?" the pimply ghost shouted at Jimmy. "Like get your throat cut open by an abo?!" He didn't follow them onto Mary Street despite several attempts to do so. Dymphna was relieved the pimply ghost really was haunting the lane and couldn't follow them any further. She turned towards the train station. The quickest way home was a train into town and then a tram. Her feet had decided on home: money, passport, and then to Glory if it seemed safe.

If the coppers didn't take her in.

If Davidson's men didn't find her.

A woman hurried past with her handkerchief held to her nose. The brewery didn't smell that bad, certainly not as bad as the room at Mrs. Stone's with Jimmy in it.

"The card," Dymphna whispered. "The one with my name on it. From *him*. Where is it?"

Kelpie put her hands in the pockets of her new coat, then into her old and new trousers. She shook her head. Dymphna didn't remember the girl transferring any belongings from the old coat to the new. Certainly not a card.

Shit.

A man in a suit brushed past them, doffed his hat. Two lorries backed into the cavernous rear entrance to the brewery. More and more people. Which was in their favour; they'd be harder to spot in the crowds around Central Station. But also bad, because there were more people to spot them.

Dymphna kept her head down and turned right on Foveaux Street.

"Nah." Kelpie came to a dead stop, causing people to walk around them, to notice them.

"Come on," Dymphna said, lowering her voice. "Don't make a scene."

Kelpie shook her head and took a backward step and then another. Bumped into a man in overalls.

"Watch yerself," he said.

Kelpie was staring at the station on the other side of Elizabeth Street.

Dymphna followed her gaze. Of course. Kelpie would be terrified.

That many ghosts all in the one place. No one had ever taught Kelpie what to do. How not to see or hear them.

Kelpie was not the only illiterate homeless child in the Hills, but most of the ones without parents were swept up off the streets by Welfare quick smart. Wasn't a child in the Hills, or all of Razorhurst, for that matter, who'd evaded Welfare for as long as Kelpie had. She was agile, fast, clever, and she had one or two ghosts on her side.

Kelpie was an ideal student for Miss Lee. Her first reading lesson began in the Darcys' backyard after Neal had gone to work, the littlies to school, and Mrs. Darcy was at the markets with little Kate. Miss Lee went inside the dunny.

Kelpie opened the door to join her.

"The smell can't be helped," Miss Lee said. "He likes to read, you see."

Miss Lee waved her hand at the back of the door plastered with pages. Some were from newspapers, some from books. Some, Kelpie knew without being able to read, advertised fights and circuses.

"It starts with letters. See that one there?" Miss Lee pointed. "That's the first letter in the alphabet, which consists of twenty-six letters. It's the letter *A*."

Kelpie already knew that. She'd seen the nuns yammering on about *A* being for apple often enough. Bloody apples.

Miss Lee traced its shape with her fingers. "This is also a letter *A*." She pointed to an entirely different shape, round with a sort of hat on top.

"They represent this sound," Miss Lee said. "*A* as in aaaapple."

Kelpie frowned. Why did it have to be apples?

"*A* as in ant and animal and ankle and apricot and arrogant and abacus and . . ."

Kelpie didn't know what an arrogant or an abacus was.

They were up to *Q*, and Kelpie was feeling pleased that she had recognised so many of the letters, when they heard Mrs. Darcy's keys in the front door. Kelpie climbed over the fence to where Tommy started chanting letters like a song and laughing at her for not knowing anything.

Miss Lee led her to St. Peter's and into the priest's office where she continued the lesson with the Bible. These letters were much

smaller and harder to see in the gloom. They would have gone to
the library after that, but by that time it was closed, so they went
to the richest man in the Hills's house: Old Man O'Reilly's.

He didn't act like a rich man. He had no live-in help, not even a
cook. Just Mary Sullivan, acting maid for him. She came once or
twice a week. When O'Reilly deigned to let her in, and only when
he seemed calm. She warned him the minute he started throwing
things she would go and never come back no matter how much he
paid her.

He was a big man with a red, veiny face who was rumoured
to have put a knife through Bluey Denham's shoulder, and Bluey
never went after him, which showed you how tough O'Reilly was.
Almost as bad were the rumours that he killed his wife because he
didn't like the way she made soda bread. Now he made his own.

But O'Reilly had more books than anyone else, was asleep
more often than he was awake, and had electricity and the fortunate drunken habit of leaving the lights blazing all night. Biggest
drinker in the Hills, everyone said. Kelpie wasn't sure how you
could tell. There wasn't a man in the Hills who didn't get drunk
when he could, not even the priests. O'Reilly had the money to get
drunk whenever he pleased, which was most of the time.

Miss Lee led her to the library. O'Reilly was so rich he had his
own room of books. Miss Lee pored over the shelves but did not
find a copy of *Great Expectations*. There were plenty of other books.
Even a shelf of them for children. Kelpie pulled down the kids'
books and turned the pages, gawking at the pictures of women
with impossibly long hair and men on horses, dressed in shiny
metal.

"Fairy tales," Miss Lee announced, and had Kelpie hold the
book open to a story called "Rapunzel." Kelpie didn't think much
of Rapunzel's name, nor of her lack of gumption. She preferred
Darcy's stories. But at least the pictures were beautiful, and Kelpie
couldn't help feeling proud when she recognised words and when
she knew it was time to turn the page.

O'Reilly also had paper and pencils. So Miss Lee showed Kelpie
how to make letters and words, not just read them. The first word
she wrote was her own name: *K-E-L-P-I-E* and *K-e-l-p-i-e*.

He had a kitchen too. With more food in it than any other
kitchen Kelpie had ever seen, which admittedly wasn't many. Miss
Lee might not need food, but Kelpie did. She stole bits of cheese

and sliced ham from the icebox. Taking only a little to make sure he wouldn't notice.

They would go back to O'Reilly's many times. Even though he was scary, Miss Lee made her feel brave. Sometimes it seemed being near a ghost made the living less likely to see you. O'Reilly never gave any sign of knowing that Kelpie spent so much time in his house.

KELPIE

Kelpie never went near that end of Foveaux. Too close to Central Station. Too close to more ghosts than Kelpie had ever seen in one place. She kept her eyes on the ground.

"Do what she says." Palmer was glaring at her. "You're going to get the both of youse caught."

"We're almost there," Dymphna said, softening her voice. Coaxing her, Kelpie could tell, the way Miss Lee used to. "Once we're on the train, we'll be at my place in no time. Safer there."

"No, it's not," Palmer said. "Tell her not to go back. Everyone will be looking for her there."

Kelpie shook her head again and pulled in the opposite direction. She tried to think of some reason Dymphna would accept for not going near Central. "I don't like trains. I don't like Central."

"We'll get the tram then. You don't have to go into the train station. Come on." Dymphna grabbed both Kelpie's arms and hauled her closer to Foveaux. "You said you were hungry, didn't you? I've got loads of food. Bacon, eggs, bread, tomatoes, whatever you want."

Kelpie tried to dig her feet in, but they slid along the footpath.

A man in a threadbare suit and a cap glanced at them.

"Stop it," Dymphna hissed.

Miss Lee had never hissed at her.

Kelpie did not want to be noticed, but she didn't want to go anywhere near Central either.

Dymphna dragged her down Foveaux past two young men who dipped their hats. Dymphna gave a quick smile and again hissed at Kelpie to stop drawing attention.

And there they were.

At the bottom of the hill on Elizabeth Street. Kelpie tried not to look, but she could feel them, an uncomfortable heat along all her nerve endings, tugging at her, making her look at the thousands of ghosts moving in and out of the entrance to Central Station. Some seemed to be floating above, some walked straight through it. There were far more dead than living. Miss Lee said it was because there used to be a cemetery under the trains. But Kelpie thought it was something worse. Something terrible had happened over there.

One or two ghosts was normal. Every street, every lane, every park, every house had its share. Even as many as a dozen in the same place. But Central, Central was a swirling grey mass of the dead. You couldn't tell where one ghost ended and another began.

Palmer stared. "Jesus."

Kelpie thought she was going to be sick. First dead Palmer and all that blood and that smell, and now this. She could *not* cross that street. Too many of them. One ghost sliding through her felt bad enough, but dozens? Hundreds? All of them talking at her at once? She could already hear the gentle roar of all those voices.

"Why are there so many?" Palmer asked. "What are they doing?"

Kelpie's muscles tightened, ready to run, but Dymphna kept pulling her along with the steady stream of foot traffic towards more ghosts than had a right to be together.

"Can ghosts kill?" Palmer asked. "Other ghosts, I mean. I don't fancy going over there."

"Look, it's not going to kill you to leave the Hills," Dymphna said. Kelpie wished they'd both stop saying that word *kill*. It felt like they were inviting more killing. "It's not 'here be dragons' on the other side of Elizabeth Street."

Kelpie tried to slip her hand from Dymphna's grip. The problem wasn't dragons, it was ghosts. Knowing they couldn't hurt her made no difference. They could do your head in. Much worse than a cut or broken bone.

Dymphna tugged harder.

Kelpie shook her head.

"That ain't right," Palmer said, staring at the swirling mass. "Tell her you don't want to catch the tram there."

"Not there," Kelpie whispered. "Don't want to catch the tram there."

"Good girl," Palmer said.

"She speaks! We'll go up to the next tram stop then." Dymphna turned her head. Kelpie thought she heard a siren. It was hard to tell over the din of the traffic. "Right, then," Dymphna said, quickening her pace. "We'll cross further up. That suit you better?"

"Yes." Kelpie's back prickled from all those ghosts behind her on the other side of the road.

They stayed on the Hills side of Elizabeth Street as a tram rattled by.

"We could have been on that one," Dymphna muttered.

When they were far enough away from Central, Kelpie let

Dymphna pull her across the street. They dodged the motor-cars and people, and Kelpie dodged the few stray ghosts always in the middle of the road, dead from a motor-car or a tram, spending the rest of their existence with the things that killed them whistling through them every day.

Kelpie looked towards Central and wished she hadn't. From this side there were even more of them, weaving so close together they looked like storm clouds.

They stood at the tram stop and waited for the next tram. There was only a grey-haired couple waiting with them.

"You'll tell me what that was," Palmer said, "when Dymph can't hear you."

Kelpie nodded her head slightly, though she didn't really know.

A fancy motor-car slowed, and someone in the back rolled down the window.

"Dymphna, angel," said a deep, oddly accented voice, "what are you doing on this side of town? Need a lift?"

The man's hat kept his face in shadow, but Kelpie knew who it was from his voice alone. Everyone knew who he was. The arm that rested on the motor-car door had a large watch on it. It shone.

"No, thank you, Mr. Davidson."

"You sure, darling? An angel like you is too refined for the tram."

Dymphna laughed, shaking her head. "I'm not sure Glory would approve. You know I don't like to get in trouble."

The man laughed hard. "Weren't you born in trouble, young Dymphna? Why, haven't you heard? You're the Angel of Death! Is there anything more troublesome than death? Do get in. I've got a present for you. You'll like it."

The man smiled. Kelpie thought he looked like a dragon. Someone moved behind Mr. Davidson, but the windows were too dark for her to make out who it was.

Dymphna shook her head and took a few steps further away. The motor-car rolled along beside her. "Terry, why don't you give Dymphna here a hand getting into the car?"

The motor-car stopped, and the driver, a large man in a suit much shinier than Mr. Davidson's, got out. He moved towards Dymphna, who increased her pace and pulled Kelpie closer to her. Several motor-car horns sounded.

"You should do what Mr. Davidson says, Miss Campbell," the driver said.

"You should fucking run," Palmer said. But he was looking at Kelpie.

"Oh, look," Dymphna said, smiling brightly, "here's our tram." She twisted past the driver, holding Kelpie's hand so tight it hurt, and dashed out onto the street. More horns sounded, someone yelled abuse, but Dymphna had pulled Kelpie up onto the back of the tram, where Dymphna paused to ask if she was all right, before waving to Mr. Davidson.

Kelpie wasn't. She didn't like the look of that Mr. Davidson. Or the sound of him. Or anything about him. It wasn't safe with Dymphna.

Mr. Davidson

No one knew Mr. Davidson's first name. Or where he came from. Or anything about him. Except for the little you could glean from looking at him. His accent was faintly foreign. But local too. Just more Point Piper than Millers Point.

He never got into fights. Not like Glory, who'd been known to go the biff more than once. With her own husband, even, and every one of her lovers. Mr. Davidson never raised his voice. The only sign he was angry was that he smiled more. Or so said one of his razor men. Long gone now. So who knew if that was true?

He didn't have a wife or children. As far as anyone knew, with few exceptions, he lived like a monk. A monk with a taste for caviar and champagne—in small amounts. No one had ever seen Mr. Davidson drunk or even slightly tipsy.

He was unfailingly polite to everyone, and yet no one in his domain would defend him the way those in Glory's defended her. No one trusted him. His hands were never dirty. He didn't drink beer. He spent more time at the high end of town than the low. "Looking after his *legitimate* business interests," Glory said, scoffing, "as if he has any of those. Or have smoke houses, sly grog shops, and two-up parlours gone and got respectable while I wasn't looking?"

The one thing Mr. Davidson could not be accused of was running a brothel. The niceties of the law meant that men could not profit from women selling their bodies. But women could. Hence Glory's rise to power. The cops couldn't take away her money from running girls.

Still, running sly grog shops and nightclubs and gaming houses and peddling illicit drugs were also against the law, and yet Mr. Davidson saw that as no barrier to his involvement. The answer to the conundrum was easy: the cops raided the houses of ill repute far more often than the illegal casinos. All those shapely women dragged out onto the street in dishabille meant better newspaper coverage.

As it happened, much of Mr. Davidson's profits from the low end of town supported his licit activities at the high end of town running legal nightclubs and restaurants and even clothing factories in Surry

Hills. Glory's territory, yes. But she didn't know he'd invested in the rag trade. *She* certainly hadn't. A pub in Woolloomooloo and some flats in the Cross were all the legal real estate she'd managed thus far.

Mr. Davidson wasn't like anyone else in their world. His ambitions were larger. The aim wasn't merely to run all of Razorhurst—Davidson wanted the entire city, hell, the rest of the country too. He wanted onward and upward and an enormous bag of respectability.

He also wanted Dymphna Campbell.

✕ KELPIE ✕

Dymphna took a seat at the back of the tram, pulling Kelpie beside her. Kelpie's feet did not reach the floor. She kicked them back and forth. Dymphna let go of her hand at last and patted her shoulder. Dymphna was breathing hard, and her cheeks were flushed. Her eyes glittered, and for a moment Kelpie thought she might cry.

"I've managed to stay out of gaol this long," she whispered. "And alive. I'm not about to go back there now. We'll be all right, Kelpie. If we can get home."

Palmer sat opposite them next to a small boy ghost.

A man in uniform came up to them, and for a moment Kelpie thought he was a copper, but then Dymphna handed him money, and he handed her two small pieces of thin paper. She gave one to Kelpie, who stared at it.

"Your ticket, silly."

Dymphna stared out the back window, probably checking that Mr. Davidson was not following them. Kelpie didn't know how she could tell. All those motor-cars looked pretty much the same to her. Black and shining and metallic. She had no trouble imagining Mr. Davidson ordering Palmer's death. Or anyone else he didn't like.

Across the aisle the small boy stared at them. Kelpie wondered why he wasn't ignoring her and Dymphna. Most ghosts ignored the living. She smiled at him. He did not smile back.

Kelpie had never been on a tram before. She'd thought they'd be free of ghosts. She didn't know why. Trams were filled with people. People could die anywhere.

Next time the tram stopped, she was going to run. She hoped it wouldn't be too hard to find her way back to the Hills.

"Dymphna's scared," Palmer said as they rattled along.

Every time the tram shuddered, Kelpie bounced on the hard wooden seat. There were already plasters on her fingers from Mrs. Darcy's scrubbing—soon she'd need them on her bum.

The tram stopped. Now was the time. They were only a block and a half further along. Easy to get back along Elizabeth Street to the Hills.

Kelpie pushed herself up.

Dymphna pulled her down.

"You'll have to be quicker than that," she whispered, holding Kelpie's hand firmly.

Kelpie was plenty quick. She'd just timed it wrong. She knew she could outrun Dymphna, especially in those heels she was wearing. No one could run in those things.

Loads of people crowded on board, filling the aisle, holding the leather straps that hung intermittently from the railing down the centre aisle. A big fat man leaned over her, so close she could smell his tobacco breath. Kelpie couldn't see a way to push past him without Dymphna catching her.

"I've never seen her this scared," Palmer said, peering over and through the fat man, who shifted uncomfortably.

She didn't look scared to Kelpie. Dymphna caught Kelpie looking. She smiled and squeezed her hand. Kelpie felt herself smiling back.

Dymphna smiled as if she wasn't worried that they were being followed by Mr. Davidson. As if she hadn't seen a man with his throat cut open that morning. Kelpie wondered what it would be like to stay with her. Dymphna had given Mrs. Darcy ten pounds like it was nothing! And those clothes she wore. She probably had more money than Old Man O'Reilly. It would be nice to have someone with money looking out for her. She'd never be hungry.

But with the coppers and Mr. Davidson after her, how long was Dymphna going to be able to hang on to that money?

Palmer again pushed through the fat man, who stumbled. Kelpie could see the ghost boy. He hadn't moved.

"He's dead, isn't he?" Palmer asked. "Because he's got that sickly look. Like there's no blood in him. Miserable."

Kelpie nodded slightly then turned away. She thought about asking Dymphna where she was going. Where was her home? Somewhere safe, she hoped. For Dymphna's sake. She was still going to run, but she wanted to believe Dymphna was safe.

The tram stopped again. Out the back window, the Hills was now three blocks away.

She didn't try anything. Too many obstacles, and Dymphna hadn't let go of her hand.

It didn't take long before Kelpie stopped recognising anything out the window. The buildings were tall and fancy with giant awnings overhanging shops selling so many different things Kelpie didn't know how anyone could use it all. There were more people than at Paddy's Markets.

Kelpie'd never been this far into town before. The city was full of men in clean suits and hats who worked at the kind of places Surry Hills people would never set foot in. Like banks, where they stole your money. Only the police never called bank people thieves or robbers. All her life Kelpie had been hearing people in the Hills complain about banks, starting with Old Ma.

Kelpie was glad Mrs. Darcy had made her wash and wear shoes. She would have stood out something awful if she hadn't. Everyone on the tram wore shoes. They were all clean too, faces scrubbed, hair untangled. Most had hats on. The men wore ties and the women gloves.

But even after running from the police and climbing through fences, Dymphna Campbell looked more of a lady than any of them. Kelpie felt a little flush of pride. The fancy lady was holding *her* hand, not any of theirs. Even if she was holding it to make sure Kelpie didn't run away.

Kelpie was the only kid. Well, her and the ghost, and even he had shoes and a little tie. Hat as well. If he was from the Hills, he must've been from one of the few posh places left up near O'Reilly's.

Palmer tried to talk to him, but the boy didn't respond. Maybe he was frozen. Kelpie'd never come across a ghost who didn't move. But why not? Maybe he sat on the tram all day staring at whoever was opposite. Never moving an inch. The thought gave her the shivers. She decided not to look at the little boy ghost again.

She didn't see any kids out the window either. She'd heard that in town kids without parents were gathered up by Welfare in huge black trucks. She'd never seen one, but then she didn't hardly ever leave the Hills.

Town wasn't safe. Kelpie wasn't sure this tram was safe. Dymphna definitely wasn't safe. But if Kelpie ran off on her own in town, she could be nabbed by Welfare.

"That's David Jones," Dymphna said, pointing out the window. Kelpie saw a sea of hats bobbing up and down, dotted with the occasional grey of ghosts. She didn't know why Dymphna thought Kelpie should know who David Jones was or how Dymphna could spot one man in such a crowd.

"The store, silly," Dymphna said. "It's the best in the city. Anything in the world you want is at David Jones, and this is where we change trams." She led Kelpie from the tram. Kelpie turned to catch a last glimpse of the boy, but Palmer blocked her view. The boy probably hadn't moved. It made her sad.

Elizabeth Street wasn't as wide here, but it was much more crowded. Kelpie didn't know how they'd make it across. Dymphna gripped her wrist and pulled her past the people and around the motor-cars and trams until they were on the other side of the street in a park that wasn't as big as Moore Park or Centennial Park and had stunted little trees and no grass, but had many more people.

Kelpie turned to look down Elizabeth Street while Dymphna dragged her in the opposite direction. Surry Hills was back that way. All she had to do was twist her hand from Dymphna's and run in the direction the tram had come from. Run until she was clear of Dymphna, then walk. Otherwise Welfare or the coppers. She'd have to be sneaky.

"You need to stay with Dymphna," Palmer said. Kelpie ignored him.

Dymphna's grip had slid from her hand to her wrist. Much harder to twist out of that grip. Dymphna moved fast, dragging Kelpie with her, looking every which way. For Mr. Davidson, Kelpie was sure. If he grabbed Dymphna, Kelpie could escape.

"Faster, Kelpie," Dymphna said. "That's our tram."

Dymphna pulled Kelpie up onto the tram and then along to the back while it headed away from the city and even further away from the Hills, rattling along a street Kelpie didn't know. She worried that she wouldn't be able to get back home without help. Kelpie wished Miss Lee was there to give her a plan for getting away from Dymphna. She looked at Palmer. He shook his head. But she had no idea at what.

The second tram was no more comfortable than the first, but at least it wasn't crowded. The aisle was empty, and no one sat in front of them. Dymphna stopped peering out the back window and turned to Kelpie.

"Where's your mum?" she asked.

"Dunno."

"What about your dad?"

"Dunno."

Kelpie didn't like those kinds of questions. Ghosts never asked any of that. That's why Kelpie was better at talking to ghosts than people. No ghost had ever tried to round her up and put her in an orphanage or make her go to school. Not that she thought that's what Dymphna Campbell was going to do. But she was asking the same questions as those who did want to ruin her life. Kelpie gave her the same answer.

"Why don't you answer her questions?" Palmer asked. "You're being rude."

Kelpie ignored him.

"Where are you from?" Dymphna said.

"Dunno."

"From Surry Hills?"

"Dunno."

"How old are you?"

"Dunno."

"Why do they call you Kelpie?"

"Dunno."

"Do you know anything?"

"Dunno."

Dymphna laughed. "Do you really not know how old you are?"

Kelpie didn't say anything. Wasn't fair asking the same question twice. Why were the living so obsessed with how old she was? How old anyone was? She hadn't asked Mrs. Darcy or Dymphna how old they were. She'd never asked anyone that question. Why did it matter? Ten, thirteen, fifteen, twenty, it was all the same if you lived on the streets. Ghosts never cared how old she was.

"Anything you tell me is a secret, Kelpie. Who would I tell? I don't like the coppers, and they don't like me. I don't like any authorities. They're all rotten."

Kelpie didn't say anything. She didn't want to encourage more questions.

"I want to help you."

Kelpie wasn't convinced. Wasn't Dymphna helping herself? She didn't want anyone to know that she'd seen Palmer dead on that bed before the police had—and Kelpie knew. She wouldn't tell, but she didn't know how to make Dymphna believe that.

That man, that Mr. Davidson, was chasing Dymphna, and he was probably going to catch her. How was Dymphna helping Kelpie when she didn't seem to be able to help herself?

"You're like me," Dymphna said.

Kelpie couldn't see how.

They got off the tram, Palmer behind them.

Dymphna looked around carefully. There were as many people as in the Hills, but it wasn't as crowded as it had been back in the city where they changed trams.

"Almost there."

Dymphna stopped at a cart, had Kelpie select two packets of chips and paid for them without letting go of Kelpie's wrist. The man selling them blushed and mumbled his thanks to Miss Campbell. Dymphna smiled graciously. Two ghosts, so old and faded that Kelpie couldn't tell if they were boys or girls, lurked behind the cart, but neither of them had eyes for anything but each other.

"Any news, Stanley?" Dymphna asked quietly.

"I hear Glory's looking for you. Urgent-like, I heard."

"That's not good," Palmer said. "I don't like an unhappy Glory."

Kelpie didn't want to think about Gloriana Nelson. Or about how many ghosts she'd created. Kelpie'd heard too much bad about her. Some good, though. Kelpie'd even gotten Christmas presents and free Chrissie lunch. More than once.

Miss Lee called Gloriana Nelson a common, uneducated, dull-witted savage but mostly preferred not to talk about her.

Old Ma had been more than happy to gossip about Gloriana Nelson. She would always press her lips together when Glory was mentioned, rant about how Glory was no better than she should be, about how throwing parties and giving away sausages and beers and toys didn't mean you were good—killing was killing, and no amount of money could buy real decency—and how it was people like Gloriana Nelson who'd destroyed Frog Hollow and how she was going to destroy all of the Hills so no decent people would ever live there again. Old Ma swore Gloriana Nelson reeked of the badness inside her, that was why she had to spray herself with oceans of perfume.

Glory was always driving around the Hills in her fancy motor-car with her driver in his fancy black uniform and shiny black cap, smiling and waving, calling out to people by name, showing that she knew everyone and would look after them if they needed it. Old Ma said, "Too right, she'll look after youse. Look you right into your grave and then dance on top of it."

Everyone knew Glory liked to laugh. But once Kelpie had seen her stop laughing abruptly, turn, and cut one of her men a look that'd made Kelpie creep away and hide. Short fella, he'd been, stocky with faded red hair. Kelpie had never seen him again.

"Anyone else looking for me?" Dymphna asked. Kelpie knew she meant Mr. Davidson.

"I seen plenty of cops around."

"If anyone asks, Stanley?"

The man nodded. "Same as ever. I haven't seen you."

Dymphna smiled at him so radiantly Kelpie thought he might faint. "Just around the corner."

Kelpie tried to open the chips one-handed but only managed to drop both packets. She bent slowly to pick them up. Dymphna's grip loosened, just enough, Kelpie hoped, pushing forward off her feet with all her strength. Her hand slid from Dymphna's. Ha! She would—

Dymphna had her by the waist, knocking out her breath and using her momentum to swing her around as if she were a rag doll, while managing to scoop up the chips with her free hand.

"I'm not letting go," Dymphna said.

Kelpie didn't quite believe what had happened. Dymphna was all blonde hair and delicate skin and fancy clothes. She didn't look strong, but the arm around Kelpie's waist might as well have been made of iron.

"I'm putting you down now. You'll behave?"

Kelpie said nothing. She was too angry. She thought about kicking Dymphna. Instead, she smiled.

Dymphna let Kelpie slide to the ground, keeping a firm grip on her wrist and handing her the chips.

"What was that for?" Palmer asked. "She's on your side, you know. All you have to do is tell her what happened to me, tell her to get out of here. She'll take care of you. She bought you chips, didn't she? She likes you."

Kelpie didn't see why Dymphna liked her or why she wanted to look after her. Dymphna was like a creature from a different world. A cleaner, shinier place. Neal Darcy hadn't been able to take his eyes off her, and Darcy wasn't easily impressed. Dymphna'd been looking at him too.

Palmer walked beside Dymphna, and his greyness made her colours more vivid: she was all blues and golds and creams. It felt good to be near someone that beautiful, as if somehow her magic could rub off on Kelpie. She would love a world where Dymphna and Darcy were together and looked after her. But this wasn't that world. Dymphna's magic got people killed. She was the Angel of Death, wasn't she?

Palmer reached out to touch Dymphna's hair. His hand went straight through. "Don't you think she's gorgeous? She glows." He sighed and then turned to Kelpie, all the softness gone from his face. "You can tell her about Mr. Davidson and Snowy soon. We're almost at her place."

Dymphna patted Kelpie's head as if she hadn't just stopped her from running away. "Why does no one look after you? Where are your people? Are they all dead?"

"Dunno." Why did it matter? Dymphna of all people knew that everyone dies.

"I want to help you. I'm not . . ." Dymphna trailed off. Kelpie could feel her looking at her. "I know things that . . . I can help you. Really help you in ways no one else can. You need me. I know you don't believe it, but you do. I could look after you—if you want. You could be my little sister. I'd get you decent clothes. Pretty clothes from David Jones. You'd always have a safe place to sleep. What do you think?"

"Orright," Kelpie said, though she still planned to scarper and didn't see how Dymphna could guarantee a safe place to sleep for herself, let alone anyone else, what with two gangsters and the police after her.

"Good." Dymphna gave her a little squeeze. "Your parents are dead, aren't they?"

"Are they ghosts like me?" Palmer asked.

"Dunno."

Dymphna snorted. "Liar."

Standover Man

Not all the standovers were like Snowy Fullerton or Jimmy Palmer, working for someone like Gloriana Nelson or Mr. Davidson. Some worked for themselves, leaning on individuals rather than a whole establishment.

Stanley Leatherbarrow was one such. It was admittedly a name that did not evoke a hard man—it would have been better suited to an accountant. But Stan was hard indeed. Also strong and fast and persistent.

Also polite.

His usual method was to go up to the person he suspected of having money. Usually bookies, but he also put the touch on the florist at Taylor Square and the elderly sisters Smith in the mansion next to Old Man O'Reilly's. He would smile, make conversation about the weather, and then he would observe that they seemed to be a bit off balance, and perhaps it was the weight of their wallets weighing them down. He would then offer to relieve them of part of their burden. His target would comply, knowing that Stan did not go anywhere without brass knuckles in his right-hand pocket and a razor in his left.

But knowing, too, that he was most reluctant to use them. *Blood is the last resort*, he would always say mournfully, shaking his head.

Until the day pale-eyed Bluey Denham walked into Molly's Flowers on Taylor Square and demanded five pounds. The girl didn't hear the actual amount, but she knew who he was and handed over ten pounds quicker than blinking.

Then she sent a boy out to find Stan, which the boy did. Then Stan found Bluey. At which point, well, no one knows what happened after that except that Stan disappeared.

Stan's four bookies and one florist—but not the Smith sisters; for some reason Bluey didn't know about them—were now paying Bluey—guessing as to the amount because no one wanted to get close enough to actually hear what he said. Bluey was acting on his own, and he kept the lot, until Glory found out and penalised him with unconsciousness—courtesy of a conk to the head—at which point he commenced handing over the 70 percent that he should have been passing to her since day one of his takeover.

That was the standover ecosystem: they took from you until someone put them out of the taking business, at which point you gave to the new standover. Every so often the powers that be— Glory or Mr. Davidson or whoever was the current monarch of Razorhurst—co-opted the independent standovers or put them out of business, at which point the take went up. Usually the big bosses' protection lasted longer than the independent standovers. You lost more money, but you had less headaches.

What Stan's targets minded most was not so much the money— they'd lived in the Hills all their lives, they expected to pay such local taxes—but that Stan had been a gentleman. Why, half the time he'd stood them a pint out of the money he extorted. So at least they got a small part of it back.

Bluey'd never bought anyone anything in his entire life.

⇾ DYMPHNA ⇽

Dymphna led Kelpie into her apartment building. A thicket of flowers crowded the lobby. White lilies among them. The perfume was overpowering.

"Mr. Davidson," Raymond the day doorman said in lieu of good morning. "Bit more of them than usual." He handed her the card.

Flowers for my flower

"Those are funeral flowers," Jimmy said. "The bastard."

"Cops been looking for you," Ray said. "And two of Davidson's men."

Dymphna didn't say *shit* out loud. She didn't want him to see how rattled she was. Ray was one of Glory's. As was everyone who worked in this building. Most of the tenants were too. Glory owned the entire building with the exception of only one or two flats. It was the first of her legitimate holdings.

"Thanks, Ray," Dymphna said, pointing her chin towards the stairs.

"No one there now. But I reckon they'd be watching the building. They'll be here soon." He nodded at the flowers. "Send them to St. Vinnie's?"

"Find a funeral for them."

She'd made it this far without Mr. Davidson, or one of his men, or one of Glory's men, or the coppers snatching her.

She couldn't help but look behind her. No coppers stormed the entrance. Instead Jimmy stood amongst the flowers, shaking his head.

Less than twelve hours since she'd seen him alive. Less than twelve hours since they'd been preparing to make themselves King and Queen of Razorhurst.

"If anyone else shows up, you'll ring me, won't you?"

"If they let me. Couldn't have earlier. One stayed in the lobby and give me the devil's eye when I reached for this 'phone here."

"I understand." She hoped Ray didn't notice her hands shaking. "Thanks."

"Who's the kid?"

Dymphna patted Kelpie's head. "My nephew."

"Looks like a girl."

. . .

Dymphna half expected to find her door ripped from the hinges. It wasn't. She led Kelpie in then closed it, locked it, pocketed the key, and drew the bolt across for extra security. The bolt was Gloriana Nelson's idea.

She leaned there a moment, catching her breath, looking around. She didn't think anyone had come in. Nothing looked disturbed.

Dymphna's heart beat too fast, sending blood to pound in her temples.

Jimmy was badgering Kelpie to tell her about Snowy. Kelpie hissed at him.

Jimmy hadn't been much of a talker when he was alive. He'd been more like that Neal Darcy, though nowhere near as handsome.

She'd never get used to how much some of them changed between breathing and being a ghost. Or how much some of them stayed exactly the same. Her father being the worst. She shook her head, pushing the thought of him far away.

Dymphna slipped her jacket off and went to hang it on the coat rack. She missed. Tried again. Missed again. The tremor that had been in her legs was now in her hands. She concentrated on stilling them, hung her coat properly, and thought about how to get everything she needed without Kelpie seeing.

Her hands started shaking again.

"You see?" Jimmy said. "She's shaking."

Trust bloody Jimmy to haunt her. None of her other dead boyfriends had. Why couldn't he not have been a ghost? Or haunted where he fell? Or where he was born? Or any damn place as long as it was far from her.

"It's dead nice," Kelpie said, looking around.

"Thanks."

Dymphna *was* proud of her place. She'd removed herself from living in one of Glory's houses within months. None of the other girls had managed that. They were still stuck living in a brothel while Dymphna owned her own flat in Kings Cross with built-in wardrobes in the bedroom, an indoor toilet, and water that flowed from the taps clear and odourless. She was not stuck in a rat-infested hole in the Hills.

Like where Jimmy had died. Not that it mattered if you died somewhere squalid. The point was to put off dying for as long as possible.

She had to focus, grab what she needed, ring up Glory.

"Tell her now," Jimmy said to Kelpie. "About Mr. Davidson. About Snowy. Why's she even here? Ask her. Tell her to get a move on. Coppers were here before. They'll be back. Tell her!"

Kelpie looked away.

Dymphna's hands were still shaking. She hadn't decided where to go. Jimmy was right. She wasn't moving fast enough. She *had* to calm herself.

"There's two rooms and my own telephone," Dymphna said, pointing with pride at the telephone resting on the hall stand, which had a cord so long she could talk on it while sitting on her chaise lounge. She should be using it right this second to 'phone Glory.

She didn't know why she was telling Kelpie any of this. It was like the words were shaking out of her to match the tremors in her hands.

But the girl's eyes widened at the 'phone. Perhaps that was why. To impress Kelpie. Next she'd be boasting about having her own bathroom and toilet to a girl who, as far as Dymphna knew, had never lived indoors. A broken shack in the remains of Frog Hollow would impress Kelpie. Dymphna's kitchen, with its two burners, sink, icebox, and cupboard against the wall, would seem grand as Buckingham Palace.

It seemed that way to Dymphna too. Her own place! It was almost brand new, and no one had died during construction, which meant no ghosts to speak of.

Before Jimmy, anyway.

Now she had to run away.

Kelpie was still gawking.

"You'll sleep on the couch," Dymphna told her, even though Kelpie almost certainly wouldn't be sleeping there. This might well be the last time Dymphna ever stood here in her own home.

Kelpie smiled.

The contrast between Dymphna's flat and the little girl was stark. Kelpie wasn't dead nice. Even with her face and hands washed and some clean clothes, she looked like something the streets had spat up. But bringing her here was worth it. Dymphna'd finally found someone who was like her. Now all she had to do was make sure neither one of them was killed.

If she could get Kelpie into the bath, that would give her time she needed to ring up Glory.

"Strewth, woman!" Jimmy yelled. "What the fuck are you playing at? Tell her, Kelpie. Does she even know it's all gone bung? Christ on a crutch!"

Kelpie winced at Jimmy's shouts, following Dymphna into the pink and white bathroom. Everything was curvy and modern and beautiful. The tiles shone; the taps gleamed. Dymphna turned the taps, running her fingers through the water invitingly. The steam rose. Kelpie stared.

Dymphna laughed. "You've never seen a bath with running water before?"

Kelpie shook her head. Dymphna didn't doubt her. Half of Surry Hills didn't have electricity yet. Almost all of it had outhouses. The Darcys didn't have running water. Not in the house.

"Do you want to get in?"

"There's no time for a fucking bath!" Jimmy screamed. His face was incandescently darker. Dymphna could imagine how red it would be if he wasn't a ghost. Like he would explode with his rage.

Kelpie told Jimmy to shut up under her breath. Dymphna pretended she couldn't hear over the sound of the water. She knew Jimmy was right. But if Kelpie was in the bath, it would give her time to line her coat with more money, her passports, to call Glory out of Kelpie's range of hearing.

Kelpie took a step closer and looked from the bath filling with water to Dymphna. Dymphna wondered again why the girl had come with her. Why she asked no questions. Snowy had told her the little girl didn't trust anyone.

"We can add bubbles."

Dymphna took her precious bottle of bubble bath from the mirrored cupboard above the sink and poured two capfuls under the taps. Glory had given it to her last Christmas. Dymphna had never heard of such a thing. The bubbles sprang into life instantly. Kelpie didn't smile, but her eyes widened and she shivered a little.

"If you get in, you'll warm up."

Kelpie kicked off Seamus Darcy's shoes and carefully removed his socks.

"Let me take your coat?"

Kelpie turned so Dymphna could help her out of it and then Seamus's clean shirt underneath. His trousers too. She hung them on the hook behind the door.

"Fucking madness," Jimmy muttered.

Kelpie stood in her ratty clothing, eyeing the growing bubbles. Dymphna debated trying to get those off her, then decided they'd probably disintegrate on contact with the water. Kelpie stepped in, swishing her feet through the water and bubbles.

"It's deep enough now that you could sit down."

Kelpie looked at Dymphna and then at the water. She sat, hesitantly reaching out to touch the bubbles. Her wet clothes rippled around her in waves.

Which was when someone started pounding on Dymphna's door. Had to be the coppers or some other muscle. The doorman wouldn't let anyone else in. Not without asking her.

"You could have been out of here already!" Jimmy yelled. "You and the little one!"

Jimmy was right, but that didn't make her love him for screaming it at her.

She was making mistakes, losing her nerve. She had to pull herself together.

She shut off the taps. Kelpie started to climb out of the bath.

Dymphna shook her head, pushed her gently back in, signalled her to be quiet, and closed the bathroom door.

She adjusted her hat, straightened the collar of her shirt, ran her hands along her skirt. If this was the end, she didn't want to look shabby.

∽✤∽ *Gloriana Nelson* ∽✤∽

When rankled, Gloriana Nelson had a voice that could strip the bark from a fig tree. She had once told a high court judge to go fuck himself. The poor man reared back so shocked his white curly wig fell off, and the whole courtroom near exploded from laughing.

Glory paid a fifty-pound fine and spent ten days in His Majesty's Finest for the privilege. When asked if it was worth it, she nodded grimly. "Insulted me, he did. Calling me a madam. I never."

Gloriana Nelson *was* a madam. Even if she didn't agree with the nomenclature. She was a lot of other things too. Besides her women there was the illegal grog, the gambling, and the drugs, mostly cocaine, but some opium as well.

Then there were her legitimate real estate holdings, which she held because of Mr. Davidson. He thought he could turn legit? Then she would do likewise. He was no better than her even if he did give himself airs.

People who got in her way had a habit of disappearing—into the harbour with shoes made of lead, it was whispered. Girls as young as thirteen; men as old as ninety. If you crossed Glory, you were gone.

But the same could be said for Mr. Davidson, and he didn't have a good side.

When Glory wasn't angry, her voice was gruff but somehow soothing. She could be charming. There were many in the Hills who wouldn't hear a word against her. *A good sort*, they'd swear blind. *Wouldn't hurt a fly.*

She told anyone who asked that she gave 20 percent of her income to charity. This was no lie. Or, rather, it was a decent stab at the percentage. Glory's accounts were not what you would call regular. Certainly no tax man had ever had a look. She ran through accountants faster than standover men.

Chances were some years she gave away more like 30 percent and others more like 10 percent. "Tithing," she called it. "Got to help the nuns and the little children and the blind. Imagine stumbling around in the dark all the time! And them poor boys come back from the war all broken and muddled. It ain't right. I bin fortunate, ain't I? I likes to do me bit."

Every Christmas Glory put on her finest gown, usually bought special for the occasion in either red or green—never the both together because that would be common—she had her hair dyed fresh and done in nice big curls, and she and her husband, Big Bill, who always dressed up like Santa, stood on the balcony of her finest terrace in the Hills, the one on Lansdowne Street with the authentic ironwork brought in on the boats from New Orleans, and handed out Chrissie pressies to every kid in the Hills, and likely many from outside them too. When the presents ran out, they showered the remaining kids with lollies and handed their parents bottles of beer. Her kitchen churned out sausages wrapped in bread for every comer.

Glory and Big Bill always smiled their brightest, biggest smile for the photo that would go in the papers. Gloriana Nelson loved to throw a big party.

That was why she was having another one on that fine August day. What better excuse for festivities could there be than getting shot of her husband, Big Bill? And who did she most want by her side to celebrate?

Why, Dymphna Campbell—Glory's best girl: her most popular and her biggest earner. Gloriana Nelson had no intention of ever letting her go. No matter how unlucky the poor girl was in love.

DYMPHNA

Dymphna put the door on the latch and opened it the full extent of the chain.

Inspector Larry Ferguson smiled and doffed his hat. He was a detective with the Criminal Investigation Branch. Around six foot, broad shouldered, and dressed in the same suit, overcoat, and hat that all the detectives wore. They were like a tribe, each instantly recognisable as what he was: a detective complete with notebook and gun. Ferguson, unlike at least one of the other detectives, was rumoured to be honest. Dymphna knew for certain he was not on either Glory's or Mr. Davidson's payroll.

She did not show her relief that he was neither Glory nor Mr. Davidson.

A little behind him stood a constable who, she was pretty sure, *was* on Glory's payroll. Of all the coppers who could have come to the door, Ferguson and one of Glory's boys were the least troublesome. Or so she hoped. Just because Ferguson wasn't on a payroll didn't mean he wouldn't arrest her.

"Fuck," Jimmy muttered behind her.

"An inspector coming to visit," Dymphna said. "I'm honoured."

"Had to send our finest to chat with the Angel of Death," Ferguson said, holding his hat to his chest as if he truly did respect her.

"Don't call me that." She wished she could slap him and all the others who called her that. It wasn't funny. It had never been funny.

"Sorry, Miss Campbell," he said, pronouncing the honorific as if it had gone bad in his mouth. "But you know everyone calls you that."

"Not to my face."

"My apologies. So how are you, Dymph?" he asked, returning his hat to his head. It was clear that he felt half her name was more than she deserved.

"I'm well, thank you. Though I was even better before you showed up."

Behind her Jimmy laughed.

"You been up to something, have you, Dymph? Funny how a guilty conscience will make a girl nervous around the law."

"I'm not nervous," Dymphna said, and she realised she wasn't. Her hands had stopped trembling. Her chin was high. "It's merely that I don't like you."

Inspector Ferguson seemed not to be mortified to hear it. "How's that fella of yours?" he asked. "What's his name? Jimmy something or other? Pritchard? Palmerton? Palmer? Palmer. That's right. He's a tough one, isn't he? Huge too. Must be the tallest man in the city. Glory's best man, I hear. Which makes him one of the most powerful men in the Hills too. Tall *and* powerful. Quite the combination. A one, two without even raising his fists. Lucky you, having him for your man."

"Bastard's lucky I'm not still alive," Jimmy said. "Talking to you like that. He'd be deader than a maggot."

Dymphna couldn't help wondering about all the live maggots who would ruin Jimmy's comparison.

"How's he doing then?" the detective asked as he unbuttoned his overcoat and pulled out his notebook. "Your man? Looking after you? Keeping you safe from all the other fellas who'd love to have you?"

"Jimmy's a good man." He had been a man, that was certainly true, and good could mean many different things.

Ferguson made a note. Dymphna imagined the words *says victim was a good man* noted neatly on the page.

"Is he? When was the last time you saw him?"

"Last night," Dymphna said, because that was certainly true. She didn't think she needed to mention having seen his dead body or that his ghost was behind her. "Not that it's any business of yours."

"Oh, it's my business all right, Angel. I'm sorry, *Dymphna*. It's very much my business."

Dymphna let her face show shock at the implication of his words. "He isn't . . . ?" she began before trailing off.

"He is. Dead as your last boyfriend. And the one before him and the one before him. How many's it been now, Dymph? Seven? Eight?"

Dymphna let her eyes fill with tears and covered her mouth with her hands.

"Your man Jimmy Palmer was killed. Brutally."

"I guess you could call a throat slashing brutal," Jimmy said.

Dymphna looked down. The detective's shoes must have been polished that morning. They gleamed. Unlike those of the constable.

"I hear you were over in the Hills today. Right where Palmer died, in fact. The Angel of—"

"Don't call me that!"

Ferguson held up his hands. "Sorry, Dymph."

"You heard wrong. I've been here all morning."

"That's funny. You weren't here earlier when we came calling."

"I was asleep. I'm a heavy sleeper. Just ask the doorman. He'll tell you I was here."

"Will he? Your doorman told us he didn't think you'd come in last night."

Well, that was a lie. Ray would never tell the cops anything. Dymphna didn't bother to tell Inspector Ferguson so.

"Did you kill Jimmy, Dymph? We heard you were covered in blood."

Dymphna was indignant. She had *not* been covered in blood. There was not a drop on her. But she couldn't say that. Nor could she point out that she didn't have the strength or reach to cut Jimmy's throat. The detective hadn't said how Jimmy had died other than brutally.

She let her eyes well up again. "I did not," she said. Her lower lip trembled as if she were barely holding back tears. Jimmy made a sound of derision.

"Did someone else kill him for you?"

"No," she said, letting that bare syllable be edged with her sad disdain.

"You'll be needing a new fella, won't you? In your world, it's not safe to be without a strong bloke for long."

Dymphna wiped at her eyes. "Why?" she asked. "Are you offering?" She let her lip tremble again. "Jimmy's not even cold yet."

Ferguson laughed. "I'm a married man, Dymphna. Not to mention that you're a touch too young for me. Man of my age prefers a woman of his own vintage."

Dymphna almost snorted. That was not something she had ever noticed.

"Can we come in?" Ferguson asked.

"Why would you want to interrupt me in my time of mourning?"

"So we can continue our friendly chat."

"My man's dead." Dymphna finally let a tear roll down her cheek. "I don't think I have the strength."

"It will go better for you if you let us in."

"Do I have to?"

Behind Ferguson the constable shook his head. He *was* one of Glory's. She knew it. He tipped his head in the direction of the fire stairs that led out onto the back lane. Dymphna hoped it wasn't a nervous twitch but him pointing her to the best escape route.

"It's in your own interest, Dymph," Ferguson said.

"Then, no, you can't come in."

The telephone rang. Loud and brassy, making the receiver rattle in its cradle. Dymphna felt her heart beat faster. The tremor returned to her left leg. That would be Glory. *She* should have called Glory. Not the other way around.

Ferguson was asking another question. Dymphna closed the door on his surprised face and the constable's sly one. She drew the bolt and picked up the receiver.

"Hello?" she said, fearing the response.

"Glory wants to see you," Lettie said.

Of all Glory's girls, Lettie was Dymphna's closest friend. She was who Dymphna turned to when she needed cheering up. And vice versa. Lettie had a terrible habit of falling in love with the wrong girl. Always a working girl more broke than she was. Her latest, Dazzle, was the worst of the lot.

"Did she ask you to call? Or are you warning me?"

"Glory asked," Lettie said, and Dymphna didn't know whether to be relieved or more frightened that Glory had made Lettie call her. Was she too angry too pick up the 'phone herself? Or was it not important enough for Glory to call her directly?

"She's at Palmer Street."

Dymphna bit back a laugh. Of course she was, on the day that Jimmy Palmer died.

"She's not happy. I haven't seen her this ropeable in ages. You there, Dymphna?"

Ropeable. That meant she knew, didn't it? Or did it? Glory flew into rages most days. Dymphna had seen her throw a teapot because one of the girls brought her Earl Grey when she had asked for Darjeeling.

"I'm here, Lettie. Shouldn't she be over on Lansdowne? The party's today, isn't it?"

"She's letting Connie and Johnno be the bosses over there. Came here 'cause she said it was like a flock of galahs in heat. Apparently the butcher delivered the wrong sausages."

Dymphna could hear the suppressed giggles in Lettie's voice and smiled, imagining the scene. She and Lettie had always been able to have a laugh together at Glory's expense.

"She wants to see you right now, and it's not to talk about the party. It's about Jimmy. Who killed him, Dymphna? It wasn't you, was it?"

"Of course not! She doesn't think that, does she?" Dymphna asked, almost hoping that she did think that because then Glory couldn't possibly know what she and Jimmy had plotted, could she?

"Glory doesn't know what to think, Dymphna. There's that many rumours flying around. Some are saying the truce is broken and it's war again."

"Oh, no! Tell her I'm on my way. I'll be there soonest." Dymphna was feeling hopeful. Perhaps Glory didn't know. Perhaps Mr. Davidson didn't know either.

"She's *really* not happy. She's got people out looking for you." Lettie lowered her voice. "She's scaring us, Dymphna. She was so happy about the party, about being shot of Big Bill and it being in the papers. You know how she loves being in the papers."

"Tell her I'm on my way, Lettie. Tell her I'm sorry."

"I'll tell her. But she's not much for listening right now. She's been like this all morning. She's not herself. She was talking about cancelling the party, and you know how she's been looking forward to it. I'm starting to wonder if she'll even listen to you, and you're her favourite."

"Sounds bad." It sounded very bad. Her hands started to shake again. It was not like Glory to stay in a rage for this long. Usually the storms came and went in a matter of minutes.

"It is. See you when you get here, which should be *soon*, Dymphna. Get here for us if you won't do it for yourself. She's that cranky, Dymphna. It's no joke."

"I will, Lettie. I'm sorry. Thanks."

"Be careful. You promise?"

"I will. I'll see you soon."

"Bye then."

The 'phone made a clicking sound, and Dymphna replaced the receiver.

She stumbled to her bedroom, started stripping off her clothes and changing into fresh ones. No time to wash. She stuffed her passports and money into her purse and grabbed her warmest winter coat, the one with the ermine collar and cuffs, the one she had already lined with money as part of her and Jimmy's contingency plan.

Glory could be this incandescently angry because her best man was dead. Three years it had been since Glory'd lost a lieutenant. She had been furious for days.

It was also conceivable Glory was enraged because she'd found out her best man and her best girl had been plotting against her.

King and Queen of Razorhurst. Dymphna had to laugh. Had they both gone mad? How had they believed for a second they could succeed?

The tremor was back in her hands.

"Get moving," Jimmy said. "You stay here, you're dead."

Dymphna knew he was right.

Should she go to Inspector Ferguson, tell him Davidson had killed Jimmy? He was honest. An honest, nasty piece of work. But too many of the cops around him weren't, too many of the courts. If she turned dingo, she was dead. If Davidson caught her, she might not be dead, but she'd want to be.

If Glory caught her, she had no idea what would happen. But dead was a possibility.

She had to be calm. If Glory knew, why hadn't she sent someone after her? Why hadn't Bluey Denham been waiting for her, razor in hand?

If she ran, where would she run to? Nowhere in the city was safe. But she'd never been anywhere else. Another city? Overseas?

If she ran, she was dead. If she stayed, she was dead.

Glory. Glory was her best hope.

Kelpie came dripping out of the bathroom, her disintegrating wet clothes clinging to her. Dymphna realised she'd been pacing. She stopped.

Kelpie reached out to awkwardly pat Dymphna's hand. She must look demented. She breathed in deeply. She would not cry. She would go to Glory, and they would fix this. "Why do they all die?" she whispered.

Language Acquisition

Before Miss Lee, Kelpie had never thought about words or language. Words were how you communicated with people. When you *had* to. Kelpie could go days, weeks even, without using any. Often running away was all the communicating Kelpie needed.

She'd never heard of poetry until she met Miss Lee. Even though Old Ma used to ease her into sleep with lullabies often enough. According to Miss Lee, songs were poems set to music.

Miss Lee—and Neal Darcy—made Kelpie aware of the pleasure of words, made her want to start collecting them, whispering them to herself. *Squelch, wheeze, ooze*—all of which sounded like what they meant. Miss Lee said there was a word for that too: *onomatopoeia*, which sounded like an explosion of worms in your mouth.

There was even a book that was for finding words and discovering their meanings. The dictionary. Kelpie could open it on any page and find a treasure. There was a word for everything. *Disembark*—which Kelpie had thought meant removing a dog's bark, but instead meant getting off a ship. One word instead of four!

Then there were all the words—loads of them—that meant more than one thing. *Dislocate* meant when your arm came out of your shoulder and hung there like a dead rat till someone pushed it back in. Stuart O'Sullivan had a lot to say about dislocated shoulders and how they hurt like hell. But *dislocate* also meant how a person could feel when they didn't belong in a place. As if they were the arm hanging like a dead rat not connected to the body anymore. Like how Kelpie would feel if they ever caught her and put her in an orphanage and forced her to live anywhere but Surry Hills.

Kelpie loved the sound of the word *scarification*—which had been done to more than half the men in the Hills, much to Miss Lee's disapproval—and *unctuous*—yet another word that sounded like what it was, as well as *smoodge*—which Miss Lee said wasn't a real word, but Kelpie had heard it said, and even if she couldn't find it in the dictionary, if people said it, then surely that meant it was a real word? Besides, Neal Darcy had used it in one of his stories. So it was also written down, and once it was written down, it would find its way into a dictionary. Kelpie was sure of it.

That was Kelpie's first argument with Miss Lee about language. Kelpie was worried Miss Lee would be annoyed, but instead she was thrilled that Kelpie was *thinking about vocabulary and had an opinion of her own, even if it was a wrong opinion.*

"Smoodge," Kelpie said, drawing the word out, "is a glorious word." *Glorious* was one of Miss Lee's favourites. "I shall smoodge my way back into your affections."

Miss Lee laughed so hard that if she was alive she would have fallen over.

>⊀ KELPIE ⊁<

Kelpie squeezed Dymphna's hand. Why did they all die? Kelpie knew the answer wasn't *because someone slashed their throat open* or *because there wasn't enough food* or *because they got sick*.

Dymphna meant why did she keep losing people she cared about. Kelpie wanted to know the same thing. Why had her parents died? Why Old Ma? Why did ghosts fade away? Why wasn't Old Ma still around to help her? Or Miss Lee?

Why did they all—living or dead—abandon her?

"I like your place," Kelpie said, because she was afraid Dymphna was going to start crying. Because if she did, then Kelpie would too. It was clean and new. Shiny. Just like Dymphna. Other than Palmer there were no ghosts. Kelpie'd never been in a place too new for ghosts.

"Ta, love. I never cry."

Dymphna's eyes were red, but she wasn't crying. Kelpie never cried either. Tears were useless. But right then she felt like it. She bet her own eyes were red too.

"Have to get those clothes off you." Dymphna disappeared into the bathroom. She returned with a large white towel and Seamus's clothes. "Dry yourself, get dressed."

Kelpie wrapped herself in the towel. Her shirt and trousers were more holes now than clothing. Bits of them were floating in the bath.

"How do you feel about travelling?" Dymphna asked.

Kelpie loved the idea of getting far away from coppers and Welfare and Mr. Davidson and Glory and anyone else who might lock them up or hurt them.

"I've been thinking about taking a trip on an ocean liner. Going to the old country. Seeing the sights. Learning a new language. What do you think?"

"Say *yes*," Palmer said. "You don't have much time."

Kelpie said, "Yes."

Dymphna went into her bedroom.

"Snowy didn't do you," Kelpie whispered to Palmer. She dropped the towel and peeled off what remained of her old clothes and put Seamus's clothes back on. She took a piece of her once-white shirt about the size of her palm and slipped it into her trouser pocket. Miss Lee had found that shirt. She put one of the packets of chips on top of it and the other packet in her other pocket. "Who was it really?"

Maybe it was Bluey Denham. He was the scariest man in the Hills. Eyes so pale they seemed colourless. Him working for Glory wouldn't stop him killing one of her men. Not if he had it in for Palmer.

The ghost shook his head. "I told you. It was Snowy. Mr. Davidson told him to. He's the one to blame."

"She already knows to avoid Mr. Davidson. You saw her." Kelpie finished getting dressed, buttoning the coat all the way to her chin.

"You need to make sure she gets moving! Tell her you can see me. Then I can tell her what to do, where to go. She needs more money. I can help."

"I can't."

All that telling the living about ghosts did was get them thinking you were mad, which made them want to give you to Welfare even faster.

"Fucking tell her, you little shit. It's not just her life we're talking about. It's yours too."

"I can't tell her! She doesn't know about ghosts. She'd think I'm mental. Ghosts aren't real. Don't you know?"

Palmer leaned in so close that her stomach began to roil. "Tell her about the tattoo of me mum on my back. No way you could know about that. She'll believe you."

Kelpie shook her head.

"I could scream again," Palmer said, moving even closer.

A fraction more, and he'd be leaning through her. "Right in your ear and not stop. You didn't like it when I screamed before, did you? I can yell bloody loud and bloody long. Was a cockatoo when I was wee, keeping watch for Glory. Me yelling me arse off and only you hearing it. That'd be bad, I reckon."

"I'll run."

"I'll follow."

"You can't. You have to stay with Dymphna. You're her haunt. You can't go anywhere she ain't." Kelpie was tempted to stick her tongue out at him.

Palmer's face darkened. He looked like he was going to say something. Yell something, more like. He disappeared.

Dymphna came out of the bedroom with her lips redder than before. Kelpie realised she was wearing different clothes and shoes, but still matching, all in black, with a necklace of small white balls at her throat. She had a bigger, warmer coat. Her bag was bigger too, hanging on a metal strap from her shoulder.

"Ready to go?"

Kelpie nodded and knew that she wasn't going to run from Dymphna. Not right then. It wasn't because of anything Palmer had shouted at her. It was because . . .

Dymphna needed Kelpie. She could see that.

Somehow Kelpie was starting to need Dymphna. The way she had needed Old Ma and Miss Lee. The thought scared her.

Dymphna led Kelpie down the hall into the back stairway, which was cold and smelled of dust and old cigarette ash, then out through the tradies' entrance into the back lane where two sleepy coppers stood smoking. Kelpie tensed, ready to run, but at the sight of Dymphna, the cops smiled. The handful of ghosts in the lane paid the living no mind.

"They're Glory's," Palmer whispered, appearing behind Dymphna and scaring Kelpie half to death. "You were right, Kelpie. I can't go anywhere unless she's close by."

Kelpie would have loved to snort at him.

"Why's that one looking at me?" Palmer asked. How would Kelpie know what a ghost she'd never seen before was thinking? People's thoughts were their own, living or dead.

"Best to go this way," the taller cop said, ushering them to a door at the back of a building on the other side of the lane. A large plaque above it was emblazoned with the words REGENCY LODGE. The copper pulled out keys to open it.

"She's at Palmer Street," he said, holding the door open. "Waiting for you."

Dymphna didn't ask who "she" was. Kelpie guessed that it was Glory.

"Come on, Kelpie," Dymphna said, walking through the door the cop held open for her. "Too much irony for me," she said under her breath.

"Take care of yourself," the copper said behind them.

"I will."

Kelpie kept her eyes down. Even crooked cops made her nervous.

Palmer was shaking his head. "What's she find ironic?" He let out a sigh. "Why am I talking to an illiterate tyke like you? Do you even know what 'ironic' means?"

As it happened, Kelpie did. It had been the subject of a long lecture from Miss Lee. Although Miss Lee preferred to call it "a disquisition." Kelpie agreed. She liked the sound of "disquisition" better than "lecture." They'd been reading *Pride and Prejudice*, and Kelpie had wondered why the book kept saying one thing when it really seemed to mean another. Irony was why, it turned out. But Kelpie was not going to explain that to Palmer.

The door opened onto a hallway with fancy red gold-trimmed carpet and walls papered with entwined green and gold leaves. On each door was a number and a letter in gold like where Dymphna lived.

At the end of the corridor, the carpet turned into shiny big white-and-grey tiles. Dymphna nodded to a large man sitting at a brown desk that curved all the way around him. Kelpie wondered how he got out of it. Did he have to climb over the top?

There were no ghosts. Kelpie decided that she liked new buildings.

The man grunted at Dymphna. "Glory's waiting for you, Miss Campbell. Word is she ain't happy. Tell her I'm doing like she said."

He put his hand on the big, black telephone on his desk, which was even bigger than the one at Dymphna's flat.

"Tell her I'm on my way."

Palmer shook his head. "Glory's got too many men. Don't know how Dymphna's going to give them all the slip. She'd be best off heading to the Quay. Bound to be a boat that'll take her on. Even with no luggage. Tell her, Kelpie."

Kelpie kept her mouth closed.

Dymphna led her briskly past the huge curved desk, through a double set of huge wood and glass doors and out onto a street almost as crowded as Elizabeth Street. Horns blared, a tram rattled past. They had to thread their way through the crowd. Many of them said hello. Hats were doffed, heads nodded, kisses were blown. Kelpie increased her stride to stay beside Dymphna.

"Ah, the joys of the Cross." Dymphna laughed. "Glory owns most of those apartments, you know," she continued, as if she was giving a tour of Kings Cross and wasn't on the way to meet her angry boss, who was known to make people disappear. "In my building too."

"Is that where we're going?" Kelpie asked. "To Gloriana Nelson?"

"Of course not," Palmer said. "Glory might kill her."

"Is Glory going to kill you?" Kelpie asked.

Dymphna squeezed Kelpie's hand and slowed her pace.

"No, silly. Of course not. I'm her top earner. She won't kill me."

"She's not going to Glory," Palmer assured her. "She just had to tell Glory's boys that."

"Where are we going then?"

Dymphna smiled brightly at two men who'd raised their hats. "Somewhere safe."

"Ask her where," Palmer said. "The Quay is in the opposite direction."

"Not to Glory?"

Dymphna said nothing, but increased her pace.

"Will Glory kill *me*?" Kelpie asked, scrambling to keep up.

"No, Kelpie. You're with me. I'll tell her how helpful you've been. How much I need you. Glory likes me. She's cranky right now, but she's been cranky with me before."

Palmer shook his head. "She's not going to Glory. You notice Dymphna didn't say you were going there."

Kelpie hoped Palmer was right. She did not want to meet Glory.

"Glory's a scary woman," Dymphna continued. "She's powerful. I told you—she owns all those flats, but she wasn't born with money. She had to make her own way. She did it the same way I have, but now look at her! I'm going to be like her. Not just own my own place but other people's places too. No one will ever think they own me again. You've got to be strong for that. You've got to be able to scare people. Especially if you're a woman."

Kelpie had never scared anyone. She'd never owned anything neither.

Owning took money, and Kelpie had never had any save the occasional penny, or twice a trey and once a zack she found on the streets. Another bonus to keeping your eyes down: you avoided trouble with the living and you found coins. She spent the zack on hot fish and chips with salt and vinegar and cake and a loaf of bread. Nothing had ever tasted as good as those fish and chips. But even a penny could buy a couple of bread rolls or a bag of mixed lollies. If the shop owner would sell them to her. Sometimes they didn't want money from her because she was dirty.

"It will be all right." Dymphna sped up again, smiling briefly at yet another man doffing his hat. She ignored the man who whistled and the man who called out something nasty about her tits.

Palmer didn't ignore them. "They should show more respect. How can they talk to her like that? Can't they see she's in mourning? Even if she wasn't. It ain't right. Not that the ones lifting their lids like they's all respectable are any better. Look at the leers! Not fooling anyone. Bloody maggots. She shouldn't be smiling at men like that."

Kelpie wondered if there was any way a man could look at Dymphna that wouldn't set Palmer off.

"You're doing well, Kelpie," Dymphna said, touching her shoulder briefly. "Not making eye contact is good. Very good. We don't want to have any trouble if we can avoid it."

"She's right about that," Palmer said. "But might happen anyway. Ask her why she's still going the wrong way."

Kelpie risked a glance at Palmer. His face was darkening again. He was scaring her. Kelpie didn't want to be scared.

"Does she *want* to die?"

Kelpie didn't think so, but she didn't get why Palmer thought Glory wanted to hurt Dymphna if she was her best girl. Dymphna had said so.

"You can at least tell her she's being followed."

Society

Back in those days, the crème de la crème of the city's society would barely admit to knowing the name of someone like Gloriana Nelson. To make such an admission would be to acknowledge reading a low rag such as *Truth*, which they would never. Nor would they read the unsavoury parts of the much more refined *Herald*.

Yet many of the city's best people went to the nightclubs owned by either Glory or Mr. Davidson, and all too many of their menfolk made their entrance with Dymphna Campbell on their arm. In her working capacity, of course.

Dymphna had never liked the better sort of man. Her father had been one of them: respected, well dressed, powerful. She would never knowingly take one of them as her man. But she would sit and smile with them, drink their champagne, and dance with them—if they could meet her not inconsiderable price.

It *was* inconsiderable to them. For even though the rest of the city—no, the rest of the country—starved and searched fruitlessly for work and slept in a humpy in a park, society's finest could still squander their money however they saw fit.

The unemployed, they would say, were lazy. If they worked harder, they'd do as well as Mr. Harry Moneypants was doing, who'd earned his vast fortune by having the foresightedness of selecting rich parents, who had, in their time, also cleverly selected rich parents.

Dymphna despised them almost as much as they wanted her.

She enjoyed taking them to Glory's club on William Street where the punters were not only charged an entrance fee, but also a steeply rising price depending on how good the table—the most expensive being close to the band, but not so close that you couldn't speak to each other. They were charged to order a drink, charged to receive it, charged when the glass was taken away. All of that on top of the charge for the actual drink. There was a charge to enter the gentlemen's room, to be given soap and a fresh towel, and then another charge to leave.

The biggest charge of all, however, was for being allowed to leave the club.

Woe betide those who couldn't pay at any point in the proceedings. If they were lucky, they were set to washing dishes in the kitchens.

Yet not once did the stupid rich boys complain.

Well, if money was nothing to them, it was something to Glory and all her boys and girls. And they were more than happy to relieve them of it, thank you very much.

Glory and her kind were grateful to society folk, who reminded them of why they kept their lives outside the confines of the law. Any law that protected the interests of such lazy parasites was an ass.

✂ KELPIE ✂

Kelpie turned to look behind her. The street was thick with people, living and ghosts, as well as motor-cars and trucks and trams.

"Don't look back," Palmer said, his voice getting louder and more agitated. "Go on, tell her. That Neal Darcy's been following her ever since she left the Hills. He's not a danger, but she needs to know. But Snowy? Snowy worries me."

Darcy was back there? Kelpie craned her neck. She couldn't see him. Why would he be following them? Neal Darcy was at the brewery, working, not here. The Darcys needed the money too much for him to skip a day's work. Mrs. Darcy would be ropeable if he took a day off. Kelpie wondered if the shock of being dead had pushed Palmer clean off his pannikin.

"Tell her! While you're at it, ask her why she's heading to Glory's. She needs to be heading the other way."

"Is something wrong, Kelpie?" Dymphna asked.

Kelpie shook her head then turned to look again. If Darcy was back there, she wanted to see him.

"I told you, don't look!"

She wanted Palmer to shut up. His voice was getting louder, and his orders were jumbling together as his face darkened. She wished he'd disappear again.

"Kings Cross isn't as dangerous as they say," Dymphna said.

Kelpie hadn't realised this was Kings Cross. She didn't trust Dymphna's idea of what was dangerous. They'd met over Palmer's corpse. Besides, everyone knew Kings Cross was dangerous. Even during the day. Old Ma had said it was full of bad men and bad women, who'd snatch a tyke like her off the streets and sell her to the Chinamen as soon as look at her.

Kelpie hadn't seen any Chinamen today. She mostly saw them at Paddy's Market buying and selling fruit and veggies—not kids. Then there was Mr. Sung and his family, who owned the grocery shop on the corner of Foveaux and Riley. They always accepted her found pennies. She liked them. Especially Mrs. Sung. She never yelled at Kelpie.

Kelpie looked back again. But there were too many people and she was too short.

"I said don't look," Palmer said. "Tell her about Darcy and about Snowy. Ask her where the hell she's going. What the hell is she doing?!"

"What are you looking at, Kelpie?" Dymphna asked.

"Never been in Kings Cross before."

"It's not a place for children."

"Thought you said it wasn't dangerous."

"No, I said that . . ."

Kelpie didn't hear the rest.

A man whistled at Dymphna. Palmer bristled. "Not a place for ladies neither," he muttered, speeding up. Palmer punched the man full in the face with such force that he went sailing through him and several other people—including Dymphna, who barely shivered.

If Palmer was still alive, Kelpie figured the impact would've killed that bloke.

Dymphna quickened her pace. "It's quieter on the other side of William Street," she said, leading Kelpie across.

"Why are we in Darlinghurst?" Palmer asked. "She can't be going to see Glory, can she? Does she want to die? Tell her to turn around and head to the fucking harbour. Jesus fucking wept!"

"That wasn't so bad, was it?" Dymphna asked, wiping her hands on the sides of her skirt. "Not long now, Kelp. Be quicker now we're in Darlinghurst. Quieter too. More like the Hills around here."

Kelpie'd never thought of the Hills as quiet before. Or peaceful. But now she knew they were.

"I wish that Snowy Fullerton could fucking see me," Palmer said. "I'd give him an earful. Why's he still following her, eh?"

This, Kelpie believed. But it made her nervous. Why *was* Snowy following them? Did he still want to take her to the orphanage? Snowy had lied to try to get her to go with him. She'd thought he'd never lie to her.

Snowy'd betrayed her.

Dymphna was exchanging greetings with a brightly painted woman in a shiny blue dress.

"I don't like it," Palmer said. "You know who Snowy works for. Killed me, didn't he? She's not thinking straight. She's got two fellas following her, and she hasn't even noticed them, let alone given them the slip. It's like she *wants* to die."

Kelpie was pretty sure Dymphna didn't want that. She looked back again. But she couldn't see Snowy or Darcy.

"I'd best get going," Dymphna said.

"Grand to see you, love," the woman said, kissing Dymphna's cheek. "I'm just around the corner. Why not come and have a cuppa? Or something stiffer. I'm all set up. You'll like it."

"I'm in a hurry, Cait. Perhaps some other time."

"Glory can wait," the woman said. Her hand was on Dymphna's arm. "It's not far." She pulled Dymphna towards a narrow lane.

Palmer tried to grab Cait from Dymphna and roared with rage when his hands went through her.

"Let go, Cait. I mean it." Dymphna pulled away, dislodging Cait's hand.

"Come on, Kelpie." Dymphna sped up, Kelpie's hand tight in hers.

Cait slipped in front of them. She was holding a knife. She was holding it so tight her hand shook. "There's money in it for you, Dymph. Lots of money. Mr. Davidson will look after both of us. He's just round the corner."

"Don't, Cait," Dymphna began. "You know what Glory will do to you. It's not worth it."

Kelpie kicked Cait hard in the shin. The toe of Seamus's shoe made a loud sound on impact. She followed up the kick with a hard punch to the solar plexus like Stuart O'Sullivan had taught her. Cait dropped the knife and screamed.

Dymphna ran. Faster than she should have been able to in those heels. Kelpie snatched up Cait's knife and ran after her, grinning at the look on the woman's face. Her heart was beating too fast, she could feel it in her ears. She risked another glance back. This time she saw Snowy. He was leaning over Cait.

Kelpie slipped Cait's knife into Seamus Darcy's coat pocket. If she'd been wearing her old coat, it would have fallen through to the ground. If she'd been barefoot like she usually was, kicking Cait would have been useless.

"Good work," Palmer said. "Now tell her to get to the Quay."

"She's not following!" Kelpie called to Dymphna, who was half a block ahead of her.

Dymphna sprinted around the corner. Kelpie followed. They were running past terrace houses, each with the same iron lace-work and brown tiled roof, identical down to the flowerpots on the sills and red lights in the windows.

Dymphna stopped outside the second-last one. There was nothing to distinguish this one either, not even a number. She bent over, panting, looking back the way they'd come. "Used to run all the time. Not as fast as I used to be."

Kelpie thought she was plenty fast, especially wearing them shoes.

Dymphna straightened, patting her hair. "You ready?"

"She can't be serious," Palmer said. "She can't be walking straight into the lion's den."

The front door opened and a man with a scarred face leaned out, holding on to the door. "That you, Miss Campbell?"

"Hello, Joe."

"She's expecting you." Joe hopped from the front door to open the front gate. He only had one leg, and the scars on his face weren't from a razor. He was one of the broken men from the last war that Old Ma used to take in and feed. Kelpie wondered if he was a screamer. Probably not. She couldn't imagine Gloriana Nelson keeping someone around who jumped every time someone dropped a cup.

"I'll be right in." Dymphna bent to whisper in Kelpie's ear. "If Glory asks you any questions, don't tell her 'Dunno.' All right?"

Kelpie thought about saying *Dunno* to be cheeky. It was fine to be cheeky to ghosts who couldn't do anything to you, much riskier with the living.

"I'll be good, Dymphna. I'll smoodge my way into her heart."

Dymphna laughed and put her hand on Kelpie's still-damp head. "Thank you."

Glory Days

The first time Gloriana Nelson realised money couldn't buy respectability was when the Big Man himself wouldn't accept her donation to his re-election campaign. Glory loved the Big Man with all her heart and soul. He was the best premier they'd ever had. She loved him sticking it to the old country, defying the federal government and London both, refusing to pay the bankers, caring about the workers more than the establishment. He was a fine Labor man even if most of his party hated him half the time.

Glory had never hated him, not for even half a second.

Then he wouldn't take her money.

She sat down and cried.

Gloriana Nelson never cried.

Then they sacked the Big Man without a by-your-leave from the people what had voted him in. He should have taken Glory's money.

The second time was when they wouldn't sell her first-class tickets for the Queen Mary on her triumphant journey to the old country to show them what a rich colonial looked like. Glory was that rich she could have bought the bloody boat. But they'd only sell her second-class steerage.

This time Glory did not sit down. She did not cry. She cursed them inside out and sideways. She raised her fists. She was ejected from the ticket office still screaming her head off.

Davidson travelled first class. Rich bastard politicians took *his* money. Didn't drop his haitches, did he? Knew when to doff his hat. Knew how to eat in one of them fancy restaurants with waiters dressed better than any of the men in Glory's life. Didn't matter that bloody Davidson made his money same way she did. He didn't call a spade a fucking spade. Not a single bloody swear word ever dropped from his fucking lips.

Wasn't just money you needed in this world. You had to have polish too.

That's why Glory took on Dymphna Campbell. It wasn't because she was so beautiful she shone. Not because of her breasts, her gold hair, her fine long legs. All of that was well and good, but beauty faded. And even the most gorgeous girl wasn't to the taste of all the clients. She'd heard one bloke claim Dymphna's chin was too pointy. Another that her breasts were too small.

It was Dymphna's voice that won Glory over.

Posh girls never lasted in the trade. Too delicate. Too used to being treated well. Glory had never had a bar of them. Besides, working men were intimidated by the posh ones, and the top of the town didn't come slumming to run into one of their own. They saved those women for seducing and for marriage. When they laid down cash, toffs wanted a rough-as-guts pretty sort who'd do anything they paid for.

Glory was a rough one come up from nothing, and she'd done fine. Owned her own houses now. Ran her own women. Why would she waste her time on a girl too posh to know how to boil an egg—let alone make a man cry out in pleasure?

Dymphna could do both.

And her voice.

Soft and silky. She should have been an actress.

Glory started watching her, listening. She collected up Dymphna's haitches and relinquished the ones that she never said. She observed the way Dymphna dressed. The way she painted her face. None of it loud. None of it too red. Watched the way Dymphna drank tea. Practised it when she was alone. Not in front of Big Bill or any of her men or women—she wasn't going to have them laughing at her.

The next time she wanted to travel first class, they would damn well let her.

But to be safe, she sent Dymphna to buy the tickets.

The two went shopping together at David Jones to buy her wardrobe for the voyage.

People who weren't born rich and came to their money by less-than-respectable means had to be unobtrusive in dress and quiet in manners. Glory bit her lip for the first week of the voyage—watching rich young men chasing waitresses and vomiting over the side. In the second week, she clipped the most obnoxious one across the ear with her fifty-pound purse.

The stupid boy didn't report her, and she wasn't made to decamp to second class. Though the toffs talked to her and Big Bill even less than before. Didn't matter, because the waitresses took to making sure she got the most attentive service and the best cuts of meat.

By the time they reached London, Glory was ready to never see or hear another toff-nosed, rich bastard ever again. She threw away the clothes she'd worn at sea and bought up all the reddest, loudest clothes London had to offer.

Glory had always known exactly who she was, but now she knew she preferred herself that way.

DYMPHNA

Gloriana Nelson sat in her large cushioned chair in the roomy kitchen at the back of the terrace. She was in her usual red and gold finery, with her fingers and mouth painted fire-engine red to match. Her feet rested on a velvet stool. Her elbows rested on the kitchen table. She had a cigarette in one hand and a cup of tea in the other.

Glory didn't look like a woman planning to kill her best girl, though she didn't look pleased to see Dymphna either.

Dymphna paused in the doorway to favour Glory with her most radiant smile. Glory loved Dymphna's smile. *Makes you look like a queen*, she had said often enough that some of the other girls called her Queenie. They didn't mean it kindly. Kelpie ducked behind her.

Glory did not return the smile. Dymphna decided not to see that as a bad sign.

Beside Glory, Lettie half smiled and gave a little wave, and her horrible girlfriend Dazzle smirked.

"She's ropeable," Jimmy told Kelpie. "Why the fuck did Dymphna think it was a good idea to walk into Glory's den?"

Because, Dymphna wanted to tell him, they wouldn't have made it to the Quay without someone nabbing them. Glory was the safest option. She had to be.

"I hear Davidson's looking for you and me best man is dead," Gloriana Nelson said. "'Course, I would've liked to've heard that from yourself."

"I'm sorry, Glory. It's been . . ." Dymphna trailed off because Glory wasn't listening.

"And the coppers!" Glory continued, her voice rising. "Bloody coppers going after you when anyone with half a brain could tell a slight thing like you couldn't do for an ox like Jimmy. Not without help. My boy Palmer's dead! My right-hand man! Whatcha want to tell me about that?"

"You'd almost think she was upset," Jimmy said. He leaned against the wall behind Glory, beside a painting of a racehorse. "You better be ready to scarper, Kelpie. I don't trust this."

Kelpie slid further behind Dymphna.

"Can we sit down, Glory?" Dymphna asked, bracing herself for more yelling.

"'Course you can. Lettie? Make 'em some tea. This pot's cold."

Lettie winked at Dymphna and leapt up to set water on the stove.

Dymphna guided Kelpie by her elbow towards a stool, but Kelpie wouldn't sit down. Likely making it easier for herself to escape. Dymphna couldn't blame her. She sat, holding on to Kelpie's elbow. Neither one of them was going to run until Dymphna knew what Glory knew.

"It's going to ruin me party. Finally get shot of that bastard— divorce papers signed and everything. I told you, didn't I?"

"You did." Glory had told everyone. Including the newspapers.

"Palmer gets murdered the very morning of me big celebration. There's a cake, you know? Made special. Six tiers. Bigger than most wedding cakes. Divorce is a lot more special to a lady like me than marriage. I'll tell you that for free. There'll be no one bludging a few pounds here and a few pounds there no more. Taking me money without doing a lick of work. Big Bill was a fat old leech. I am well shot of him."

Dymphna could not disagree. She had always avoided Big Bill. He had wandering hands and did not believe he had to pay for any of Glory's girls.

"What's her name then?" Gloriana Nelson asked, pointing her chin at Kelpie. She stubbed out the cigarette and picked up her polished black stone, running it back and forth between her fingers.

"Kelpie," Dymphna said.

"Ha!" Glory let out a giant roar of laughter. Kelpie took a step backward. Dymphna pulled her forward.

"Well, of course that's her name. She's a wee puppy dog, ain't she?"

Dymphna smiled at Kelpie, who was decidedly not smiling. Dymphna prayed that she wouldn't say anything to rile Glory.

"Oh, and look, now she's baring her teeth. Adorable. She's a brown little thing, isn't she? I hear she's been following you around, Dymph. Where'd you find her? She might be a bit small to work. But there's all sorts, aren't there? Have the doctor check her out."

Dymphna stood up, horrified. "I didn't bring her here for that, Glory."

"Don't rile her, Dymph!" Jimmy shouted. Dymphna wondered when Jimmy was going to get it through his thick head that she wouldn't hear him.

Glory laughed. "I'm joshing you, love. Still, want the doc to look her over. Don't want the wee doggie giving you no fleas. It'll bring your price down. You're my best girl. Ain't no rival for you. Sorry, Dazzle. You're lovely, but *your* hair comes courtesy of a bottle."

Glory smiled at Dazzle, who made a sound that did not resemble a laugh. Dymphna could not resist smiling at her.

"I don't mind," Dazzle said, even though she sounded as though she'd as soon stab Dymphna as praise her. "She's the Angel. Everyone knows she's the best."

Dymphna smiled wider. She loved Dazzle as much as Dazzle loved her. Dymphna had caught her going through her things more than once. Complained to Glory too, who'd thrashed the girl and elicited the promise she'd never do it again, which had lasted a couple of days. Perhaps. Dazzle couldn't help herself. One of the many reasons Dymphna was delighted to have her own place.

Dymphna had no idea what Lettie saw in Dazzle. Her taste in women wasn't great, but it wasn't usually this terrible. Dazzle would only use Lettie. If—no, *when* this mess was over, Dymphna would do what she could to break them up. Lettie needed protecting.

"Shall I take Kelpie to the doctor then?" Dymphna asked.

"Not right now! Got more questions for you, Dymph; don't you know? Though some are the same questions I've asked you already. The ones you ain't answered yet."

"Sorry, Glory. It's been a long day."

"You say that, but it's not even noon yet, love. Some of us only just woke up. Isn't that right, Lettie?"

Lettie laughed and winked at Dazzle. "It was a long night and all."

Dymphna looked at her watch. "Noon," she repeated.

"I ain't even been dead a whole day," Jimmy said, sounding as bemused as she was.

"Tea ready yet, Lettie? Good-oh. Pour us all a cup. Plenty of lemon for our Dymphna. Milk and sugar for the rest of us and for the doggie too."

Kelpie scowled. Dymphna patted her shoulder, though that probably wasn't the best way to let Kelpie know that she didn't think she was a dog.

Glory laughed. "I like her, Dymphna. Lots of spirit. Look at that expression! Would melt the eyes of an arse-faced judge, that would. Or turn them to stone." She accepted her tea and took a sip. "Thanks, Lettie love. Nice and hot. Can't beat a cuppa, can you?"

Dymphna murmured her agreement as she took her own cup. Sipping it calmed her.

"Be careful," Jimmy said. "Wouldn't put it past the old bird to poison you."

"Lettie, Dazzle?" Glory jerked her chin towards the door. "You two lovebirds can make yourselves useful elsewhere."

The two women jumped up, closing the door behind them. Dymphna felt colder and wrapped both hands around the teacup so Glory wouldn't see her shiver.

"Tell me about Palmer," Glory said without a trace of laughter.

"I'm dead," Jimmy said. "You can tell her I don't like being dead. You can tell her if I'd had my way, *she'd* be dead."

Dymphna closed her eyes. He'd never said that before. Killing Glory had never been the plan. Sidelining her had been, easing her out of power, but Jimmy had sworn that Glory didn't need to die.

Kelpie pressed closer to her. Dymphna took another sip of her tea and wished she could say something to reassure the girl. She wished someone would say something to reassure *her*. "Jimmy asked me to meet him at Mrs. Stone's."

"Bit of a rough place for you, ain't it, Dymph?"

"You know I like rough men, Glory. Always have. Same as you."

It wasn't true. Dymphna wasn't entirely sure what kind of men she liked. Ones that smiled and laughed. Though she'd known few like that. She wondered if Neal Darcy laughed. Strong, tough men were a necessity that had nothing to do with liking.

"Rough men, yes, but not dirty, run-down places. You're like me that way too. Mrs. Stone's ain't that far off being demolished."

"I had to, Glory. Jimmy said it was urgent." He was supposed to have killed Davidson that night. She was supposed to have given Glory the news.

"Must've been. He was meant to be doing a job for me over in the 'Loo last night. Never showed up." Glory tossed the black stone from one hand to the other.

"That doesn't sound like Jimmy, does it? He was steady."

"For his kind. When he didn't have a drink in him. He said it was urgent?"

"I never drank when I was working," Jimmy said. "But she kept calling me in when she'd given me the day off. Can't expect a man to be sober on his day off."

"Yes," Dymphna said. "Though things were often urgent with Jimmy."

"I was in a hurry! Can't blame a man for that!" Jimmy spluttered.

"But not why it was so urgent?" Glory asked.

Dymphna shook her head. "And when I arrived . . ."

"And when you arrived?"

"His throat was slashed. No, not merely slashed. You could see his spine. His head was almost completely off. His face was cut up. Blood everywhere." Dymphna blinked, letting her eyes water, though there were no tears in her.

"Well, that wasn't necessary, was it?" Glory pursed her lips disapprovingly. As if Jimmy's death would have been all right if it had been done more genteelly. "How'd you get in, then?"

"Get in?"

"Into Mrs. Stone's. Be a bit tricky for Palmer to open the door with his head half off."

"Door wasn't locked."

"The door to one of the most notorious boarding houses in the Hills—a place filled to the rafters with thieves, bastards, and rotters who'd kill you soon as look at you—and the front door wasn't locked?"

"No." Dymphna cursed herself. Why hadn't she said that Jimmy gave her the key?

"Didn't strike you as curious?"

"No. I was running late. I was tired. I didn't notice, really. Besides, I knew Jimmy was there and he'd look after me. Everyone was scared of him. You know that."

"Big boy, our Palmer. It's why I kept him. Seen him scare folks without even lifting a finger. All he had to do was stand and glower. Makes me wonder how many it took to kill him. Was he alive when you got there?"

"With his head half off?"

"That is unlikely, isn't it? Was he still warm?"

"Very," Dymphna said, thinking about how warm the room had been despite it being the coldest time of the night. It was as if his body's receding heat had filled it. Or his panic and fear and rage at being murdered.

"Couldn't have been dead long then."

"Could Glory really not know that Davidson had me butchered because I was going to kill him?" Jimmy asked. "Does she really not know what we planned?"

"That's why I ran. I didn't want anyone to find me." Dymphna wished she could ask Jimmy why he thought Glory didn't know anything. She wished she knew what Glory was thinking, what she knew.

"Of course you didn't, love," Glory said. "'Cause then they might start thinking that you had something to do with Jimmy Palmer winding up dead."

Glory smiled at Dymphna like a snake before it ate you.

Kelpie discovered that she loved words and sentences and stories. If she'd thought about them at all, she would have thought they had no place in her life. But there was the story Old Ma had told her over and over and over about her parents. The story that Kelpie had to badger Old Ma into telling right. Learning to read meant learning to write. It meant that she could write down the story of her parents so it could never be told wrong again.

The morning after Kelpie's first reading lesson, Miss Lee was back in Kelpie's ear again, talking faster than Kelpie had known anyone could talk.

She ungummed her eyes. She'd slept heavier than usual, exhausted by all the new: Letters! Words! Writing! Reading!

Miss Lee insisted that they had to go back to Neal Darcy at his typewriter. That they had to find a copy of *Great Expectations*, that they should start from the beginning because Kelpie would need to know the whole story.

Miss Lee had heard that the owner of the flower shop at Taylor Square was quite a reader. Maybe there'd be a copy there?

On and on went Miss Lee's flood of words.

Kelpie gave in to them, gave in to Miss Lee leading her back to Darcy, ignored Tommy's sarcastic comments about Darcy's appearance and Irishness, and fell into the spell of Darcy's stories.

"You see? You see? This is him making a book! Right in front of us. A miracle."

Darcy's story was not nonsense about Rapunzel, with her long, long hair that could be climbed by a full-grown man without any of it tearing out. None of the women in Darcy's stories lacked fight. The men didn't either. If anything there was too much fight. Exactly like the streets of the Hills and, it would seem, out bush too. Kelpie had always thought bush people would be different, but not according to Neal Darcy.

Sadly, though, Darcy didn't write in a straight line. For some stories, they never found out what happened at the beginning or the end. Darcy would work on the one scene, the one paragraph, writing it over and over until he was satisfied. Only then would he move on. Miss Lee read Kelpie the same description of rainwater pouring down Foveaux Street so many times she wanted to scream.

Kelpie loved watching Darcy at work and hearing his words. But she couldn't help wanting to read complete stories too, like the ones they found at O'Reilly's.

Before too long, Kelpie was reading almost everything. Any word she didn't recognise Miss Lee would explain. Reading was okay, Kelpie decided.

Reading was better than okay.

Though not okay enough that she enjoyed sneaking into the public library.

They hadn't found a copy of *Great Expectations* anywhere else. Not at the florist's. Not in O'Reilly's attic or his library or at any of the churches or schools they snuck into.

The library felt dangerous. Even when it was summer and school was closed until the autumn. Kelpie was still an unaccompanied child.

The librarians were too vigilant. Too ready to hand her over to Welfare.

Kelpie would only venture in on Tuesday mornings when the blindest librarian had her one shift. Getting past her did not require sneaking. It was slow going getting through *Great Expectations*. Sometimes they read only a chapter a week. Even so, Kelpie had been glad that Miss Lee started from the beginning. *Great Expectations* was a fine story. She liked Pip and Estella. She even liked that mad old woman Miss Havisham.

They'd started *Great Expectations* at the end of spring when Kelpie could barely recognise a handful of words. When they'd finished, the days were turning cold, and Kelpie could read about Pip all on her own.

Which was as well because when they finished *Great Expectations*, Miss Lee disappeared.

She had been getting fainter for that last week. Kelpie pretended to herself it wasn't happening. But then Miss Lee was gone, and no amount of pretending had brought her back.

Kelpie stopped sneaking around after that. It wasn't as much fun without Miss Lee, and the thought of the librarians or O'Reilly catching her was too terrifying.

But she missed the stories. She missed Pip and Estella. Even stupid long-haired Rapunzel in her tower.

Kelpie missed them that much she started to tell herself those stories to keep them from fading away the way Miss Lee had.

KELPIE

Gloriana Nelson had a red-and-gold shawl around her shoulders, though its red seemed muted compared to her hair, which was the brightest red Kelpie had ever seen. Her cheeks and lips too. She sat in a chair that was almost like a throne. It made her seem taller than everyone else. Scarier too.

The everyone else when they'd first entered the room was four ghosts paying no mind to each other or to the living and two women sitting side by side on stools, both of them younger than Glory, one with shiny yellow hair and the other with hair so black some of it had leaked out over her temples.

Even if Kelpie'd never seen Gloriana Nelson before, she'd've known that Glory was the boss. The other women's heads weren't held as high. They slouched and sat closer to each other than they sat to her. One was called Lettie and the other Dazzle. Kelpie wondered how you got a name like Dazzle.

She also wondered if Snowy had been helping or killing that Cait woman who'd tried to grab Dymphna. Kelpie didn't think he'd been killing her, but she wasn't certain. She had the growing feeling that she knew even less about Snowy than she had realised. It was an uncomfortable feeling.

There was a gap between knowing that Snowy had killed people and seeing someone that he might have maybe killed. It was more than an uncomfortable feeling.

Palmer kept saying he'd done it because Mr. Davidson told him to. That it was Snowy's job. Like it had been Palmer's job to kill for Gloriana Nelson.

But Palmer said he'd been planning to kill Glory. That *wasn't* his job.

Did Dymphna know about that? Palmer had killed people before. Had Dymphna? Kelpie looked at her. There was no way of knowing. Snowy had always been kind to Kelpie. Even when he wanted to take her to the nuns, to the orphanage. He thought that was being kind. Now Dymphna was being kind. But that didn't mean she hadn't thought about killing. Or hadn't actually killed.

People who killed weren't good people. Kelpie knew that from

Old Ma, from Miss Lee, from all the stories they'd read together. From everything she'd seen in her short life. But she also knew that the world would be better if certain people weren't in it. Like Bluey Denham.

Old Ma had said Snowy was good. But he killed people, so he couldn't be, and he had lied to her to try to get her to go with him to the orphanage. Then there was Dymphna, who did many of the things Miss Lee and Old Ma did not hold with. Possibly killing too.

Kelpie didn't know what to think.

Was Glory going to kill Dymphna?

Since Lettie and Dazzle had left the room, Glory hadn't smiled once, and Dymphna's leg was shaking under the table.

Kelpie fought the urge to slip her hand into Seamus's coat pocket and touch the knife. It was dead sharp. If Glory tried to kill Dymphna, Kelpie would stick it in her.

Glory asked if Dymphna had anything to do with Jimmy Palmer being killed. Palmer yelled at her.

Dymphna was staring at Glory, her mouth a little open. "I did not," she said, rising from her seat.

Gloriana Nelson's left eyebrow went up.

Dymphna sank back. "Sorry, Glory."

Palmer was still shouting. His face was getting darker.

Dymphna took a sip of her tea. Kelpie did the same, copying how Dymphna held the cup. She'd not had tea before. Didn't taste that good, but it was hot and sweet. Kelpie had been feeling cold since Glory first looked at her.

"I know you didn't do him," Glory said. "Stands to reason. You're not tall enough to slash the throat of a man that size. But a man can be killed without the person who wanted them dead raising a finger." Gloriana looked down at her own painted hands. Her nails were as bright red as her hair. There was a ring on every finger.

Kelpie wondered how many people she'd killed with those hands. According to Old Ma, the harbour was half full with people Gloriana Nelson had done in. But then Glory had said she didn't need her own hands to make people die. However she did it, Kelpie was surprised there weren't more ghosts here. Surely at least some ghosts would haunt their murderers? Someone like Glory should have a swarm of them following her wherever she went.

But Snowy didn't. Or Dymphna. Well, just the one. She wondered if Palmer had been haunted when he was alive. She'd never seen any ghosts following Bluey Denham.

"Perhaps," Glory suggested, "something you said or did . . . might have given someone the wrong idea?"

Dymphna shook her head. "He was my man. Everyone knew I wanted him to stay that way."

Palmer grunted as if to say *Too right.*

"Youse were thick as thieves. No doubting that. Did anyone see you there, Dymph? At Mrs. Stone's?"

"Someone might have seen me leaving the house."

"*Might have* or *did* see you?"

"Might have. The police were asking for a well-dressed woman but not for me, not by name. Ferguson asked me about it, but he didn't try to arrest me. I don't think they know much."

"Did he ask you who did Jimmy?"

"He asked if I had. I told him no."

"Do you know who done him?"

Dymphna shook her head. "Mr. Davidson's been after me. But I thought you and he—I thought the truce still held? He tried to get me into his motor-car when I was heading home."

"Did he? Cheeky bugger."

"One of his girls tried to nab me on the way here."

"That's a lie," Palmer said. "Cait works for Glory, not Davidson. Why's Dymph protecting that dingo?"

"Now that's disrespectful," Glory said. "I've a mind to have a word with Mr. Davidson. Going after my best girl. If he killed my man Palmer, it'll be more than words we'll be having. Do you think it was him?"

Dymphna looked as if she was trying to decide what to say. Kelpie reckoned she'd be better off not saying anything.

"Him trying to nab you—you, my very best girl—has Davidson ever tried that before?"

"He's offered me work. You know that."

"I told him you weren't for sale. Seemed to accept it."

"He's been sending me flowers."

"Flowers? Cheeky bugger. That's just greedy, him going after the best girl in town."

"She knows," Palmer said.

Knows what? Kelpie wondered. That Palmer wanted to kill Glory? But how could Palmer know that from what Glory said?

"Who do you think killed your man, Dymphna?"

Dymphna glanced at Kelpie.

"What?" Glory said, looking down at Kelpie so hard Kelpie felt her cheeks growing warm even though she was chilled all the way through. "Does the little doggie know who done Jimmy?"

Kelpie wanted to yell at her that she wasn't a dog. Instead she looked at Dymphna's leg shaking under the table and her hands pressing against it trying to keep it still.

"'Course not, Glory. Kelpie doesn't know anything."

On that, Kelpie agreed. So much of what they were saying to each other made no sense. She was lost and scared.

"Except where to hide in an emergency?" Glory asked.

"Well, yes, she's been living on the streets. She knows a lot about that."

"She's small, isn't she? How old are you, little doggie?"

"She doesn't know, Glory," Dymphna said, patting Kelpie's head, which made Kelpie want to bark at them both. She was not a dog or a littlie.

"Is that right, doggie?"

"Yes, Glory," Kelpie said. Why did everyone care how old she was? It wasn't like it would change anything. She'd still be scrawny and little whether she was as old as Dymphna or even Glory.

"Not much to look at."

Kelpie wanted to tell Glory she wasn't much to look at either. Though it wasn't true. Glory was like a living Christmas tree.

"I bet she sees things people don't realise. They'd hardly notice you, would they?"

Dymphna nudged Kelpie.

"No one notices me," Kelpie said. She felt even colder. *Except Glory right now, and Dymphna, and before her Snowy, and ghosts.*

"Useful skill. You seen anything today that no one else noticed?"

Kelpie didn't know what to say. She'd seen a lot of things. Starting with Palmer's dead body, then his ghost, then Snowy following them. She was sure Gloriana Nelson would want to hear about that. Instead she shook her head.

"Are you sure? Did you see Palmer dead, little doggie?"

Kelpie wished she could bite her. Glory's gaze was still fixed on her. She lowered her head even more.

"Answer her, Kelpie."

She swallowed the strong desire to say *Dunno.* "His feet were dangling over the edge of the bed," she said, not looking up. "He weren't breathing. There was lots of blood."

"Did Jimmy look like he'd put up a fight?"

"His hands were cut," Kelpie said. "His shirt was torn. There was blood everywhere. Even on the walls."

"On Dymphna?"

Kelpie shook her head.

"What were you doing there, Kelpie?"

"Looking for food."

"That's curious. Not known for her housekeeping, Mrs. Stone. Did you find any?"

Kelpie shook her head again. Not even bloody apples.

"See that?" Glory pointed to a tin on the other side of the sink. Birds were painted on the lid. "Bring it here."

Kelpie looked at Dymphna, who nodded. She took the tin and handed it to Glory, who opened the lid. "Bickies, see? The good kind with jam. Take one."

Kelpie reached in and took one, trying not to think about what Palmer had said about poison. Dymphna smiled at her. Kelpie took that to mean she should eat. The bickie melted on contact with her tongue, coating her mouth with the taste of butter and sugar. If it was poisoned, Kelpie didn't care.

"Oh, go on, take another," Glory said.

Kelpie did and retreated to Dymphna's side to eat it.

"I wonder," Glory began. She shook her head. "How *did* you manage to get all the way home from Mrs. Stone's without being seen?"

"Kelpie knows all sorts of places to hide. We were in and out of hidey-holes, backyards, laneways. She knows where to hide in the Hills better than anyone else."

"Lucky you ran into her."

Dymphna nodded. Kelpie felt Glory's eyes on her. She shivered.

"Where *did* you run into her?"

Dymphna didn't answer straight away. As if she was considering whether to lie or not. "Over Palmer's dead body. I was standing there staring at him. In shock, I guess. Then she was there. It woke me up."

"Well, thank you, doggie girl. Lucky you were looking for food in such an unlikely place, isn't it?"

Kelpie didn't say anything, since Glory hadn't asked her a question.

"Where'd you go? After Mrs. Stone's? Can't have been straight back to your place."

"No. Kelpie showed me where to hide. O'Reilly's place up the hill. Old bastard's always passed out and leaves the back windows open. It's posher up there. Less people to see me."

Kelpie wondered why Dymphna lied and how she knew that about O'Reilly's. Kelpie watched Glory store that bit of information away. She seemed to pay attention to everything. She wasn't at all how Kelpie had imagined. She always looked bigger than life. Gaudier. Louder. Stupider too, Kelpie had thought.

But she wasn't. Miss Lee said she was common and didn't have anything but rat cunning, but Miss Lee was wrong. Kelpie suspected Glory was every bit as smart as Miss Lee. Smarter, maybe.

Old Ma had been wrong too. She said Gloriana Nelson was a dirty slattern. But this kitchen was clean and tidy. No tell-tale damp rot smell underneath. No dust on the table or any of the other surfaces. The tiles under her feet gleamed. Much cleaner than Old Ma's home had been. The outside hadn't looked like much, but inside all the walls were fresh painted. Kelpie could smell tea and milk and behind it all eucalyptus. She did not smell the oceans of perfume Old Ma had told her about.

"Bless you, Kelpie, looking after my best girl like that. You help yourself to as many bickies as you want."

"Thank you," Kelpie said, but she didn't feel brave enough to venture closer to Glory and her biscuit tin.

"I'll be honest with you, Dymphna. I don't like it. Weren't no reason for Davidson to get rid of Palmer."

"We don't know for sure that he did."

Except that they *did* know that for sure. Kelpie realised that she believed Palmer after all. Snowy had killed him. She wasn't sure what to make of the realisation. As far as she could tell, everyone in this room was a killer. Except for her and maybe Dymphna. But maybe not.

"We all know he fancies you. Doesn't shut up about it. But going after my best girl? He knows I can't let that ride. And me not letting it ride? Well, that's not good for business. It's why we got the truce in the first place. Under Ferguson cops aren't as easy to lean on as I'd like. Goes same for Davidson as it does for me. Bodies lying around? Oceans of blood? Cops can't ignore that."

"She seems right cut up about me, doesn't she, Kelpie?" Palmer gave a short bitter laugh.

"I'll see what I can find out, Dymphna love. It doesn't make sense. Sure Davidson'd like to have you working for him. Who wouldn't? I'm thinking this goes deeper than that. Deeper! Ha!" Glory laughed loudly. Dymphna smiled. Kelpie had no idea what was funny.

"But if Davidson's circling, best I protect you. Lettie! Lettie! Get your arse back in here!" Glory threw her stone at the door. "Lettie!"

The door opened. "Yes, Glory?"

"Go get Bluey Denham."

Palmer swore.

Lettie paled, then closed the door behind her.

Kelpie heard Dymphna gulp. "Do you think that's nec—"

Glory shut off Dymphna's words with a hard look.

"Could you find my stone, little doggie dear?" she said, giving Kelpie a wolfish smile.

Bluey Denham was the ugliest man anyone in the Hills had ever seen. His nose was smeared halfway across his face from all the fights he'd gotten into. His ears were giant cauliflowers. His left eye was bigger than his right, and both eyes had irises barely darker than the whites, almost like a fish's. There were uneven scars on both his cheeks. He spoke with a rasp so quiet you had to lean forward to hear him. But no one wanted to get that close to Bluey.

His disposition was worse than his looks.

He was probably the most feared man in the Hills. He wasn't anywhere near as tall or big as Jimmy Palmer or Snowy Fullerton. But it didn't matter. He had no limits. You riled him, he would kill you. There was no arguing, no paying him off.

Done was done.

Bluey didn't like anything or anyone. He hated animals and children. But he wasn't thrilled by adults neither: the women were hideous and too loud, the men stupid and boring. Everyone talked too much. The beer was too warm. The soup too cold. Newspapers were full of lies, and no politician or policeman or pianist or plumber was worth tuppence, and nothing was ever worth the time or the effort.

Except for hurting people.

Bluey could get behind that. In his own way, he respected Glory Nelson because she understood the value of pain and she was never afraid. He wouldn't have worked for her otherwise.

He had no respect for Mr. Davidson. Had point blank asked Glory if he wanted him done for. "I'll do him," he'd said in his raspy whisper. "Whenever you like. He'll be deader than Phar Lap."

He liked to take things away from people simply because they prized them. He'd take whatever it was and then break it, whether it was a hat, a car, a cat, or a woman or a man. He didn't value what he took. He valued the pain in the former owner's eyes when he broke it.

Bluey had great bushy ginger eyebrows that hung so low over his pale eyes it was a wonder he could see. He could, though. When he had a gun—which wasn't often, guns being scarce in the city—he shot straight and accurate. Learned how to do it on the farm he was on until he ran away at ten. He perfected the art during the war. Liked to boast about how many Turks he'd done for.

He was even better with a razor.

Half the scars in the Hills were put there by Bluey. He liked to carve a big *L* from ear to mouth on everyone who riled him. There were plenty that swore it was Bluey that started that particular fashion.

He'd kicked Kelpie once. Down in Frog Hollow. Not too long after Old Ma had faded. When Kelpie didn't understand what fading meant and wouldn't leave the Hollow because she kept hoping Old Ma would come back.

Bluey'd found her curled up asleep in the ruins of what had been Old Ma's home. He'd pulled the blanket off and kicked her hard in the ribs and then kept walking. The bruise had taken months to disappear. Took weeks before she could breathe without pain.

Kelpie was mostly grateful he hadn't killed her. He'd killed plenty of others for being in his path.

When Bluey Denham said to nick off, Kelpie nicked.

He was the baddest of all the bad men.

KELPIE

Bluey Denham stomped in sullenly with an almost-burnt-down-to-the-end cigarette dangling from his lips. He stood barely a foot away from them and stared at Gloriana Nelson.

Kelpie slid closer to Dymphna and made a show of clutching at her arm. She wanted Bluey to know that she was scared of him. Bluey liked to go after those who didn't show fear and teach them to be afraid. He wanted everyone to tremble when they heard his name. So Kelpie trembled.

Gloriana Nelson smiled. "My favourite boy!" She clapped her hands. "G'morning, Bluey."

"I thought *I* was her favourite boy," Palmer said. "How can she like this miserable bastard?" He spat. But of course no spittle went anywhere. Palmer looked in disgust at the floor where his slag should have been. "Ghosts are useless. Look at this mob." He pointed at one of the ghosts in the corner of the room, who sang tunelessly and skipped back and forth. Kelpie assumed it had once been a girl, but it was too faded now to know for sure. "How do I stop being a ghost?"

Bluey raised his head, looking at where Palmer lounged against the wall.

Palmer disappeared. It was the first time he had disappeared without his face darkening first. He must have gotten the knack of it.

"Well, that's not a very effusive greeting, is it, Dymph? What's the matter, Bluey? You forgot how to speak during the night?" Glory sipped her tea and didn't invite Bluey to sit down.

"Only woke up, didn't I?" Bluey said so quietly Kelpie wondered how Glory could hear.

"Sorry to wake you, my boy. But I got a job for you."

Bluey grunted.

"Bluey here is going to keep an eye on you, Dymphna. That right-o with you, Dymph?"

Dymphna said yes, even though Kelpie knew it wasn't. It wasn't right-o with Kelpie either.

"He's going to make sure no one lays a hand on you. I want no blemishes—not even a scratch—on that skin of yours. That's the most expensive skin in the city, that is."

Dymphna didn't say anything. Kelpie wondered what it felt like to have valuable skin. Probably Dymphna's hair and eyes were expensive too. All of her, really.

"That mean she's my woman now?" Bluey grunted. "I heard Palmer was dead."

Kelpie squeezed Dymphna's hand. If Glory said yes, Kelpie would help Dymphna find a place to hide.

"No, Bluey, Dymphna is not your woman now."

Bluey glared, not at Glory but at the floor. Kelpie reckoned Glory wouldn't tolerate anyone who glared at her directly.

"Do you work for me, Bluey?"

Bluey grunted.

"Have I been paying you good money for easy work since you was a tyke?"

Bluey mumbled something that sounded like a yes. But he could also have been telling Glory to get nicked. Hard to tell with Bluey.

"Dymphna here—my top earner—is being threatened by Davidson. Isn't that right, Dymph?"

"Yes, Glory."

Kelpie could feel Dymphna wishing she was anywhere but here.

Bluey spat hard on the floor. Spittle bounced up to hit the back of Seamus's trousers. If she'd been wearing her old pants, some of it would have hit her bare legs.

"I want you to stay close to Dymphna and keep Davidson—or anyone else, like the cops—from doing anything they shouldn't. It's not that hard, Bluey. Keep Dymphna safe. You think you can manage it?"

Bluey spat again. Even harder this time. Kelpie wondered if he understood.

"Let me put it this way, Bluey. If you don't keep Dymphna safe, if something happens to her, there will be consequences. You know how unhappy that makes me."

"Consequences?" Bluey rasped as though the word didn't fit in his mouth. Kelpie didn't think he'd come across it before. If it weren't for Miss Lee, she wouldn't have either. She only knew it from *Great Expectations* where *consequences* were almost invariably bad. Seemed like they were that way outside of books too.

"I know you're slow, Bluey," Glory said softly. Kelpie glanced up to see her looking directly into Bluey's eyes. If anyone else had commented on his stupidity, he'd've flattened them. If anyone else had looked him in the eye, they'd be dead. "Not your fault. But you're a strong boy, and that makes up for any shortcomings. That's why I trust you, Bluey. You've always been solid with me. Which is more than I can say for some of my smarter men. Brains are wasted on standovers."

Bluey said nothing. Kelpie didn't think he was angry with Glory. He seemed to accept that what she said was true. Even though he wouldn't have if Kelpie had pointed out to him that he wasn't the full quid.

Kelpie tried to imagine what it would be like with Bluey glowering at them throughout the day. All she could think of was how long her side had hurt the last time she'd failed to stay out of his way. Of how careful she'd been to avoid him since. Bluey Denham was exactly the kind of bad man Old Ma was always warning about. Not caring any more for a person than he would for a fly. Men like that weren't right in the head, Old Ma said. They *looked* for trouble. They *wanted* to hurt people.

Neal Darcy might be following Dymphna. Palmer had said he was, and it had turned out to be true about Snowy. Bluey would love hurting Darcy. Bluey especially hated men he thought were soft. Men who weren't scarred and savage like him. Kelpie decided she would stab Bluey if he hurt Darcy. She didn't care what he did to her.

"You think you can cheer Bluey up a little, Dymphna?"

Bluey growled. Kelpie started to wonder if he hated animals so much because he wasn't that much different from a dog himself. Well, except most dogs were smarter and less vicious.

"On the house, possum."

Dymphna didn't say anything, but Kelpie could feel her tension. Bluey growled again. Kelpie wondered if it was because Glory called him *possum* or if he just growled a lot.

"Just a little, Dymphna." Glory made a gesture with her hand that Kelpie didn't understand.

"Yes, Glory."

"That's a one-off, Bluey. Don't start thinking it's a perk of this particular job, you hear?"

Bluey didn't say anything.

"Do you hear, Bluey? Just this once."

"Yeah, Glory."

"I need your word on that, Bluey."

Bluey paused. Dymphna seemed to stop breathing. Her leg shook harder than ever. Kelpie could feel it vibrating against the chair.

"Bluey?" Glory said in an ugly tone of voice.

"On me word. Just the one."

"And, Bluey, keep the little girl safe too."

"What for? 'M I her keeper?" Bluey said, sounding like he was Glory's disobedient son. Kelpie wouldn't have been surprised if she'd belted him one. She wished she would. She could feel Bluey looking at her. She shifted even closer to Dymphna, who slid her arm around Kelpie's waist.

"Because I want the little one safe. That's why."

He grunted again.

"No marks on them neither. You and Dymphna go upstairs, and when you're finished, I'm sending her and the little one to the doctor. Escort them. Wait outside until they're finished and then bring them back here. Dymphna'll work the afternoon shift, but you'll be outside her door."

"What about when I got to pee?"

"One of the other boys will spot you. But make it quick. Don't let none of Davidson's men near her. I don't care how much money they've got. Today she's not doing them nor coppers neither. Just her regulars. Got that?"

"Yeah."

Kelpie was not entirely convinced Bluey did follow. It was a lot for such a small-brained man to remember. What if he forgot and kicked her again? Or worse?

"Send anyone to me who wants to squall about it. Then you'll head over for the party. I think it's right that Dymphna here say a few words about Jimmy. Raise the toast. That okay with you, Dymph?"

"Of course, Glory," Dymphna said.

"Wish I had some chocolates. Lettie. Go find me some. You know the kind I like. Get rid of the nasty peppermint ones before you hand me the box." Glory shuddered.

Lettie jumped up and exited as quick as she could. No one wanted to be around Bluey.

"I'm not asking much, Blue. Keep Dymphna and the little one safe and unharmed. That's it."

Kelpie wondered if he was going to argue. He looked like he might. His lips were pressed together and his hands clenched and then unclenched and then clenched again. His hands seemed more comfortable as fists.

"I'll keep 'em safe."

"You promise?"

"I promise."

Kelpie didn't believe him.

"Cheer up, Bluey," Glory said, leaning forward to pat him on the shoulder. "Someone might try to snatch 'em. You can hurt whoever tries that as much as you want. But don't leave no bodies lying about. Don't want any more attention from the coppers than we got already."

Glory smiled at Dymphna. "He means well, he does."

Kelpie knew that wasn't true.

No one called the doctor anything but *Doctor* or *Doc*. Better no one knew his real name—that way they couldn't look into why he'd been struck off. Most assumed it was the drinking what done it. Seemed unfair. What man didn't drink too much?

Mostly, though, people didn't want to know why he wasn't a proper doctor anymore. Same way they didn't want to know how someone as rough and ready as him became a doctor in the first place. All that mattered was how he'd kept plenty of Glory's people alive who wouldn't be otherwise. If he'd done anything worse than fancy a few too many drinks, he'd more than made up for it.

When the doc took care of girls who'd been careless, he left them alive and unbroken, which was a lot more than you could say for most of the back-alley practitioners of Razorhurst. He'd fixed Dymphna Campbell and made sure she healed whole and clean. He'd left her almost as if nothing had happened.

People were grateful.

The doctor was showered with gifts: freebies from Glory's girls whenever he was up for it, a necklace of shark teeth, several beautiful gleaming razors, almost (but never quite) as much whisky and beer as he could drink, a diamond necklace, gold rings, silver rings, a parrot, several motor-cars, a top hat and tails (several sizes too big), and more cakes and biscuits and home-baked casseroles than any one man could eat.

As the doctor would rather drink than eat, the comestibles were redistributed among his many patients. The noncomestibles he parlayed into cash at the pawnshop. The cash turned into drink.

He saw whoever came to him. Glory's people always had priority, but after them, it was first come first served. He'd dosed almost every kid in Darlinghurst with cod-liver oil at one time or another, patched up their cuts, splinted their broken bones.

He drew the line only at animals. Dogs and cats were a menace as far as he was concerned, and he wouldn't allow them near him. They were only good for killing rats, the doc maintained, and from the state of things—more rats than people—they weren't much chop at that.

⤐ DYMPHNA ⤏

Dymphna was grateful Bluey didn't say a word as they left Glory's. She'd seen to him before. At least this time he hadn't hurt her. She didn't trust Bluey to keep his word even to Glory.

He grunted, grabbed his crotch, and grimaced at her. Dymphna suspected that was his version of a smile. Kelpie was on Dymphna's other side, carefully keeping herself out of Bluey's range. Wise.

Had she made a mistake? Trusting that Glory didn't know, trusting that sticking by Glory was her safest path through this mess, trusting that Bluey was her bodyguard and not a veiled threat? Or an unveiled one?

He could be both.

Glory could know and still not intend to kill her. Glory had said it herself: Dymphna was her best girl. What did it matter if she had plotted to take Glory's empire from her? She'd failed and her co-conspirator was dead. There weren't many men with Jimmy's strength and brains. She glanced at Bluey, who had neither.

"What?" he grunted.

"Nothing."

They walked two blocks before turning into the narrow lane behind Palmer Street. So narrow Dymphna could easily reach out to touch the houses on either side of her. She and Kelpie dropped behind Bluey.

The lane stank as always, but not as foully as it did in summer. There were no flies to swat away. The backs of houses were never as pretty as their fronts, but on this block half were collapsing, sinking in on themselves, no glass in the windows, doors gone, half the roofs gone too. None of these houses had yards. Many of the dunnies were on the verge of subsiding into the lane. The houses that were intact were small one-up, one-down cottages. All had seen better days.

Dymphna stepped over a pile of rusted tins with sharp, serrated edges.

"Doc's a good man," she told Kelpie, because it was true. She squeezed the girl's hand.

She'd played nurse for the doctor on more than one occasion. She'd watched him pull a bullet out of one man and stitch up several razorings, trying not to think about the damp rising up the walls or the cockroaches scuttling across the floor. Open wounds became infected. She knew that. She also knew he doused them all in disinfectant. Alcohol at the very least. He was a good doctor. Considering.

There was no harm in him checking Kelpie, making sure she was all right. It was another sign of how well Glory treated her people. Mr. Davidson did not employ his own doctor. If any of his people were broken, he discarded them.

She and Jimmy, they'd vowed to do the same as Glory: look after people, show their appreciation. Ironic that they had begun by plotting to take over from Gloriana Nelson. Dymphna doubted Glory would have felt appreciated if they had succeeded.

It was another reason she'd wanted Davidson dead but not Glory. Dymphna had been certain she could manage Glory. Though after today's display, Dymphna was less sure of that than she had been.

Had Jimmy truly planned to kill Glory? Would she have been able to stop him? How much would Jimmy have listened to her if he'd succeeded in killing Mr. Davidson?

They hadn't even discussed killing Glory. Jimmy had agreed that Glory wasn't a threat. Her old man, Big Bill, was gone, and while he was a worthless human being, he had been Glory's muscle.

But now Big Bill *and* Jimmy were out of the picture, which left, who, Bluey? Too stupid, too hard to control. Johnno Bailey? Didn't have the heart for it. He cared more about cooking than keeping people in line.

Of Glory's remaining men, if they were smart enough, they weren't strong enough. And vice versa.

Dymphna imagined trying to rule Razorhurst with Neal Darcy by her side. She smiled.

There wasn't anyone else. Not who worked for Glory.

Jimmy's death left Mr. Davidson in a much more powerful position than before and Glory in a much more vulnerable one.

As soon as she could do it safely, Dymphna needed to scarper. Glory was only temporary shelter. She squeezed Kelpie's hand. The girl looked up at her.

"It'll be all right, love," Dymphna said, though she feared that wasn't true.

She should have told Glory that it was Mr. Davidson who'd had Jimmy killed. But she could hardly tell Glory that dead Jimmy

Palmer told her. Besides, Glory was already certain it was Davidson. Gloriana Nelson was wary. She was prepared.

Bluey waited outside the grog shop, arms crossed. It was the sturdiest building on either side of the lane. Bars at the window and a steel-reinforced door.

Dymphna knocked on the door.

Bluey looked back the way they'd come. "Reckon someone's following us."

Dymphna followed his gaze, worried that he'd spotted Snowy or Neal. "I don't see anyone."

Bluey grunted and pounded on the door.

A small boy opened it, saw Bluey, and scampered up the hall.

They followed him. The place was empty except for him and another small boy doing a haphazard job of mopping the floor and wiping down the walls. It was hours till the pubs closed and men desperate for more grog started piling into the illegal joints.

The two boys goggled at Dymphna as she smiled at them, then froze when Bluey strode in behind her.

"He won't hurt you lads," she told them. "Glory told him to be on his best behaviour."

Bluey walked up to the smallest of the two, picked him up by his collar, and threw him against the wall. The boy slid to the floor, his eyes watering with pain, but he said nothing.

Dymphna turned on him. "What was that for?" She pulled Kelpie closer to her side.

"Said I wouldn't hurt youse two," Bluey said in his barely audible voice. "Didn't say nothing about them."

"Animal."

"Whore."

Dymphna thought about slapping him. He wasn't worth it. Someone else would do for him soon enough. Sooner rather than later if Davidson decided to keep picking off Glory's muscle.

She turned away and walked through to where the doctor worked out of the largest storeroom. Bluey pounded so hard on the doctor's door it shook on its hinges.

"What?" said a voice from inside.

The door opened and Doc stood wiping his glasses. "You been stabbed again, Bluey?" He peered beyond him. "You messed up another girl?"

Bluey pointed at Dymphna and pushed Kelpie at the doctor.

Dymphna cut a look at Bluey, which she wished could hurt him, and walked through with her head high and her back straight. None of this was going to touch her. She put her hand on Kelpie's shoulder. The girl was trembling.

"Glory said wait outside, Bluey."

Bluey slammed the door then leaned against it, making it bow inward. Much as Neal Darcy had when he was hiding them. But this time there was nothing magical about it. Dymphna could hear Bluey breathing heavily, panting like a dog, blocking the only exit.

The room was messier than the last time she'd been there.

"You let your maid go, Doc?"

"Funny."

One corner was piled to the ceiling with wooden boxes labelled QUALITY WINE and DOUBLE DISTILLED SPIRITS, but there were less than the last time she'd been there. Some must've been hauled over to Lansdowne Street for the party.

The rest of the room was a desk, two chairs, and a bookcase filled with battered medical books and the doctor's supplies. There was bedding on the floor and two buckets under a leak that had grown considerably. It hadn't rained in weeks, yet the mould on the walls had now reached the ceiling over his desk.

Jimmy reappeared next to the liquor. Dymphna did not groan. She didn't even blink.

"I think Bluey can see me," he told Kelpie, who was staring at the floor. "He was looking straight at me earlier."

Dymphna knew for a fact that Bluey Denham did not see ghosts; he barely saw people. But his disconcertingly pale eyes made everyone think he could see more than he could.

"Why you here, Dymphna?" The doctor sank back into his chair and put his feet on his desk. "Neither of you appear to be bleeding. You clapped up?"

Dymphna shook her head and put her hands on Kelpie's shoulders. "She's feral. Glory wants to know if she's got any diseases."

The doctor yawned. "She's a bit young for it, isn't she?"

"She's not going to work for Glory. She's my niece. We want to see if she's all right." Dymphna decided it was best to start calling Kelpie her niece straight away. It would make explaining Kelpie being with her easier.

"Thought you said she was feral? How'd that happen to your niece?"

"Same way I started working for Glory. Things fell apart. I expect it was the same way for you."

"You're not wrong."

The doctor took a swift swig of a bottle, then stood up, stretched, and became the doctor he used to be before the medical board took his licence away.

Boxing Ghost

Stuart O'Sullivan had tatters for ears and a nose that had been broken three times. He made sure Kelpie knew that it had *only* been three times. *Number of fights I had? Three broken noses is nothing. Most boxers had their noses smeared across their ugly mugs a million times more than that.*

Stuart O'Sullivan was prone to exaggeration.

He haunted the cinema on Crown that was once the gymnasium where he'd trained and had almost become the best fighter the country had ever seen. *Almost*, because he'd been beaten down in Frog Hollow by five jumped-up pedlars who'd decided to switch to being outright criminals, starting with robbing him. *Before the war, that was. Five of them and they still didn't do the job right. Took me a week to die. Bastards.*

He was a small, wiry man who'd started as a flyweight and ended a bantam because of a growth spurt in his twenties. *Oh, the growing pains. Swear I could feel me bones moving. Kept me up nights for months. Then me coordination was all out of whack. That's when me nose got broke second and third times.*

At first he'd thought she was a boy. When Kelpie corrected his misapprehension, he said he would no longer teach her "the fine art of pugilism." He didn't approve of a girl learning. Women were built too delicately and lacked the endurance for such a rigorous, manly sport. But he loved to teach, and in all his many years of ghosting, he had never come across another live one who could see and hear him well enough for lessons.

He taught wee lass Kelpie because there was no one else.

Most of the dead weren't interested in learning. Those that were had no interest in learning anything physical. What was the point? They could feel nothing. Touch nothing. They were zephyrs unable to deliver a knock-out punch to a gnat.

He taught Kelpie whenever she visited him, which was not as often as O'Sullivan would like. He was a yeller, and Kelpie did not enjoy being yelled at. Each time she'd storm off, and he'd promise not to yell again, but the second she did something wrong, there he was yelling again. He couldn't help himself.

Miss Lee never yelled.

When Kelpie was with Miss Lee, she did not visit O'Sullivan. She hadn't been back since Miss Lee faded, but she remembered what he'd taught. Not just the fine pugilistic art, but the much more useful sneaky fighting tailored for someone small and quick: like O'Sullivan had been and like Kelpie was.

Most of it below the belt.

Kelpie practised because you never knew when running away wouldn't be enough.

DYMPHNA

"How old are you, girl?"

The doctor peered at Kelpie's face as if she were deaf. Dymphna half expected him to knock on the girl's skull and ask if anyone was home. She had a mind to tell him off if he did. After everything that had happened that day, Dymphna was more than ready to start yelling.

Kelpie said nothing.

"She doesn't know how old she is. I was hoping you'd be able to tell."

"You don't know how old your niece is?"

"Things fall apart, Doc. I've a younger brother I've never seen. I don't know how old he is either."

"Well, she doesn't look much over eleven or twelve. Is that how old you are, girl?"

Kelpie looked past the doctor to the wooden crates.

"She doesn't talk much," Dymphna told him.

"Does she talk at all? Could she be dumb?"

"She talks."

"Right then. Let's get her shoes off and measure her. Against the wall."

Kelpie looked warily at the doctor then removed her shoes. Dymphna led her to the only clear bit of the room, which was the back of the door.

On the other side of the door, Bluey made a sharp barking noise. They all three startled.

"He was next on my list," Jimmy said. "Doing for Bluey was going to be such a pleasure. Now the most I can hope for is to lead him off a fucking cliff."

The doctor made a mark above Kelpie's head, then pushed her onto the scale, sliding the weights until they balanced.

"Four feet nine inches, weighing a smidge under five stone. Round here that's about average for a ten- or eleven-year-old. Are you eleven, girl?"

Kelpie didn't even blink at him.

"Sit down."

Kelpie sat. The doctor bent over her.

"She's not as clean as she could be."

Dymphna was indignant. Mrs. Darcy had washed her. She'd been in a bubble bath. Dymphna doubted Kelpie'd been this clean in years.

"When's the last time *you* had a wash?" Dymphna asked, eyeing his crumpled suit. The tie was barely four inches long and had a half-moon stain below the knot. Even so it was cleaner than his face. Dymphna did not want to think about his teeth.

A loud, vibrating snore came from the other side of the door. Then another. Bluey was asleep. Glory would be pleased he was so vigilant in his guard duties.

The doctor held a stethoscope to Kelpie's chest. "Nothing wrong with her heart." He shifted it to her lungs. "Breathe in deep." Kelpie did. "And again." She did.

"Surprisingly clear," he told Dymphna, "for someone living on the streets. Stick your tongue out."

Kelpie did. The doctor grunted.

He shone a light in her eyes, had her sit so he could hit her knees with a tiny hammer. "All better than it has any right to be," he said. "Let's get her clothes off then."

Kelpie looked at Dymphna. Dymphna squeezed her hand. "He's a doctor and I'm right here. But he has to check you."

Kelpie shook her head.

Dymphna bent to put herself level with Kelpie's eyes. "If you don't do what Doc says, he'll tell Glory, and then she'll have Bluey make you do what he says. Neither one of us is going to enjoy that."

"Orright."

Kelpie took off her clothes. Politely Dymphna stared at a notch in the wood of a crate of quality liquor several inches above Kelpie's head.

"She's brown as a nut. You sure she's your niece?" Doc looked from Kelpie to Dymphna's pale skin.

"Her dad was foreign and she's been living on the streets. What did you expect?"

"Her mammary glands are coming in."

"Her what?" Dymphna asked for Kelpie's benefit.

"Tits," the doctor said, pointing. "Her tits are starting to grow."

Kelpie put her arms across them.

The doctor shot a triumphant look at Dymphna. "She might be dumb, but she can understand."

"She's not dumb. I told you, Doc. She can talk."

"Lift up your arms."

Kelpie did, glaring at the doctor. Dymphna couldn't help thinking that Glory was right: Kelpie had a fearsome glare.

"There's the beginnings of adolescent hair growth. On her pudenda and underarms. You got your monthlies yet, girl?"

Kelpie didn't respond. Dymphna wondered if she knew what that meant.

"Probably too undernourished. Look at those ribs. She has to be at least twelve to have breasts and pubic hair growth."

Dymphna didn't correct him. She'd had hers by the time she was ten.

"But the malnourishment has probably stunted her growth. I'd say she's probably older. Could be as much as sixteen."

"She can't be," Dymphna said in shock. This little girl? Sixteen? She didn't come up to Dymphna's collarbone. Kelpie looked and sounded like a child. "*I'm* sixteen. How on earth could she be sixteen too?"

"You're not!" The doctor was staring at her.

"Shit," Dymphna said. She hadn't meant to say it out loud. But she'd been shocked. Kelpie could *not* be the same age as her. "You can't tell anyone, Doc. No one knows but Glory."

"Sixteen?" Jimmy shouted. "You could be me own kid!"

She could not be his child. Jimmy wasn't thirty yet—*hadn't been* thirty yet.

Kelpie was staring at her too. Directly. It unnerved Dymphna. The little girl was usually careful not to meet anyone's eyes.

"You look like a lady," Kelpie said, her gaze still on Dymphna. She hugged herself tighter as if to fend off that piece of information. "You *can't* be sixteen. You're not a kid."

Doc was still staring too. "How many dead boyfriends you got? You're the Angel of Death, and you're telling me you're only *sixteen*?"

"Don't call me that! They weren't *all* my boyfriends. People exaggerate. Not that it's any business of yours. You can't tell anyone how old I am!"

"*Sixteen*." Doc's face drooped. "You can still get out of this life, you know, love. You've got time. Keep at it and you'll be old beyond your years. Old*er* beyond your years. Right now you look twenty—all well and good—but soon you'll be looking fifty. I ain't even thirty-five yet and look at me."

Almost the same age as Jimmy Palmer. But he looked like he could be Jimmy's dad. Doc was a wreck. But that had nothing to do with Dymphna. She didn't drink every minute she was awake. She ate right, looked after herself. She was careful.

"Shall I tell Glory you're encouraging her best girl to leave her?" Dymphna stared at the doctor so hard he backed up a step. "I pull in fifty pounds a night *after* she's taken her cut. What are you making?"

The doctor closed his mouth, swallowed. "Forget I said anything."

"Do you promise not to tell?"

"Not a soul. On my word."

"Because I will find out, Doc, and I will make you pay."

Now Doc looked more tired than afraid. She felt a moment of resentment that he was more afraid of Glory than of her.

"I won't tell anyone," he said. "I stay out of trouble. You know that."

Dymphna did. "You neither, Kelpie."

Kelpie nodded but did not stop staring at her. Dymphna had to hope that Bluey hadn't heard. That he really was asleep. Though if Glory or Davidson had her killed, it wouldn't matter if she was ninety. Shit.

The doctor turned to Kelpie. "How often do you eat?"

Kelpie didn't answer.

Dymphna suspected Kelpie ate more than Doc did. The way the cheekbones stuck out on his face, it was a safe bet she'd be able to count his ribs too.

He pulled out his bottle of cod-liver oil and measured out a dose. Kelpie eyed the doc and then the slimy liquid on the spoon. Dymphna almost laughed. Kelpie looked like she'd rather eat her own foot.

"Open up," the doc said.

"Bluey," Dymphna reminded her.

Kelpie's eyes narrowed, but she opened her mouth and swallowed.

"Paint the abrasions and rashes with gentian violet. Dose her with cod-liver oil once a day. Makes sure she bathes at least two or three times a week and brushes her teeth daily. You'll have to take her to a dentist. Make her eat apples too. Good for the digestion and the teeth. Also red meat."

"Don't want no apples." Kelpie started pulling her clothes back on.

"She'll eat apples," Dymphna said, smiling at Kelpie. "I'll make you an apple cake."

"If you want her to eat them without any nutritional value, go right ahead."

Dymphna didn't ask what *nutritional value* was.

The doctor sat down again and put his feet back up on the desk.

"That's it?" Dymphna asked.

"She's not going into the life? Then that's all needs checking."

Dymphna thought about objecting but then grabbed Kelpie's arm and led her to the door.

"Doctors. I could have worked most of that out for myself," she muttered. Well, not that Kelpie could be the same age as her. She still couldn't believe that was true.

"I'll see you at Glory's party tonight," Doc said, closing his eyes. "Should be a bosker."

Before Kelpie learned to read, the outer limits of her world had been Centennial Park, Paddy's Markets, Central Station, and Cleveland Street. A world of no more than a handful of square miles. She'd never seen the ocean, a desert, or inhaled mountain air. She hadn't so much as crossed the Harbour Bridge. Kelpie had not known such experiences were a possibility. Then she learned to read, and the boundaries of her imagination, if not her actual world, slowly began to expand.

Miss Lee had revelled in Kelpie's quick transition from illiterate to voracious reader. *Such a quick study you are!* she'd cry. *You are far and away my finest student, and you know I taught at the finest girls' school in Surry Hills.*

Kelpie did know that. Miss Lee had often told her.

The school, Lady Cheltenham's School for Young Ladies, had since moved further east. Surry Hills had become too dangerous for the sensibilities of innocent young ladies.

Miss Lee loved that Kelpie was now able to read anything.

But it did not follow that she thought Kelpie *should* read anything.

There was a pile of magazines in the living room at Old Man O'Reilly's with titles like *Photo Bits*, *Spicy Adventures*, and *Modern Art for Men*. Miss Lee's face changed when she saw them: lips thinned, nostrils flared, eyebrows raised. "These are not for reading. In fact, let's avoid this room. On general principle, one should avoid reading magazines. There's nothing in them to broaden the mind. But these are the worst kind of magazine there is."

After that they stuck to Old Man O'Reilly's library and attic. Kelpie didn't mind. She loved the library.

Though there was one shelf Kelpie wasn't allowed to touch. The books on it had interesting names such as *The Satyricon*, *The Decameron*, *The Kama Sutra*, and *Les Liaisons dangereuses*. Kelpie couldn't find any of those words in the dictionary. A book called *Ulysses* was also on that shelf, which puzzled Kelpie, as he was a character in *Greek and Roman Myths & Legends*, which Miss Lee had encouraged her to read, despite the stories making no sense.

Some of the other titles made it clear why that shelf was forbidden to her: *Sex-Love, and Its Place in a Free Society, A Bibliography of Sex Rites and Customs, The Marriage of Near Kin, La Prostitution, The Amatory Experiences of a Surgeon* (amatory was in the dictionary), *The Romance of Lust, The Sexual Side of Marriage, The Life and Amours of the Beautiful, Gay and Dashing Kate Percival,* and *Raped on the Railway: a True Story of a Lady who was First Ravished and then Flagellated on the Scotch Express.*

Then there were the books that sounded innocent and made Kelpie wonder why they weren't: *The Colonel's Daughter, The Life of Fanny Hill, The Butcher Shop, Capital Volume I, The Well of Loneliness, A Farewell to Arms, Dubliners, All Quiet on the Western Front, Woman's Destiny and Birth Control,* and *The Diary of a Smut-Hound.*

That shelf had horrified Miss Lee even more than the magazines. She had yelled at Kelpie to get down from the stepladder. Gestured for her to sit down on the comfy leather couch.

"Not all books," Miss Lee said, once her lecture face was in place, "are good for us. There are some that are shoddily written. Mysteries, penny dreadfuls, and the like. Books like those are not educational and are full of vulgar notions and expression. But they are unlikely to be harmful. At least not if read in moderation.

"However, there are other books, which, well. It would have been better if they were not written in the first place, and once written they most definitely should not have been published. They are deeply harmful. That shelf is full of such books. It is saddening to learn that Mr. O'Reilly is a degenerate."

Kelpie had no idea what a degenerate was. She looked it up first chance she got. The description seemed to fit most of the men of the Hills. Very few of whom were fine examples of their species.

"You must promise never to read those books."

Kelpie solemnly promised with her fingers crossed behind her back. She fully intended to look at each and every volume the second Miss Lee wasn't around to see.

But then Miss Lee faded, and Kelpie did not have the heart to return to Old Man O'Reilly's.

⟩⟨ KELPIE ⟩⟨

Kelpie didn't know what to do with the knowledge that Dymphna Campbell was sixteen. The woollen hat Snowy had given her for her tenth birthday had long since fallen apart. Could it really have been six years ago?

But how could she and Dymphna be the same age? Sixteen was Maisy O'Keefe who haunted Devonshire Street below Crown and was skinny and loud and had hair in dirty blonde plaits and was not much taller than Kelpie. Maisy was always singing about her run-away lad whose name changed on a daily basis. *That* was sixteen. Not Dymphna Campbell.

Wasn't Tommy sixteen? He didn't look nearly as grown up as Dymphna. He had pimples, and his voice bounced up and down like the Adam's apple in his throat.

Apples. Ugh.

Dymphna was much taller than she was. She had bosoms and the kind of arse all the men looked at. She talked and walked and looked like a lady. Like a fully grown woman. *Not* a sixteen-year-old.

Dymphna shoved the doctor's door hard. It wouldn't open. Bluey was snoring, asleep on the other side, his full weight against the door.

"Bluey?" Dymphna called out. "Bluey!"

Kelpie wondered if he was pretending. If this was his way of getting at them because Glory wouldn't let him hurt them. The doctor roused himself to add his weight to the door. All three of them pushed. It budged but not enough for them to slip through. Now Kelpie was sure Bluey was pretending.

"Wake up, Bluey!" Dymphna cried.

"Whaa?" The door opened. Bluey stood blinking. He wiped his mouth with the back of his hand and eyed Dymphna slyly. He didn't look like he'd just woken up.

Kelpie stayed behind Dymphna.

"Bye, Bluey," the doctor said, closing the door as quickly as he could.

For a moment Kelpie wished she could hide in the doctor's office. Even with her clothes off, which had been awful, it was better than being near Bluey. She wouldn't put it past him to accidentally fall on her and break as many of her bones as he could.

Palmer had disappeared again. Though what he thought Bluey could do to him even if he could actually see him, Kelpie had no idea. Palmer was the only one who *wasn't* in danger from him.

Bluey led the way through the shop without saying a word. Kelpie needed to pee but didn't want to say so in front of him. The two boys were sensibly hidden. Kelpie wished she was too. There was a big bowl of peanuts on the bar. She'd been hoping to palm some, but no chance with Bluey marching them through this fast.

Bluey's fists were clenched again. Kelpie wondered how long before he gave in to temptation and thumped her and Dymphna like he wanted to.

Once again, she considered running. She'd be safer in the Hills. Well, except that Glory knew about her now and would send someone to find her. Once she was found, would Glory still protect her? Or would she throw her in the harbour? Mr. Davidson probably knew about her too. He'd seen her with Dymphna. Maybe Kelpie wasn't safe anywhere. The thought made her feel colder than Glory's looking at her had.

Did Bluey hold a grudge? If she ran away, would he find her and break her into tiny pieces?

Bluey opened the front door, and Dymphna followed him out. Kelpie looked behind her to see if the boys would emerge from hiding. Maybe she could run back and sneak the peanuts now.

"Hurry up, Kelpie," Dymphna called.

Kelpie saw someone moving in the abandoned house on the other side of the lane. The house was a roofless mess of fallen bricks and timber, with no doorway and a window that had neither glass nor frame.

Bluey leapt across the narrow lane and in through the window, fists flying. "I see ya! Ya fucking mongrel!"

Kelpie heard a dull smack that meant that Bluey's fist had connected. Neal Darcy came tumbling backward out the same window, rolling over and onto his feet.

He grinned at Dymphna. "Shoulda ducked."

Bluey climbed out after him. "Following us like a mangy fucking dog. Ya think I'm fucking blind or somethink?"

Darcy backed away, panting, his right cheekbone red and his fists raised.

"Leave him alone, Bluey. He's harmless," Dymphna said. "We've got to get back to Glory."

"He was following youse. Glory said I could kill 'im."

A window went up two houses down. "What's the barney?" a large man called, leaning forward on his elbows. Then he saw Bluey. He ducked back in faster than a rat up a downpipe, slammed the window, and closed the curtains.

Bluey swung at Darcy again, who danced backward, nimbly jumping over a brick. Bluey had his fists high. He threw a cross, missing by a fraction of an inch.

Darcy ducked, then pivoted, scraping along a cottage wall and out of the way before Bluey could land a kick, but Darcy didn't swing back at him.

Bluey was wide open. His chin was up. One punch to the throat would fix him. Then follow it up with a few blows to the head. This fight was Darcy's. Kelpie bit her lip to keep the instructions she wanted to yell at him inside her.

Bluey threw a roundhouse, wild and off balance, missing Darcy and hitting the broken post of a crumbling house.

Bluey screamed, shook his hand. Kelpie saw blood. Bluey curled it into a fist again and threw a wild hook at Darcy's head. Darcy was out of range before Bluey finished his wind-up. His knuckles slammed into a wall.

Darcy made Bluey look slow and old. Bluey was neither.

He threw another cross. Darcy swayed out of its path. He had plenty of time to return a blow of his own. Instead he danced backward, agilely avoiding colliding with the flowerpots in front of one of the intact homes.

Stuart O'Sullivan would have been appalled. Kelpie *was* appalled. She'd've liked to scream at Darcy to smash him one. O'Sullivan would've approved of Darcy's footwork but would have wondered what the point of it was if the kid couldn't bring himself to go for the kill.

If Darcy wasn't going to fight Bluey, why didn't he run?

Bluey jabbed and missed, hooked and missed. Sweat ran down his now-red face. "I'll fuckin' kill ya!"

"Run, Darcy!" Kelpie yelled, hoping Bluey was too ropeable to hear her.

Darcy tripped over one of the flowerpots, landed on his arse, picked up a broken shard, and rolled out of Bluey's way.

Bluey flicked his razor open. It gleamed.

"Bluey!" Dymphna called. "Put it away! Glory said no trouble."

Kelpie was pretty sure Bluey wasn't listening.

"Run!" Dymphna screamed.

Why wasn't Darcy running? He could outrun Bluey easy.

A whistle blew down the lane. Kelpie turned. A copper.

Dymphna said, "Shit."

The copper had something dark and heavy in his hand. He ran towards them, yelling at Bluey not to move. His copper's hat fell to the ground. He had a gun. He pulled up less than a foot from Darcy.

Kelpie had never seen a gun this close before. The metal was dull, not shiny like she'd imagined. Bluey's razor shone more brightly. Even so, the gun looked dangerous. Kelpie shrank back.

Bluey slowed. He looked at the gun in the copper's hands, the razor in his own, and at Darcy in the dirt between them. Bluey did not look afraid or even wary. Not like the copper or Darcy.

Or Kelpie.

"Don't move, Bluey," the copper repeated. He had more pimples than Tommy.

"They're mates, Constable," Dymphna said. "Bluey was putting the razor away, weren't you, Bluey?"

Bluey nodded, but he didn't close his razor.

Dymphna edged away from the men.

"You stay still, Miss Campbell."

That didn't mean Kelpie. She took a step back to the sly grog shop, keeping her eyes low, willing them not to see her. The door was still open. She could escape out the back. She didn't slip her hand into the coat pocket to feel the knife—Kelpie didn't want to draw any attention—but she was glad it was there.

Further down the lane, a woman opened her front door and peered out.

"Get back inside, Missus," the copper yelled, his authority undermined by his voice going up half an octave.

The woman retreated. But her front window went up an inch. Kelpie noticed other open windows. She wondered how many were staring from behind curtains. She backed up half a step.

A few more and she'd be inside.

Two houses up from the one with the flowerpots, on the narrow path between two houses, Kelpie saw someone tall move. She couldn't make out the face, but it had to be Snowy.

"It's not a fight, Constable," Dymphna said. "They were mucking about. Bluey, close your razor."

Bluey closed his razor but didn't put it away and didn't take his eyes off the cop. He stepped towards him, almost standing on Darcy's feet as if he didn't see him there. Darcy dropped the flowerpot shard, scrambling from Bluey on his hands and heels.

"Stop right there. Both of youse!" The copper's voice shook.

Darcy stopped. Bluey took another step.

"I will fire." The copper sounded uncertain. Air moved against Kelpie's back as the grog-shop door slammed loud behind her.

The gun and closed razor were now pointing at her and Dymphna. Kelpie heard a tiny squeak for half a second. She didn't realise she'd made the sound. Dymphna held her palms out, smiled. "Really, Constable, there's no need—"

Bluey took another step towards the cop. Darcy scrambled out of the way.

The copper swung his gun back at Bluey.

"Don't!" Dymphna yelled.

Bluey took another step.

There was smoke and then a loud bang. Kelpie didn't quite connect them. Except that the copper staggered backward and the hand holding the gun dangled by his thigh.

Kelpie tried to figure out how Bluey could have hurt the copper without touching him when it was the copper who had the gun.

Bluey grunted, took several steps backward, clutched at his left shoulder. Darcy retrieved the shard and stood up.

The cop stared at his gun in disbelief.

Shearing Shed

Neal Darcy was fourteen when he went shearing. Legged it away from school with his youngest uncle and went bush to learn a trade. He sent back almost every penny he earned. Six months he was at it until the letter begging him to come home arrived from his ma.

The old man had abandoned her again. But not before losing most of their money on the trots. Most of it the money Darcy had sent back seeing as how, his ma wrote him, the old man lost his job for getting stuck into the boss to his face. She and the kids were near starving and they would lose the house if he didn't do something. *That house is all we have.*

Darcy went back as soon as he could. Was lucky enough that Father O'Brian found him a job at the brewery. He'd been looking after his ma and the littlies ever since.

But he'd loved the shearing life. He'd even loved it when he was a mere roustie picking up the wool as it fell from the shearer's blades, sweeping the floors. He loved the feel of the fleece in his fingers. The swag on his back. Bathing in a billabong. Sleeping under the stars. Not having to worry about his family. He knew that made him a bad son. He worried it made him as bad as his father.

Every night he wrote down what had happened. He wrote about his first lesson from one of the big guns, a bloke who could shear more than two hundred sheep a day. His notebook was so small he had to cramp his writing and fill it all the way to the edges and write in between the lines.

He wrote about his first fight. How his knuckles had turned blue and had swollen so much that holding the shears the next day was agony.

He learned that he loved writing more than anything in the world. Back in the city, it had been something he was good at, not something he couldn't live without.

Darcy even loved the sheep, though they were the stupidest animals he had ever come across. Too stupid to know what was in their own interest. Driven by fear but without the brains to survive. He figured they'd have gone extinct long ago if they hadn't been useful to humans.

He loved the camaraderie. Old, young, didn't matter. They were all blokes working together to bring in the most wool they could and getting full as a tick at the pub afterward. Telling stories by the fire. Singing together. Ogling the same girls.

At first he was the worst shearer who ever drew breath. Cut the sheep to pieces. Nearly took his own fingers besides. The more experienced guns laughed till they fell down. Turned out they'd given him the most obstreperous sheep they could find. That rare cussed, angry sheep with a will to kill. They did things like that to all the newies.

Before the first week was done, you wouldn't know Neal hadn't always been shearing sheep. The ones who didn't learn as fast as him were out quick smart on their backsides.

That was the life. Going to bed each night weary with a bone-deep ache. A good ache, not the soul-sucking ache of the city. Not the ache throughout his body and mind and heart and soul each evening as he returned from the brewery stinking of hops and yeast and wanting never to drink a drop of beer ever again.

Going back to the city—to his ma and brothers and sisters and to that stinking fucking brewery—had been the worst time of his life.

The only thing that kept him going was knowing they had no one else.

That and his stories.

DYMPHNA

Dymphna watched Bluey steady himself against the wall, wiping his right hand, sticky with blood from where the bullet hit his left shoulder, on the bricks. He pushed off, flicked open his cut-throat again, then took a heavy step towards Neal.

Why hadn't Neal run while he could? She couldn't stand to watch Bluey slash up his beautiful face.

But Bluey wasn't looking at Neal, who weaved gracefully out of his way. Bluey's eyes were on the copper. Dymphna reminded herself that that was worse. A dead copper was far more of a worry for Glory than a dead Neal Darcy.

"Stop that," the copper mumbled. "Don't come closer."

Dymphna wished he'd shoot Bluey again, wished she could tell him to, but the boy didn't raise his gun.

Bluey's razor was held high.

"Get back," the copper said. He tried to lift his hand, but it dropped back to his thigh. The recoil must have hurt it. Dymphna knew a bloke who'd broken his shoulder that way. But that had been a shotgun. She prayed that he'd pull himself together and take another shot. Instead the boy took a step backward, stumbling on something underfoot.

Dymphna grabbed Kelpie's hand. Time to get far away from this mess. To Circular Quay even.

"This way," she hissed, dragging Kelpie away from Bluey and the cop.

Neal smiled at her and followed. Dymphna tried to shrug off the way his slow smile made her feel. There was no time for any of that. For this brief moment, they were allies, but as soon as the three of them were away, he had to go back to his family. Neal had no idea what he'd walked into. Bluey could have killed him; Bluey still could kill him.

Kelpie dragged her feet, craning her neck to watch as Bluey slashed at the copper, his left arm still dangling. The razor sliced through the copper's hands brought up to protect his throat. He screamed and dropped the gun. Blood ran down his chin onto his arms.

Dymphna kept moving, dragging Kelpie behind her, but the little girl kept turning to look. Bluey slashed again, diagonally across the copper's face and then back across his throat.

"Jesus," Dymphna whispered.

Blood squirted across the lane. The copper pressed his hands to his neck, trying to hold the blood in. His screams wound down. He dropped to his knees.

Someone yelled. More than one person it sounded like. The news would be out soon. Glory would know. The coppers. Davidson.

"We've got to move," Neal said.

Dymphna stepped around a large pile of bricks; Kelpie stumbled on them. Dymphna righted her. Neal was just behind them.

Bluey roared.

Kelpie twisted around and shook off Dymphna's grip. "It's Snowy."

Dymphna turned.

Snowy was standing between them and Bluey. He had to have a full foot on Bluey—who lurched another half step towards them, waving the razor at waist height. Blood dripped steadily from his left sleeve.

"Put it down," Snowy said quietly.

Bluey kept moving.

Snowy brought his fists down hard on Bluey's head.

Bluey swayed, his eyes rolled up so they were mostly whites, but he did not fall. His right arm with the razor staccatoed through the air.

"Bloody, bloody . . ."

Dymphna couldn't hear the rest of what Bluey was saying. She held on to Kelpie with both hands.

Snowy picked up the copper's gun and hit Bluey hard on the head with it. Bluey went face first into the dirt, razor still in hand, and tried to push himself up.

"Bloody, bloody . . ."

Snowy belted him over the head again. This time Bluey stayed down. Snowy pocketed the gun.

Jimmy Palmer appeared beside Kelpie. "He's not dead yet. More's the pity."

"Oh, Christ," Dymphna said. "Glory's going to kill us. Bluey's not dead, is he?"

Snowy shook his head. Bluey's chest was moving.

"But the cop is," Snowy said. "Are you all right, Kelpie?"

Kelpie squeezed Dymphna's hand. Snowy patted her head.

Bluey groaned.

"Help me," Dymphna said, stepping closer. "Got to get him to the doctor."

"Better off scarpering," Neal said.

"Boy's right," Snowy said.

Dymphna ignored them and took one of Bluey's arms. If she carried Bluey to the doctor, it would look better with Glory. She still had a chance to stay in good with her, to not have to flee to another country. It would give her time to think.

Neal hesitated, then took the other arm; Snowy grabbed Bluey's legs.

"You should run," Snowy said. "How long do you think Glory's going to last without Bluey up and about?"

"She's got other men," Dymphna grunted. Bluey was surprisingly heavy for a man who was shorter than she was.

His eyes weren't properly closed. His eyelashes fluttered revealing whites but not irises; with all his scars, it made him look even more monstrous. Dymphna didn't see the razor anywhere. She wondered if Snowy or Neal had taken it.

Blood poured out of Bluey's head, but he was breathing evenly, and there was no blood coming from his mouth.

Kelpie danced ahead to the grog shop. One of the boys opened the door. Doc was already there; he'd put an apron on.

"He dead?" Doc didn't sound much concerned.

Kelpie shook her head and followed him back to his office where she hovered by the door, watching them carry Bluey in and lay him on the doctor's desk. His head and legs dangled over the edges.

Dymphna stood beside Kelpie at the doorway, putting an arm around the girl's shoulders. They could not be the same age. The doc had to have been mistaken.

Neal stepped back from Bluey, wiping his hands. He gave Dymphna another wry smile and slid past her to stand in the corridor.

The doc was already bending over Bluey. Snowy stepped away to lean against the crates of liquor.

"Pass me one of them bottles," the doc said. Snowy did.

The boy who'd opened the door whispered to Kelpie, "You sure he's not dead?"

"He's breathing," Kelpie whispered back. "Lot of blood. Could still die."

She sounded happy about it.

"Hope so," the boy whispered. He stayed by the door.

Jimmy appeared inside the doctor's office watching the doc examining Bluey.

"Go get water," Dymphna told the boy. He blushed. Dymphna smiled at him, and he went even redder. "Get your mate to help. Clean up that trail of blood so it doesn't lead in here. Wet up and down the lane. It'll stay the cops for a bit. Go on, both of you. You want the cops on us as well as Glory? Do it fast!"

The boy ran.

"I'll need some of that water," the doctor shouted after him.

"You should go," Dymphna told Neal. He was leaning against the wall rolling a cigarette back and forth between his fingers. His eye was nearly swollen shut. "Before anything else happens."

"I'll be all right. I'll nick off when I have to." He grinned.

Dymphna bit back the urge to snap at him that this was not a lark, that he could have been killed.

"Hope Bluey dies," Jimmy said. "Even if it does leave Glory exposed."

Dymphna was fairly sure everyone hoped that. Except her. Gloriana Nelson exposed right now meant Dymphna with little protection from Mr. Davidson.

"Though if he dies," Jimmy asked Kelpie, "is there a chance Bluey could haunt Dymphna too? Fucked if I want to spend the rest of me days listening to that stupid mongrel bastard."

Dymphna kept herself from shuddering.

"Now's the time to get away," Snowy said.

"Pass me towels," Doc said. Dymphna grabbed a handful from the pile by the door and tossed them to Snowy, who handed them to the doctor.

"Where's that water?" the doc asked.

"Coming," Dymphna told him. "What about the constable?" she said to Snowy. "Can't leave him on the lane."

Snowy stared at her. "Not our worry. We need to get out of here."

Dymphna stared back at him, wanting to question his use of the word *we*. He was Davidson's. They weren't a *we*. "Glory said no bodies."

"Not our lookout."

There he was again, talking as if they were in this together. The dead cop might not be Snowy's lookout, but it was definitely

Dymphna's. She didn't want to think about how many had seen Bluey kill the cop or how many had already run around the corner to tell Glory. She certainly didn't want the cops finding the body. A dead copper? Even such a young one. They'd tear Razorhurst apart until they found the culprit.

It wasn't a full day since Jimmy had died, and now another dead one. Bluey had better stay alive.

The smaller of the boys returned with a bucket of water for Doc, who commenced washing his arms past his elbows.

"Glory didn't want any bodies," Dymphna repeated. "There's a dead cop out there. I think that counts." She turned to where the doctor was working on Bluey. "She'll be none too keen on Bluey dying either."

"He'll live," Doc said, removing Bluey's jacket and tearing away his shirt, both soaked with blood. But not as badly as Jimmy's clothes had been. Bluey was sweating, which Jimmy Palmer would never do again.

Snowy left the room.

Outside a police siren sounded.

Neal Darcy flinched but didn't say a word.

Snowy returned. "The body's been shifted. Glory's boys, most like. Or the boy's mother had him brought in. He lived with her down the other end of the lane."

Which was why the copper was there, Dymphna realised. Home for lunch. He hadn't been much older than she was.

"Those two boys did what you said. Neighbours are helping. Water's everywhere."

"Great. Now we can go," Dymphna said. Back to Gloriana's, she decided. If she went straight there, she could explain. How Bluey had lost control, attacked unprovoked. Glory knew how he was.

Neal said nothing. But there was a hint of a smile in his eyes. Dymphna couldn't believe he was enjoying this.

"We'll go out the back way," Snowy said.

"Don't bloody go with him," Jimmy said. "Tell her, Kelpie. She can't go with Snowy. He's as good as said he'd take her to him!"

Kelpie said nothing. Dymphna itched to tell Jimmy that Snowy had been far more concerned about Kelpie than he was about Dymphna. She wished he'd be quiet; she had no intention of going with Snowy.

"What do you mean *we*?" she said to him. "I'm going out the front. Same as I came in."

2 gtt

"Into the arms of the coppers?"

"Almost everyone who lives around here is Glory's. They're not going to tell the police anything."

"What do you think Glory's going to do to young Darcy here?"

"I'm not afraid of Gloriana Nelson," Neal said. He didn't sound afraid. Though he should have been.

"Nothing," Dymphna said, which was what she hoped, but she had no idea. Glory was unpredictable. "He didn't do anything. Didn't lay a finger on Bluey. Besides, he'll head home."

"He was following you."

"I was looking out for her," Neal objected.

Snowy snorted.

"You didn't hear that," Dymphna told Doc. "You're not hearing any of this."

"I don't hear nothing. I don't tell Glory nothing. She knows that. I don't know who either of these gentlemen are, and I don't care. Though the one in the corridor should get some ice on his face. Icebox is behind the bar. You'll have a shiner otherwise." He resumed his work on Bluey.

"You were following us too, and you're Davidson's, Snowy." Dymphna lowered her voice. "You killed Palmer."

Snowy did not respond.

"Didn't hear that neither," Doc muttered, cleaning the hole in Bluey's left shoulder. The edges of the bullet hole were black where the bullet had burned its way into his body.

"Glory's out for me whatever happens," Snowy said. "But she doesn't have to get her hands on Darcy. Let's go."

"Where's Snowy going to take her? To Davidson. She needs to get down to the Quay and on a boat." Jimmy was yelling at Kelpie, his face darkening. "Tell her!"

"I'm heading back to Glory's," Dymphna said. "She's expecting me. I'm telling her what happened."

"How do you think that's going to work?" Snowy asked. You don't think she has eyes? Who do you think moved the copper? Glory's not going to be pleased when you lie to her."

"I'm not going to lie to her."

"How you going to explain Bluey attacking Darcy?"

"Bluey's not right in the head. Everyone knows that."

"Then there's Davidson. He's not going to let any of this go, Dymphna. He'll drag you out of Glory's if he has to."

"He wouldn't."

"Maybe not before. But Bluey's out of action now."

Another siren sounded. Kelpie eased closer to the back door, tugging at Dymphna's skirt. "Don't want to go back to Glory," she whispered.

Dymphna had to decide.

"Listen to me," Snowy said. "I can get you somewhere safe. Kelp and Darcy here too. Then I'll deal with Davidson. See what we can do to get the truce back in place."

Dymphna shook her head. "Glory's two men down. You really think *now* is when Mr. Davidson's going to ease off?"

"Maybe not, but you need to be elsewhere. We all need to. I know a place."

Doc looked up from cleaning Bluey's wounds. "I need to get this bullet out. I need fewer people in here. I need quiet."

Someone started pounding on the front door.

Snowy pushed past Kelpie and opened the back door, looked both ways, and then gestured them through.

Neal closed the back door behind them. There was no lane. The grog shop backed onto a dilapidated ruin of a house, sharing the one fence.

Snowy pointed to the yard next door. "We'll go over the fence, then yard to yard," he began. Dymphna heard shouting. "Reckon they're searching all the houses on the lane."

Kelpie scrambled over the fence to the ruined house. There was no door.

Snowy gave Dymphna a leg-up, and she jumped over and followed Kelpie into the abandoned house, telling herself she could still get back to Glory and explain what had happened.

Gaol Time

Dymphna had only been in gaol once. Glory had long since lost count of her stays in the lock-up. Snowy and Bluey likewise. So much so that Snowy was thinking hard on another profession, on getting out from under Mr. Davidson's control and away.

Snowy did not like gaol, not after that first long stay.

Bluey had never minded it. Didn't seem that much different to normal life. Just as many afraid of him in there as out here and easier to get at them 'cause there were that many fewer places to hide. Sure the guards'd smack you around, but Bluey didn't feel pain. Didn't bother him one way or the other, 'specially if he got to have a go at them later on the sly.

Glory had spent more than her fair share of time behind bars. But for the last decade she'd had money and connections, and gaol time had become considerably shorter and more comfortable. Now Glory treated lock-up as a holiday, using her time there to rest up and scheme and recruit new girls. They came to her in droves because she had the money and influence to protect them in gaol. So surely, they figured, she could do even better for them outside.

Women's gaol was much worse than the men's. The prisoners were at the mercy of the screws, and those who couldn't buy them off were sometimes traded for use in the men's gaol.

Gaol was where Dymphna Campbell met Gloriana Nelson. Gaol was where Glory saved Dymphna.

Before Glory took her in hand, promising to make her Glory's best girl, Dymphna's despair had grown large enough to encompass thoughts of taking her own life.

Glory had put all such thoughts from her mind. *Use what you're good at, my girl. Use it for you, not for them. It's what I did.* She didn't have to say, *And now look at me.* The diamond bracelet on her wrist glittered. No one else was permitted jewellery in the lock-up. But Gloriana Nelson could do whatever she wished.

Dymphna Campbell was impressed.

✂ KELPIE ✂

Dymphna and Darcy and Snowy followed her into the wreck of a house as Kelpie'd hoped they would. She felt more at ease than she had since . . . well, since before climbing the window into Mrs. Stone's. This was her world.

She knew those smells: dust, mildew, rot, rat dung, pigeon droppings. Spider webs everywhere. But no piles of newspaper. No signs anyone had slept there recently. Probably because the floor had too many holes in it to support the weight of a sleeping body.

The roof was gone, and wind swept through the gaps between the boards. There were no rooms anymore, not much to distinguish outside from inside. The house had subsided so much the gap between boards and dirt underneath was negligible. The glass in the windows, the wooden frames, the pipes, door-handles—everything that could be salvaged—had long since been carted away. Nothing left worth stealing.

Kelpie'd have bet anything there was a demolition order stuck to what remained of the front door. Probably the whole block had an order. Houses this bad they almost always tore down. Eventually. Like Frog Hollow.

Though this wreck looked ready to fall on its own.

Snowy stepped past her. A floorboard cracked under his weight, almost as loud as a gunshot.

They froze.

She could hear shouting but not what was being said or who was saying it. Further away, the humming clangour of traffic. Closer to them a dog barked. Someone yelled to shush it. If the coppers were chasing them, there was no point in standing still. Even if the cops didn't hear them, they might be able to see them though the gaps in the walls.

Kelpie tapped Snowy on the back, stepping quietly into a hole connecting to the next cottage. The holes were solid ground. She stepped from that hole to the next, hoping he was smart enough to follow her and that the holes were big enough for his feet.

Snowy followed quietly, Dymphna and Darcy behind him. Kelpie could hear their breathing, the sounds their shoes made flicking the edges of the floorboards. She worried they were loud enough to be heard outside.

"You'd think," Palmer said beside her, "neither of them ever had to get away quiet-like before."

Kelpie heard yelling, male voices, but she couldn't tell how far away. She heard no fences crashing in.

"That's the cops, if you were wondering," Palmer said.

Kelpie quickened her pace, bouncing from hole to hole.

"Like a bloody rabbit you are, they're more like donkeys."

She paused, touching the sawn edges of the hole in the wall. Someone had created a path through. She'd been in abandoned houses like these before.

This cottage hadn't sunk into its foundations, and remnants of the ceiling remained. Like the first house it had been stripped of everything valuable, but there were fewer holes in the floor and the walls, and there was a wall between the front and back rooms. They couldn't be seen from outside in this one.

The only cobwebs were on the ceiling. Two swags were rolled up in the far corner with no dust on them. People lived here. From the smell they were using the back room as a dunny.

On the other side was another neatly sawn hole leading to another cottage. Kelpie led the way, carefully picking out the least noisy path, avoiding planks with obvious signs of rot, nails that had worked partway out. Only Snowy matched her step for step.

The next cottage had subsided so much they had to drop down into it. What remained of the floorboards kissed the earth.

This one was almost as decayed as the first, but less porous; it reeked of alcohol. The floor was littered with broken bottles, kicked aside to clear a path to the next cottage.

A floorboard cracked loud enough to make her ears ring.

Darcy let out a half-yelp as his jaws snapped shut. She turned. He'd stepped through a rotten board and dropped an inch.

They all froze.

"Bloody moron," Palmer said. "The pretty ones are always stupid."

Kelpie could hear Darcy and Dymphna breathing. Herself too. A couple walked by outside. They were arguing. But she couldn't hear about what. Further away the traffic was punctuated by a tram bell. But no sirens. No sounds of the police. She wished she could ask Palmer what he heard.

A door slammed. Dymphna startled. Kelpie looked at Palmer. "Not here," he told her.

Darcy started to pull his leg up. The floorboard made a cracking sound. Snowy put his finger over his lips and moved lightly to Darcy, testing each board before he put his weight on it. *That was how you did it*, Kelpie thought, *not galumphing like an elephant.*

Snowy bent down and slowly pulled Darcy's trouser leg up. The trouser was torn but the skin underneath wasn't. Snowy held the edge of the broken floorboard up and Darcy eased his foot out. The shoe was half off. He bent to put it back on and lace it more firmly. He half smiled at Dymphna to let her know he wasn't hurt. Palmer rolled his eyes and Kelpie itched to smack him. Darcy wasn't stupid and it wasn't his fault he didn't know how to move around properly in an abandoned house. He had a mum and a job. He shouldn't have to.

In the fifth house Snowy whispered in Kelpie's ear, "You think this one's safe?"

"People." Kelpie pointed to the swag barely visible under a broken floorboard in the corner of the room.

"They're not here now."

Kelpie turned to stare at Snowy. "It's theirs." She would never encroach on anyone else's kipping place. It wasn't right.

"Could've been there awhile. Maybe they're not coming back."

Kelpie shook her head. There was no dust on the swags.

Snowy shrugged. "When there's one that'll work let me know."

Dymphna and Darcy caught up. Both panting.

Kelpie pushed through to the next house. From cottage to broken cottage they crept. Kelpie in front, Snowy in rear. Dymphna and Darcy were being more careful, but still did not test their weight as often nor tread as lightly as they could. They stopped half a dozen times because of too loud a creak, Darcy sneezing, Dymphna leaning on a wall that threatened to collapse.

Kelpie could have strangled them both.

She went as fast as she could without leaving them behind.

Part of her wanted to. But she didn't even know where they were. Darlinghurst, she thought Dymphna had said, or Palmer, but she wasn't sure.

The only place she knew to run to was the Hills, Glory's domain.

Snowy was an orphan. Raised in Frog Hollow by Old Ma.

As if he were her own son. Old Ma was generous that way, though she'd never admit it.

When Snowy was fourteen, he brought a girl to Old Ma because he'd got her in trouble. He should have known better than that. Old Ma had taught him better than that.

Old Ma looked after the girl while she lived, which wasn't long, and the baby after she died. That baby girl received almost every ounce of Old Ma's love. The love that had been Snowy's. Her heart had broke when Snowy became a standover man.

She understood why. Weren't a whole lot of other options for the likes of Snowy. No one wanted him for an apprentice. They'd heard that black boys didn't work hard. Old Ma'd never seen a boy work harder than Snowy, but no one would listen to her, he kept running away from the public school, and she couldn't afford to send him to St. Patrick's. Snowy was thieving when he was little, threatening when he was big. He was under Mr. Davidson's wing by the time he was fifteen and already more than six foot tall.

Old Ma wept. But she understood. Snowy gave Old Ma a big chunk of his money and visited when he could.

He was in gaol the first time when he was sixteen. At first he didn't mind. He was the biggest, strongest bloke in there. They left him alone, and the chaplain decided to teach him. The chaplain tried to teach all the boys, with many more failures than successes. Snowy was a quick learner, which made the chaplain believe he was a good teacher.

Snowy learned to read, and that was useful. But it was the numbers he loved. Under the chaplain's tutelage, he went from basic arithmetic to percentages and fractions and even the wonder of algebra.

Gaol was good to Snowy. As good as it could be, which was not very good.

Getting out was a lot better. Meant he saw Old Ma a few more times before she died, tried to look out for Kelpie as best he could. He went looking for licit work, but there wasn't any for a black man just out of prison with a scar on his face and fists bigger than some people's heads. Legitimate fighting was out 'cause white fellas wouldn't step into the ring with him.

He went back to work for Mr. Davidson. But he was stronger and smarter now. Mr. Davidson gave him more responsibilities and more money. Snowy took the work, not because he wanted it but because he couldn't find any other way of living. Passed as much of the money as he could on to Old Ma. He didn't see as much of her or Kelpie as he wanted. Mr. Davidson liked to have Snowy close at hand, called him his bodyguard, his right-hand man. Other businessmen—legit and not so legit—found Snowy bowel loosening.

He didn't want to go back to gaol. Working for Davidson meant he would definitely go back to gaol. He went back to gaol. In and out. More years in than out.

A week after Old Ma died, he bleached his hair. It was his own tribute. He kept it that way to remember that he'd failed the only mother he'd ever had, that he'd failed Kelpie too.

DYMPHNA

Dymphna had lost count of how many dirty, broken hovels they'd picked their way through. She was cold and tired and wishing she'd gone straight to Gloriana when she'd had the chance.

Cockroaches skittered away as Snowy ushered them past a torn old curtain into a back room.

Kelpie was staring up at what remained of the ceiling. Sunlight dappled her face through the holes in the roof. She was almost pretty. Dymphna didn't believe for a second that the doctor was right about her and Kelpie being the same age.

"He wants you to hide in the middle of a fucking thieves-and-hobos thoroughfare?" Jimmy asked Kelpie. "Genius plan, that is."

Dymphna had assumed they were exiting through the back door. It looked solid but had no handle or lock. Snowy was making no attempt to get it open.

"I'll be back for you soon," Snowy whispered.

Both Dymphna and Neal opened their mouths to speak, but he held up his hand.

"You have to be quiet." He pointed at the back door. "I won't be more than an hour. I'll be back with a motor-car."

Neal snorted. His eye was now swollen completely shut.

"You want us to wait here?" Dymphna said softly. Snowy and Neal leaned in to hear. "Why should we trust you?" She had no intention of waiting in this hole. She could hear pigeons cooing in the roof. She could smell them too; the floor was dotted with droppings.

"Why are you helping Dymphna," Neal asked, "when you work for Davidson? I might not be one of your mob, but I know that much."

Dymphna looked at Snowy. She wanted to know too. Snowy looked at Kelpie.

They were close enough that Dymphna could smell the tobacco on Neal's breath. The faint mint on Snowy's.

Jimmy snorted. "God. How long has it been? Last night we were going to run all this—her and me—King and Queen of Razorhurst! Now look at us."

Kelpie didn't respond. She'd become so much better at ignoring Jimmy. Dymphna was impressed.

"I'm not helping Dymphna," Snowy said at last, his voice low. "I'm helping Kelpie . . . I knew her mother."

"She'll be safer with me," Dymphna whispered. "I'm going to go back to Glory. She can protect us both. Bluey's not her only muscle."

"You're not safe with Glory. None of you are."

"You're not safe with either of them, girl," Jimmy said. "Tell her, Kelpie. She has to get out of this city. Out of this country."

"I know Mr. Davidson's trying to muscle in on Glory," Dymphna whispered. "Break the truce, take over everything. But he won't succeed. Glory's too strong."

Jimmy laughed. "She doesn't believe that. We were going to take it all over because Glory was getting weak. She has to run!"

Dymphna wished Jimmy wouldn't yell.

"Why should I wait here?" she asked.

"Because I might have to move on Davidson. He's not fit to . . . He's not what he was."

Dymphna stared at him.

"Well, that's the truth," Jimmy said. "But I don't see Snowy doing for his boss. He ain't the type."

"But I have to make sure the time is right. I have to keep his trust a little longer."

"You want us to sit here until you get it all sorted?" Dymphna said, making it clear what she thought of Snowy's plan.

"Are you looking to be Jimmy Palmer's replacement?" Neal asked.

Snowy smiled. His lips didn't just turn up; he smiled. Dymphna had never seen him smile like that before. It made his eyes brighter. She had to put her hand over her mouth to suppress a laugh.

"What?" Neal was annoyed.

"Snowy doesn't want to be my man. It's not like that. We're friends. I've never seen Snowy with any woman."

"I stay away from white women, is what I do," Snowy said softly. "Not worth the trouble."

Jimmy laughed. "But not white men."

Neal looked sulky and angry at the same time. Dymphna squeezed his hand.

Kelpie looked mystified. "I saw you kissing a woman."

"Did you?" Snowy ruffled her hair. "Can't have been recently."

"Old Ma was still alive. He did promise Old Ma," Kelpie told Neal.

"Snowy's been keeping an eye out for me for years. He's saved me before."

Neal looked at her. Kelpie returned the gaze, which was unlike her. Neal nodded briefly. He believed her. Dymphna did too. Snowy had always treated her well, but he would not go out of his way for Dymphna Campbell. Kelpie, it was clear, was another matter.

Dymphna found herself looking from Snowy to Kelpie and back again. They couldn't be, could they?

"Why are *you* here?" Snowy asked Neal. "Are *you* looking to be Jimmy Palmer's replacement?"

Neal's fists clenched.

Dymphna sighed. They did not have time for the two of them to be squaring off against each other. Neal might know some boxing, but Snowy was twice his size and knew how to hurt a man. How to kill him too.

"He's a writer," Kelpie said quietly. "He's here for an adventure. You saw him grinning, didn't you, Dymphna? He's going to write about everything that happened today."

Now it took two hands to keep the laughter in. One of the worst days of her life and Neal Darcy thought it was an *adventure*?

Neal blushed, but his fists unclenched.

"Adventure?" Dymphna asked in a low voice. "Is that what you call this, Kelpie? Jesus Christ."

"Makes sense," Snowy said. "We all want to rescue the maiden."

"I can rescue myself," Dymphna said. If they'd let her.

"Maybe," Jimmy said. "But not if you stay here."

"I gotta get back to Mr. Davidson," Snowy said. "Keep it down. Stay away from the windows, the door. I'll be back soon."

Snowy ducked past the curtain before Dymphna had time to object. She did object. She turned to stop him and say so, but Kelpie was faster, following him past the torn curtain.

Dymphna watched as Kelpie tugged Snowy's arm, so that he bent all the way down to her level, and whispered something softly into his ear that Dymphna couldn't hear.

"It's July," Snowy said, his words barely carrying to her. "You'll be sixteen in two weeks. Sixteen. You wouldn't think it to look at you, would you? Better find you more food."

He tousled Kelpie's hair and made his way out of the house.

For half a second, Dymphna thought she might throw up. She and Kelpie truly were the same age.

Cockatoos

It's remarkable how many standover and razor men got their start as cockatoos, keeping an eye out for the cops. Or the boss while cards were played, after-hours grog was imbibed, or the sweet heaven from China was smoked.

A good cockie was keen eyed, fast, stealthy, with an earsplitting whistling technique. It was all about the lungs. Cooees emitted had to be loud and long. A cockie kept his eyes peeled, ready to give the alarm when the coppers or other ingressors showed and then scarper swift and loud as possible.

The best cockies were young. No more than twelve or fourteen. If you were standing cockatoo when you were a full-grown man, well, then everyone knew you weren't ever going to amount to anything. Not in the straight world and definitely not in the bent. Might as well kill yourself and be done with it.

Both Palmer and Snowy had started as cockatoos. Both were done with it long before they turned twelve. They'd already grown to a man's height and would only get taller. There were plenty of more profitable ways to use big, strong men than having them standing lookout.

Bluey had also tried to be a cockatoo. He lasted exactly one job.

He was keen eyed and swift, and a total failure as a cockie. He thought it was funny, at the age of six, to run in, kick a copper in the shins, and then scarper. Then there was his voice: he was hard pressed to speak too much above a whisper and could manage only the breathiest whistle. He was much better at thieving and smashing.

But Glory found uses for him. Even then she could see that Bluey's evil would be useful.

>— KELPIE —<

Kelpie was sixteen years old. She'd been born in the month of July. She wondered why Snowy'd never told her before. She counted backward on her fingers. In 1916. That was right, wasn't it? This was 1932. Sixteen years ago was 1916.

How did he know? Had Snowy known her parents? Had he seen her born? He must have been remembering what Old Ma had told him. He'd known when it was her tenth birthday.

"Wish I had a cigarette," Darcy whispered. He looked funny with one eye red and purple and swollen shut.

Kelpie was glad he didn't have a cigarette. Tobacco smoke made her eyes water.

Kelpie and Darcy stood in the middle of the room. Kelpie had hidden in worse places. There was plenty of light, not that many cockroaches, and no mould growing up the walls. The floorboards weren't rotten.

Dymphna paced, the floorboards sighing and shifting and creaking under her weight.

"Why did you tell them about me writing?" Darcy asked Kelpie, watching Dymphna go back and forth.

"It was true, wasn't it? If you wrote about what happened today, it would sell for sure, like that one that's going to be read on the radio."

"How'd you know about that?"

"I heard it somewhere." She hadn't heard that *somewhere*. Miss Lee had told her, proud as punch.

"Ma must've told people." For a moment Darcy sounded as young as she was—*and Dymphna too*, Kelpie reminded herself.

"Would have been because she was proud," Dymphna said. "How many people do you know who've had something they wrote on the radio? I don't know anyone who has."

"Hasn't happened yet. But I got paid already."

Outside there was a loud sound like a gunshot. Kelpie held her breath. Darcy and Dymphna reached for each other's hands. Then there was the sound of a motor-car driving away.

"Motor-car backfiring," Palmer said. He leaned against the back door, his head not far below where the ceiling used to be, watching the three of them. Kelpie could tell he wasn't happy with what he saw. But at least they were alive. "Hope that's enough to get her arse in gear before Snowy gets back here with Mr. Davidson in tow." For once he wasn't shouting. "Doubt it. Starting to think she wants to die."

"Backfiring," Kelpie whispered. Dymphna didn't want to die. Kelpie was sure of it.

Dymphna pulled her hand from Darcy's. Her cheeks were pink. She resumed her pacing.

"Phew, eh?" Darcy said. He smiled at Kelpie. It was a lovely smile. Made his eyes seem brighter. She couldn't help smiling back. Kelpie wanted to ask him more about his stories. How'd he know where to begin? Who to tell stories about? Were they only about real people? She thought of his Kitty Macintosh, who was a gangster's girl and looked exactly like Dymphna Campbell and who died. Killed by her own man.

Dymphna kept pacing. She hugged herself with her gloved hands. "We should go," she said. But Kelpie wasn't sure who she was saying that to. She wasn't looking at Darcy or Kelpie.

They hadn't heard any yelling for a while. Just the wind, people passing by. It made Kelpie more nervous. It shouldn't be this quiet.

"It doesn't sit right. Waiting like this," Dymphna said. "We should go back to Glory. Me and Kelpie should. You can go home, Neal. I'll make sure it's all right for you."

"How's she going to do that exactly?" Palmer asked. "Glory'll want somebody's blood."

"Not leaving," Darcy said. He smiled. "It's the most excitement I've had since I was out bush."

"Excitement—" Dymphna broke off because her voice was too loud. She quieted. "You going to write a story about all of this? Being attacked by a razor man? Hiding from criminals with a fallen woman?"

"You're not a—"

"I am."

"How old are you?" Kelpie interrupted in a whisper, looking at Darcy. She didn't want them fighting. They'd get loud. She didn't know why she was asking. Just that she had to.

"Nineteen," Darcy said.

"Tell her you dunno," Dymphna said at the same time.

Kelpie sighed and dropped into a cross-legged position, not caring about the pigeon shit or that they should be on the run like Palmer said. She felt as if someone had let the air out of her. Nineteen wasn't much older than sixteen.

Darcy and Dymphna seemed old to her. They were grown up and she wasn't. They weren't part of the same kind of people as she was. She was little. They were big. Welfare would never pull them aside for walking down the street when school was on. They would never be asked where their parents were.

Kelpie had never thought about people's ages before. People were either grown-ups or they weren't. She only thought about it if they said, like Tommy and Maisie had. Ghosts who died young always told you their age. They were the ones who found it hardest to be dead. Always moaning about how young they were, *Only eleven! Only fifteen! Only seventeen! Only twenty-one!* And how much they were missing out on. *No one ever kissed me! I never got rid of me virginity! I was about to get married! I wanted to have bubs!*

But she had no idea how old Miss Lee had been. Or Old Ma. Or her ma and pa. She didn't know how old Snowy was, except that he had to be older than Darcy. That doctor said he was thirty-five, and he looked much older than Snowy. Did that make Snowy twenty-four? Twenty-eight?

"How old are you?" she asked, looking straight at Palmer.

"Thirty-six. Though I started to lie about me age. Doesn't matter anymore, does it? I could be your dad. Dymphna's too. Not to mention that Darcy fella there." He looked sad.

"I told you," Darcy said. "Nineteen."

Kelpie started.

She had asked a ghost a question in front of the living. Something she had not done since she really had been little, back when Old Ma was still alive.

She hadn't forgotten Dymphna and Darcy were right there, standing over her. She wasn't being careless. Not exactly. It was more like there were worse things. Gloriana Nelson worse. Mr. Davidson worse. Blood everywhere worse.

Still, slipping up like that worried her.

She breathed like Old Ma taught her. But it didn't help.

Jimmy Palmer was older than the doctor even though he looked younger. Kelpie didn't know what to do with that information. She didn't know what to do with any of this information.

She felt more upended by the news that she really and truly was the same age as Dymphna Campbell than she had been by Palmer's dead body, or the copper's, or by running from the police. Meeting Glory. Having Bluey for a guardian. Seeing a man get shot. None of it made her feel this way.

She felt like . . . She didn't know how she felt. Her world wasn't the way it had been. She wasn't who she thought she was.

If Kelpie was sixteen, that meant she was almost a grown-up. If she'd lived a life like Darcy had, with a family, she would have finished school by now. She'd be finding a job in one of the factories, making clothes, shoes. Or working in a shop selling them. Or she'd be working for someone like Glory or Mr. Davidson.

Though probably not. If you had a family, they protected you from having to do work like that, and even if they couldn't, she wasn't pretty like Dymphna. She wasn't even as pretty as Lettie or Dazzle.

Or she'd be trying to find work. Half the grown-ups in the Hills were looking for work. But most of them didn't find any.

What else did girls do?

They got married. But then their husbands beat them, or ran away, or the wives did. Like the lodger at the Darcys'. Or the husbands drank all the money they made so there wasn't enough for food.

Kelpie did not want any of that.

Kelpie never thought about the future. Why would she? She didn't have a home. She didn't have people. She didn't have a future.

Except as a ghost. Kelpie thought about *that* future often. She knew what could happen when she was dead. She didn't know what could happen to her alive and fully grown. She was sixteen. Could be that she wouldn't grow another inch.

What did it mean not being a kid anymore? Even if she still looked like one? How long would that last? She crossed her arms to cover her—what had the doctor called them?—mammary glands. They were tender. The doctor was right.

Dymphna sat down next to her. "Are you all right, kiddo?"

Kelpie said yes, though it wasn't true. Darcy sat down. The sun shone in through the broken roof. She could smell dung and urine. Probably possums up there too. They'd be asleep. Possums slept during the day and screamed like banshees at night.

"We're the same age," Kelpie said to Dymphna.

Darcy gasped. "You're sixteen?" he said, looking at Dymphna.

"I am," Dymphna said.

"But that's imposs—"

Dymphna cut him off with a look. The way Glory had cut Dymphna off earlier. For a moment, Kelpie could imagine Dymphna turning into Gloriana, ruling Razorhurst.

"Kelpie, you wanted to say more?" Dymphna said.

Kelpie didn't know what to say, or how to say it. She had spoken more today than she had since Miss Lee faded. Even then she'd never spoken *this* much in one day. She'd asked a ghost a question in front of the living. She was breaking all the rules. It felt like a bad omen. She held her hands wide in front of her. "There's so much I don't know."

Palmer sat in front of them, angled for the best view of Dymphna. He hadn't said anything since he told Kelpie his age. Him being quiet unnerved her.

"I can read. But I don't know my numbers. Not like they teach them at school." Kelpie could count and do a little bit of adding and minusing, but she'd had a squiz in the windows of every school in the Hills and seen how much she didn't know. Blackboards covered in big numbers mixed with letters and symbols she didn't recognise.

Back then it hadn't bothered her. She hadn't known the point of letters until Miss Lee taught her. But once she'd learned her letters, she could tell that numbers were important too.

Miss Lee was the beginning of learning how small her world was. She had told Kelpie to keep reading, but Kelpie was increasingly sure she needed to know more than she could glean from discarded newspapers and chance encounters with books. She hadn't dared the library since Miss Lee faded.

Most of what Kelpie didn't know wasn't in books. She didn't even know enough about living people to tell how old they were. She hadn't even known how old *she* was. She still didn't know. Not for sure. Snowy could be wrong.

She didn't know how to buy a ticket on a tram. She didn't know how to dress. Even if she'd had the money, she had no idea how to go about buying clothes. How did you take pieces of fabric and turn them into something you could wear? How did you know what would fit you? She didn't know how to turn raw food into something more wonderful, like a pie or fish and chips. She didn't even know how to make porridge.

"I don't know how . . ." She was going to say *how the living live*. But she couldn't say that because then she'd have to explain about ghosts. Funny how the things she *did* know were all things the living didn't. "What's going to happen to me?"

"I'll look after you, love." Dymphna put her arm around Kelpie. Kelpie leaned into her, appalled to realise that her eyes were stinging the way they did when tears were trying to slip out. "Glory always forgives me, no matter what happens. She likes you. I could tell. It will be all right."

"We'll both look after you," Darcy said, sitting on her other side. For a moment, Kelpie felt like they were her parents. "Ma likes you too. She'd already decided to keep an eye out for you."

"She was going to send me to the sisters. Put me in an orphanage. Make me go to school."

"She would never," Darcy said.

Kelpie wasn't sure of it. Maybe Darcy believed what he said, but she was not at all convinced about his ma.

"Well, school, yes," Darcy continued. "But not an orphanage."

Kelpie wished that was true. "Will you let me read your stories?"

"'Course."

She wanted to tell him how much she liked them. How much she wanted to read them all through from beginning to end.

"Teach me how to use your typewriter?"

"If you want."

"I want to write stories. Like you."

Darcy smiled at her. "I bet you've got plenty."

Her stories would be about ghosts. If she wrote 'em down everyone would think she'd made them up for a story, not that she was touched in the head. Miss Lee had always marvelled at the things Darcy made up, and everything he wrote was normal everyday living-people things. She could work the same trick.

Kelpie closed her eyes and went to sleep. Not all the way down. She had long since learned to sleep when she could, as lightly as she could. It was something else she knew that most people didn't.

The kind of talent that you learned when you grew up among ghosts.

Neal Darcy's Typewriter

Neal Darcy saw the typewriter on display at Gold's, the smallest pawnbroker on Oxford Street. It was as if she was calling to him. Rays of sunlight through the grimy window made the glass keys of the typewriter glow. Golden dust motes danced in the air around it as if to say, *Here she is, your typewriter, the essential tool in your journey to becoming the famous writer that you know you must be.*

Neal had to have it.

But it cost almost a brick—eight pounds.

Eight pounds was more money than Neal Darcy'd ever had, more than three weeks' wages. Those eight pounds that Neal did not have weighed him down for the rest of the week as he went to work each day and then home the long way via Gold's on Oxford Street because he couldn't not make sure that the typewriter was still there.

The typewriter never glowed again as it had that first day. But Neal didn't care. It was the most glorious thing he had ever seen.

He thought about stealing it. But smashing a window and taking a typewriter was many steps up from a little shoplifting. Where would it lead? His family couldn't afford to have him in gaol, and even if he wasn't caught, his ma would want to know where it came from. She almost always knew when he was lying.

There was no space in Neal's life for mistakes. He couldn't afford to sleep in or get sick, let alone serve gaol time. Not being able to work meant no money, which meant his family would be one step closer to living on the streets. He still wanted that typewriter. He *needed* that typewriter. With it he could type his stories so they looked classy enough for publication. He was still smarting from the neatly typed letter that deemed his handwritten story unprofessional and illegible.

That Sunday, Neal went to church. He rarely did. Sundays were Neal's writing days. Church was hours of wasted writing time and far too much temptation. There were too many flirtatious, curvy, laughing girls in church. Especially Lettie Ryan, who glowed almost as much as his typewriter had. Wasn't right for her to be that pretty, and prettier every time he saw her, and smiling at him that way. Neal couldn't afford to get into trouble and wind up married with five kids of his own and no way of ever affording a typewriter.

Neal listened to the father's sermon, kept his eyes steadfastly away from Lettie Ryan's, took communion, confessed, and then did something he'd never done before: asked Father O'Brian to lend him money.

"A typewriter, is it?" Father O'Brian said, looking at Neal as if he was asking to borrow money to buy the Taj Mahal.

"It's for my stories," Neal said. The father knew he wrote. He'd won best essay at St. Peter's three years in a row and once for the whole district. "I want to send them out." Neal paused. "For publication, for money. There are places, Father, that will pay for stories." Neal wasn't sure if the father would believe him. He was fifteen years old, and he found it hard to credit that anyone would ever pay him for a story, but it wouldn't stop him trying.

The father didn't say anything.

"But some of those places, they won't accept my stories—not if I write them by hand."

"Your handwriting is fair," the father said.

"They'll say they don't look right if they're not typed."

"On a typewriter?"

"That's right. It's not professional."

"Professional, is it?"

Neal nodded. "I'd pay you back. A pound a week."

The father held out a wadge of money. Coins wrapped in notes. It looked to be closer to a brick than eight quid.

"Father, that's too much."

"You'll be wanting paper as well, won't you? And other matter to keep the machine running? Ribbons, isn't it?"

"Yes," Neal said. He stared at the money as if it might turn into straw in his hand.

"You'll pay me back when you sell one of your stories."

Neal blanched.

"You can give me a little back with each story you sell," the father clarified. "And that way you'll remember to tell me of your progress."

"But what if I don't . . . ?"

"I have faith, Neal Darcy."

Neal bought the machine the next day instead of going home for lunch. He bought ribbons and two reams of paper. Then he took it home, told his mother exactly where the money had come from, put the paper and ribbons high out of the littlies' reach, and warned them upon pain of death not to touch the machine itself. When he was stern enough, they almost always listened.

He named the typewriter Lucy after the first girl he'd ever kissed. It hadn't been much of a kiss. They were five-year-olds with dry lips and runny noses. Lucy was his best friend. Until she died of polio a year later. While she was alive, they'd held hands and played on the street with her older brother's "borrowed" marbles and billycart, and there'd been that one kiss.

Neal hadn't forgotten. Naming his new machine would keep him from forgetting. It would also keep his attention on this one girl he could never get in a family way, and that would—he hoped—help him earn enough money to leave the brewery but still look after his family.

Lucy was good for Neal Darcy. And he was faithful to her.

He sold his first story at sixteen and paid Father O'Brian back in full before his eighteenth birthday.

>— KELPIE —<

Kelpie woke with her head in Dymphna's lap, her arm resting partly on Dymphna's legs and and partly on Darcy's knee.

Dymphna's and Darcy's quiet murmurs flowed around her. Kelpie kept her eyes closed and didn't stir. She didn't want them to stop talking. The way they'd been looking at each other had turned into a feeling that filled the room.

She felt warm and safe, but she knew she wasn't. They could be found. Snowy could lead Mr. Davidson to them. Kelpie didn't think he would, but she hadn't believed he killed Jimmy Palmer either, and Snowy had lied to her.

Kelpie opened her eyes a crack. There was a ghost in the corner. An old man. He wasn't looking at them. He was bent over examining something on the floor, poking and prodding at it, even though he was a ghost, and neither of those actions could affect anything.

Palmer sat cross-legged in front of them, wretched and grey.

Kelpie didn't think she'd been asleep long. The sun still shone brightly. Her eyes still ached with how tired she was. She closed them again. This was her first chance to lie down since she'd met Dymphna. She tried to relax herself back into sleep. But she was starting to pick out the words amid the murmurs.

"Did you see Snowy kill him? Your man?"

"No," Dymphna said too loud. Then more softly. "No. I just found the body."

"Was it . . . terrible?"

Kelpie felt Dymphna's nod.

"I've never seen a dead body," Darcy said. "Not outside of an open casket. My gran. Two of me uncles. But that's not the same as finding them dead."

"There was a lot of blood."

That was true. There had been so much blood on those walls, on that bed, on Palmer, it was hard to imagine it had all once flowed inside his body.

"How do you know Snowy killed him?"

Dymphna paused. Kelpie had wondered about that too.

"Good question," Palmer said.

Kelpie opened her eyes a sliver.

"Snowy's Mr. Davidson's right-hand man. Like Palmer was for Glory. Seemed likely. He didn't deny it, did he?"

"We could light out of here," Darcy said. "I know shearing. We could go bush. I'll work the sheds and—"

"What about your ma? Your brothers and sisters?"

"I'd send money back."

"Is that what your pa does? I didn't see any men's clothes where your ma sleeps."

Darcy stiffened. "I'm not like my old man."

"I believe you. I'm not like mine either."

"Where—" Darcy began.

"Does your eye hurt?"

"It's okay. Just can't see much out of it. It'll go down."

"Why didn't you hit Bluey?" Dymphna asked.

"Didn't seem like a good idea. He's got a reputation. If I hit him, I'd have to kill him or he'd kill me."

"But what about after he was shot? You could have knocked him out."

"Didn't seem fair. Besides, he wasn't right, saying mad stuff."

"Like what?"

"Dunno. He was whispering and that. He's dead hard to hear."

"Glory says his voice got like that 'cause someone tried to choke him to death when he was little."

"Now there's a surprise. How does Glory explain his dead-fish eyes?"

Dymphna laughed briefly.

"Someone's coming," Palmer said, his voice sounding like a dead man's. No emotions.

Kelpie blinked her eyes rapidly, hoping to attract his attention, get him to tell her more. *Who's coming?* she mouthed.

All she could hear were Dymphna and Darcy, the cooing of the pigeons above, a motor-car passing by on the street outside, wind blowing through the abandoned houses, the scuttle of insects, cockroaches most likely, but not people approaching.

"Might be Snowy," Palmer said in the same flat voice. "Might not. Could be someone worse."

Kelpie wanted to yell at him. Palmer had to know who it was. Why was he mucking about?

"You know what they call me? Angel of Death. You're not afraid?"

"No."

"You should be."

"Very afraid," Palmer whispered.

"I'm not."

"You can't be my man. Not ever."

"I don't believe that about them all dying because of you."

"You should."

"Well, I don't. It's superstitious."

"You can kiss me if you like."

Darcy didn't say anything, but Kelpie could hear his breathing. She heard a soft sound. They were both breathing faster. She heard cloth move against cloth.

"How long did that take?" Palmer demanded. "I haven't been dead a day, and she's already kissing another man. And such a man! He's a kid!" He stopped. "But then so is she." He looked past them as if he'd heard something. "Getting closer," he said and grinned.

Kelpie hadn't known he could smile. Was he teasing her? She stared straight at him, willing Palmer to tell her more.

Is it Snowy? Kelpie mouthed.

The room got warmer. It was like Darcy and Dymphna ushered summer in. Dymphna exhaled, and Kelpie knew she was smiling.

"Do you like it?" Darcy asked quietly. "The life you live?"

Palmer laughed. "Now he's fucked himself. Never ask that question: *Are you happy being a whore? Never.*"

Dymphna didn't say anything, but she drew away. Kelpie's arm slid from Darcy's knee. They didn't notice.

"I . . ." she began. "I make a lot of money. That's all you need to know."

"I'm sorry," Darcy said.

"Do you like working at the brewery?"

"No, and I don't make a lot of money. I'm sorry."

"Closer," Palmer said.

Who is it? Kelpie mouthed.

"Does it matter?" Jimmy Palmer said. "Eventually you're all going to be ghosts like me, so why not now?"

Because, Kelpie wanted to shout, *it's too soon!*

"You awake, love?" Dymphna asked her.

Kelpie closed her eyes, trying to decide whether Palmer was teasing her or not. Surely he was. He was devoted to Dymphna. Had been screaming for her to escape. Why would he change his mind?

Dymphna shifted. "When I was a kid, I loved to run. I was faster than anyone. Boys too. But girls weren't supposed to run like that. They can now. I saw a girl I grew up with on a newsreel winning a championship. I was always faster than Suzy."

"You're sixteen. You could still run."

Dymphna sighed. "It's not like that anymore. I left that world behind. Oh, I don't mind. This world's better."

Kelpie wondered what she meant. Some of the scariest people in the city were looking for them, not to mention the police. Why would Dymphna prefer this world to the one where she could run, and had parents looking after her, and didn't have to fend for herself all the time? Palmer said she was from the North Shore. Everyone was rich over there.

There were more soft noises and sighs.

"I shouldn't be jealous," Palmer said. "I'm dead."

Kelpie wanted them to stop, wanted their warmth and electricity to disappear. They were relaxing. This wasn't the place to relax. Or the time for it. She should not have let herself fall asleep.

"This won't end well," Palmer said. "Knew I wouldn't be the only one dead today. That copper's not going to be the last one neither."

That was it. Kelpie sat up. "I think someone's coming."

They all three stood slowly and eased away from the curtain hanging in the doorway.

A floorboard creaked. Kelpie couldn't be sure if it was in this house or further away. Then another and another. Snowy wouldn't be that careless.

Dymphna picked up a piece of broken wood. Darcy brought his fists up in front of his face and lowered his chin. A fighter's stance.

Kelpie slid her hand into her coat pocket and gripped the handle of the knife.

Sex

Even had Kelpie grown up with two parents inside a home with brothers and sisters, odds were her sex education would have been incomplete. Growing up on the streets, she knew both more and less than that imaginary Kelpie would have, the one who grew up with a roof over her head.

Kelpie knew about sex but not in any detail. It wasn't something Old Ma or Miss Lee had ever talked about. She wasn't about to ask Tommy or Stuart O'Sullivan. Or Snowy, for that matter.

Neither Old Ma nor Miss Lee had ever uttered the word or any of its many synonyms. Kelpie knew sex was why Miss Lee kept her away from those books and magazines at Old Man O'Reilly's. She knew you weren't supposed to read about it or talk about it. Though men at the pubs often did. Sometimes the women coming out of the ladies' lounge would too.

What Kelpie knew was what cats did, what dogs did, what humans did in back lanes or in the parks in summer.

She knew it took two people squishing up close together. She knew that it made people go red in the face and sweaty, that sometimes it hurt and led to tears and other times led to giggles and laughter. She knew that it could lead to babies.

She knew that sometimes men gave women money to do it. That sometimes men did it with men. She had also seen two women with their faces pressed close together, kissing. So she assumed that women could do it with women too.

Kelpie knew it was often hard to tell the difference between sex and a fight.

And that both were to be avoided: fighting and sexing.

She knew that men wanted it all the time and women hardly at all. Women who did it were bad women. But men who did it were just men. She'd heard that priests and sisters didn't do it ever. But she knew that wasn't true. There were rumours that Father Kelly did it with all the widows in the Hills and was a very bad priest indeed. (There were no rumours about Father O'Brian.)

Kelpie had seen Father Kelly kissing a woman in the rectory when Kelpie'd been trying to sneak in to find something to read.

She knew, too, that sex was messy. The girls in Moore Park walked away with leaves on their clothes, twigs in their hair, and their lipstick half across their faces. The boys were no better.

She didn't know that sex was related to the way Neal Darcy and Dymphna Campbell made her feel. She didn't know it had anything to do with the electricity that prickled in the air between them.

She didn't know it had anything to do with love.

But then Kelpie knew as little about love as she did about sex.

KELPIE

Kelpie was afraid, but as Stuart O'Sullivan had taught her, she put the fear away and ran through her options: run away, hide, or surprise them. O'Sullivan said those were the best strategies when smaller than your opponent, which Kelpie always was.

The windows were boarded, which had been helpful for trapping their noise inside when they were hiding, but now it made their escape difficult.

Kelpie tried the back door. It didn't budge. Darcy lowered his fists and joined her to put his shoulder next to hers and shove. The door creaked, loudly, but did not move.

There'd be no running away. Not in that direction.

Darcy went back to his position beside the curtain.

There was a hole in the floor big enough for Kelpie to squeeze through, but she wasn't sure if there was enough space between the floorboards and the foundations. Even if there was, she'd make too much noise getting there.

Nowhere to hide.

Another floorboard creaked. She heard displaced air. The rustle of fabric. A male voice.

It didn't sound like Snowy. Dymphna and Darcy glanced at each other.

When you can't run or hide, O'Sullivan had taught her, go for the knees, between the legs, the feet, and if the bastard falls, go for the eyes. A bottle of acid would be best, but the odds were low of ever having one of those to hand.

Kelpie had assumed he was joking about that last, but O'Sullivan swore he'd known a man who always had a bottle of acid on him. He used it to break into houses. Dissolving locks was quieter than breaking windows. Kelpie had no idea how to get hold of acid.

She crept quietly to Dymphna's side. Dymphna smiled at her before turning her eyes back to the curtain.

Somewhere in one of the houses on the other side of the back door, a radio came on. The unmistakeable sound of a race being called. This time of year, Kelpie figured, it had to be the dogs. Was hard to hear anything over the screaming of the dogs' names.

"There are two of them," Palmer said.

So he had decided to help. Sort of. Kelpie didn't doubt that he could identify who they were by now.

Kelpie held up two fingers to Dymphna and Darcy and gripped the handle of the knife tight, wishing she could sink back into the wall. Her nose itched. She put her hand over it. She could not sneeze.

"Bad time to sneeze," Palmer said, helpfully. "I don't see a good end to this."

The announcer on the radio was screaming now. Kelpie concentrated hard, trying to hear beyond the race. More creaking floorboards, she was pretty sure.

Abruptly the radio shut off.

Kelpie could hear male and female whispered voices, overlapping. Outside a horse blew air past its lips. It was pulling a cart. One of the wheels must be out of kilter—it made a loud clicking sound as it turned.

Kelpie's hand started to sweat where she held the knife.

"Snowy sent me," a female voice called. "It's just me. I brought some food."

Palmer shook his head. Kelpie repeated the movement. Though surely Dymphna and Darcy knew the woman was lying.

Dymphna put her fingers to her lips, handed Darcy her bit of floorboard, and pushed through the curtain.

"Hello, Cait," Dymphna said softly.

"You don't have to whisper," Cait said. "There's no one about."

"Even so," Dymphna said, "best not to attract attention. Walls are thin. Houses close together."

"You are a nervy one," Cait said no softer than before.

"How's your stomach?" Dymphna asked.

"Where's that little horror then? She punched me, she did."

Kelpie half hoped she'd get to punch Cait again.

"What are you doing here, Cait? How'd you know we were here?"

"I told you. Snowy sent me. Got some food for youse."

Kelpie heard a tapping sound.

The radio came back on again. Not so loud this time. Music. The kind of stuff without words that Miss Lee had loved.

"The cops are on the warpath. They know their constable's dead, but they don't know where the body is. They know Bluey killed him, but they don't know where Bluey is."

"They don't know where Bluey is?" Dymphna repeated.

Kelpie found that as hard to believe as Dymphna. The cops had been pounding on the grog shop's front door. It wasn't like Bluey could go anywhere. He'd been unconscious.

Cait ignored Dymphna's question. "The coppers know you was seen nearby. So they want to talk to you. They demanded Glory hand you over. She was not pleased."

"Where's Snowy?"

"Glory's furious," Cait said, once again not answering.

Kelpie started to doubt that Snowy had anything to do with Cait being here.

The floorboards creaked. Cait's skirts swished. Sounded like Cait was moving back and forth without a care for how loud she was. "All this fuss? It's ruining Glory's big day. She's still going to have the party, though. Everyone's invited. Even the coppers. Well, except Big Bill, of course. You don't think he has something to do with what's been happening, do you? He can't be pleased that his gravy train's roared out of the station. Maybe he's the one that killed Palmer? To punish Glory. Maybe he's done a deal with Mr. Davidson."

Kelpie wondered why Cait was talking so much, so loudly.

"I'd be worried about Big Bill if I was you, Dymphie. He's—"

"Big Bill's long gone. He was never much of a man. Just another lazy bastard leeching from his wife."

The floorboards fairly screamed from the impact of heavy stomping into the room.

"Is that what I am?" asked a deep, booming voice.

Kelpie had only ever seen Big Bill from a distance. She imagined him towering over Dymphna, smiling at her like a threat. He wasn't as tall as Palmer or Snowy. But he was big enough.

"How you going, Dymph?"

"All right, Bill. What are you doing here?" Dymphna's voice did not shake. She sounded like she'd been expecting Big Bill.

"Come to collect you, ain't I? Present for me wife."

Kelpie tried to remember what she'd heard about Glory's husband. Old Ma had said he'd slap Glory around when he was drunk, but that's what husbands did. Kelpie'd never heard he was mean like Bluey. He'd started as one of Glory's razor men, which meant he was hard. Even if he had gone soft after he married the boss. Kelpie didn't know if he killed people. But wasn't that what razor men did?

Kelpie kept her breathing as quiet, but her heart was beating too

234

JUSTINE LARBALESTIER

loud. She worried it alone was enough to give her away. She gripped the knife tighter.

"Ex-wife," Dymphna said. "I heard it was official today."

"Don't matter what she calls herself. We was married in church. Can't undo that. She might have forgot, but I haven't. I'm a good Catholic, I am. Ain't no such thing as divorce."

"I was on my way to see Glory, Bill. I don't think I need an escort. But thank you kindly for the offer."

Dymphna sounded as if this was a normal conversation. A raising-your-hat-and-how're-you-going-on-a-Sundee-afternoon kind of conversation. Kelpie couldn't tell from listening, but she feared Bill had a razor in his hand.

"Thank you kindly for the offer," Big Bill said in falsetto. "You are high up, ain't you? Is that what gives you the right to call a hard-working husband a bastard leech? Well, Glory, she thinks you need an *escort*." He emphasised the word as if there was something wrong with it.

"But Cait here said Snowy sent her."

Kelpie heard a smacking sound. Cait yelped.

"She gets confused. You know how it is with the older chromos. Work too long and your brains start to go soft."

Cait made a noise halfway between spitting and hissing.

"Too much bother about, Dymphna. Not safe for you. You heard Cait, didn't you? Coppers looking for you. That Mr. Davidson too. Got me auto outside. Won't take a jiffy. We can start the party early. I always liked you, Dymphna. Pretty face you've got."

"I don't think Glory will like that."

"I don't give a fuck what that old slut likes."

The floor was all creaks. Dymphna gasped. On the other side of the doorway, Darcy raised the jagged piece of floorboard.

"Stop it, Bill!"

It sounded like he was dragging her.

"Don't hurt her, Bill. Mr. Davidson won't pay as much if you hurt—"

"Shut it, Cait." He raised his voice. "Youse others in there can come out. I know you're there."

Kelpie and Darcy looked at each other. Kelpie showed him her knife.

Darcy nodded. "We're coming through."

"Slowly," Big Bill said.

Darcy raised the tattered curtain, and Kelpie walked through, both hands in her pockets.

Big Bill was holding Dymphna by the waist. She was kicking back at him. He glared at Darcy, not bothering to look at Kelpie. "I'll break her in two if you try anything."

"He won't," Palmer said. "She's too valuable."

Dymphna shook her head. "He's working for Davidson now. He has to keep me safe."

"I'm not working for anyone," Big Bill yelled.

Darcy rushed at him, punched him in the kidneys, and then side-stepped to kick him hard in the back of his knees. Big Bill bellowed but didn't let go of Dymphna.

Cait came at Kelpie with her bag flying. Kelpie ducked, then stepped out of her way. Cait's eyes were narrowed and her teeth bared.

Wood splintered and Bill roared. Darcy must have let him have it with the board.

Cait turned and swung the bag at Kelpie again, using both hands. Kelpie ducked and stuck out her foot. Cait tripped and went flying into the wall.

Kelpie moved in and kicked Cait's left knee, grateful again for Seamus Darcy's heavy shoes. Then she hit Cait as hard as she could with her elbow. She was aiming for her solar plexus but hit bone. Something snapped. The jarring went all the way up Kelpie's arm. She staggered backward.

Cait gasped and slid to the floor, her eyes filling with water. "You little shit! Broken me fucking ribs!"

"Well done," Palmer said. "Though you should have stabbed her."

"Come on!" Dymphna yelled.

Big Bill was down. Blood poured out of the side of his head.

Dymphna and Darcy were bolting. Kelpie ran after them, looking down to make sure she didn't put her foot through any of the holes. Behind her Bill was swearing and Cait was screaming her head off.

Kelpie's arm felt like it was on fire. She should have used the knife.

She followed Dymphna and Darcy through to the next house and then out the front and onto the street. All three of them were breathing hard.

"Jesus's tits and Mary's balls," Darcy said.

Kelpie almost laughed. Old Ma used to say that and then make Kelpie promise never to blaspheme.

"This way," Dymphna said, eyeing the motor-car parked two houses over and leading them in the opposite direction. "Don't run, but don't dawdle. Kelpie, hold my hand. You're my niece."

"Where are we going?"

"To Glory. I've got to tell her about Big Bill."

Earlier that same year the whole city had had a party. There was a new bridge to span the sparkling water between the meat of the city and its northern outpost.

The folks of the Hills didn't give too much of a shit about the proceedings, but they were proud in a general sense because they knew there wasn't another city in their fine country that had a bridge as big or as beautiful. So they partied and then they pretty much forgot about it. Wasn't like any of them would ever use it. Who wanted to go that far from the Hills?

The morning after the official opening, they were as one in outrage to learn that some jumped-up squatter type on an old nag had taken it upon himself to embarrass the Big Fella, who presided over their fine state and who everyone knew to be a friend of the working man. The bastard on the clapped-out horse had presumed to cut the ribbon before the Big Fella could get to it.

The nerve of the mongrel!

He was even wearing a sword. Rich-toff weapon if there ever was one. He was arrested forthwith. Wouldn't you know it, this interloper and enemy of the working man had some kind of fancy Frenchy name. Well, of course he did. Should transport everyone with a name like that back where they came from. They weren't fit for the new world.

Gloriana Nelson spoke for almost everyone in the Hills when she said that hanging was too good for him. Hadn't many of their fine boys died in making that damned bridge? Then they should throw this bastard off the bridge first thing. How dare he embarrass the Big Fella?

There were roars of approval, and Glory shouted everyone a beer.

DYMPHNA

Dymphna had never wanted to scream so much. She held Kelpie's hand tightly and kept her moving forward, though Kelpie twisted to see if they were followed. Perhaps she *was* sixteen, but she surely didn't act like it. Dymphna realised she felt almost angry with Kelpie, as if the girl had tricked her. She pushed those feelings away. There wasn't time.

Neal Darcy strode along by her side. She'd been hoping he'd have the sense to go home, or off bush, or somewhere, as long as it was far away from her.

They'd kissed, and it had been delicious. But now she had to make him go. He was too young to die.

Jimmy was, of course, still with them. Bastard could have warned them it was Big Bill. Though that wouldn't have mattered if she'd run as soon as Snowy left. Cops be damned. But she was tired. All she'd wanted was to stop for a moment. Then Kelpie had fallen asleep. Then she and Neal had talked and kissed, when she should have been running, should have been getting them as far from this mess as she could . . .

Even now it was probably not too late to head to the Quay. But Dymphna had realised she needed to square things with Glory.

Glory would be at Lansdowne Street already. Sunset wasn't too far off, and that's when her parties always began. Glory loved sunsets. So that's when she always cracked open the first bottle of beer, or, more recently, as her money had swelled, the first bottle of champagne that meant, yes, the party has begun.

Much as Dymphna hated Glory's Lansdowne Street home, that's where she had to go. She wished there was some way of preparing Kelpie. But with Jimmy and Neal by her side, that was impossible.

"I know how to get us out of the city," Neal said.

"We're not hiding," Dymphna said. "I've had enough hiding. Do you see anyone? Is Big Bill following us?"

"Not yet," Kelpie said.

"We'll be fine up on Oxford Street. Too busy for even Big Bill to try anything."

"You can't go to Glory," Neal said. "It's not safe. You heard what Snowy said."

"I'm not arguing," Dymphna said in the same hard voice Glory used when she would hear no arguments. "You don't have to stay. Be better if you went back to the brewery."

"Glory could kill you," Neal said.

Dymphna wanted to scream. Couldn't he hear that what she said was final? Why did she have to point out the obvious? "She's not going to kill anyone at her own party. Besides, who do you think told Big Bill where we were? It had to be Snowy. You can't forget who he works for. Mr. Davidson ordered Jimmy dead. Snowy's hardly the best guide to who's safe and who isn't."

"Snowy never . . ." Kelpie began. The little girl—well, no, not little. Again, Dymphna felt that jolt of surprise and anger at discovering Kelpie was the same age as her.

Kelpie pulled her hand out of Dymphna's. "Snowy wouldn't. You heard him. He doesn't think Mr. Davidson's right in the head. Cait must've been following us. She's sneaky."

"Could be." Dymphna wanted to believe her. But she didn't. Snowy must have told. Perhaps he had a reason. But that didn't matter. Everyone had reasons for what they did—including Mr. Davidson and Glory and, hell, her and Jimmy. Good reasons didn't stop people from winding up dead.

"None of that mob can be trusted," Neal said. "We have to get away from all of them."

"*I* am one of that mob."

Neal had the grace to flush.

Dymphna was not going to waste breath explaining that of the two crime bosses Glory was the sane one. The safer option. Dymphna was her best girl. Glory wouldn't kill her. The problem was whether Glory was still capable of protecting her with Jimmy, and now Bluey, out of action.

"He's right," Jimmy said. "She should be heading to Circular Quay and purchasing a berth out of here. Tell her, Kelpie."

So now he wanted her safe again, did he? When he could have warned them in time to get away before Big Bill and Cait showed up . . .

"I didn't mean . . ." Neal paused. "It's not safe for you here right now, that's all. We could go bush until things cool down."

Why were they both so stupid? Her odds of getting out of town or to the Quay safely were terrible. Every standover, razor man, cockatoo, errand boy, chromo, and cop in the city knew Miss Dymphna

Campbell. Word would get back to Glory, or Davidson, or the coppers, or all three before they'd made it to Hyde Park.

To prove the point that she hadn't made to anyone but herself, as they turned into Oxford Street, two of Glory's bookies walked past, both dipping their hats. The street was packed with people, mostly men, hurrying from their place of work to the pubs in the narrow window before six o'clock closing.

"Gentlemen," Dymphna said.

"Heading to Glory's party, Miss Campbell?" the taller one enquired.

"We are," Dymphna said, smiling and resisting the urge to check if Cait and Big Bill were behind them. "Should be a ripper."

"Hope to get there later," the taller one continued. "Glory's parties are always bonzer." The two men nodded and moved on.

Kelpie held Dymphna's hand tighter and pushed closer to her side. The little girl did not like crowds. Not *little*. She had to stop thinking of Kelpie that way. Kelpie was someone her own age, who could see ghosts same as her, who'd been living on the streets so long it had stunted her growth. She was *not* one of her little sisters. They were dead.

Dymphna held her hand out for a taxi. One pulled up beside them seconds later. Oxford Street was always awash with cabs, and, she had found, they were always likely to stop for her first.

Before she opened the door, she lowered her voice: "Get ready to run if we have to."

Neal nodded. Kelpie muttered what sounded like a yes. They slid inside the cab.

"Going to Glory's party, Miss Campbell?" the cabbie asked.

"Of course," Dymphna said.

She wanted to sit back and close her eyes, but she couldn't resist looking out the rear window for Big Bill and Cait. Kelpie was looking too.

"We'll be all right," Dymphna said, hoping that was true.

As the cab turned into Crown from Oxford, Dymphna and Neal were pushed against one another. Warmth radiated from him even on this cool day. What Dymphna wanted more than anything was for none of this to be real, so they could go back to her flat.

But if none of this had been real, they wouldn't have met. She would have spent the day doing her shift for Glory and helping with the set-up for the party. She would not have finally met Kelpie.

Neal was a wonderful kisser. She hadn't been with someone who made her feel that way since Danny Dunbar, her first man, who died in Long Bay lock-up. Slipped in the shower, the coroner said, but everyone knew the screws had done for him. And good riddance. Nasty piece of work Danny had been for all he made her tingle.

Dymphna had to work out how to stay alive, how to protect Kelpie and now Neal. No doubt Glory already knew that Neal had been there, that Bluey had tried to kill him. She'd want to know why and whether she should finish the job for Bluey, and she'd *really* want to know why Snowy had intervened.

The cab was almost at Lansdowne. Dymphna's heart beat a little faster. Was she making a mistake? Betting wrong on Glory?

And Glory's house. Dymphna really hated going to her Lansdowne Street house.

"Can you pull up for a moment, driver?"

"Yes, Miss Campbell. Be happy to."

Dymphna leaned past Neal to open the door. She said quietly into his ear, "Hide at St. Peter's. You know how the father feels about Glory. He'll hide you."

Neal shook his head, turning towards her, leaning closer. "I'm not leaving."

Dymphna put her hands to his chest and pushed. There wasn't time for this. Should she make him take Kelpie with him? That would probably be best. The girl was not ready for Lansdowne Street.

"Please, Neal, for me?"

"What's she doing now? I know Neal's soft, but he's better than having no man at all," Jimmy told Kelpie. "Look at that mob."

Dymphna didn't have to look—with the door open, she could hear them.

"Is there a problem, Miss Campbell?" the cabbie asked, turning around.

"No, no problem. Thank you."

She wanted to tell Kelpie to go with Neal but found she couldn't. Kelpie *had* to stay with her. Otherwise . . . Dymphna wasn't sure what, but she knew she couldn't let Kelpie go.

"I can look after myself," Neal said.

"I know you can. From what I saw, you look after your whole family. But this is different. I need to handle Glory on my own. She's apt to take one look at you and have you knocked about because she can. Or worse, decide that you should be working for her. I'll meet you here after. Please?"

Neal leaned into Dymphna and kissed her mouth. She wanted to lean back into him, but she pulled away.

"Okay," he said, sliding out of the cab. "But it doesn't sit right."

"Go," she said, closing the door on him. She did not look back to see if he was going to do what she said. Her leg began to shake. She gripped Kelpie's hand. Kelpie returned the squeeze. "Be strong," Dymphna told her, though she knew it was meaningless.

"I never knew she was such an idiot," Jimmy said. "Right into the lion's den. Not once, but twice."

The driver, having the luxury of not hearing Jimmy, continued on as close as he could to Glory's place.

On Lansdowne Street, the crowd, mostly men, spilled from the footpath onto the road. Noisily jostling each other, yelling decreasingly witty demands for beer even though Glory's people wouldn't start distributing said beer for an hour or so. Not till the sun went down.

"How much?" Dymphna asked.

"I don't need your money," the cabbie said. "Glory looks after me."

"Well, at least take this." Dymphna pressed a shilling into his hand. "Thank you."

Dymphna kept a tight hold on Kelpie as she led them through the rowdy men. Even on such a cold day, she could smell the sweat on them, the stale beer. Mostly the men made way for her, nodded, lifted their hats, but a few grabbed at her with lecherous hands, whispered nasty words.

"Bloody stop it," Jimmy said, putting his fist through their faces to no effect.

Were he still alive and towering by her side, they would not have dared. Dymphna never enjoyed the time in between boyfriends.

Someone pinched her arse so viciously she knew there'd be a bruise. She said nothing and showed no reaction, though her eyes watered briefly. She wished she could have them all killed.

"Filthy bastards," Jimmy said, throwing more futile punches.

No one ever touched Gloriana like this. Or said such foul things to her. Not to her face. One day they wouldn't dare do it to Dymphna Campbell either.

"It'll be all right, Kelpie," she said, though she doubted Kelpie could hear. She pulled the girl in front of her, and they walked in step. She didn't rule out the possibility that one of Mr. Davidson's men would snatch them right here under Glory's nose. It felt like a thousand people were looking at her, trying to touch her.

"Dymphna," little Stuey Keating said, grabbing her arm and steering her through the crowd. He was one of Glory's. Not big enough or old enough to do standover work, but he ran messages and stood cockatoo.

A large man made a grab for Dymphna's waist. Stuey slapped the man's hands away. "Oi, you. Get your fucking hands off her. You want beer or not? Think Glory'll thank you for roughing up her best girl?"

"Thanks, Stuey." Dymphna couldn't be sure he'd heard her.

"What the fuck is that?" Jimmy asked. Dymphna followed his gaze to Glory's balcony then quickly looked away. It was better not to look.

Jimmy stopped. "It's like Central. I'm not going in there."

Good, thought Dymphna. She wished it was possible to keep Kelpie from going in as well.

Stuey cleared their path by shouting at everyone who stood in their way and giving them what for if they didn't shift. The threat of no beer proved effective. Stuey practically lifted her and Kelpie up to the steps leading into the yard. He was stronger than he looked. He'd be a standover in no time.

Dymphna weaved her and Kelpie's way around the kegs crowding Glory's front yard. The beer was doled out in front and the food in back. The back lane would already be packed with hungry Hills people. The first year Glory had a party for the whole community, she'd tried to serve both the food and the beer from the back of her place. It was a miracle none of the littlies had been trampled.

"Glory's in the fancy room with the chandeliers," Stuey said. "Could you tell her I haven't seen any coppers yet?"

Dymphna blew Stuey a kiss. She smiled as his blush crept down from his cheeks to his neck. He turned towards the crowd, keeping his eyes peeled for the next set of proper guests trying to make their way inside.

Dymphna turned to Kelpie, bending a little. "It's best not to look Glory directly in the eye. Probably safest to look down," she said, though Kelpie had already met Glory.

The advice was not for coping with Glory but for coping with her house. She had to hope that Kelpie would understand.

"You ready? You can do this. You're strong." Dymphna wished she could tell Kelpie the truth. But Jimmy had not left them alone for long enough.

"Yes," Kelpie whispered. Dymphna hoped she was ready because Glory's house would test her.

Many people had died here. It was a house full of ghosts.

Kelpie's First Ghost

Those who are gifted—or cursed—with seeing ghosts lay eyes on the dead not long after they behold their first living person. It can take time to learn to distinguish between the two. Some never do. Giggle houses around the world have more than a few inmates who see the dead as well as the living.

Kelpie began seeing ghosts before she could hold her neck up properly.

Old Ma said that little baby Kelpie's eyes would stare off at nothing and follow that nothing around the room. Once she started walking, Kelpie began following things that were not there and, once she had words, asking them questions.

It was eerie, Old Ma said. *Just like me mam. She had the sight, she did, and now you do too.* Old Ma was proud of it, though she told no one. *You can't be telling everyone about a thing like that. They'll find ways to make use of you. They'll find ways to turn it wrong and try to make money. Don't be telling no one. Not ever.*

Kelpie didn't.

By the time Kelpie could talk, she'd met more ghosts than living people.

The first ghost she remembered was so faded Kelpie couldn't tell if it was a woman or a man or if it was old or young. The ghost could have been Irish or Italian or Chinese. There was no way of knowing.

Her first ghost was a talker.

But Kelpie couldn't understand the words; they were as faded as the ghost. They might even have been in a different language. Old Ma spoke Irish. She taught Kelpie how to say "I am cold" in Irish because she was sick of hearing it in English. So Kelpie took to saying *"tor may fooar"* until Old Ma got sick of that too and begged her to go back to English.

Some of Old Ma's lodgers were German; they'd bark at each other in their yelling language. Kelpie had also heard the priests speaking their secret language. Old Ma said it was how they spoke to God, which was why only priests learned it and why all the services in church were in that language too. It did sound like God's words: big and strong and incomprehensible.

The ghost's words didn't sound like they came from any of those languages. They weren't singsong like Old Ma's Irish, or barking like German, or cranky like the priest language. They were gentle and whirling words. Like the kind of wind that came out of the northeast in spring. Soft and warm. Not raging and cold like a southerly buster.

When Kelpie walked through her first ghost, she didn't feel sick. There wasn't enough of the ghost left for that. Though it did raise the hairs on her arms a little. Like when there was an electrical storm.

A few days later, the ghost was gone. But by then Kelpie'd already met the Frog Lady who camped out where the stream through Frog Hollow had once been. She wasn't a talker, but Kelpie could tell she was looking for the frogs that had disappeared in the last century. Old Ma had told Kelpie what good eating frogs were.

Many ghosts forgot that they didn't need food; ghosts could only eat air.

✂ DYMPHNA ✂

Dymphna paused in the doorway and focused on the living. The trick was to consign the swirling, translucent grey mass of ghosts to the periphery of her vision, to close her ears to their whispers and moans, to see only the living, to hear only the clink of champagne glasses and Glory's dulcet tones telling her waiters exactly how they were doing everything wrongly.

With Gloriana Nelson dressed in her party finery, it was easier than usual. Glory wore green and gold velvet, which contrasted strikingly with her hair and mouth and nails, all of which were crimson. On every finger was a different jewelled ring: sapphires, rubies, and, of course, diamonds. There were more diamonds in her ears. But the diamonds at her neck were the most brilliant, falling in tiers, sending reflected light around the room.

Almost as brilliant as the many-tiered chandelier, hanging from the centre of the ceiling rose.

Glory hovered over her three waiters, all of them wearing lustrous black tuxedos only surpassed by the lustrous blackness of their hair. They almost looked like the genuine article.

The living were glittery eyed and pink cheeked; they glowed. The dead were all matte greys.

Kelpie held Dymphna's hand so tight Dymphna had to resist pulling away. Kelpie's head was down, her eyes staring at the floor. Much better than making eye contact with the ghosts. As soon as they were alone, Dymphna would start teaching Kelpie how to not see them. Finally let her know she wasn't the only one. She cursed Jimmy for dogging her every step since she'd found Kelpie so that she couldn't tell Kelpie without letting him know she could see him. For now all she could do to help was let Kelpie bruise her hand.

The waiters were arranging champagne glasses in a tower. Dymphna had seen it done in a talkie: the champagne was poured from the top and cascaded down like a waterfall to fill all the glasses. Yellow and sparkling. It would match the necklace glittering over Glory's large bosom.

One day, Dymphna was going to have enough money to have tricks like that at her own parties. She wouldn't be holding them in a terrace house in the Hills; her parties would be in a mansion in Elizabeth Bay or perhaps even Vaucluse.

Her waiters would not be as nervous as this lot: rough young men who had waited about as often as Dymphna had sailed around the harbour on a yacht. One of Glory's wee boys was sweeping up the shattered remains of one of the waiters' mishaps. Dymphna wondered how many champagne glasses had been lost already.

Dymphna coughed. "Glory?"

Glory turned and her eyes narrowed. She stepped forward and put her hands, gently, against Dymphna's jaw and neck. Dymphna could see the green, brown, gold, and black striation that made up Glory's irises, the tiny red veins that threaded her whites. There was a smudge of red lipstick on one of her front teeth.

Glory's hands slid down from Dymphna's jaw to encircle her throat. Dymphna concentrated on not swallowing, on not letting Glory know how afraid she was, though Glory could likely feel the quickening of her pulse.

Glory's fingers squeezed tighter. Dymphna fought a desire to cough, but not to run. She looked into Glory's eyes and told herself that Glory would not do this, not here, not in front of so many witnesses. She repeated it to herself over and over.

Glory's hands pressed tighter. Dymphna felt pressure build around her eyes, tiny dots starting to appear. Her head began to hurt. The desire to cough became stronger. She was Glory's best girl. Glory would not kill her. Not here. Not with this many people watching. Would she?

More dots, crowding together and blurring Dymphna's vision. All she could see now was Glory's eyes, though somehow they had turned black.

Then the pressure eased from her throat. She could see Glory's face change to milk and honey and kindness.

"You look gorgeous, my love!"

"So do you, Glory." Dymphna's voice was a little raspy, but she was startled it worked at all, that she had managed to keep from coughing, from rubbing her throat. "Those diamonds! They're like a river."

Kelpie's hand was still holding hers, still squeezing her fingers almost as tight as Glory had squeezed her throat. Kelpie was breathing fast with her head held low. The gratitude she felt to Kelpie right then for not screaming, for not trying to hurt Glory—there weren't words.

They could have both been dead.

Glory adjusted the diamonds on her bosom with her now–mottled pink hands. Dymphna wondered if her own throat was as pink.

"Cost a fortune, these did. Bought 'em for meself. You don't think Big Bill ever gave me anything this fine? If he had, he woulda bought it with me own money." Glory laughed. "So glad he's done with. This is going to be my best party yet. Towers of champagne, those are going to be."

"Wonderful," Dymphna breathed.

Her leg was shaking again. If she wasn't strong, Kelpie could fall apart under the weight of all these ghosts. She breathed deeply and put her hands on Kelpie's shoulders, hoping that would still her own body's reaction. She was Glory's best girl.

She could still feel where Glory's fingers had pressed at her throat.

"Someone take Dymphna's coat."

One of the waiters, still clutching champagne glasses, turned to do Glory's bidding.

Dymphna pulled her coat tighter around her. She was not taking it and all that money off, no matter what Glory said. "Not right now, thank you," she said, smiling sweetly. "I'm still feeling a little chilled."

"I hear things have been rough since I saw you earlier, my love."

"Yes, Glory."

"My poor Bluey, eh? Lucky to be alive."

Dymphna murmured something that she hoped sounded sympathetic.

"Come through and you can tell me about it." Glory put her hands around her mouth and yelled, "Connie!"

Connie came running from the kitchen. Her hair was a mess, and she was wearing an apron. She gave Dymphna a little half wave.

"I'll be upstairs having a little natter. Make sure the bubbly is done right and those little hors d'oeuvres"—Glory made it sound like *whores doovres*—"are ready to go. Give us a shout if we're not back down at sunset. Right-o?"

"Yes, Glory. See you later, Dymphna."

"Oh, and, Connie. Make sure you're cleaned up for when the important guests get here. Your face all painted and nice. Got that?"

"Of course, Gloriana."

Dymphna followed Glory to the stairs. Kelpie's hand trembled in hers. Dymphna squeezed it and stroked the girl's hair briefly, hoping that it would give Kelpie strength. "It will be all right," she told her softly.

"'Course it will, my lovelies." Glory looked at her watch. "There's enough time. You can come too, little doggie." Kelpie scowled and Glory laughed. "I do like you, puppy. I really do."

Dymphna had never been upstairs before. As far as she knew, Glory didn't invite anyone up there. Except for Big Bill, and his invitation had long been rescinded. Dymphna's hope that there would be fewer ghosts dissipated as they climbed. She focused on Glory's green and gold back and her words. She was not going to flinch, or shudder, or move out of their path, no matter how many there were or how awful they made her feel. She pulled Kelpie closer. The girl was shaking. Oddly enough, that seemed to drive the tremors from her own body.

Glory led them into what could have been an elegant sitting room. Two large windows opened onto the ample backyard. The ceiling was high. The floorboards did not squeak or groan as they walked in. The settees were large, as were the lounge chairs.

Both matched Glory's gaudy dress, upholstered in green velvet with gold tassels. The wall was papered in a velvet wallpaper of gold and a red as brilliant as Glory's hair. The room was more showy than any of Glory's brothels.

Dymphna felt like she had stepped inside a gilded womb. Under any other circumstances, she would be anticipating describing it to Lettie later. But today, well . . .

Glory gestured to the closest settee. Dymphna sank onto it, and Kelpie sat beside her, her legs too short to touch the floor.

There were too many ghosts, more than downstairs.

Dymphna wasn't sure that Kelpie could endure it. She'd refused to go anywhere near Central Station, which was not as hideously packed with them as this much smaller space.

Central Station was built on an old cemetery, one of the oldest in the city, but Dymphna was fairly certain that wasn't why it was like that. She'd been to other cemeteries. None were as thronged with ghosts. The ghosts at Central were like the ones here, grey and meshing together, losing their solidity, losing, too, what Jimmy Palmer still had: humanity.

Only a few bore any resemblance to the living person they'd once been.

Dymphna had a theory for both Central Station and Glory's house. Violence. A massacre. A fire. Something that killed many. All becoming ghosts at once, jumbling together and, she was fairly sure, calling out to other dead to join them.

She'd passed in and out of Central Station many times since she was a child and seen how slowly more ghosts accreted.

It was the same at Glory's house.

Dymphna did not want to think about what had happened here. But she didn't think it had happened under Gloriana Nelson's rule. She may have added ghosts, but the initial terrible thing must have happened a long time ago.

"Not happy about that copper. Bluey had no business doing that. I told him no bodies. There's nothing worse for business than dead coppers."

"Bluey's a bit hard to control, Glory."

Glory smiled. "At least we got rid of the body. What a bother that was. I've had words with Bluey. Stern words."

Dymphna didn't doubt it. She took a deep breath. "Big Bill tried to grab me."

Glory's face tightened. Dymphna realised that she looked tired. Glory rarely looked tired. She was the one who drank and laughed and kept the party going and was still at it as the sun came up.

"Cait was working with him."

"Never trusted that girl. Even for a chromo." Now was not the time to point out that Dymphna was also a chromo or that back in the day Glory had been one too.

"Dazzle might be a thief, but she's loyal. Cait would sell you out as soon as look at you. Trust her and Big Bill to be together. Like finds like."

"He was going to—"

Glory smacked her hands together. "It's beyond all get out. I knew he was no good—but this? And on the very day I celebrate being shot of the bastard forever! I could kill him."

Dymphna hoped she would.

"Go on then. What did the bastard say?"

"He was going to take me to Mr. Davidson. To spite you. I think it might have been Bill who killed Jimmy." Dymphna was improvising. *This* was how to get Snowy out of Glory's sights. Perhaps Kelpie was right. Why would Snowy hand them over to Big Bill when he'd already put himself to so much trouble to make sure they were safe? She wouldn't wager much on Snowy doing too much more for her, but there was no mistaking his concern for Kelpie. "Perhaps to prove to Davidson he isn't yours anymore?"

"The nerve."

"Perhaps that's why Big Bill didn't contest the divorce? He was already planning a different kind of revenge."

"Planning? He's not much of a planner. Someone smarter must have put him up to it. Though someone smarter would have left well enough alone."

"I think Snowy's jack of working for Mr. Davidson. That man's too crooked, too twisty. I think Snowy's ready to switch to a fair-dealing boss. Like yourself."

"Been doing a lot of thinking, haven't you, Dymph?"

Dymphna wasn't sure about Glory's tone, but she ventured on. "There's a lot to think about."

"You know what thought did, don't you?" Glory chuckled. "I hear Snowy helped you move Bluey's body into the doctor's. That was good of him. Mind you, I also heard Snowy knocked Bluey out first. Less good of him, that—coshing my strongest man."

"Bluey was trying to kill Neal. Snowy stepped in."

"*Neal*, is it?" Glory said. "I heard *Neal* attacked my Bluey first. Bluey's doing a lot better, you'll be pleased to hear. Said he'll join us here later." She didn't wait for Dymphna to respond. "So why'd your *Neal* Darcy attack Bluey?"

Kelpie shifted herself closer to Dymphna; she was almost burrowing into her side.

"He didn't. Bluey went after him."

Glory nodded. Clearly, Dymphna was not the only one to tell the tale that way.

"Why'd the copper shoot him, then? It wasn't to save that Darcy's life? Because that's what I'm being told. Apparently your *Neal* Darcy is in thick with the coppers."

Dymphna didn't pause, didn't breathe deep, didn't give Glory any indication that this was important to her. "Well, whoever's keeping you informed is blind as a bat. Bluey went after Darcy, and then the copper pulled the gun on both of them. Screamed at all of us to stay put."

"The copper just showed up? Handy, that."

"The copper lived on the lane with his mum. He heard the fight and came out to put a stop to it."

"Then what was Neal Darcy doing there? He's a Hills boy, ain't he?"

Dymphna let herself blush.

"Got a crush has he? Following you about? Well, he isn't the first, and he won't be the last. He should join the bloody queue! He can step in right behind bloody Mr. Davidson."

Dymphna managed a laugh.

"Was like that with me, you know. Back in the day. Not that you'd credit it now."

"You're still a handsome woman, Glory," Dymphna said, because it was true.

"Aye, I am. But it ain't the same. Takes a while to get used to that. You'll find out. I *hope* you'll find out. So you don't want me to kill this Neal Darcy?"

Dymphna shook her head, hoping she seemed calm. Next to her, Kelpie froze, and she prayed the girl would say nothing. Dymphna could barely trust herself to speak. Neal was a kid. He had little idea of the mess he'd become involved in. He wrote stories. He'd been away shearing once. He was kind to Kelpie. He didn't deserve to die because he'd stumbled into Dymphna's world.

What would become of Mrs. Darcy and the younger ones if Glory killed Neal? It was going to be hard enough to keep Bluey from going after him. One crack to Neal's eye was not going to be enough to appease Bluey's bloodlust.

"Is he interested in this line of work? I wouldn't've pegged him for the type. Works at the brewery, doesn't he? Supporting the whole family 'cause the da ran off. Bloody men. He's a good boy from what I'm told, that Neal Darcy."

"Yes."

Dymphna wasn't surprised Glory knew so much. She liked to know about everyone in her empire. Even those, like Mrs. Darcy, who wouldn't give her the time of day if it was a choice between that or setting their own hair on fire. Didn't matter. Glory still needed to know her name, those of her children, how long her man had been away. Where her oldest boy worked. What brand of cigarette he smoked too. If he did. Most of the Hills were more roll-your-own fellas. Ready-made cigarettes were expensive.

It was something else that set Glory apart from Mr. Davidson. Rumour had it he didn't even know the names of half his own men. He might pay for their funerals, but unlike Glory, he rarely attended them.

Funeral.

She hadn't given a thought to Jimmy's funeral. She had no idea if he had living parents and, if he did, whether they had been told. She looked at her watch. Not even five yet. Jimmy hadn't been dead a whole day.

"But the Darcy boy knows how to box. I'm told he was quite the quick one avoiding Bluey's blows. Mind you, Bluey did have a bullet in him. Slows a man down."

"If you heard how good he was at avoiding Bluey's punches, you'll also know he didn't lay a finger on him. He could have."

"That was smart. I wouldn't feel at all kindly towards him if he'd hurt my Bluey. You looking at this Darcy boy to be your man?" Glory snorted. "Wouldn't last a day."

"Oh, no." Dymphna smiled to show she thought it was absurd too.

Glory clapped her hands. "Right-o then. I won't touch him." She stood up. "Almost time to get the party started. Let's have some sherry."

Dymphna went to the liquor cabinet. It was made of a hideous dark walnut with red glass behind iron latticework. She opened the doors. There were more than a dozen bottles.

"The ones with JEREZ written on them. That's Spanish for sherry. I want the oloroso. The *seco* one. Had them brought in from Spain, I did. Tried it when I was on the *Strathnaver*. You know, when I went over first-class? Never knew there were sherries that weren't sweet before that boat ride. Revelation, it was. Much better than the sweet kind."

Dymphna sorted through the bottles until she found it. She poured Glory a glass and handed it to her.

Glory drained it in one swallow. Dymphna poured her a second. She drained that one too. The third glass she took a sip from and then placed gently on the table beside her.

"Pour yourself one too." It wasn't a question.

Dymphna splashed a little into a glass and wrapped her hand around it to prevent Glory from seeing how little she'd poured. She sank back onto the couch and faked taking a large gulp. Kelpie's eyes fluttered. She looked pale.

"I'll have Snowy kill Big Bill. That'll see everything neat and tidy, won't it? Snowy can prove he's up to working for me, and Big Bill will pay. What do you think, little puppy dog? Does Big Bill deserve to die?"

"Yes," Kelpie whispered. "He was going to hurt Dymphna."

"Well, then," Glory said, taking another sip of her sherry. "We can't have that."

Dymphna's First Love

The first man Dymphna ever cared about was stabbed to death in the shower at his boarding house.

The killer, who was never caught, dragged Larry Simcoe's body from the shared bathroom back to his room, leaving a trail of water and blood along the corridor, and shoved the body into the bottom of Larry's own wardrobe, wrapped in an old sheet stripped from the bed. The door to the wardrobe would not close. Blood and water dripped out onto the floor.

The clothes in the wardrobe, his precious suits and ties and bone-white shirts, the clothes he had been so proud of: they were all of them ruined.

The killer fled, slipping and sliding down the corridor and out the front door, and disappeared.

Everyone in the boarding house had been home when Larry was stabbed twenty-eight times and his body shoved into his wardrobe. The bathroom was opposite the dining room. Around seven o'clock at night it had been, and most of them were eating. None of them saw or heard a thing.

Larry Simcoe was a strong man. He would have fought back. He would have screamed.

A neighbour called the police on seeing a man covered with blood, holding a knife, running out of the boarding house.

When the police arrived, Larry hadn't been dead more than an hour. There was still blood in the corridor. Had the landlord and his residents really seen and heard *nothing*?

So they insisted.

In the detective's notebook, scribbled over and over again, were the words *saw nothing, heard nothing, smelled nothing, felt nothing. Nothing. Nothing. Nothing.*

Larry Simcoe was twenty-two. He was one of Glory's top stan-dovers. Not as big a man as Jimmy Palmer or Snowy Fullerton, but give him a few more years, and he might get there.

He hadn't been a good lover. His kisses were too hard and too sloppy, and the whole thing was over too fast. He didn't make her tingle. But he loved to dance. He was good at it too. They were at the

Palais Royale twice a week, dancing and laughing until they barely had the energy to stand up.

Larry also loved to listen, to hear Dymphna's gossip and her plans, her jokes and observations. They would laugh at Glory and Big Bill together. Dymphna hadn't known men could be like that: funny and wry and interested in more than sex and killing and drinking. Larry didn't drink. There were some that held that's why he was killed: because it wasn't natural.

Dymphna Campbell loved Larry Simcoe. Though she hadn't realised that until she heard he was dead.

When they told her, a tear almost slipped from her eye. She and Larry had been together two months.

Her next man, Ray White, was another one of Glory's. He slotted right into Larry's place, took over his duties and Dymphna too.

Ray hadn't liked Larry. There were more than a few to tell Dymphna that, the night of Larry's death, Ray had celebrated in a little too much detail. *As if he'd been there in that shower delivering those twenty-eight blows with that knife*, they said, looking at Dymphna knowingly.

Ray White lasted less than a week. Perhaps because Dymphna had intimated to whoever would listen that she would not be sorry if Ray were to have an accident.

He did, and she wasn't.

⊁ KELPIE ⊁

Kelpie was beginning to trust that Gloriana Nelson wasn't going to kill Dymphna. Though when Glory put her hands around Dymphna's throat and began to strangle her, Kelpie had been very afraid. But then Glory was smiling, and Dymphna too, like nothing had happened. So Kelpie let herself relax about *that*. Glory wasn't going to kill Dymphna.

Or Darcy. Or Snowy. Or Kelpie herself.

Not that minute anyway. But that was about the only thing that was keeping her panic at bay in that stuffy, overwhelming red room.

She tried to attend to their conversation, to concentrate on the whys and wherefores of what they planned to do about Mr. Davidson and Big Bill. But all she could hear was the overlapping voices of all the ghosts in the room.

She'd never seen so many in one house before, almost as if they'd become one huge ghost. Hardly any space in the room wasn't taken up by ghosts. Kelpie had had to walk through them on the stairs and now in this room.

She wanted to turn and run. She wanted to scream.

So many of them staring at her, and pointing, and too many of them talking at her. Even though she couldn't tell where one began and the other ended and none of what they said made any sense. She couldn't even be sure they were real words.

It was like Central Station, only worse because she was inside it.

These ghosts looked like the ones at Central too. Washed out, almost clear, and cobweb grey. Even when Old Ma and Miss Lee had been fading, they were never like this. Stuart O'Sullivan wasn't like these ghosts, and he'd been dead since before the war. He was even older than Old Ma.

They kept moving through Kelpie, making her insides curl. Her heart was beating too fast, she was sweating, and her stomach would not be still.

Kelpie thought she might be sick. She thought she might die.

Someone asked her something.

Kelpie couldn't speak.

A face with overly large eyes and wild hair was hovering barely an inch from her, poking fingers in and out of Kelpie's face. A cluster of ghosts shadowed Glory's every movement. When she sat, they sat. Inside and outside of her. As if they were a part of her. Or packed into some other space that happened to be where she was.

It hurt Kelpie's head to think about it.

She had always been afraid that if ghosts intruded on the space she was in, they could turn her into a ghost. Every part of her they had contact with would turn grey and fall from her body. She couldn't shake the fear that every time a ghost made her shudder they were breaking her into tiny pieces.

But Glory wasn't shuddering. Neither was Dymphna. Though the ghosts were pushing through Dymphna's head.

Kelpie wanted to be deaf to the ghosts, like Glory and Dymphna were.

She wished she could use the knife in her pocket to cut the damn ghosts to ribbons.

"Perhaps if you closed your eyes," Dymphna said, "and laid down for a moment?"

Kelpie close her eyes. She could still feel them.

"It's been a long day for the little pup," Glory said. "Though the pup's not as little as we thought. Doc says you and her are the same age." Glory grinned, looking from Kelpie to Dymphna and then back again. "Shows what a good feed'll do for you. You've got a full foot on that one, Dymphna, and Lord knows how many pounds."

Kelpie had never felt so little, so skinny, so insignificant. If she stayed much longer in this room, there'd be nothing left of her.

"You sure you don't want to lie down, Kelpie?"

"I'm okay," Kelpie managed to say. "A bit hungry." That was a lie. The shudders in her stomach had chased all desire for food away.

"Why don't you run down to the kitchen?" Glory said. "Have one of the boys give you something. Tell Johnno I sent you. You can eat whatever you like. The icebox is full to the gills."

Kelpie quailed. She did not know how to leave the room, how to push through all the ghosts. She could barely see beyond them. She would miss a step, fall down the stairs, break her neck, die.

"Why don't we all go down?" Dymphna said.

"It's getting on, isn't it? Sun'll be setting in no time. You've got the right of it. I do need a bit of food to layer me stomach. Though there won't be as much drinking as I was planning. What with recent events. Got to keep a clear head. We all need that, don't we, girls?"

"Yes, Glory," Dymphna said, knocking back the rest of her drink. Many shimmering hands copied the gesture.

These were the ghosts Kelpie'd always avoided. The ones who never helped you. The ones who were so far removed from when they'd been alive that they'd forgotten what it was like. The ones who had nothing left of being human except mischief and spite.

Dymphna turned to help Kelpie up, taking her hand firmly, and she tried to take courage from it. There were even more ghosts on the stairs. They came out of the walls. Thronged on each of the steps, on the railing too.

Glory was already downstairs. She'd walked through them without faltering, as if they weren't there. Kelpie closed her eyes. If she couldn't see them, then . . .

She could feel them.

Her stomach clenched, shifted. She swallowed and opened her eyes. Large eyes were looking straight at her. She squeezed Dymphna's hand even tighter.

"Come on, Kelpie," Dymphna said.

Glory was talking to one of her men at the bottom of the stairs.

Kelpie kept her gaze down. She tried to slow her breathing, to take that first step and keep on going. Another ghost walked straight through her. She felt like a littlie. Not a grown-up like Dymphna. She reminded herself that they were the same age. If Dymphna was grown up, then she had to be too. Dymphna would not quail at a house full of ghosts. Nothing scared her.

Dymphna leaned down to whisper in Kelpie's ear, "Look down. Say nothing. Don't look at them. Don't think about them. Walk as if you and I are the only ones here."

Dymphna took a step, pulling Kelpie with her. But Kelpie felt herself floating.

Dymphna knows. Dymphna sees them too.

Kelpie could not hold on to that.

How could Dymphna know? How could Dymphna see? How could she not even flinch?

Dark spots filled her vision as if the air was full of holes, but then everything was light, floating upward, unanchored. Kelpie could not stay conscious in such a dislocated world.

She fell into weightlessness.

Betting Shops

Gambling was everywhere in Razorhurst. In every pub, every gentlemen's establishment, as well as the establishments of the not-so-gentle men. Rumour had it that the gentlemen's lavatories on the top floor of David Jones were run by an attendant who was also an SP bookie. Marble sinks; porcelain trough; clean, fresh towels; and a chance to place an each-way bet on the nags. Or whatever else you fancied. Couldn't find better than that, could you?

Gambling was not legal. Which meant there were no regulations. Which meant being able to bet on anything.

Such as: would Glory's party end with the coppers closing it down?

How many more would be dead by midnight?

Was 1932 the bloody year of 1928 all over again? If so, how many dead razors and standovers before the end of the month? Several had money on eleven. Which was how many it had been back in '28.

Would Mr. Davidson take over all of Razorhurst? Short odds. Or would Gloriana Nelson take over the whole pie? Longer ones. Even longer were the odds on them both being gone by the end of the month. But there was plenty of money on it.

Would Dymphna Campbell make it through the day?

She was the Angel of Death, which led many to believe she was impervious to the permanent good night. How could the Angel of Death die? But plenty said, no, her days were numbered *because* she was Death's angel, and Death always came to claim his own. She'd been the best girl in the entire city for how long now? Almost three years. It was clear as day her number was up.

Dymphna would have been saddened to know that the book was running heavily against her. She'd be even sadder to know that Neal Darcy had once killed her himself, under the name of Kitty Macintosh.

She might not have tickets on herself, but everyone else did.

⤛ DYMPHNA ⤜

Dymphna saw Kelpie's eyes roll back. She slipped her arms around her before Kelpie could tumble down the stairs. The girl weighed disturbingly little. Dymphna put one arm under her back and the other under her feet and carried her down. She vowed that she would feed Kelpie more than three times a day—ten or a dozen times—as much as it took for her not to feel hollow boned like a bird.

She vowed, too, to teach the kid everything she knew about ghosts. She should have told her back at the flat. But Dymphna had been rattled, and Jimmy had barely left her side. She could not do anything that would encourage him to stay. She refused to have him haunting her for the rest of her life.

Even so, she should have told Kelpie.

The time to tell her was not at Glory's house caught in a swarm of ghosts.

Dymphna doubted that Kelpie had ever known anyone else who saw them. She had seen only one other person who did, before Kelpie that was. They were rare, Kelpie and her.

She'd handled it all wrong. Might have lost Kelpie forever, she'd made such a mess of things.

Glory looked up. "She fainted?"

Dymphna nodded.

"Take her to the kitchen. We'll get some water and food into her. That'll bring her round. She's practically starving, poor wee pup. I should've had food brought up first thing. I wasn't thinking. Sorry, Dymphna."

Dymphna would almost have believed that Glory hadn't placed her bejewelled hands around her throat and squeezed. She wondered how close Glory had been to killing her.

She followed Glory into the kitchen, Kelpie limp in her arms. Mercifully it wasn't like the rest of the house. There were only two ghosts.

"Hello, Johnno," Dymphna said to Glory's head chef.

Though they could not look less alike, Johnno Bailey reminded Dymphna of Isla, her family's cook. Johnno Bailey cared about food the way Isla had. It was why Dymphna had stepped out with him.

He was the only man she'd been with who was alive to talk about it. Not that anyone knew. Because he was a decent bloke, he'd kept his mouth shut.

"Johnno, clear that crate."

It was an order Johnno would only take from Glory. He gestured the kitchen hand back to his work and gathered up a bag of potatoes so Dymphna could put Kelpie down on the crate. He handed her half an onion. "Stick that under her nose."

Dymphna did. Kelpie coughed.

"Water," Glory said. "Give the puppy water."

Johnno handed Dymphna a cup. She held it to Kelpie's lips as her eyes opened.

"It's all right," Dymphna said. "Sip the water."

Kelpie took the cup in her hands and sipped, then gulped. She held the cup out for more. Dymphna handed it to Johnno, who filled it and gave it back to Kelpie.

Unlike the rest of Surry Hills, Glory's kitchen was modern, with running water, gas you didn't have to put money in the meter for, and electricity. One of her iceboxes was electric.

"How do you feel?" Dymphna asked.

"Better," Kelpie mumbled, staring at her.

Dymphna looked across at where a ghost was sitting with its back against the largest of the iceboxes counting its fingers. She made sure not to catch its eye, then she looked back at Kelpie. Kelpie didn't say anything, but Dymphna knew she understood.

"You need something to eat," Glory said. "Then you'll be right as rain."

Johnno handed Kelpie a sandwich, bacon poking out of the sides. She took a large bite and then another and another, and then it was gone. The girl could eat faster than anyone Dymphna had ever seen.

"You're looking fine, Dymphna."

"Thanks, Johnno. You too."

"Are we ready?" Glory asked Johnno.

He indicated the platters of sausages and bacon sandwiches set to be handed out to the throngs on the back lane. "Just give the word."

Glory looked out the window. "The sun's almost low enough, don't you think?"

"Wouldn't hurt to start a bit early."

One of the waiters came through and whispered to Glory. She

turned to Dymphna and Johnno. "First of the proper guests are here, my lovelies."

Glory smiled at Dymphna, and she could see Glory's joy in all of this: the chaos of wining and dining affluent, tuxedoed men inside and the people of the Hills in back. All the while plotting how to deal with her enemies. Gloriana Nelson had no use for a quiet life.

"Yes, start feeding the proud folk of the Hills. I shall see to me honourable guests. Dymphna, join us when you think the wee one's up to it."

Kelpie still sat on the crate, slumped against the wall. She did not look like she had the energy to stand up, let alone join the party. Dymphna squeezed in beside her on the milk crate.

"I'm sorry," she said softly in Kelpie's ear. "I should have told you sooner. But I didn't want Jimmy to overhear."

Kelpie let her head rest on Dymphna's shoulder.

"The key is to never let them know that you see them. You have to learn to close your eyes to them even when your eyes are open. Focus on what you can touch and taste. Narrow your gaze and close your ears to all but breathing people. Don't see the grey. Shut out the dead."

Dymphna wished she could see more than the top of Kelpie's head. She had no idea how she was responding.

"They prey on us, you know. You can't let them. I'll teach you. Once we're away from this mess—it will be you and me, and I'll teach you everything you need to know."

"Where will we go?" Kelpie asked in a whisper.

"Far away from here. Overseas."

"Somewhere . . . somewhere there are no . . . none of them?"

Dymphna was fairly sure there was no such place. Where there were people, there were ghosts. Hell, where there *weren't* people, there were often ghosts.

"We'll see what we can do."

Johnno Bailey

Johnno was a handsome man who loved to cook.

He'd been a safe-breaker back in the day. Until he'd discovered the glories of bouillabaisse and wound up head chef at Romano's, where he stayed until the Bedford family hired him. Out from the kitchen and into their Vaucluse mansion he went, their private chef at three times his Romano's salary. Only to be let go less than a month later because he made inappropriate advances at the oldest Bedford girl.

The fact that she was twenty-one and had not rejected those advances, that she had, in fact, been ready to run away with Johnno, did not change the Bedford family's version of events. Though it was telling that they did not press charges. Even more telling that Johnno and the Bedford girl still saw each other from time to time even though she'd long since married.

Johnno left the Bedfords' fancy mansion, and Glory snatched him up.

"Always wanted me own chef," she told everyone and was pleased when Johnno's new appointment was mentioned in the gossip columns. She even let him hire kitchen hands and an assistant chef, though he called him a sous-chef, which impressed Glory.

Glory paid Johnno more than the Bedfords had, but she demanded a lot more of him too.

He didn't mind. He was allowed to cook whatever he wanted— except for the proles fed out back when Glory had one of her parties, and he delegated *that* cooking to his underchefs. Besides, with Glory he didn't have to watch his p's or his q's, and the old bird liked for him to be adventurous. She liked trying new things she'd never heard of. She appreciated his artistry.

They were a happy fit. Many suspected they were going to be together much longer than Glory had been with any other man. Big Bill taking a drunken swipe at Johnno, demanding that he cook *bloody normal food*, had been the straw that sent Bill out onto the street and in the direction of a divorce.

Glory couldn't trust a man, even if he was her own husband, who didn't appreciate a good feed.

✕ KELPIE ✕

Kelpie thought Darcy was leaning over her, offering to tell her a story about all the ghosts of the Hills, but his voice was lighter than it usually was. Her eyes weren't focusing. She closed them, counted to ten, opened them again.

It was Dymphna.

Offering her water.

Kelpie drank.

The room swirled. The light had changed colour—everything was gold and pink and red. She couldn't tell who was living and who was a ghost. She thought Dymphna was alive, but she couldn't be sure—hadn't Glory tried to strangle Dymphna, or did she imagine that?—and she didn't recognise anyone else.

Kelpie closed her eyes. Then she was drinking again. More water. It tasted cold. She could feel it slide down her throat and into her belly. It sloshed around in there even though she was sure she wasn't moving. She suspected there was a ghost in her belly. More than one. Small ones running back and forth.

Kelpie opened her eyes to food. She held it, took bites. She couldn't taste what it was. But she chewed and swallowed. There was some kind of film over her eyes, making everything brilliantly coloured. Had all those ghosts, blurred into one giant mass, broken her eyes?

No, she could see Dymphna.

Dymphna who could see ghosts same as Kelpie could.

Dymphna Campbell who was the same as her. Same age, same ghosts.

She closed her eyes again because it was too much. Dymphna Campbell was exactly like her. Kelpie hadn't thought there was anyone like her. She'd thought maybe she was the way she was because her parents were dead almost as soon as she was born and they'd infected her with their ghostliness.

She would have to ask Dymphna if that was true. If that was what had happened to her. Because it could have happened that way, couldn't it? So many mothers died having babies.

Kelpie thought about asking her, but it seemed too hard. Her mouth was heavy. Everything was heavy. But then Dymphna was beside her and whispering, answering her questions. Telling her about ghosts.

The ghosts that Dymphna could see same as her.

Then there was an earsplitting crack. A gunshot. Glass breaking.

Kelpie leapt up. Her ears hurt, but everything was clear. She was in a kitchen. There were two ghosts and eight living, if she included herself. The kitchen looked over a yard that was full of people lining up behind trestle tables piled with food. Everything was gold and pink and orange because the sun was setting over Glory's backyard.

A gunshot.

Someone screamed. Dymphna turned to where the sound of the shot had come from.

Stuey Keating, who had led them through the crowd in front of the house, came running into the kitchen. He was smiling. "False alarm. One of the O'Hannagan kids let off a firecracker. Scared one of the old fellas so much he dropped his glass."

He ran out onto the back balcony and repeated his tidings.

"Which doesn't mean there won't be the real thing later on," Dymphna said.

The tall man with the white hat shook his head. "Not in the Hills. Guns aren't the fashion. Haven't had a proper gunfight since '28. They'll come on us quiet-like, with a blade in hand." He smiled. "Don't worry, Dymph. It'll be right as rain. Glory's tough as nails. Tougher. Every man in this kitchen can more than hold their own. She's got more fellas stationed out front and in back. This place is a fortress with several hundred guards."

He turned back to where he was stirring a reddish-brown sauce that smelled delicious.

One of the other kitchen people opened the icebox. Inside was a giant pink-and-white construction.

"What's that?" Kelpie asked.

The tall man laughed. "That, my girl, is Gloriana Nelson's I-am-shot-of-that-bastard cake. Six tiers, it's got. Pretty impressive, eh? Even if I do say so myself."

Kelpie had never seen anything like it.

"You ready to face Glory and her party?" Dymphna asked.

Kelpie nodded. She had herself back. She hadn't made eye contact with either of the ghosts. She could stand up now. Focus.

She wondered where Palmer was. She hadn't seen him since they'd entered Glory's house.

Kelpie wondered if there really was a place in the world with no ghosts.

Newspapers

Before Miss Lee taught her to read, Kelpie collected newspapers. They could be used for almost everything.

They kept you a lot warmer than you'd expect. You could use them to line your shoes and your coat and your hat—if you had one. You could tear off strips and stuff them into too-big shoes or wrap them around your feet if you didn't have shoes, which Kelpie almost never did. They were excellent ground cover, keeping the cold and the damp further away. You could use them to pad the bench or the tree you kipped down in. You could use them to wipe your nose or your arse.

They absorbed blood and pus.

They worked well, too, for wrapping up the useful things you found: string, sticks, stones, bits of food, a wrench. Kelpie had carried that wrench for months before Mr. Sung agreed to swap it for a fresh loaf of bread. It was a good wrench; but that still-hot bread in her belly had been better. You couldn't eat a wrench.

One old man who always dossed down in Moore Park dressed entirely in newspapers, swore they were warmer than cloth. But at the end of every day, he had to fashion a whole new newspaper suit. Besides which, every time he fell asleep on a bench, the pigeons would start to eat his clothes. Sometimes possums too. If he was lucky, he would wake up in time to grab one. More meat than you'd expect on a pigeon. A possum was three, four meals, easy.

After Miss Lee, Kelpie had a whole other use for newspapers: she could read 'em.

So many strange and wonderful things in newspapers. Reports of police, fires, love gone wrong, and the strange goings-on in the capital and far away over the ocean where the foreign king had sacked the Hills' beloved Big Man without asking a single denizen of the Hills what they thought on the matter. Though from those same newspapers, Kelpie learned that not everyone loved the Big Man. She hadn't realised that was possible.

Newspapers were full of advertisements for everything you could ever imagine wanting, including a cream that made men's hair grow and one that made women's hair disappear and another that faded freckles and warts and made your nose smaller. All it cost was more money than Kelpie had ever had.

The one thing you couldn't do with newspapers was eat them. Though Kelpie had heard some of the older hobos had done that when desperate.

But, like eating dirt, all it did was make you sick.

DYMPHNA

The room was thick with cigarette smoke. A few more hours and it would almost obscure the swirling mass of ghosts.

All the men were in tuxedos. Aside from Glory's men, there were lawyers, respectable businessmen, three senior coppers, two politicians, a judge, and a mining magnate. The tuxedoed men who had never paid for Dymphna's time were uninterested in women.

Glory's waiters weaved their way through the crowd with silver trays of hors d'oeuvres.

Dymphna wished this was one of Glory's girls' parties. No men of any kind, not even standover boys. Those were always the best. Parties of friends. Even when Dazzle was there.

This party was almost all men. Of the worst kind. Old society men. Not that their sons were much better. But at least some of them were pretty.

Dazzle was playing the piano. Lettie turned the pages for her with one hand, playfully fending off one of the respectable businessmen with the other. She winked at Dymphna and gave Kelpie a cheerful wave.

Dymphna couldn't help noting, once again, that it was the society men who were free to venture into the dragon's lair, the den of iniquity. Society women almost never attended Glory's parties, and when they did, it was the beginning of the end. The sure sign that they were losing their grip on the upper echelons and sliding into a far less salubrious life. Only men could cross between the worlds and return unscathed.

There were a few of Glory's old mates from back in the day, their hair as gaudily dyed as her own. Some with husbands, some not. Those not seemed particularly keen on toasting Glory's excellent judgement in finally getting rid of that parasite Bill. "Changes your life, it does, getting rid of your husband. Haven't had a shiner in years," Peggy O'Hara told her.

The woman in question had painted her legs brown to make it appear that she was wearing stockings. It had been many years since the dress she wore was new. It dripped with deteriorating lace, too many layers, all of it concealing corsetry so tight it creaked. No one had dressed like that since before the war. She wore no jewels, having likely hocked even her paste jewellery.

This was how most of the girls wound up. It was only Glory's generous heart that let an old chromo like Peggy attend her parties. The old girl was painfully aware of it too. The sight of her made Dymphna cringe. She knew Peggy's was the more likely trajectory for her kind than Glory's riches.

Dymphna would not allow that to happen. She forced herself to give Peggy a hug, though she was none too clean and smelled like bad gin.

"Who's the wee one?" Peggy asked.

"This is Kelpie, my niece. I'll be looking after her from now on."

Peggy drew a breath and lowered her voice. "Did the poor thing's mother pass?"

"She did."

"Oh, I know what that's like. Me old mam died before I was ten. Never recovered. None of us have. Well, those of us what's alive. I had six brothers and four sisters once." Peggy sniffed. "What about you, little one? How many brothers and sisters have you got?"

Kelpie didn't respond.

"She's shy," Dymphna said as the judge pinched her arse. It hurt, but she didn't flinch. She turned to him smoothly and said, "How are you, Your Honour?"

He slid his arm around her waist and squeezed hard. "Very well, my dear, and you are as beautiful as ever."

He was not. He reminded Dymphna of nothing so much as a warthog. She wished men of this kind spent their time killing each other at the rate that the men from her world did. Or that she could set Bluey loose on the lot of them.

For half a second she saw the room splattered with wide arcs of blood. Dripping down the walls. Red, still many hours from turning brown. She tried to imagine how much blood there'd be if she took a razor to each and every one of their throats. The blood from Jimmy Palmer had splattered across three walls.

Jimmy had shown her his razor. Taught her how to hold it. How to wield it if she had to. Had given her one of her own. She kept it in her handbag just in case. She'd never had to use it. Not even to talk a bloke down. Dymphna had been lucky with her customers, not a one had ever smacked her around. Though many had wanted her to hurt them. That was fine. That was easy.

This was not.

She did not want to talk to these men.

They weren't all bad. The butcher smiled at her. He was a decent man. Even though he had butcher shops all across the city and was richer than he'd ever dreamed. He was still a butcher, and he did not forget it. He was one of those who turned to women like her because his wife was an invalid. Not all these men were terrible. Just the truly powerful ones. And the Mr. Davidsons of the world, who golfed and lunched with these men. They recognised each other, smelled the corruption, smiled. Dymphna wanted to be teaching Kelpie and spending time with Neal. She didn't know much about him. Neal Darcy had no reputation. She hadn't known he existed until she saw him sitting on his back steps smoking a cigarette.

She'd heard all about all her boyfriends long before she met them. Knew who they worked for, who they'd killed, who they'd robbed, how long they'd been in gaol, how they'd received most of the scars on their faces, who their previous girl was. They went after her because they knew who she was, what having Dymphna Campbell as their woman meant: Glory's best girl was only ever with the toughest man in Razorhurst.

Maybe one day, they all figured, she'd find one tough enough to stay alive. Maybe *they* would be that bloke.

Every time one of them died, another one stepped up. As if being with Dymphna was the official trophy for their masculine domination of the worst parts of the city.

But they were also her protectors. When she didn't have a man, she was propositioned by all comers. Her arse was pinched. Her breasts fondled. She was their prize, but they warded off all the other hard men. It was a fair deal.

Neal wasn't like that. He wasn't tough. He wasn't scarred. He'd never killed anyone. He was never likely to kill anyone. He didn't even want to hurt anyone. At least, she didn't think so. He could have taken several shots at Bluey and hadn't taken a one.

Their kisses had been soft, lingering, the sensation travelling from her lips to her toes, making her face warm, her heart speed up. Bad-men kisses were bruising. Their lovemaking fast. As if the violence of their lives left them with no other way of being. They did everything that way: fast and brutal.

Then they were dead.

She couldn't be with Neal. He couldn't protect her. He couldn't protect himself. She couldn't protect him. He'd be dead quicker than Jimmy.

Little Stuey Keating slipped into the room and lingered at the doorway, contorting his face at Glory.

"One moment, sirs," Glory said to the tuxedoed men.

Dymphna pretended to sip at her champagne but drank nothing, her hand in Kelpie's. She tried to force herself not to look across at Stuey and Glory. Whatever it was, they'd deal with it. Glory was smart and well armed. The house was surrounded by her men. Nothing could happen here.

Dazzle and Lettie looked up from the piano.

Glory patted Stuey on the shoulder, then walked over and whispered to Lettie. Dazzle quickened the tempo of her song, while Lettie went to the judge and asked him to dance. Four other couples formed and began hauling themselves around the floor. Peggy and the butcher were particularly enthusiastic.

Dymphna declined a lawyer's invitation to dance. "Perhaps later."

Glory leaned in to whisper in Dymphna's ear, "Inspector Ferguson is outside. He wants to talk to you. He's threatening to raid the house despite all the exalted persons in our midst."

Dymphna pretended to take another sip of her champagne. "Can we get out the back way?"

Glory shook her head. "I can hide you upstairs."

"Hide?" Dymphna said, louder than she intended.

Kelpie squeezed Dymphna's hand. Dymphna couldn't help agreeing. Bad enough hiding in places not infested with ghosts. She was not going to hide again.

If they arrested her, Glory would pay her bail. It would not be so bad. She would not wind up in gaol. They couldn't charge her with prostitution. This was not a brothel; it was Glory's home. No one here had paid for Dymphna's services. Not recently. Nor could they charge her over Jimmy or the constable. She hadn't killed either one, and besides, the constable's body had been disposed of.

Not that the police were above charging an innocent. But she was sure they couldn't make anything stick. Not this time.

Dymphna bent to Kelpie's ear. "I don't want Jimmy to know that I can see him. Don't give me away."

Kelpie gave a little nod.

"Next time we come here," Dymphna whispered, "if there's no avoiding it, you'll know more. It won't be so bad. You can learn to ignore them. I promise."

She stood and smiled at Glory. "We'll talk to the inspector."

"You're sure, love?" Glory asked, squeezing her arm.

Dymphna wasn't, but she had no idea what else to do.

When They Died

All four of them had thought about what would happen to them when they died.

Neal Darcy dreamed of having written the great Australian novel. Many of them, in fact. When he died, he wanted to be an old man of letters, to have travelled the world, to have married a woman like Dymphna Campbell, strong and smart, and for them to have had children of their own. Three or four would be plenty. He wanted to have seen all his brothers and sisters find their own successes and have families of their own. He dreamed of having long since ended his mother's long, hard days of constant drudgery. When he died he wanted his obituary in the paper, three columns wide, with the headline FAMOUS LOCAL AUTHOR DIES. There'd be a huge funeral at St. Mary's, with so many flowers they overflowed onto the street.

Snowy Fullerton hoped to die an old man in his bed. But most days this hope was not strong. Mostly he kept his dreams smaller: to be buried in a plot with his name on the gravestone, leaving someone behind to mourn him. He hated the idea of a pauper's grave, but even that would be better than a concrete-booted plunge into the harbour. Being a practical sort, however, he didn't expect it would much bother him how his body was disposed of, what with being dead and all. Snowy did not believe in the afterlife.

Kelpie didn't care about funerals, or graves, or people remembering her; all she cared about was being the right kind of ghost. She wanted to be like Miss Lee, free to roam. Or even Jimmy Palmer or Tommy. If she had to be a ghost, she wanted to know who she was, to remember having been alive. She wanted to find one of the living, like herself, like Dymphna, and help them as she had been helped. She did not want to be stuck on the one narrow lane, or tram, or motor-car, or stuck haunting a person who could not feel, or hear, or see her. Most fervently she did not want to be trapped in a grey, swirling mass of ghosts. Kelpie would rather pass straight from death to oblivion.

Dymphna Campbell did not want to die. Did not want to think about dying. Did not want to be a ghost. Did not want to go to heaven, or hell, or the void, or nowhere at all. Dymphna Campbell did not want to ever not be.

⤝ KELPIE ⤞

Outside Glory's house, Kelpie could breathe again. No ghosts nearby except Palmer, who reappeared beside Dymphna, looking the way a ghost should: opaque, separate, himself. He was scowling, and Kelpie almost wanted to hug him. None of the ghosts in that house had had expressions of their own.

There were two policemen on the footpath, standing next to an older man in a suit and heavy coat and hat. Though he wasn't in a uniform like them, it was clear that he was their boss. One house down a paddy wagon was parked with two more coppers sitting in the front.

Glory stood beside Dymphna on her front steps. Behind them were Johnno from the kitchen and four of Glory's other men. All of them strong and scary looking. Scars on all their cheeks except Johnno's. Kelpie had to hope there was enough of them to keep the coppers from taking Dymphna away.

On the front lawn, the beer kegs lay on their sides, not even a trickle flowing out of them. Hardly anyone was left outside Glory's, just a few drunks slumped against the fence or asleep in the gutter. It was night. Despite the sun setting, Kelpie had half expected to walk outside into daylight, into this day that would never end.

Kelpie turned to look back at Glory's awful house. The place glowed at night the way Central did. Ghosts flitted past every window, like giant moths. Though moths never looked at her, never tried to fly inside her, to infect her with death. Kelpie shuddered.

"What was it like in there?" Palmer asked. "All those things crawling around."

Kelpie grimaced.

"That bad?"

She didn't want to be standing there knowing they were swirling around and through each other a few feet behind her. She didn't want to die and become like them.

But Dymphna was right: it hadn't been as bad after she'd told her what to do. Standing in that room with the chandeliers and the men in their strange suits, all of them drinking yellow liquid full of bubbles . . . Kelpie had kept her gaze on Dymphna and not the ghosts, watching her, making her the centre of what she saw, giving her her entire focus. Somehow the ghosts had faded into the background.

Her stomach still turned when they went through her. She could still hear their sibilant whispers, but it wasn't close to as horrible as it had been upstairs.

Dymphna bent to speak into Kelpie's ear. "Not a word."

Kelpie wondered how Dymphna was going to keep her secret from Palmer. He haunted her. How was Dymphna going to be able to teach Kelpie anything when Palmer was always around? Or was Dymphna planning on teaching her at Glory's house or at Central Station? Kelpie really hoped there was some other way.

"What'd you say, Dymphna darling?" Glory asked.

"I told her it's going to be all right."

"It will be," Glory said. "Though I cannot say I am entirely happy to see Davidson sitting in the back of that Rolls over there."

Kelpie turned to where Glory indicated. It looked like the same big, black motor-car Mr. Davidson had been riding in that morning. The window was rolled down. Mr. Davidson was in the back, and someone else was beside him. Kelpie couldn't see who.

"Good evening," the man in the suit said, taking his hat off briefly. "Lovely night, isn't it?"

"Beautiful, Inspector Ferguson. You come to join the party?" Glory asked.

If the man in the suit was the boss of the other two coppers, Kelpie wondered why he didn't wear a uniform.

"It's been quite the knees-up. Not every day a woman celebrates being shot of a no-good, low-down, sneaking mongrel of a husband, is it? I believe there are still some canapés left. Aren't there, Johnno?"

"Some of the prawn ones, Glory," Johnno said.

"Oh, I do like those. Very fresh, Inspector. Sweet and succulent. Would you like to come in and try? Loads of champagne and all. Or beer if you prefer."

"Thank you, Miss Nelson. I appreciate it, but I'm on duty. Just wanted a word with young Dymphna here."

Dymphna stood tall. "I told you everything this morning, Inspector."

"Indeed you did. However, a few events have unfolded since then." Ferguson took a step towards them, his two men moving with him.

"Should we be discussing important matters like this with all of Surry Hills listening, Inspector?" Glory asked.

She wasn't lying. Glory's neighbours on either side were leaning over their fences, almost falling into her front yard.

"I agree," said Ferguson. "Better we go back to the station."

"Am I under arrest?" Dymphna asked.

Ferguson considered Dymphna's question.

"Because I haven't done anything."

"It's true, Inspector," Glory said. "Dymphna here is an innocent. Wouldn't hurt a fly. I have a feeling that me and my boys would not be the only ones upset if you insisted on taking her to the police station."

Lansdowne Street was filling with Glory's neighbours. Kelpie saw one man holding a shovel, another a cricket bat. More of Glory's men joined them on her front porch.

Leaning against a fence two houses up was a man who looked a lot like Neal Darcy, wearing a cap pulled low. Kelpie felt Dymphna's grip on her hand get a little tighter.

"We don't want this to get out of hand," Ferguson said.

"Too right," Glory said. "My neighbours are mostly true believers. Still angry about the Big Fella. Longing for that revolution that never bloody comes."

"Are you threatening me and my officers, Miss Nelson?" The copper took a notebook out of the inside pocket of his coat and started writing in it.

Glory laughed. "I really am touched that you remembered to call me miss. Dead polite of you, Inspector. Much obliged. I would never threaten such a polite man. 'Course not. I was merely making an observation. I myself ain't political at all. Can't tell a Trotskyite from one of them, whatcha-may-call-it, Flabby-anns? I'm a law-abiding citizen, I am. But I do know some of my neighbours are less peace-able than meself."

Kelpie didn't think the boss copper believed her. "There are already two dead today. None of us wants the truce to be broken. Or for anyone else to die."

"Too right," Glory said. "Blood on the streets isn't good for business. Anybody's business. We could talk inside." She gestured behind her. "In my home, if that would be acceptable."

It wasn't acceptable to Kelpie. She was not ready to return to the swarm of ghosts. Dymphna didn't say anything, though Kelpie was longing for her to protest, suggest somewhere, anywhere else they could go.

"That will do," the inspector said.

Across the street a horn sounded. Mr. Davidson lifted his hat. Glory nodded. Neither one of them smiled. On the other side of the motor-car, the door opened. A man stepped out. Snowy. His hair looked bright yellow under the street light. He crossed the street.

"Good evening, Inspector," Snowy said. "Glory."

Ferguson wrote something else in his notebook.

Snowy gave Kelpie a quick smile. "Mr. Davidson wonders if you are discussing today's events. If so, he believes that he is an interested party and wonders if he might join your conversation."

Sounded like Snowy was quoting Mr. Davidson word for word.

"How does he reckon that will work?" the inspector asked, looking up. "Because I don't see how this affects him. Unless he's admitting *he* killed my constable? Or Jimmy Palmer? Or that he runs the other half of the crime in this town?"

"Who said anything about running crime?" Glory said. "I'm a respectable businesswoman."

"Of course," Ferguson said.

Snowy held his hands up. "Mr. Davidson is also a respectable businessman. He believes he can offer another perspective on this conversation."

Palmer laughed. "You know, we're only missing Big Bill. If he shows up, we'll have the full set. Can you smell it, Kelpie? Blood in the air. That's what that is."

Trust Palmer to be annoying again, though Kelpie was worried that she *did* smell blood. The inspector had a gun, his men too. The ones on the street as well as the ones in the paddy wagon. Snowy and all of Glory's men would have razors.

Kelpie's hands were in her pockets, the knife gripped tight. If anyone tried to hurt Dymphna, she'd stick it in them. Right through the coat so they never saw it coming.

"What is Mr. Davidson's interest?" Inspector Ferguson enquired.

Several of the neighbourhood men crept closer, Darcy with them. It *was* him. He smiled, looking directly at her.

"He knows who killed Jimmy Palmer," Snowy said.

Dymphna and Glory looked at each other.

Palmer laughed. "Of course he bloody does. He ordered it and you did it, Snowy! Not that I hold a grudge."

Kelpie marvelled at how Dymphna gave no sign that she'd heard Palmer. She hadn't given a sign all day.

How did she do it? *Why* did she do it? Did she tell *any* ghost she could see them? Kelpie figured she'd be dead by now if it hadn't been for Old Ma and Miss Lee. Even Tommy had helped her. Well, not today he hadn't. She wondered again what would have happened if she hadn't fallen for Tommy's false tale of apples.

"Who killed him?" the inspector said.

"Mr. Davidson will tell you privately."

"My arse he will," Glory said. "Jimmy was my right-hand man. Your Mr. Davidson will be bloody telling me and all."

The inspector held up his hand. "All right, then. Mr. Davidson may join us."

"Mr. Davidson wants me present as well," Snowy said.

Kelpie could tell he wasn't enjoying any of this.

"Does he? Why is that?"

"I also have information you need."

Kelpie watched the inspector make more notes. She could almost see him figuring out what to do, how violent this was likely to get. Already been one copper done for that day.

Kelpie didn't trust Mr. Davidson, but she did trust Snowy. Ferguson looked at Snowy and probably saw a big, bad razor man. If Snowy wanted, he could break the inspector in half. The coppers looked like boys next to Snowy. But they looked like boys next to Mr. Davidson too. Not a one of the coppers had much hardness to him. Their eyes looked capable of tears.

Kelpie couldn't help but think of how that copper's hand had shook when he'd pointed the gun at Bluey.

Glory's men would eat them for breakfast.

The inspector clearly did not like his odds. But he could hardly back down either. Backing down was the worst thing you could do in Razorhurst.

Palmer laughed even harder. "You know, it isn't the full set. I mentioned Big Bill, but I forgot one!" He slapped his thigh and continued laughing. Kelpie followed his gaze.

Bluey Denham strode down the street towards them, a double-barrelled shotgun over his undamaged shoulder.

"Blood," Palmer said. "Lots of blood."

Old Ma's Death

Kelpie had been too young to realise it, but she watched Old Ma die. Kelpie hadn't known how to read the signs of illness and decline, because everyone in Frog Hollow was ill and fading away, whether they were alive or ghosts.

Old Ma's skin was yellow. She coughed so hard her phlegm turned red. She shook. She was breathless and easily tired. But so was everyone else.

When Old Ma took to her bed, Kelpie wasn't alarmed. She'd done it before. For weeks at a time.

Then one day Old Ma stopped moving, and then she wasn't breathing, and then she was a ghost.

Kelpie was by her bed drinking the glass of milk Old Ma insisted she drink each day with a slice of bread spread thick with butter, chatting to Old Ma about the new ghost in the back of the lane who didn't yet understand that she was a ghost.

Then Old Ma was in the bed unmoving, her cheeks sunken, her eyes bloodshot, but she was also on the bed smiling at Kelpie, grey all over.

Kelpie did not know Old Ma was dead until her ghost self was attempting to pat her head, to hug her, and then Old Ma had led her away from her dead body to her last few coins, motioned for Kelpie to put on all her clothes, grab a warm blanket, and then taken her to an abandoned house on Little Riley Street to hide.

That was the last Kelpie saw of Old Ma's body. The last time a living person took care of her every day. The beginning of Kelpie's life among ghosts.

✂ DYMPHNA ✂

Dymphna nudged Glory to look in Bluey's direction. Everyone along the street was slinking into their houses or flattening themselves against a fence—anything not to be in Bluey's path. Neal and two other men slipped into a house three doors up.

Bluey strode with the urgency of someone who wanted to kill. Dymphna prayed he hadn't seen Neal.

"Well, shit," Glory said.

Inspector Ferguson turned. "I take it Bluey Denham's another interested party?"

Dymphna felt an urge to laugh. She would not have credited the inspector with a sense of humour.

"You could say that," Glory said.

"Bluey's yours, isn't he, Glory?" the inspector said. "Can you call him to heel?"

"I can try, but he's a bit cranky today. Ropeable, even. There was a bullet in his shoulder."

Dymphna wondered at Glory admitting that. The inspector had to know it was the dead constable who put it there. Perhaps Glory had decided to cut her losses. That Bluey Denham was no longer worth the chaos and death that followed in his wake. Dymphna hoped so.

"I can get him plenty of rope," the inspector said. "If he killed Constable Lewis, he'll hang. Either way, he'll be in gaol a good few years for carrying that banned weapon."

"He might, at that, but I suspect he's planning to go down fighting, taking as many of us with him as he can, which would be"—Glory paused—"unfortunate. Maybe I should have a word with him first?" She started walking down the street towards Bluey without waiting for the inspector's permission.

The inspector told one of his constables to go with her.

"No," Glory said. "Not wise."

The constable looked back at his boss, who gestured for the constable to stop.

Dymphna felt the skin prickle along her back.

"Will he kill her?" Kelpie whispered.

Dymphna shook her head. But what she really meant was that she hoped not. If Bluey shot Glory, then no one was safe. Glory was the only person alive he'd ever paid heed to.

Dymphna took a few steps away, pulling Kelpie with her, glad to have the inspector and his two constables between them and Bluey Denham. The inspector signalled to his men in the paddy wagon. She wondered if it was one of the motor-cars with a radio in it. She hoped so. For once in her life, she would be glad to see more police.

Glory stopped in front of Bluey. He didn't lower the shotgun, but he did stop.

Whatever they were saying was impossible to hear.

Snowy's hand was on the inside of his coat. Dymphna doubted he had a gun. But a razor should be enough to do Bluey. The damaged shoulder undid the advantage of a shotgun.

"Hope you're not thinking of disappearing, Dymphna," Inspector Ferguson said.

"Of course not, Inspector."

She was, though.

Bluey raised the gun. Glory was yelling at him. He fired it over their heads and let out a scream. The kick must have been too much for him with his buggered shoulder.

Shoulder or not, Bluey was lifting the shotgun again. Double-barrelled—he had another shot.

The inspector and constables were running towards Bluey and Glory.

Dymphna tugged Kelpie into motion, and they took off in the opposite direction. Dymphna heard someone running behind them, but she didn't look back. They'd turn at Riley Street. Or . . . Christ, where was there to hide around here?

"This way," Kelpie said. "There's a lane."

Behind them the footsteps were getting closer.

"It's me!" a man shouted.

Dymphna turned. It was Neal.

A motor-car pulled up ahead of them. Two men jumped out. Mr. Davidson's men. Kelpie wheeled around. Neal almost ran into Dymphna. They started back the way they'd come, but Snowy stood there with a razor in his hands.

"We can still—" Neal began.

Mr. Davidson leaned slightly out of the window. "You'll join me now, won't you, lovely Angel of Death? Your two friends are most welcome."

Snowy walked forward and opened the back door. There were two glossy, long, black leather seats facing each other. Nothing but the best for Mr. Davidson. He sat on the one facing forward, his legs crossed, revealing shoes as glossy as his car.

Opposite him sat the ghost of a well-dressed young woman, her clothes only a year or two out of date.

"We're not getting in," Dymphna said.

"I think you are, Dymphna darling," Mr. Davidson said, patting the seat where the beautiful ghost sat. "Plenty of room. I think Inspector Ferguson was quite likely to arrest you. You have been awfully close to rather a lot of violence, haven't you? Not only today, either. Consider me your guardian angel."

"If we go with you, I'll see even more violence." Dymphna turned to walk past Snowy. "Come on, Kelpie."

Snowy blocked her path, putting his hands up so his razor was in the air. "Mr. Davidson won't hurt you." He lowered his voice. "I'll see to it."

"What about Big Bill?" Dymphna asked. "He was all set to hurt us."

"That had nothing to do with me—" Snowy began.

"We'll go with Snowy," Kelpie said.

Dymphna felt her heart speed up. "No."

"I trust Snowy. He's always looked out for me. Coppers will hand me to Welfare. Snowy won't do that."

"I won't."

"You won't let that man hurt us?"

"I promise," Snowy said. "On my life."

Dymphna thought about arguing, but Kelpie's face was set. Walking away meant walking away from Kelpie. She couldn't do it. "Neal, you can go now. This is not your business."

"I'm staying with you."

"Yes," said Mr. Davidson, who'd stepped out of the motor-car. "I think your young man would do much better joining us, rather than, say, having any sort of conversation with the police."

He slid back into his vehicle. Snowy pocketed his razor.

Dymphna looked down at Kelpie. "Are you sure?"

Kelpie nodded.

Dymphna slid across the leather upholstery, holding her breath as she moved through the beautiful ghost, and over to the far window.

Kelpie sat beside her, barely shuddering at her contact with the ghost, and Neal slid in after. Snowy climbed in beside Mr. Davidson and shut the door.

Jimmy slid through Mr. Davidson to sit between him and Snowy. "I've got a bad feeling."

The beautiful ghost smiled. "You should do. Mr. Davidson blew my head off in here. Couldn't even clean all the bits of my brain from the creases in the lovely leather. Had to have all the leather replaced. Any other man would have bought a new car."

"Thought he didn't like doing his own dirty work?"

"He made an exception for me. Nasty temper, that one."

"You're Annie Darling, aren't you?" Jimmy asked.

"You're one of the Angel here's dead men, aren't you, Jimmy Palmer?"

Both ghosts laughed.

Dymphna felt sick. She knew about Annie Darling: she'd been the most expensive chromo in the city, Mr. Davidson's best girl. The city's too. Dymphna had never seen her up close, but she'd admired Annie's style. She disappeared not too long after Dymphna went to work for Glory.

For the first time that day, she truly believed that she was going to die.

"Nothing but bad feelings for everyone from here on out is what I reckon," Annie told Jimmy, who agreed. "Nothing feels good about being shot in the head. It is quick, though. I'll give it that. As I'm sure they'll all find out soon enough."

"If he doesn't have them razored. That weren't quick."

Mr. Davidson leaned forward to tap the glass between them and the driver. The motor-car drove away.

Behind them Dymphna heard a shotgun blast. Then sirens.

Perhaps, if she survived this, there would be no Razorhurst for anyone to rule over.

Family

Dymphna had loved her mother. She had loved her sisters too. Twins they were, Vera and Una.

Her father was another matter. She never spoke of him. She hardly ever thought about him. He was in the closed-off part of her mind. The part she'd bolted and nailed shut and locked and thrown away the key.

Her mother taught her how to sew and cook and balance accounts. Her mother made little sugar biscuits with a lattice pattern of icing on top. They melted in your mouth like butter. Her mother's garden was arranged around the house to attract as many butterflies as possible. Her mother loved butterflies, even though they came from caterpillars that ate up her vegetable patch.

Dymphna taught Vera and Una to dance. Barely three years old and twirling around the garden with flowers in their hair. She taught them every song she knew. But they loved the kookaburra song best.

When Dymphna thought of her home, she thought of the sea of flowers surrounding the house, making the other homes in the street seem far away. The sound of birds singing. The scent of honeysuckle and roses and her mother's cooking.

She did not think of the violence. She did not think of the way it had ended. Or of her running away.

In her memories, her mother and sisters were still alive.

In her memories, her father was buried long ago and far away, and no one remembered his name.

⊱ KELPIE ⊰

The automobile sped through the city, not stopping at intersections, not slowing for corners. Kelpie kept being thrown up against Darcy and then Dymphna, sliding through the ghost of Annie Darling. She worried she was going to be sick.

The sirens receded behind them. It didn't surprise Kelpie that Mr. Davidson could afford a motor-car that was faster than the cops'. Davidson looked like he had all the money in the world.

"This is not going to end well," Palmer said.

"It never does, my love," Annie Darling said. "The trick is to have fun while you can."

Kelpie wanted to tell Palmer that Snowy wouldn't let Mr. Davidson do anything to her, but now that she was in the fast-moving motor-car and none of them was saying anything, she wasn't certain. Snowy hadn't looked at her since he got in, and now she knew that Mr. Davidson had already killed someone in this motor-car.

Wedged between Dymphna and Darcy, it was hard to see out the window. Not that she would know where she was if she could see. It was dark, and they'd probably already left the Hills far behind.

Dymphna's hands were in her lap and her knees were pressed together. Darcy's arms were crossed over his chest. He didn't shake, but Kelpie could tell he was scared. They were all scared.

Mr. Davidson and Snowy sat at either end of their seat. Snowy stared out the window. Mr. Davidson stared at Dymphna. Kelpie didn't know how Dymphna could sit there calmly as if no one was looking at her.

"You'd have been better off with the cops," Palmer told Kelpie. "Men like Davidson don't care that you're still a kid. You could be a baby in your crib, and he'd kill you just the same."

"You are aware that none of them can hear you, possum?" Annie Darling said with a laugh. "You're dead, they're still alive, and never the twain shall meet."

"She can hear us." Palmer nodded at Kelpie. "She won't show it in front of that lot. But she can see us and hear us."

"Really?" Annie did not sound like she believed Palmer. She waved her hand in front of Kelpie's eyes. Kelpie tried hard not to blink. She focused on the carpeted floor and on the smells of this fancy automobile, of the leather and wood. They were different from the smells of cigarettes and stale beer in the taxi. It didn't help. She blinked and wondered how Dymphna managed not to.

Annie waved her gloved hand again, even closer. Despite concentrating as hard as she could, Kelpie blinked again.

"Well," Annie said. "That is interesting. I've been in this motor-car I don't know how long—"

"Three years, maybe," Palmer said. "You disappeared at least two years ago."

Annie gasped. "That long? I thought perhaps a few weeks, maybe months. Well." She paused. "Three years?"

Palmer nodded.

"Not one of them has seen me or heard me. The only dead people I've seen have been outside the car. I thought that they couldn't come inside because I was here. But now here's Jimmy Palmer, larger than death."

She reached forward to touch Palmer's shoulder. Her hand went straight through. "There goes that forlorn hope." She sighed. "No sex ever again. Well, at least we can talk. You're the first person I've spoken to in three years. Three years! How do you move around? I have tried to leave this car—a thousand times—more—but here I stay."

"I wish I could tell you, love," Palmer said.

Kelpie closed her eyes, trying not to hear Annie and Palmer talking. She was tired enough that soon their words slipped past her. She leaned on Dymphna's shoulder, almost falling asleep. She would have nodded off, but she needed to pee. She was thirsty and hungry too. But she was used to those feelings. It grew darker and darker outside. Fewer and fewer lights.

The roads were bumpy now, and she began to smell dust. Kelpie had never been outside the city before. She'd barely left the Hills. The idea made her even more nervous than she already was.

How would she ever get back?

After what seemed like hours, the motor-car came to a stop. Snowy slid out first, holding open the door for Mr. Davidson and then the three of them.

"Can't you stay?" Annie Darling said as Palmer got out of the motor-car behind Dymphna. "Your girl will be dead soon."

Kelpie didn't hear his reply. She was staring at the darkness. It stretched forever. There was nothing but the stars and a faint sliver of the moon for light. She'd never seen anything like it. It made her feel tiny and even colder. She hugged herself.

"You are my guests," Mr. Davidson said. "Terry, see to the fire." One of the men who had been in the front seat hurried away. Mr. Davidson followed. Kelpie had to stare to make out their silhouettes.

"Follow," Snowy said.

Dymphna went first, then Darcy. Kelpie looked at Snowy, who nodded. He'd promised everything would be okay. Whatever Mr. Davidson wanted from Dymphna all the way out here, maybe it wasn't so terrible. Maybe Annie Darling was wrong.

By the motor-car the driver lit a cigarette. The red glow illuminated his face briefly, then he headed after the others.

Snowy reached down to give Kelpie a hug. He'd never done that before. Instead of feeling comforted, Kelpie felt scared.

"What does he want?"

"It doesn't matter what he wants," Snowy said quietly. "He's not going to get it. Come on." He led her into the darkness, which became less dark as her eyes adjusted. Then lights came on. She saw steps. They climbed them to a broad verandah and then into an enormous house.

Snowy led her into a room where Mr. Davidson was sitting on a large leather couch, one leg crossed over the other, his arms stretched out along the back. Dymphna sat opposite on a similar couch, hugging herself. Darcy sat in a large cushioned chair. Kelpie sat beside Dymphna.

The room was very cold. Terry crouched over the fireplace, stacking paper and kindling.

On the table in front of them was a gas lantern. The chandelier was also gas. Kelpie didn't wonder at there not being electricity. Most of the Hills was without, so why would they have it here so far from the city?

There was a whoosh as the fire caught. Terry stood up, wiped his hands, nodded at Mr. Davidson, then left the room.

"I'll see to some food," Snowy said, leaving them.

"How cosy, just the four of us," Mr. Davidson said. He patted his pocket. "I do have a gun, which I am reluctant to use. But I thought it best you know of its presence. Once the fire's going, it warms up quickly in here."

Palmer sat beside him. "He's telling the truth about the gun. It's loaded. It has a gold-plated handle, and his name's engraved on it. Very showy. Doesn't stop it working, though."

"Can I pee?" Kelpie asked.

Mr. Davidson smiled. "Of course, my dear. You'll find the water closet just past the stairs. Do make sure to wash your hands before you rejoin us."

Kelpie scarpered. On the other side of an enormous set of polished wooden stairs, she opened the door on the fanciest toilet she had ever seen. Fancier even than Dymphna's. This one gleamed. The chain above it looked like it was made of gold.

It didn't change the experience of emptying her bladder. She was no more relieved than she would have been if she'd been peeing in a gutter in the Hills.

The house seemed old, but she hadn't seen any ghosts yet. Other than Palmer. That didn't feel right.

She washed her hands. Not because Mr. Davidson had requested it but because Dymphna would have approved. Dymphna liked clean things and was always clean herself, except on days like today—when she'd had to run, climb fences, and hide. Kelpie didn't think Dymphna had endured too many days like today.

She wiped her hands on the towel, then closed the lid of the toilet and sat on it for a moment. She knew she couldn't run. She didn't know where she was, and outside the house she couldn't see much further than her outstretched hands. She didn't know anything about the bush. Except that there were giant goannas. At least if Darcy's stories were true.

She couldn't leave Dymphna or Darcy behind. Or Snowy for that matter.

She wished she knew what Mr. Davidson wanted. They could give it to him and go.

She heard someone speaking loudly. Darcy, she thought.

She could hear Mr. Davidson's voice. Dymphna's also. She braced herself, hoping that she was not going to hear that gun going off.

If Darcy and Dymphna died here, it would be her fault for taking Dymphna to hide in Darcy's home. Had that copper died because of her too?

Would things have gone differently if she'd run away from Dymphna the minute she'd seen her? Or if she hadn't been tempted by Tommy to go in search of those nonexistent apples in the first place?

She would never eat an apple again.

Darcy wasn't yelling anymore.

Kelpie walked back into the living room. The fire was roaring now. Darcy was leaning back in the chair. His chin was up. He looked defiant.

Snowy wasn't back, but the other man, Terry, was sitting by the fire.

"I imagine you would also like to make use of the . . ." Mr. Davidson trailed off.

Dymphna rose. She squeezed Kelpie's upper arm as she walked by.

"You are quite the mystery, young lady," Mr. Davidson said as Kelpie sat next to where Dymphna had been.

Kelpie didn't feel mysterious.

"How is that you are acquainted with the lovely Dymphna Campbell?"

"She's my aunt," Kelpie said because that's what Dymphna kept saying.

"Is she? Where is your family?"

"Dead."

"How interesting. Where are you both from?"

"The North Shore," Kelpie said because that's what Palmer had said.

"Whereabouts on the North Shore?"

Kelpie had no idea. She wasn't entirely clear on where the North Shore was.

"Mosman," Palmer said. "Her family is from Mosman."

"Mosman," Kelpie said.

"Mosman? Quite a nice area. I have always suspected that our Dymphna came from quality stock. She has a certain air about her. Is your family still there? Yours and hers?"

"Dead," Palmer said. "They're all dead."

Kelpie shook her head. "There's only me and Dymphna left."

"Dymphna and I," Mr. Davidson corrected as Miss Lee would have. "I see that you did not have quite the same educational opportunities as your aunt."

Kelpie decided she didn't have to answer that.

"Your aunt is very beautiful. I've seen very few people with hair that colour. Does it run in your family?"

Kelpie nodded.

"But you weren't lucky."

"I got me mum's hair. Brown like a mouse."

Mr. Davidson did not laugh. "Not silver blonde like an angel. I've seen women spend a fortune trying to dye their hair that exact shade. All they get is a head full of straw."

Kelpie wasn't sure what she was supposed to say to that. She'd never seen a woman with straw hair.

"She seems fond of you, your aunt. Yet she never sought you out before today?"

Kelpie wasn't sure what to say.

"Tell him she was looking," Palmer said. "But she only found you today."

Kelpie repeated Palmer's words.

"Where were you?"

"On the streets. Didn't have no one looking after me. Had to look after meself."

"Ah," Mr. Davidson said. "Poor mite. You must have been mightily relieved to be found by your aunt."

"I was. She says she's going to look after me from now on. That I won't be hungry no more." Kelpie spoke the way she used to. The way that used to annoy Miss Lee.

"*Any*more. Does she? You are lucky."

"She says she loves me like I was her own."

"Laying it on a bit thick, don't you think?" Palmer said. "He knows you only just met Dymphna. I see what you're trying to do. You're hoping he won't shoot you. Wouldn't hold my breath on that, little one. He doesn't care much who lives or who dies. Not like Glory. This one's a lot colder."

"I do," Dymphna said, sitting beside Kelpie and hugging her. "Kelpie here is all I have left."

Unhappy Endings

None of Neal Darcy's stories set in Surry Hills had happy endings. They ended with despair or death. Because that's what the Hills did to people. The bush was where hope lay, birth and renewal, happy endings. Neal Darcy longed to live the rest of his life out bush with his own small farm, enough livestock and fruit and veg to feed his family, the money coming from his stories, and Dymphna there too.

He could only write sad stories of broken people when he set them in the Hills.

He tried not to. His stories there were either of honest people who could barely make ends meet, even if they had a job, or of criminals in flash suits with shiny cars and hard-faced women, who were better looking than any of them deserved. He tried to give the first group happy endings and the second misery.

But Surry Hills didn't lend itself to happy endings for anyone.

Besides, when he wrote about those hard men, he started to understand them as well as he understood the honest men. They were every bit as desperate, as filled with longing for the elusive happy ending. They loved and sorrowed as strongly as anybody else.

His stories about them always ended with that flash suit shot full of holes or cut to ribbons. With the dead man's family wailing, every bit as shattered as they would be by the death of an honest man. Death was death and love was love, no matter who was suffering it.

In Surry Hills—*Sorrow Hills* as so many of the older folks called it—one often led to the other. The two could not be separated: love and death; death and love.

In Neal's love stories, one of the lovers ran away, or lost all his or her money, or went to gaol, or became so sick there was no hope, or died, or killed the other, or both lovers were killed by a jealous husband.

Neal wanted to write his and Dymphna Campbell's love story. The one with the happy ending. He wouldn't call her Kitty

Macintosh this time—how had he ever thought that name was right for her?—and he wouldn't let her be killed at the end.

There would be a cottage out bush, surrounded by flowers, and her and him, and death a million miles away.

✂ DYMPHNA ✂

Dymphna had spent most of her life living with terror. She had long since learned to hide her fear. Besides, this man did not scare her as much as her father had. No one could. At that moment, her impatience was stronger than her fear. She wanted to hear him out and then get away.

Davidson only had Snowy, that Terry person, and his driver, who was yet to come into the house.

Snowy returned carrying a tray of sandwiches, neatly cut in halves, which he placed beside the gas lamp on the table. He sat on the remaining empty chair.

"You wouldn't suspect it to look at him, but Snowy is quite an adept cook," Mr. Davidson said. "He's been looking out for himself for many years now. A man alone needs to know how to prepare food as much as any woman does. Isn't that so, Snowy?"

Snowy agreed that it was.

Kelpie slipped off the couch and picked up half a sandwich. She slid back onto the couch and took a bite. Dymphna wished she could do the same. The sandwiches were fat with ham and cheese and lots of butter. From the expression on Kelpie's face, they were delicious.

Neal made no move towards the food either. Good. Neither one of them could afford to relax around this man. They could eat later.

Kelpie slipped forward to take more.

Mr. Davidson smiled. "Take as many as you want, little one. You sure you wouldn't like some, Dymphna? It has been rather a long day, hasn't it? You must be quite worn out and hungry."

"Thank you, no," Dymphna said. "I'd rather we discuss why I am here."

"Ah," Mr. Davidson said. "Would you like a drink? I can offer you whisky, wine, sherry. Even beer if you would prefer. Though surely you are too much of a lady for ale or lager."

Dymphna declined. She wasn't going to be in his debt even for something as trivial as a mug of ale.

"Straight to the business at hand then?"

"Yes."

"I wish you could tell her to turn on the charm, Kelpie," Jimmy said. "Davidson won't like her being curt. She'd be better off trying to manage him."

"You may leave us," Mr. Davidson said to Neal and Kelpie.

Kelpie didn't move. Neither did Neal.

"Would you rather I insist?" His hand slid into the pocket where Jimmy said his gun rested. "Snowy, could you escort them outside?"

"If they leave, I won't discuss anything with you," Dymphna said.

"I think you are forgetting where you are."

Dymphna almost laughed. "You want something from me. If you take them away, you won't get it. I won't believe they're safe unless they're in front of me."

"What if they're not safe even in front of you?" Mr. Davidson smiled. "Snowy, kill the boy."

"Jesus," Neal said, standing up.

Snowy stood too, but he did not move towards Neal Darcy.

Dymphna rose. Somehow she managed to keep her voice even, to sound calm. "Then it hardly makes any difference that they're here, does it? If you hurt Neal or Kelpie, you'll get nothing from me."

"I can take it from you."

Which was when she knew he was bluffing. "If that's true, then why speak to me at all? Why didn't you snatch me from the street this morning? Why didn't you have Big Bill kill me? If you can take what you want, then take it."

"You have a point." Mr. Davidson smiled. His teeth were too white and too even. "Sit down, everyone."

Dymphna did not sit. "What do you want, Mr. Davidson?"

"I'd like you to sit. We can discuss this calmly. Are you sure you wouldn't like some wine?"

Dymphna sat down. "Quite sure."

Neal did not. "Let's go, Dymphna, Kelpie. We don't have listen to a madman." He looked like he was ready to kill Mr. Davidson. Like he didn't realise that Davidson was the one with a gun. With the men.

Out of Mr. Davidson's line of vision, Snowy shook his head. Dymphna willed Neal to listen.

"You will sit, boy." The gun was now in Mr. Davidson's hand. "Or you will regret it."

Neal sat, but his face had darkened. A vein stood out above his left temple.

"I think it would behove us all to be calm, don't you, Dymphna?"

Dymphna nodded. It was about the only thing they agreed on. She needed Neal to keep his head. Kelpie too.

Mr. Davidson rested his right hand, holding the gun, on his knee. "You asked what I want, Dymphna Campbell? I want you."

He said it as if it were a great revelation. Jimmy Palmer laughed. "Show me a man who doesn't. Well, other than Snowy."

"That's flattering, Mr. Davidson, but I work for Gloriana Nelson. She pays me well and has always taken good care of me. I hear you don't even pay for a doctor for your girls. Why would I work for you?"

"If that's true, then why were you and the late Mr. Jimmy Palmer plotting to take over from her? And from myself, I might add. You wanted Razorhurst."

"That was all Jimmy's doing," Dymphna lied. Well, that answered that question. He had known. She itched to ask him how.

Jimmy laughed. "It was the both of us. Together. Though she started the ball rolling."

Dymphna would have loved to correct Jimmy. He'd made the suggestion first. But it didn't matter. They'd been equally enthusiastic about the plan.

"I was happy the way things were," Dymphna said. "But Jimmy—"

"Is dead. I am not. Gloriana Nelson and myself—we're still here, still in control. Though her position is more precarious than it was. Who knows, she may already be deceased. There was rather a lot of gunfire behind us, wasn't there? But even if she has survived . . ." He waved a hand in the air. "Jimmy Palmer was a good lieutenant. She doesn't have anyone else as smart and as strong as him. Her husband's gone. All that's left is Glory and some not-very-clever muscle. Easy pickings. So thank you for that."

"She's stronger than you think. She has me. I'm every bit as smart as Jimmy was. She'd have to be dead before—"

"She may well be. If not today, some day soon. If I were you, I would not wager on her living longer."

"Are you saying you're going to kill her?"

"I suspect I won't have to. She's a lone woman now. Vulnerable. There's an ocean of standovers out there, and far too many of them are as ambitious and greedy as your Jimmy Palmer."

"Wasn't greedy," Jimmy muttered.

"I won't work for you." Dymphna said.

"I didn't say I wanted you to work for me. I said I want you to be mine."

She failed to see the difference. Except that it was safer having many different customers. If you only had one and you failed to please him, well, she'd seen what happened to girls like that. It didn't matter how beautifully decorated the home they were kept in was, because it wasn't theirs. When it was over, they were out on the street. Whether that happened to them at sixteen or sixty.

"Yours?" she asked him, trying and probably failing to keep her contempt out of her voice. "I'm not a thing, Mr. Davidson. I'm a person."

"I'm offering to marry you."

Dymphna stared at him, suppressing laughter. Mr. Davidson *was* mad. He seemed unaware of how insane his proposition was.

No one said anything.

"I would make you my wife. Everything I have, you would have: houses, cars, horses, jewellery. Razorhurst. You'd rule it. And beyond. Like you wanted. But from a safe distance."

Dymphna couldn't help noticing that he didn't mention guns, or razors, or illicit grog, or drugs, or chromos. Would all those be hers too? Surely he was joking?

"You would be one of the richest women in the country. I would lift you out of Razorhurst and into the finest circles of society." Mr. Davidson wasn't smiling. There was no hint of irony in his words. He *had* lost his mind. How did he think their marriage would work?

"I would take you all over the world. You've never been overseas, have you? There's so much to see. So much to experience. You would love it."

Dymphna put up her hand. He had to stop. This was ridiculous. "I'm a chromo, Mr. Davidson. A whore."

"You *were* a whore."

"Am a whore."

"You're too good to be a whore."

"No, you're wrong, Mr. Davidson. I'm exactly the right amount of good. I have a talent for what I do. I'm a talented whore. It's not because I'm beautiful. Or because I'm young. It's because I know how to please a man. Any man. That's why I'm the most expensive chromo in the entire city. Probably the entire country. There's not a man I've taken on who hasn't been satisfied. It's my gift."

That and death, she thought.

"Shut up!"

Beside her Kelpie tensed. Dymphna fought to keep her own shock from showing. Everyone knew that Mr. Davidson never yelled. Never lost his temper. Yet here he was, his face red and the veins on his forehead and neck visible.

"Don't push him, Dymph," Jimmy said.

But Dymphna couldn't let Davidson see how scared she was. "Those fine society men," she said, as if she was unaware that Davidson was furious and had a gun in his hand, "I've fucked more than half of them. *Those* are the circles you want to impress? How can you with a whore like me on your arm? They would laugh at you."

"Snowy, I said to kill the boy."

Snowy did not move.

Mr. Davidson turned and shot Neal in the chest in one motion.

Someone screamed. Dymphna didn't think it was her. She was on her feet. Neal convulsed. Blood poured out of his mouth. She took a step towards him. He was still alive. She needed to keep the rest of his blood inside him.

Mr. Davidson shot Neal once more and then pointed his gun at Dymphna's stomach.

"You're not a whore."

"I am a whore," she said softly, as if he might see reason. Neal stopped moving. His eyes were open. "I like being a whore." She returned Davidson's stare. Surely he could not pull the trigger, standing so close, looking into her eyes. Not if he wanted her as much as he said he did.

He lifted the gun higher, aiming at her heart.

"Killing me won't change who I am, Mr. Davidson, and it won't make me yours."

Kelpie lunged at him.

Mr. Davidson fired.

Funerals

In Razorhurst when you died you were buried. Cremations were for heathens. Christians buried their dead. Even the indigent poor were buried.

In the Hills almost everyone was Irish and Catholic, and that meant a wake. Plenty of grog and not all of it drunk by the priest. Enough food to sink an ocean liner. Even if you were poor as church mice.

Funerals were days when everyone ate and drank and cried and didn't think about how much that coffin and the flowers and all that grog and food cost until the morning. The father might have drunk all your whisky, but he gave you a chunk of the collection to go towards your expenses. If you were really poor, the church would even give you clothes to bury your loved one in. Especially if it was your child.

Those funerals were the worst.

Hard to come back from burying your own child. Your children should not die before you. Parents die first, then children. That's the natural order of things. Not in the Hills, though. Not always. Sometimes it felt like not ever.

Flowers and a coffin and a nice little burial suit did not do a thing to ease the ache in your heart. That's what the alcohol was for.

That and to put you a few steps closer to your own grave. Why live once your children were gone?

Thank God for the music. The few fiddles that weren't in hock were brought out. Everyone sang. Everyone cried.

It was beautiful.

But your loved one?

They were still dead.

⊁ KELPIE ⊱

The knife was in Kelpie's hand, and then it was in Mr. Davidson's belly.

She pulled it out and stabbed him again. He swatted at her, but she ducked and stabbed and stabbed and stabbed, wiped the blood from her eyes, and kept on stabbing.

He grabbed at her shoulders. She didn't care. She didn't care if he shot her. She didn't care what he did. Kelpie wanted him to die. She kept stabbing at his belly. Even though the knife was slippery now and hard to hold on to. Even though the smells from Mr. Davidson's insides made her gag.

Mr. Davidson slid away from her sideways on the couch. Kelpie kept stabbing, but it was as if she was stabbing the couch. There was no resistance. She stepped back. The knife dropped from her hands.

"Cait's knife," Snowy said.

Mr. Davidson's throat gaped open like Palmer's had. Snowy stood behind the couch, a razor in one hand, a clump of Mr. Davidson's hair in the other.

"Fucking good riddance," Terry said.

Or it could have been Palmer. Kelpie wasn't sure. Her ears were filled with a roaring sound.

There was blood everywhere.

She turned to Dymphna, who'd slid to the floor. She was opening and closing her mouth. Her hands were shaking, blood all over her.

Kelpie had never seen so much blood. She could taste it.

"Are you shot?" Snowy asked.

Kelpie didn't know who he was asking. She shook her head, though she wasn't sure. There was too much blood in her mouth to speak.

"No," Dymphna said. "No, no, no, no."

Snowy moved around the couch and put his hands on Kelpie's shoulders. "You're sure you're not hurt?"

Kelpie didn't know.

Snowy patted her arms, her stomach, her legs.

"You're not hit."

He turned to Dymphna. "Can you stand?"

Dymphna nodded, but didn't move. She was shaking. "It was like watching myself," she said softly. "I used a knife . . ."

"You're stunned," Snowy said. "It's like that the first time you see someone killed. You'll be better in a while. I'll get us something to drink. That helps."

Dymphna shook her head.

"It's not the first time," Palmer said. "She saw me like this."

Kelpie knew that wasn't right. Dymphna hadn't been there when Palmer was killed. She hadn't been like this.

Outside the motor-car started up. Snowy grabbed the gun and dashed out of the room.

"It was my sisters," Dymphna said. "My mother."

Kelpie wasn't sure who she was talking to. Then Dymphna looked straight at Jimmy Palmer. "My dad did for them . . . It was like this."

"You can see me?" Jimmy said.

"I can see all the ghosts. Every single one."

"But," Palmer said. He was fading. "You never said—"

Then he was gone.

Dymphna turned to look at Darcy. Reached out her hand to touch his arm. "I killed another one, didn't I? Angel of Death."

Kelpie spat to get some of the blood out. "Mr. Davidson killed him."

Dymphna laughed. "Too right, he did."

She leaned across and closed Darcy's eyes. Her hand lingered on his face for a moment. Then she turned to Kelpie, holding out her hand, and Kelpie took it.

"What should we do, Kelpie? Run or stay? March into Surry Hills, take over Razorhurst?"

"Sorrow Hills," Kelpie whispered, because she was thinking that Old Ma had been right to call them that.

"I could be Glory's right-hand man. Snowy's proved himself killing Mr. Davidson. I'm good at numbers, at people. I'm smart. I've got polish. I could run it better than she could. I could take over Davidson's side too. I could say we were married. But then I'd have to deal with Glory. I don't want to deal with Glory. I like Glory."

She put her hands to her throat. Faint bruises had appeared where Glory had squeezed.

"Perhaps best we go. Buy our passage. See the world. Plan nothing."

"Somewhere like this? Without ghosts?" As Kelpie said it, she looked first at Mr. Davidson and then at Darcy, half expecting their ghosts to appear.

"Not everyone becomes a ghost. Mostly people just die."

"He *could* be a ghost. Maybe back at the Darcys' place. We could go there, find him. He could tell me his stories, and I could write them down." Kelpie could feel it wasn't true even as she said it. Darcy hadn't loved his home, hadn't loved Surry Hills. He hadn't been born there, and he hadn't died there. If he haunted anywhere, it would be somewhere out bush.

Or maybe it would be Dymphna, but he wasn't here.

Darcy would never write another story.

Kelpie's throat burned. She blinked. It was a weakness to cry. Dymphna wasn't crying. Kelpie wouldn't cry. She kept blinking. Her face was wet. Probably blood.

There was so much blood.

Razorhurst

Nineteen thirty-two was a banner year for blood. Worse, even, than 1928.

The year didn't start that way. In January, the heat and humidity hung like a miasma over the streets of Razorhurst, and the king and queen were Mr. Davidson and Miss Gloriana Nelson. Coppers and judges in their pockets. Houses built out of sly grog, drugs, women, and, yes, blood, but not the way it had once been.

But in the winter of 1932, everything changed.

Throughout the east of the city—Surry Hills, Darlinghurst, Woolloomooloo, Kings Cross, Paddington—blood flowed. Razors cut up faces, sliced off ears, opened up chests and bowels, went in through the eye, the ribs, the throat. They maimed, crippled, and killed.

Blood artists they considered themselves; but butchers is what they were.

Chaos is what they unleashed.

⊱ KELPIE ⊰

If Mr. Davidson had become a ghost, he wasn't anywhere Kelpie could see him. A small mercy. Terry and Sam the driver helped them drag Mr. Davidson's body deeper out into the property. They buried him near an ants' nest and didn't mark the spot.

Turned out Terry and Sam'd never liked the man either.

"No one did," Snowy said.

"Amen to that," Dymphna said.

"May he rot in hell," Terry said and spat on his grave.

"For all eternity," Sam added.

Kelpie felt the same anger rise up in her. She wanted to dig Mr. Davidson up and start stabbing him again. He had killed Darcy for no reason. Except that he could. Kelpie was glad he was dead. She hoped his ghost had ended up in the tangle at Glory's house. He would hate that.

They walked back through the long brown grass that was almost as tall as Kelpie. Even though it was cold, the sun beat down, and Kelpie wished she had a hat like the others.

Darcy would have loved it here. So many of his stories were about being out bush, looking for miles and seeing nothing but land, no buildings, no people.

Kelpie didn't like it. But she thought she might if Darcy was here to explain it to her. There were fewer ghosts, and not a one of them had tried to talk to them. That, she liked. She'd never been anywhere so silent.

No one said anything. Dymphna raised a canteen they'd taken from the house to her lips, drank deep, then passed it along as they walked.

"Will we bury Darcy too?" Kelpie asked when the house came into view. She wanted to. She hated the idea of leaving him there soaked in his own blood, flies already gathering, even in the cold.

"No," Snowy said. "The caretaker gets back in a day or two. It's better Darcy's found. So people know what happened. Think of his ma."

"And his brothers and sisters," Dymphna said.

Kelpie knew they were right. Mrs. Darcy would need to know

what had happened to her oldest boy. She'd want to sit vigil. Drink whisky. Cry. Bury her boy.

Kelpie's throat burned. She couldn't believe Darcy was dead. For the first time, she was glad that Miss Lee had faded and didn't know Neal Darcy had never written a book. She'd been sure he'd write hundreds.

Darcy had been going to teach her to use his typewriter. So she could write stories too.

All of that was gone.

"What do we do now?" Dymphna said. She brushed a stray fly from her face.

"I'm going back to the city," Terry said. "Don't like the bush."

"Me neither," Sam said. "Got a wife and a kid."

"We run or we go back there," Snowy said. "We leave this state—"

"This country," Dymphna added.

"Or we take over Razorhurst."

"I'd back you," Terry said. "All of Davidson's people would, Snowy."

"Not all of them," Sam said. "You're not white, Snowy. Wouldn't sit right with some."

Snowy nodded. Kelpie couldn't see what difference that made.

"Most would," Terry said. "More than enough."

Snowy did not look convinced.

"I'd have almost all Glory's girls," Dymphna said. "And a fair few of her men. If Glory's dead, I mean. Perhaps even if she's not. I don't want to kill her."

Kelpie was sure that Glory would kill Dymphna if Dymphna was in her way.

"I don't want to kill anyone," Snowy said. He sounded tired.

"But it can't be helped," Terry said. "Not if you want to run Razorhurst."

Kelpie couldn't figure out why they wanted to run Razorhurst. If Bluey was still alive, how would they get him to do what they said? They wouldn't. So they'd have to kill him. He wouldn't be the only one. Every death led to another. If Jimmy Palmer hadn't been killed by Snowy, that copper wouldn't be dead, and Mr. Davidson, not that him being dead was anything but good, and, and—her thoughts didn't want to go there—Neal Darcy would still be alive.

Killings multiplied.

"We could say Mr. Davidson and I were married," Dymphna said. "I know someone who could do the certificate for us."

"You'd take over," Snowy said. "I'd be your top man."

"Could work," Terry said. "If it looked like Snowy was calling the shots. No offence, Miss Campbell, Mrs. Davidson, I mean." He smiled. "But we know Snowy, we don't know you, and . . ."

"He's still black," Sam said softly.

"And what?" Dymphna asked Terry.

"Nothing."

They were back at the house. Snowy sat down on the steps. Darcy lay dead inside. His head rested on the couch, his mouth open.

"And I'm a chromo?" Dymphna said, sitting next to Snowy.

"You're a woman," Terry said, sitting on Snowy's other side. "Wouldn't sit right with some of the fellas. Way Glory doesn't always sit right. Plenty of Davidson's men won't work for a woman. I hear some of Glory's have been peeling off since she tossed Big Bill."

"Dymphna's a woman," Sam said. "And Snowy's black."

"It wouldn't matter," Terry said. "We trust Snowy."

"It would," Snowy said.

"You don't think we could do it, Snowy?" Dymphna asked.

"I think the odds ain't good. We don't know what's happened back there. Drove away from a lot of shooting. We don't know who's dead or who's alive."

"How close is the nearest 'phone?" Dymphna asked. "We could find out what happened."

"About twenty miles away," Sam said.

"Not sure I want to know," Snowy said. "Jack of the lot of them. Jack of Razorhurst and all."

Kelpie couldn't agree more. She wouldn't miss Gloriana Nelson or Bluey or Big Bill or Cait or any of that mob.

"Me and Jimmy, we were going to take over," Dymphna said. "We planned it all out. Seemed real before we'd done a single thing. Mr. Davidson has a mistress in the city."

Sam nodded. "Donna. I'd always drop him off in the lane behind the house."

"Then you'd drive away. Mostly before he'd gone in. It's a quiet lane. Jimmy was going to jump him there. But he found out."

Sam's cheeks got a little redder. He pulled out a cigarette, started to say something.

"I don't want to know how he found out," Dymphna said. "Davidson's dead. Doesn't matter anymore, does it? He's dead. Jimmy's dead. That constable. Neal Darcy . . ." Dymphna paused.

Kelpie slid her hand into Dymphna's and squeezed it.

"Who knows," Dymphna said more firmly, "who else is dead? Bluey? Glory? Johnno? Those coppers? Could be we'd be walking into a bloodbath. The cops already going in hard to clean up. Like they did back in '28."

"Let's go somewhere else," Kelpie said. "Some place without . . ." She trailed off because she couldn't say *ghosts*. Dymphna reached out to touch her face.

"Violence?" Snowy asked. "Wouldn't that be grand?"

Dymphna wrote a letter for Terry to give to Mrs. Darcy. She gave him ten pounds for delivering it and sealed one hundred pounds in the envelope with the letter. Snowy said Terry could be trusted. Kelpie hoped so.

Kelpie thought about that hundred pounds. She couldn't imagine how Mrs. Darcy could ever spend it all.

After Terry and Sam left, Dymphna cut her hair short and put on some of the caretaker's clothes. She didn't look like a man, but she didn't look rich anymore either.

Snowy shaved his hair off. Made him that little bit less visible. A six-foot-four black man with blond hair they'd find in seconds. A six-foot-four black man with a shaved head didn't stand out as much.

They would stay off the main roads. Work their way north. Way, way north. Then find a boat to some other country. They had money. All the money Dymphna had hidden in her clothes and bag. There was more money hidden away in the house. Mr. Davidson's stashes, Snowy called them. They hid it in their clothing, the lining of their hats, in the swags Snowy put together.

Dymphna said she'd always wanted to travel. Kelpie hadn't realised it was a possibility. Kelpie had thought she'd live her whole life in the Hills, and that was a step up from living her whole life in Frog Hollow.

"You'll love it," Dymphna said. "Seeing the whole wide world."

"Mango trees," Snowy said.

Kelpie had no idea what mangoes were.

"Coconut trees," Dymphna said.

Or coconuts.

"Yes, and monkeys," Snowy added.

"Monkeys, really?" Dymphna asked. "Have you ever seen a monkey, Snowy?"

He shook his head. "But we will."

"I'd like to see a monkey," Kelpie said, and Dymphna hugged her. Kelpie realised that it didn't make her feel strange anymore. She liked it.

Snowy ruffled her hair. "You can be my daughter."

Dymphna smiled. "I was going to be her aunt. But we're the same age."

Snowy stared. "*You're* sixteen? Jesus Christ."

Dymphna laughed. "I am sixteen and now I can *be* sixteen, can't I? I can stop pretending."

"You can," Snowy said. He still looked stunned.

"Are you old enough, Snowy?" Kelpie asked. "To be my da?" She paused. She still didn't quite believe that she and Dymphna were the same age.

Snowy and Dymphna both laughed. Kelpie'd never seen him laugh before.

"I'm an old fella," he said, the laughter gone from his voice. "I'm old enough to be your dad."

"But you're black."

"We'll say you had a black father and a white mother. Can lead to a light daughter. You're plenty brown for a white girl. Besides, people see what you want them to see. If we say I'm your da, you'll look even browner to them. It's always that way. We just need to get away from this country, or they'll take you away."

Dymphna was looking at Snowy differently than before and then back at Kelpie. "Been watching over her all her life, haven't you, Snowy?"

Snowy nodded. "I'm not proud of the job I've done."

"Old Ma asked him to," Kelpie said. "Like I told you. You've been good, Snowy. Lost count how many times you helped me out."

Snowy shook his head. Dymphna didn't say anything else.

"I want to leave," Kelpie said, though what she was feeling was bigger than that.

She also wanted to go back to the Hills because that's what she knew. Here she could see for miles, and there was not another house. It made her feel almost as strange as Central Station did, like something was wrong. But she didn't want to see Glory again. Or Big Bill. Or Bluey Denham. Or Cait. Or Tommy, whose lies had started this whole mess.

No apples. Not ever.

She wanted to go somewhere without ghosts. Or at least fewer ghosts than the city. Somewhere her heart wouldn't hurt with every step. She didn't know where that place was. She didn't know if such a place existed.

"Will you buy me a typewriter?"

Snowy laughed again. Kelpie liked the sound.

"Soon as we get settled," he said.

"We'll buy you a dozen," Dymphna said.

"Right-o," Snowy said. "We'll buy you all the typewriters in the world."

Kelpie smiled at that, even though it hurt. She only wanted the one.

GLOSSARY

Note: This glossary gives a definition for each word as it is used in *Razorhurst*. Some of these words have other meanings and many of them are no longer used in Australian or any other kind of English.

abo: a racist term for an Australian Aboriginal person

barney: a fight

bickie(s): a cookie

billabong: a pond or lake cut off from a main river

billycart: go-kart

bludge/bludging: to obtain by taking advantage of another's generosity

bonzer and bosker: excellent

to bottle: to attack someone with a broken bottle

brick: £10

bub(s): a small child

bung on: to put on

the bush: the remote countryside, far from the city; often used in an idealised sense as the Bush in opposition to the City

(to go/gone) bung: broken down, not working, fallen apart

(to go/went) bush: to run away, disappear; to abandon the city for the remote countryside

(out) bush: living in a remote area

chiack: tease

choko: chayote; a bland green fruit often used to replace apples in cooking

chook(s): chicken(s)

Chrissie: abbreviation of Christmas

chromo: prostitute

cockatoo/cockie: a lookout

cooee: a bush cry to attract attention

crim(s): abbreviation of criminal

damper: a bread made without yeast

dingo: someone who can't be trusted

to turn dingo: to betray someone; to inform on someone to the authorities

dropped her bundle/to drop one's bundle: to lose it

dunny: toilet (usually outdoors)

(not the) full quid: someone who is not all there

galah(s): a fool

get(ting) stuck into: to attack someone either physically or verbally

goal: jail

goanna(s): monitor lizard

good-oh: okay

guns: experienced shearers

haitch(es): letter h

humpy: a temporary shelter; originally a temporary bush hut made by Australian Aborigines

jack of: sick of

kookaburra: a common Australian bird with a distinct call which sounds like a human laugh

lookout: one's own business and thus not anyone else's responsibility

newie(s): rookie

nick (off): piss off

pannikin (as in "off his pannikin"): A metal pan or small metal cup, typically used out bush. Often used in the phrase "off your pannikin" crazed, deranged, out of your mind

Phar Lap: Australia's most famous racehorse, though she actually hailed from New Zealand

proddie: derogatory term for a protestant

right-o: okay

ropeable: very angry

rouseabout (or "rousie"): someone who does odd jobs, usually out bush

sly grog shop(s): an unlicensed bar or liquor store where you can buy alcohol outside the legal hours for the purchase of alcohol

smoodge: to ingratiate yourself into someone else's affections

southerly buster: the cold wind that blows in from the antarctic

spear/speared: sacked

squatters: privileged landowners who may or may not have acquired their land legitimately who now consider themselves to be Australia's aristocracy. Or, at least, are considered to believe that of themselves by those who are less well off

(to have a) squiz: to take a close look

standover men/man: someone who uses the threat of violence to extort

strewth: interjection

swag: one's personal belongings rolled up in a blanket and carried over one's shoulders in order to travel through the bush

tradie(s): tradesperson

trey: threepence

trots: harness racing

two-up: a gambling game involving two coins

zack: five-cent piece

◦ ∾∾ *Acknowledgments & Influences* ∾∾∾

As usual my agent, Jill Grinberg, has been both supportive and encouraging as I worked on this book. And patient, *really* patient. Her editorial comments were invaluable.

This book was marvellously well edited in Australia by Jodie Webster and Hilary Reynolds. And for this US edition by the eagle-eyed Daniel Ehrenhaft.

Thanks to Daniel, Meredith Barnes, Rachel Kowal, Amara Hoshijo and everyone at Soho Press. You've been fabulous to work with.

Thank you to my first readers, Scott Westerfeld, Megan Reid, Alaya Dawn Johnson, and Jan Larbalestier.

K. Tempest Bradford helped keep me going with our weekly chapter exchange.

Thanks to Donna Nelson for allowing me to borrow her surname, suggesting the first name Gloriana, and telling me tales of her family's years of living in Surry Hills.

Thanks to Gwenda Bond and Christopher Rowe for typewriter research.

This book would not exist if Johnny Heron hadn't insisted that I read Larry Writer's *Razor: Tilly Devine, Kate Leigh and the Razor Gangs*. You were right, Johnny, it's a wonderful book.

Razorhurst was also inspired by my move to the venerable Sydney suburb of Surry Hills. Although I grew up in inner-city Sydney, I had never lived in any of the suburbs that made up Razorhurst until 2005.

My Surry Hills home is around the corner from what was once Frog Hollow. Several signs there commemorate the fact. Although now it's thoroughly gentrified, I'd known that when I was a kid Surry Hills was considered to be a dangerous area. It was where criminals and poor people and weirdo bohemians lived. It was not a neighbourhood full of million-dollar-plus flats, fancy restaurants, coffee shops, boutiques, furniture shops, and hair salons. (Seriously, what is it with all the hairdressers in Surry Hills? I swear there's one per block.) Most of the poor have been driven out, though fortunately there are still Housing Commission flats, homeless shelters, and needle exchanges. May they never be forced out. Most of the remaining criminals are decidedly white-collar and own some of those million-dollar-plus properties.

Then I read Larry Writer's *Razor*, a non-fiction account of inner-city Sydney's razor gangs in the twenties and thirties. Which led to other splendid books such as Larry Writer's own *Bumper: The Life & Times of Frank 'Bumper' Farrell* and Vince Kelly's *Rugged Angel: Australia's First Policewoman*. Around the same time, I came across *Crooks Like Us* by Peter Doyle and *City of Shadows* by Peter Doyle with Caleb Williams. These are two books of Sydney Police photographs from 1912 to 1960. The photos of crime scenes, criminals, victims, missing persons, and suspects are extraordinarily vivid black-and-white pictures, which evoke the dark side of Sydney more richly than any other resource I have come across. Some of the faces in those two books I will never forget.

As stated in the dedication, the novels of Ruth Park and Kylie Tennant were a huge influence on this book. They are two of Australia's finest writers and should be much more widely read and loved than they are. I read and re-read their books published in the 1930s and 1940s throughout the writing of *Razorhurst*. Kylie Tennant's *Foveaux*, a fictionalised history of Surry Hills, was particularly inspiring.

Although this novel was inspired by an actual time and place, that's the beginning and end of the resemblance. None of the events in the book are based on real events. I have taken liberties with some of the geography, ghosts aren't real, and my characters are wholly their own selves.

Though a few had starting points with real people:

Dymphna Campbell started with Dulcie Markham and Nellie Cameron, two young, beautiful prostitutes who were Razorhurst's best girls during their time. Dulcie Markham was dubbed the "Angel of Death" because, according to Larry Writer in *Razor*, at least eight (!) of her lovers were murdered. Markham was able to get out; Cameron was not so lucky.

Gloriana Nelson was inspired by Tilly Devine and Kate Leigh, who were rivals and ruled various parts of Razorhurst, making what would be millions of dollars in today's terms. I decided to combine them in homage to Ruth Park, who invented Delie Stock as her Tilly Devine/Kate Leigh character in her wonderful novel, *The Harp in the South*. Miraculously both Devine and Leigh lived into old age. Though neither had much money or influence at the end.

I use the term *Razorhurst* with great frequency, but it was not generally used. It was a beat-up term coined, and mostly deployed, by the Sydney *Truth*. But I love the term, and the fact that Razorhurst was in many ways an imaginary place fits well with my wholly imaginary book. The Sydney *Truth* has also been inspiring. What a wonderfully overwritten, addicted-to-alliteration, sensationalist tabloid it was. Sydney is the poorer since its passing.

I used the *Oxford English Dictionary* online, the *Macquarie Dictionary* online, Google's Ngrams, the National Library of Australia's Trove online repository of digitised Australian newspapers, G. A. Wilkes's *A Dictionary of Australian Colloquialisms*, and Hugh Lunn's *Lost for Words: Australia's Lost Language in Words and Stories* to make sure the words and phrases I used in this book were in use in Sydney in 1932. Any remaining anachronisms are entirely my own lookout. Please don't chiack me over my mistakes. But I'd love to hear about them.

Other inspirations for this book are the film noirs I obsessively watched and rewatched as a teen and, well, as an adult too. *Out of the Past* and *Gilda* remain two of my favourite movies. I was especially fascinated by those glorious femme fatales and have always wanted to write a book from their point of view. Dymphna Campbell is my homage to all of them.

That's why she gets to live.

ABOUT THE AUTHOR

Justine Larbalestier is the author of the award-winning bestseller *Liar* and several other novels. She also edited the collection *Zombies vs. Unicorns* with Holly Black. She lives in Sydney where she gardens, boxes, and watches far too much cricket. Justine has been obsessed with the 1930s since she saw her first Jean Harlow movie as a littlie. *Razorhurst* is the result. You can find out more about Justine here: justinelarbalestier.com.